# ADELINE MOWBRAY

broadview editions
series editor: L.W. Conolly

NPG 765, *Amelia Opie* by John Opie, oil on canvas, 1798. National Portrait Gallery, London.

# ADELINE MOWBRAY,
## or THE MOTHER AND DAUGHTER;
### A TALE

Amelia Alderson Opie

*edited by Anne McWhir*

broadview editions

**Library and Archives Canada Cataloguing in Publication**

Opie, Amelia Alderson, 1769-1853

    Adeline Mowbray, or the mother and daughter : a tale / Amelia Alderson Opie ; edited by Anne McWhir.

(Broadview editions)
Includes bibliographical references.
ISBN 978-1-55111-452-1

    I. McWhir, Anne, 1947-  II. Title.
III. Series: Broadview editions
PR5115.O3A75 2009       823'.7          C2009-904314-9

**Broadview Editions**
The Broadview Editions series represents the ever-changing canon of literature in English by bringing together texts long regarded as classics with valuable lesser-known works.

Advisory editor for this volume: Michel Pharand.

Broadview Press is an independent, international publishing house, incorporated in 1985. Broadview believes in shared ownership, both with its employees and with the general public; since the year 2000 Broadview shares have traded publicly on the Toronto Venture Exchange under the symbol BDP.

We welcome comments and suggestions regarding any aspect of our publications—please feel free to contact us at the addresses below or at broadview@broadviewpress.com.

*North America*          PO Box 1243, Peterborough, Ontario, Canada K9J 7H5
                     2215 Kenmore Ave., Buffalo, New York, USA 14207
                     Tel: (705) 743-8990; Fax: (705) 743-8353
                     email: customerservice@broadviewpress.com

*UK, Ireland,*          NBN International, Estover Road, Plymouth, UK PL6 7PY
*and continental Europe*   Tel: 44 (0) 1752 202300; Fax: 44 (0) 1752 202330
                     email: enquiries@nbninternational.com

*Australia and New Zealand*   NewSouth Books
                     c/o TL Distribution
                     15-23 Helles Ave., Moorebank, NSW, Australia 2170
                     Tel: (02) 8778 9999; Fax: (02) 8778 9944
                     email: orders@tldistribution.com.au

www.broadviewpress.com

Broadview Press acknowledges the financial support of the Government of Canada through the Book Publishing Industry Development Program (BPIDP) for our publishing activities.

This book is printed on paper containing 100% post-consumer fibre.

PRINTED IN CANADA

RECYCLED
Paper made from
recycled material
FSC® C103567

# Contents

# Acknowledgements

For the help I have received in preparing this edition, I want to acknowledge my gratitude and appreciation. To the University of Calgary Library, and especially to its Interlibrary Loans department, thanks for efficient and kind help in tracking down primary materials. To Jeannine Green and Apollonia Steele, Special Collections librarians at the University of Alberta and the University of Calgary respectively, thanks for sending books from one library to the other (and sparing me unnecessary drives to Edmonton and back). The Thomas Fisher Rare Book Library at the University of Toronto and the Firestone Library at Princeton University offered me wonderful places to work and very generous photocopying privileges. I am very grateful to these institutions and the staff members who made them a pleasure to visit.

I would also like to thank the British libraries where I read some of Opie's manuscript correspondence: the Library of the Society of Friends, London; the British Library; Special Collections at University College London; and the Bodleian Library, Oxford. Special thanks to Dr. Bruce Barker-Benfield of the Bodleian Library for allowing me to quote from some of Opie's letters to Godwin and Wollstonecraft in that library's extraordinary collection of late eighteenth- and early nineteenth-century literary manuscripts.

While working on this project I was particularly fortunate in being able to refer to the excellent edition of *Adeline Mowbray* by Shelley King and John B. Pierce (Oxford: Oxford UP, 1999). Their fine notes and illuminating introduction were a great asset to me: I am very aware that editorial work is a particularly collaborative kind of scholarship, and I hope that I have been able to build on their work and not merely to depend on it.

Thanks are also due to the Department of English and the Faculty of Humanities at the University of Calgary, and to the staff of Broadview Press. In particular, for help ranging from financial assistance to checking footnotes to moral support, I acknowledge the kind help of Julia Gaunce, Don LePan, Lorne Macdonald, Marjorie Mather, Susan Rudy, Saroj Tiwari, Amy Tureen, and Angela Waldie. Special thanks to Leonard Conolly, Series Editor, Broadview Editions, for helpful suggestions in the final stages of revision, and to Michel Pharand for his eagle-eyed copy-editing.

Finally, thanks, as ever, to my family: David, Catherine, and Stephen Oakleaf. While I hope that this edition of Opie's novel about a mother and a daughter will reach a wide readership, it is especially for my daughter, Catherine, who thinks as much as I do about the issues it raises.

# Introduction

In July 1811, Percy Bysshe Shelley, recently expelled from Oxford University for atheism, wrote to his friend and partner in crime Thomas Jefferson Hogg: "Miss Westbrook, Harriet, has advised me to read Mrs. Opie's 'Mother and Daughter.' She has sent it hither, and has desired my opinion with earnestness. What is this tale? But I shall read it to-night."[1] We do not know what Shelley thought of Opie's novel, but we can speculate about the sixteen-year-old Harriet Westbrook's intentions in recommending it. The next month, Shelley helped Harriet to escape from her boarding school, and the couple eloped to Scotland, where it was possible to marry without a licence or the reading of the banns. While Shelley shared Opie's heroine's distaste for the institution of marriage, his marriage to Harriet may have been inspired by the first marriage of Charles Berrendale, that heroine's future husband: Berrendale had "r[u]n away, about four years ago, with the only child of a rich West Indian from a boarding-school" (177). Curiously, Opie's tale of desire, transgression, principle, and remorse resonates with the lives of the Shelleys as well as the Godwins, looking forward to lives not yet lived, as well as backward to the institutions, debates, and revolutions of the second half of the eighteenth century.

*Adeline Mowbray, or The Mother and Daughter; A Tale* begins and ends with the relationship between Adeline and her mother, Editha—but encompasses just about every other possible relationship and destination in the long journey between their rift and their reconciliation. It is a colonialist novel in its relation to the Other: the dress of Turkish women, the self-immolation of Hindu widows, and the passionate decadence of Creole ladies provide at various points ways of thinking about the experience and virtues of English women.[2] Major Douglas, one of the most decent men in the novel, has made his fortune in India; Charles Berrendale goes to Jamaica to manage an estate (including, inevitably, its slaves). Yet the most potentially dramatic event in the novel—the journey of a freed slave back to Jamaica—is almost parenthetical, recounted with neither drama nor specific detail. The central plot focuses on the failure of the mother-daughter relationship ("it was decreed that every thing the mother of Adeline did should accelerate the fate of her devoted daughter" [93]), and its trajectory is directed relentlessly at the daughter's repentant homecoming.

---

1  *The Complete Works of Percy Bysshe Shelley: Vol. 8, Letters, 1803-1812*, ed. Walter E. Peck and Roger Ingpen (New York: Gordian, 1965), 129.
2  See pages 79, 124, and 222-23.

In this sense, the novel is a romance turned inside out: adventure happens somewhere else, to someone else; marriage is a source of suffering, not an occasion for a happy ending; women learn to live without men, forming primary relationships with one another; and the final deathbed scene—one of several—is the fulfillment of Adeline's longing throughout the novel, a closing in of the world of travel and adventure on a central interior space. Adeline is, as a literal reading of the title might suggest, both a mother and a daughter; ultimately, through her child, she gives her own mother a second chance. The untold story of the grandmother and the granddaughter, presumably a positive echo of Adeline's relationship with her mother (and also with her own grandmother), is left for the reader to imagine.

Opie had already written about the relationship of a father and a daughter.[1] Her relationship with her own father, James Alderson, a Norwich physician, was central in her life. Dr. Norberry, the heroine's surrogate father in *Adeline Mowbray*, may be a comic—but genuinely affectionate—version of Dr. Alderson, in spite of Norberry's evident failings. Opie's mother had died when she was fifteen, and Amelia Alderson had become her father's hostess. After her marriage in 1798 to the fashionable painter John Opie she lived in London, rarely visiting her father's home (perhaps because Dr. Alderson disapproved of the marriage). She had no daughter of her own: the Opies's rather brief marriage was childless. After her husband's death in 1807, she returned to Norwich, where, apart from trips to London, to other parts of England, and to France, she lived with her father until his death in 1825.

About Opie's early relationship with her mother we know little except that she gave her daughter a certain perspective on empire. Amelia Briggs Alderson's father had been a servant of the East India Company: as a little girl, she had been sent to England in the care of her black nurse following the death of her parents. Upon her arrival, her uncle wrote to her friends in India as follows:

> [Amelia] is a charming child, and the country agrees very well with her. The black girl, her nurse, is not reconciled to England; and, thinking she never shall be so, she is determined to return to Bengal by the Christmas ships.... I believe her design is to enter into service, as other free women do. If it be in your power, you are very much desired by all my niece's friends to prevent Savannah's being bought or sold as a negro.[2]

---

1   See *The Father and Daughter* with *Dangers of Coquetry*, ed. Shelley King and John B. Pierce (Peterborough: Broadview P, 2003). This edition brings together two texts: Opie's first novel, *Dangers of Coquetry* (1790), and *The Father and Daughter* (1801).

2   Cecilia Lucy Brightwell, *Memorials of the Life of Amelia Opie, Selected and Arranged from her Letters, Diaries, and Other Manuscripts* (Norwich: Fletcher and Alexander, 1854), 8.

From this story, certainly, comes part of the idea for Savanna in *Adeline Mowbray* (and also a hint of the abolitionism to which Opie remained committed throughout her life). The fact that Amelia Briggs Alderson died young makes it inevitable that her daughter should have found the influence that mothers' lives and attitudes have on their daughters particularly poignant. It also makes Mrs. Mowbray's inadequacy as a mother all the more striking, perhaps in contrast to Mrs. Alderson's recollected competence.[1]

Furthermore, motherhood was a crucial theme in contemporary writing by and for women. Mary Wollstonecraft, like most writers on education, is particularly concerned with the mother's role in educating her daughter. Her early *Thoughts on the Education of Daughters* (1787), rather a conservative treatment of the subject, is followed in *A Vindication of the Rights of Woman* (1792) by pointed criticism of mothers ill-equipped to teach their children. Her unfinished novel *The Wrongs of Woman, or Maria*[2]—an important influence on *Adeline Mowbray*—includes a long letter written by an oppressed mother to her infant daughter. *Letters Written During a Short Residence in Sweden, Norway, and Denmark* (1796), which Opie particularly admired, addresses Wollstonecraft's lover, Gilbert Imlay, and contemplates the future of their daughter, Fanny, who accompanied Wollstonecraft on her journey to Scandinavia:

> You [Imlay] know that as a female I am particularly attached to her—I feel more than a mother's fondness and anxiety, when I reflect on the dependent and oppressed state of her sex. I dread lest she should be forced to sacrifice her heart to her principles, or principles to her heart. With trembling hand I shall cultivate sensibility, and cherish delicacy of sentiment, lest, whilst I lend fresh blushes to the rose, I sharpen the thorns that will wound the breast I would fain guard—I dread to unfold her mind, lest it should render her unfit for the world she is to inhabit—Hapless woman! What a fate is thine![3]

---

1  Brightwell speculates as follows: "From the occasional glimpses we catch of the mother in her daughter's short record of her own early days, it is evident that she was possessed of firm purpose and high principle; a true-hearted woman, and somewhat of a disciplinarian. Her steady hand would have curbed the high spirit of her child, and softened those ebullitions of youthful glee, which made the young Amelia such an impetuous, mirthful creature: she would have been more demure and decorous had her mother lived, but perhaps less charming and attractive" (6-7). See also Opie's poem "In Memory of My Mother" (1834), Appendix F2.

2  First published in *Posthumous Works of the Author of "A Vindication of the Rights of Woman,"* (London: J. Johnson, 1798), vols. 1 and 2.

3  Mary Wollstonecraft, *Letters Written During a Short Residence*, letter 6, in Mary Wollstonecraft and William Godwin, *A Short Residence in Sweden, Norway* (Continued)

Caught between cultivating reason and principle (conventionally masculine and therefore at odds with the space women were expected to inhabit)
and sensibility and sentiment (conventionally feminine and therefore a
source of vulnerability), mothers have a difficult task in bringing up their
daughters. Adeline Mowbray, both as daughter and as mother, illustrates
precisely this tension between reason and feeling. Amelia Opie, perhaps
more interestingly, struggles with the tension between the domestic space
where Adeline reconciles herself to dying, and the wider world of journeys,
commerce, slavery, revolution, and imperial adventure and exploitation.

★ ★ ★

Opie's novel begins some time before the American War of Independence
(1775-83). Adeline, raised on an idyllic country estate by her rich widowed
mother, Editha, suffers neglect because of her mother's intellectual preoc-
cupations. Although she is given some practical training by her uneducated
but sensible grandmother, Adeline is mostly left to her own devices and
learns revolutionary principles without the maternal guidance that might
have put them in context. By the time she is a teenager, immersed in pro-
revolutionary philosophy and politics and largely ignored by a mother who
adopts fashionable opinions the way other women adopt fashionable dress,
Adeline has become a quietly fervent supporter of the "new philosophy."[1]
She may, to some degree, be Opie's representation of her own youthful
self: enthusiastic, curious, educated without a mother's consistent guidance, and inexperienced in the ways of the fashionable world.

From the outset, this is a novel about false learning. Editha Mowbray,
in spite of her reputation as a "learned lady" (47), seems to have learned
little from her reading but a sense of her own importance. While she frets
about whether children should go barefoot or wear shoes, and while she
imposes on her daughter a meager diet she has no intention of following
herself, narrator and reader agree that she is ridiculous. Whether her ideas
are right or wrong is beside the point: Adeline's feet are bleeding on the
rug while Mrs. Mowbray ponders whether or not children should wear
shoes. The mother's self-indulgence while her daughter lives on "pudding
without butter, and potatoes without salt" (44) teaches a deeper lesson
than any textbook. Opie's satire in these early chapters focuses not on

---

*and Denmark* and *Memoirs of the Author of "The Rights of Woman,"* ed. Richard
Holmes (London: Penguin, 1987), 97.

1  There are hints in the text that Opie may have deliberately confounded the periods
   of the American and French Revolutions. See, for instance, the reference to "spies
   and Jesuits" at the beginning of chapter 5 (see 62 and note).

any particular educational school, but on bad education—which appears to mean education based primarily on theory, not on human needs and practical considerations.[1] Mrs. Mowbray's inconsistency, vacillation, and impracticality make her an inadequate parent, a foolish woman, and an irrational thinker, as the narrator emphasizes:

> ... after haranguing with all the violence of a true whig on the natural rights of man, or the blessings of freedom, she would "turn to a tory in her elbow chair," and govern her household with despotic authority; and after embracing at some moments the doubts of the sceptic, she would often lie motionless in her bed, from apprehension of ghosts, a helpless prey to the most abject superstition. (43)

This is satire that cuts both ways. As a female philosopher, Mrs. Mowbray is perhaps vaguely associated with Mary Wollstonecraft; but Editha Mowbray is also a shameless coquette, and therefore more convincingly associated with the women whom Wollstonecraft criticizes so forcefully in *A Vindication of the Rights of Woman*.[2] Her allegedly intellectual pursuits are just as frivolous as more conventional female pursuits—and she falls well within Wollstonecraft's critique of the ill-prepared, irrational mother. Governed by whims and fears rather than by principles and convictions, she is, from any rational viewpoint, an injudicious parent. Caught between "the prejudices of an antient family" (42) and her own literary ambitions, even more delusional about her intellectual powers than she is about her youthful attractiveness, Mrs. Mowbray is rendered unfit for either contented life in her social station or for a successful career as an intellectual woman.

Or perhaps this is an unfair reading, for Mrs. Mowbray is also a loving mother: Adeline is comforted even at the worst moments in the novel by her memory of her mother's concern during a childhood illness. In comparison with Mrs. Norberry, who raises her daughters to be conventional and judgmental, or with Berrendale's mother, who raises a spoiled

---

1 Mrs. Mowbray is eventually described as having been "a neglecter of that practical benevolence which can in days produce more benefit to others than theories and theorists can accomplish in years" (266).

2 E.g., chapter 4 ("The State of Degradation to which Woman is Reduced"), where Wollstonecraft counters the conventional admiration of female sensibility by arguing that women of sensibility make poor mothers (*The Vindications: "A Vindication of the Rights of Men" and "A Vindication of the Rights of Woman,"* ed. D.L. Macdonald, and Kathleen Scherf [Peterborough: Broadview P, 1997], 166–97). For all her intellectual pretensions, Mrs. Mowbray turns out to be governed by flights of feeling more than by rational conviction.

glutton, Mrs. Mowbray is an admirable parent. Perhaps Opie means us to recognize her as a more complex character than I have so far described—a Wollstonecraftian heroine whose gifts have been blunted and distorted by "things as they are."[1] She has been overindulged; society offers few outlets for her talent and ambition. Having married to please her parents, she finds herself widowed in her late thirties—hardly an age when most modern women are willing to retreat from life. Yet, however we might want to sympathize with her, Editha Mowbray is condemned from the very beginning of the novel, where the narrator takes a stern look at the effect of her intellectual interests:

> Fatal and unproductive studies! While, wrapt in philosophical abstraction, she was trying to understand the metaphysical question on the mechanism of the human mind, or what constituted the true nature of virtue, she suffered day after day to pass in the culpable neglect of positive duties; and while imagining systems for the good of society, and the furtherance of general philanthropy, she allowed individual suffering in her neighbourhood to pass unobserved and unrelieved. While professing her unbounded love for the great family of the world, she suffered her own family to pine under the consciousness of her neglect; and viciously devoted those hours to the vanity of abstruse and solitary study, which might have been better spent in amusing the declining age of her venerable parents, whom affection had led to take up their abode with her. (42)[2]

Words like "culpable," "neglect" (used twice), "viciously," and "vanity" leave no doubt as to the moral perspective of the narrator.[3] Yet in tension

---

1   William Godwin's novel *Things As They Are, or The Adventures of Caleb Williams* (1794) explores the relationship between social institutions and individual experience and aspirations. Godwin insisted that his intention was not to attack law and custom, but to encourage his readers to think for themselves about the institutions and ideas they were accustomed to take for granted. Cf. *Adeline Mowbray* 157, for Opie's adoption of the phrase.

2   The reviewer in the *European Magazine* 47 (1805) quotes this passage approvingly. See Appendix A5.

3   On this point I must disagree with Jeanette Winterson, who in her introduction to *Adeline Mowbray* (London: Pandora, 1986) claims that the novel "makes no moral judgements." There are, she says, "no omnipotent author passages, so beloved of the Victorians, to tell us what to think or to ram home how disgraceful everyone is" (vi). On the contrary, there is no reason to think that the narrator, whose views are expressed frequently in the course of the novel, does not represent Opie's own reflections and opinions. A useful question, however, is the extent to which the narrator blames individuals for their own misery and the extent to which she deplores the social and intellectual influences that can distort their lives.

with that perspective is the novel's social determinism (or even fatalism): how could Editha Mowbray be different than what she is, and how can the reader not extend criticism beyond the individual to the family—and even to the "great family of the world"—that can shape such a woman's life? The problem for the modern reader is separating the carefully explicit moral criticism of individuals from the subtle social criticism that might, to some degree, indicate Opie's silent sympathy with ideas and practices she explicitly rejects.

Adeline, the daughter, is even harder to read than her mother. Unburdened by the label of "genius" applied to Editha, Adeline learns practical skills (cooking, nursing, accounts). But she also models herself on her mother, reading the same books and engaging in "abstruse speculations," "new theories," and "romantic reveries" (52). Significantly, she does this without guidance (her mother is too remote, her grandmother too uncultivated). The "new theories" in which she dabbles appear to include not only the revolutionary discourse on the "rights of man," but attacks on such central institutions as marriage. The writings of Godwin, Wollstonecraft, Thomas Paine, and other radical writers of the English 1790s, with their "French" ideas, appear (anachronistically) to form the mind of this young woman raised at the time of the "American War": chronology is disrupted so that ideas the reader may agree with (for example, sympathy with the American Revolution) mask Adeline's immersion in opinions regarded by 1805 as more dangerous. Perhaps we are encouraged to read Adeline's education through that of Amelia Alderson, who grew up in Norwich in the 1780s and who participated in the radical debates of the 1790s. Yet later in the novel we discover that Adeline (unlike Amelia) has read little poetry and no plays or novels except Voltaire's *Brutus*[1] and the romances of Scudéry (see 92). "[R]epublican ardour" (92) and philosophical speculation seem to be the main directions of her "romantic reveries." Opie's education, influenced as she was by the lively political culture of Norwich, by Quaker friends, and by a growing circle of writers and actors, was much more extensive and eclectic.

Like many another mother and daughter, Editha and Adeline head off to Bath, equipped for disaster by inexperience. The mother's intellectual pretensions being a mere façade, she is looking for love. The daughter's principles having been formed in isolation from the practical world, she is looking for the romance of realized ideals. Mrs. Mowbray is thirty-eight

---

1  Associated in France from 1789-94 with anti-monarchical feeling: see Kenneth N. McKee, "Voltaire's *Brutus* During the French Revolution," *Modern Language Notes* 56 (1941): 100-06.

(as, strikingly, Mrs. Alderson was at the time of her death);[1] Adeline is eighteen. Both expect to find suitors. Adeline first meets an Irish colonel, Mordaunt, who, having no intention of marrying, does the honourable thing and leaves town. Second, she meets Frederic Glenmurray, the author of the very books that have already persuaded her that marriage is a corrupt institution. Innocent to a fault, Adeline has no idea that her opinions are socially repugnant. Her mother is appalled when she finally realizes that Adeline means what she says: ideas are for Adeline principles of action, not merely clever forms of words.

When Adeline and Glenmurray fall in love, Mrs. Mowbray (to Adeline's surprise, but not to the reader's) will not consent to them living together outside of marriage. Even Glenmurray seems to realize, perhaps for the first time, that theory may not provide the best practical model for life in a world of prejudice—or, at least, of principles different from his own. The ambiguity that confuses high-minded principle with vice is highlighted by Sir Patrick O'Carroll, a handsome young Irishman who has his eye on the mother's fortune and on the daughter's beauty. When Adeline expresses her view of marriage and states her unwillingness to submit to such a degrading institution, she expects Glenmurray to be pleased. However, "[t]o her great disappointment ... his countenance was sad; while sir Patrick, on the contrary, had an expression of impudent triumph in his look, which made her turn blushing from his ardent gaze, and indignantly follow her mother, who was then leaving the room" (66). Principle strong enough to be consistent with practice dooms Adeline to be regarded as and treated like a prostitute. The novel critiques both her principles *and* the social prejudices that justify others abusing her.

Adeline's blindness to the tension between principles and practice operates in almost every episode. Although Glenmurray has written a book against duelling, he accepts a challenge from Sir Patrick, is wounded, and must bear Adeline's rebuke. "Alas! I am a man, not a philosopher, Adeline!" (73), he tells her, admitting, perhaps (as Adeline is rarely able to do), that human experience cannot be governed by reason alone. Once again, Glenmurray has discovered the strain between theory and practice— though in this case, his theory appears to be less controversial than his attack on the evils of marriage.[2] Editha Mowbray, on the other hand, gives up her dream-world of theory and speculation for a new dream-world

---

1   The age is perhaps significant for other reasons: cf. Charlotte's Smith's poem "Thirty-Eight, Addressed to Mrs. H——y," in *Elegiac Sonnets and Other Poems*, 8th ed. 2 vols. (London: Cadell & Davies, 1797), 1: 82–85.

2   For other contemporary views of marriage, see Appendix D.

of sexual fantasy. Revealing the conventionality and naïveté that under-lie her studied eccentricity, she falls for Sir Patrick O'Carroll. Before the Bath season is over, she has married her Irishman and gone with him and Adeline to live in Berkshire. Predictably, Sir Patrick attempts to seduce—probably more accurately to rape—Adeline (now his stepdaughter). She escapes and is reunited with Glenmurray. The lovers flee and eventually, driven to find a warmer climate by Glenmurray's declining health, they move to Portugal.

Opie seems to think it important to emphasize that Adeline's elope-ment is reasonable. Adeline, she persuades us, is not another frail heroine driven by passion, sensibility, and delusion into her lover's arms; she has no other recourse than Glenmurray's protection if she is to avoid Sir Patrick's aggression, for her mother cannot or is unwilling to help her. Adeline loves Glenmurray—but the reader may suspect that she loves her self-defined virtue and principle more. And here again the novel's ambiguities and paradoxes tease the reader and—slowly—become apparent even to Adeline. Glenmurray may think marriage a foolish institution; but his be-lief does not make it possible for him to introduce Adeline to his acquaint-ances. Either she must be introduced as his wife (a lie), or else she must be introduced as his mistress (an insult to any respectable woman who may meet her—and a justification for both men and women to treat her with disrespect). Running away from such a social impasse, the lovers move from Portugal to France. When Sir Patrick is accused of bigamy and acci-dentally drowns, Adeline and Glenmurray return to England in the hope of being reconciled with Adeline's mother. Adeline, now pregnant, sees her mother only to be driven away: blaming her daughter for Sir Patrick's rejection, Editha vows never to see her again until she is on her deathbed. This rejection, rather than the elopement with Glenmurray, appears to be the turning-point in Adeline's fortunes.

The lovers settle in Richmond, where Adeline once again sees Colonel Mordaunt, the confirmed bachelor (and libertine) who was her first suitor in Bath. Significantly, it is Mordaunt who makes her aware of her own degradation and Glenmurray's real situation: no longer just an interesting invalid, Glenmurray is dying of tuberculosis. Various other episodes make Adeline increasingly aware of what it means to be the pregnant mistress of a dying man. She watches the funeral of a seducer who has left his child penniless; she observes the lonely anger of a boy who is called "bastard" by his classmates. Glenmurray has by now given up his own theory and has expressed his desire to marry, realizing what Adeline's future will be when he dies. Nevertheless, almost driven to the altar by the horrors she observes, Adeline has a miscarriage and—with her usual principled per-versity—changes her mind.

Having dismissed a servant, Mary Warner, for insolence, Adeline is approached by Rachel Pemberton, a Quaker woman who wants to hire the girl but who needs a recommendation from "Mrs. Glenmurray." Mrs. Pemberton's eloquent preaching and her role as surrogate mother contribute to Adeline's gradual change of mind about marriage. The other significant meeting in this part of the novel is with Savanna, the "mulatto" woman whose sick husband Adeline rescues from a cruel creditor and who, at an earlier stage of her life, has been a slave in Jamaica. (Later in the novel Savanna returns to Jamaica, where she is sold back into slavery and must once again escape.) Opie's Victorian biographer Cecilia Brightwell quotes a story from Opie's papers about Opie's childhood fear of a black servant in the neighbourhood:

> Aboar (as he was called) used to come up to speak to little missey as I stood at the door in my nurse's arms, a civility which I received with screams, and tears, and kicks. But as soon as my parents heard of this ill behaviour, they resolved to put a stop to it, and missey was forced to shake hands with the black the next time he approached her, and thenceforward we were very good friends. Nor did they fail to make me acquainted with negro history; as soon as I was able to understand, I was shewn on the map where their native country was situated; I was told the sad tale of negro wrongs and negro slavery; and I believe that my early and ever-increasing zeal in the cause of emancipation was founded and fostered by the kindly emotions which I was encouraged to feel for my friend Aboar and all his race. (13)

Opie's "zeal in the cause of emancipation" informs her sympathy for Savanna;[1] however, her ignorance of the lives and language of actual slaves means that Savanna's speech is a travesty ("Me be name Savanna" [280]) and that her love for Adeline (with a few wonderfully outspoken exceptions) is expressed in unbearably sentimental terms.[2] Opie's representation of the racialized Other, typical of liberal views at the time, may well offend modern readers. Yet her sympathy for people of colour and for the slaves she had read about since childhood would be a guiding principle throughout her life.

---

1   However, in a later novel, *Temper, or Domestic Scenes: a Tale*, 3 vols. (London: Longman, Hurst, Rees, Orme, and Brown, 1812), the "woman of colour" is an "artful Indian" who agrees to help the man she loves get rid of his lawful wife. She is a negative version of Savanna, though her story is even more deliberately reminiscent of the story of Amelia Briggs Alderson's nurse.
2   In 1844 Opie did make some effort to move Savanna's language (like that of the other lower-class characters) closer to standard English.

Since the Mansfield decision of 1772,[1] slaves could not be taken back to the colonies against their will—a ruling that "severely undermined slaveholders' power in England."[2] But the institution of slavery contributed a problematic but pervasive metaphor to the discourse of writing on women's rights, and the fact that Savanna is a woman of colour makes the metaphor all the more insistent: a free woman in England, Savanna is nevertheless figuratively enslaved by her race, class, and gender. Wollstonecraft extends the metaphor to all women, who, she argues, "may be convenient slaves, but slavery will have its constant effect, degrading the master and the abject dependent."[3] Opie is less clear about the extent to which Adeline (or Savanna) is a "slave" in this figurative sense. Even as a woman on the brink of poverty, in comparison with Savanna Adeline is relatively powerful, relatively wealthy. Savanna herself, sold back into slavery during a visit to Jamaica, is relatively privileged in comparison with those who have never known freedom.[4] The price of Savanna's freedom from debt and of her enduring devotion to Adeline is the cost of a pineapple—an extremely precious commodity because Glenmurray, now seriously ill, desires one so ardently. Savanna and her son, "the Tawny Boy," come to live with Adeline, and they pledge allegiance to her in terms of the highest chivalric devotion—with more than an echo of the ideal marriage vows which are never exchanged in this novel (where weddings are furtive and often legally uncertain).[5] Savanna helps to nurse Glenmurray, who dies, having recanted many of his radical opinions. She is to some degree Adeline's alter ego: both women love men who die; both are socially marginalized and oppressed. Their relationship recalls the mutual devotion of an idealized marriage in which, at least on the emotional level, Savanna appears to be the protector, Adeline the more vulnerable party.

---

1  See Appendix G1.
2  Carol Howard, "'The Story of the Pineapple': Sentimental Abolitionism and Moral Motherhood in Amelia Opie's *Adeline Mowbray*," *Studies in the Novel* 30.3 (1998): 358.
3  Dedication to *A Vindication of the Rights of Woman*, in *The Vindications:"A Vindication of the Rights of Men" and "A Vindication of the Rights of Woman*," ed. D.L. Macdonald and Kathleen Scherf, 104.
4  One argument of the abolitionists was that even relatively mild enslavement was infinitely worse than hard servitude, because unlike the slave the servant remained in possession of his or her right to freedom.
5  "Here, child, tawny boy," says Savanna, "down on knees, and vow wid me to be faithful and grateful to this our mistress, till our last day; and never to forsake her in sickness or in sorrow!" (174). Curiously, the word "health" in the marriage service is changed to "sorrow" both here and in another allusion to the marriage service, when Adeline agrees to marry Berrendale (199).

Yet (whether or not Opie intends this), the relationship between the two women also points to some telling similarities between devotion and enslavement. Adeline buys Savanna's love—if not her person—for the price of a pineapple. On her deathbed, she "bequeaths" both Savanna and little Editha to her mother's "care and protection," just as Glenmurray had earlier intended to "bequeath" Adeline herself to his cousin, Charles Berrendale, who has fallen in love with her and who resembles Glenmurray in appearance, though not in character. Neither slaves nor servants, Adeline and her daughter are, nevertheless, commodities to be exchanged: like Savanna, they are defined in terms of their relationship to those who protect, govern, and pay for them. Yet Adeline's relative power comes from her ability to pay for and control the fate of others, rather than merely being controlled herself: economic exchange makes benevolence possible, and one of Adeline's last acts is to request that her mother continue to support an unmarried mother and her child, the objects of Adeline's charity. Opie's critique of corrupt institutions aims at a change of heart, the individual conversion of those with the power and money to make a difference. In this sense, *Adeline Mowbray* echoes the views of the evangelical Hannah More more emphatically than those of Mary Wollstonecraft, who emphasizes social and political change. Adeline is far more powerful than Savanna, who, seeing the provisions made for Adeline in her final illness, says, "This it be to have money ... poor Savanna mean as well—her heart make all these, but her hand want power" (280). Savanna is an opportunity for benevolence: her unequal social station is not fundamentally questioned and—in spite of Adeline's self-proclaimed colour-blindness—Savanna remains, in Berrendale's words to Adeline, "your mulatto" (212).

Temporarily mad with grief following Glenmurray's death, Adeline recovers and sets up a school outside London. Mary Warner turns up in the village to reveal the story of Adeline's past. Forced to move on, Adeline finally marries Berrendale more than two years after Glenmurray's death. He turns out to be selfish and greedy, ruled by unrestrained appetites for food and (barely disguised by Opie's reticence) also for sex. Their daughter Editha is born some fifteen months after the marriage; but by then Adeline has suffered from Berrendale's unfaithfulness, neglect, and unkindness. When Editha is two years old, Berrendale leaves for Jamaica, where he is to manage the estate of his first wife's father. Berrendale clearly benefits economically from the institution of slavery, although he does not own slaves himself. Even in England, he tends to treat people as mere commodities: his son by his first wife is the prospective heir to a Jamaican fortune—and has, in effect, been sold to his colonial grandfather in exchange for an annuity. In Jamaica, as if to emphasize his similarity with Sir Patrick, Berrendale eventually enters into a bigamous marriage. Challenged by an agent of Colonel Mordaunt's, he is driven by fear of prosecution to declare little Editha his legal heir before he dies. But "this circumstance ... did not take place till long after Adeline took up her abode in Cumberland" (246) at the end of the novel.

Meanwhile, back in London and unaware of Berrendale's adventures and difficulties, Adeline is determined to prove for Editha's sake that her marriage to Berrendale is legal. For the second time, she goes to see a lawyer called Langley—a notorious libertine and the lover of her former servant Mary Warner. Mary's infant son has smallpox: Adeline realizes that her contact with Mary Warner means that she may carry the infection back to Editha on her clothing. She dashes into the street, where Colonel Mordaunt comes along in time to rescue her from the gallantry of strangers. He takes her to the house of a friend, where once again he tries to persuade her to be his mistress. Adeline refuses, manages to get Editha inoculated in time—and contracts smallpox herself.

When she recovers, Adeline, Savanna, and Editha set off for Cumberland, where Adeline's mother now lives. The novel seems to draw in on itself: the larger world—India, Jamaica, even London—seems no longer relevant. By now, Adeline is entirely persuaded that her earlier opinions and convictions were false. Far from advocating independent thinking, she has come to believe that children should be taught "sympathies with general society" (275). She no longer wants even reconciliation with her mother on her own account, but only for the sake of her daughter, little Editha. For Adeline is by now convinced that she is dying—and there is more than a hint that she has contracted the tuberculosis that killed Glenmurray.[1] Once Adeline arrives in Cumberland, the reader learns that Mrs. Pemberton has settled near Mrs. Mowbray, and that the two women have become friends. They are looking for Mrs. Mowbray's lost daughter, not realizing that Adeline, seriously ill, is confined at a poor man's house in the neighbourhood.

A rather awkward subplot informs us that Colonel Mordaunt has changed his ways and married a good woman, Emma Douglas, who defends Adeline against mean-spirited gossip. We also learn that Adeline's

---

1   The causes of consumption were thought to include "[v]iolent passions, exertions, or affections of the mind; as grief, disappointment, anxiety, or close application to the study of abstruse arts or sciences.... Consumptions are likewise caught by sleeping with the diseased; for which reason this should be carefully avoided. It cannot be of great benefit to the sick, and must hurt those in health" (William Buchan, *Domestic Medicine: or, A Treatise on the Prevention and Cure of Diseases ...*, 17th ed. [London: A. Strahan, T. Cadell, Jun., and W. Davies, 1800], 175-76). Infection—whether with smallpox or with tuberculosis—appears in the novel to signify moral as well as physical disease.

scheming cousin has been intercepting letters between her and her mother. The novel ends with Adeline's death in her mother's house, surrounded by her mother, her daughter, and Savanna, her surrogate parents, Mrs. Pemberton and Dr. Norberry, looking on. Perhaps significantly, the house in Cumberland is her *maternal* home: Adeline does not return to her father's house, Rosevalley, the lost home of her childhood, but to a community of women where, we seem to be expected to believe, the child Editha can be educated to make happier choices than her mother.

★ ★ ★

Having travelled from home to home through a series of wanderings, Adeline leaves the two Edithas, grandmother and granddaughter, to practice the lessons the novel has taught. Yet those lessons are elusive ones, and the relationships of mothers and daughters can easily be forgotten in the other issues the novel raises. Before her marriage to John Opie, Amelia Alderson had been sympathetic with many radical causes: in November 1794 she had attended the treason trial of leading "English Jacobins," or supporters of revolutionary ideas, including the novelist Thomas Holcroft and the philologist John Horne Tooke. She and her father had considered emigrating to the United States if the trial turned out badly, but fortunately the defendants were acquitted. Moving between Norwich and London in the 1790s, Amelia Alderson had befriended Holcroft, William Godwin, Mary Wollstonecraft, the playwright and actor Elizabeth Inchbald, the actor Sarah Siddons, the poet Anna Laetitia Barbauld, and a number of refugees escaping from the Reign of Terror in France. She may have been for a time romantically involved with Godwin: her letters to him are occasionally flirtatious and remarkably unrestrained.[1] However, Godwin, radical philosopher and novelist, author of—among many other works—*Enquiry Concerning Political Justice* and *Caleb Williams*, and Wollstonecraft became lovers in 1796 and, against their own principles, married the following year. When Wollstonecraft died in 1797 following the birth of her second daughter,[2] Godwin sent Opie a lock of her hair. Opie replied: "should I ever be the mother of a daughter, I shall have a pride in shewing it to her as a memorial of a woman, who nobly, & incomparably fought for the

---

1 See, for example, this excerpt from a letter of 1 November 1796: "I hate you for always throwing *Coquette* in my teeth—it is a bad habit—& you have lately acquired a worse—you call me a bitch the last time I saw you—but no matter—" (Oxford, Bodleian Library, [Abinger] Dep. b. 210/6). Adeline would never have written such a letter as this!

2 The future Mary Shelley, most famous as the "Author of *Frankenstein*."

violated rights of her sex, but died alas! before she could see the victory which she so well deserved to obtain——."[1]

By 1805, Opie was certainly less committed to that victory than she had been eight years earlier. Married to John Opie[2] and part of a fashionable London circle, she had distanced herself from her radical friends. Godwin had published his *Memoirs of the Author of "A Vindication of the Rights of Woman"* (1798), which—in an attempt to present Wollstonecraft sympathetically—had badly misjudged the attitudes of the reading public.[3] He himself, abandoning principle yet again, had remarried in 1801. Yet *Adeline Mowbray* has long been read as a novel based on the relationship of Godwin and Wollstonecraft; indeed, this association is one reason for its continuing interest to modern readers. Nevertheless, the similarities are not particularly pointed: Adeline, unlike Wollstonecraft, is the daughter of a wealthy heiress, a heroine of sensibility who might have made even the author of *Letters Written During a Short Residence* cringe. Glenmurray is a gentleman of property, not a professional man of letters like Godwin. Already ill with tuberculosis when he meets Adeline, he, not she, is the one who dies first. Opie's fictional lovers are young, inexperienced, and doomed. In contrast, Godwin and Wollstonecraft were no longer young when they became lovers, and Wollstonecraft, at least, was by no means inexperienced, having lived with Gilbert Imlay in France and having given birth to their daughter, Fanny, in 1794. While there is no doubt that Opie drew on her personal and intellectual interest in Godwin and Wollstonecraft to write her novel, *Adeline Mowbray* is not simply a *roman à clef*.

Nevertheless, Glenmurray's ideas about marriage and duelling coincide in many respects with Godwin's. "[N]othing can be so ridiculous upon the face of it, or so contrary to the genuine march of sentiment," writes Godwin in his *Memoirs*, "as to require the overflowing of the soul to wait upon a ceremony, and that at which, wherever delicacy and imagination exist, is of all things most sacredly private, to blow a trumpet before it, and to record the moment when it has arrived at its climax" (see Appendix E1). Glenmurray similarly regards the institution of marriage as "at once absurd, unjust, and immoral": "the sacred ties of love" are, he believes,

---

1  MS letter to Godwin, 11 October 1797 (Oxford, Bodleian Library, [Abinger] Dep. b. 210/6).

2  Divorced from his first wife in 1796 by Act of Parliament, John Opie had married Amelia Alderson on 8 May 1798. One wonders what he thought of the heroine's arguments against divorce in *Adeline Mowbray*; see, for example, 238.

3  See, for example, the responses in *Anti-Jacobin Review and Magazine* 1 (July-December 1798): 91-93; and Robert Bisset, *The Historical, Biographical, Literary, and Scientific Magazine ... for the Year 1799*, vol. 1 (London, [1800?]), 27-35 (Appendix E2).

profaned by "so odious and unnecessary a ceremony" (65). Godwin's (like Glenmurray's) condemnation of marriage recalls some of the criticism levelled at Lord Hardwicke's Marriage Act of 1753 ("An Act for the better preventing of clandestine Marriages"). The Act had attempted to regularize and control marriage, previously an area of legal and social confusion, and to prevent property falling into the wrong hands through elopements and other clandestine marriages outside the control of parents and legal guardians.[1]

As Shelley's 1812 marriage to Harriet Westbrook demonstrates, such marriages were still performed in Scotland (hence the popularity of Gretna Green, just over the Scottish border, as a destination for runaway lovers). But Hardwicke's Act put a stop to clandestine marriages in England. Before 1753, practices ranging from a simple exchange of private vows to undocumented ceremonies by unlicensed clergy (including so-called "Fleet marriages," conducted within the precincts of the Fleet Prison) had been accepted as legal marriages: the definition of legitimacy and the determination of bigamy had been at the heart of tangled legal cases. The poor, according to Lawrence Stone, had resisted public marriages for the very reason Godwin mentions: they tended to consider marriage as a private matter, and new requirements, such as the reading of the banns in churches, were regarded as embarrassing.[2] Far from establishing practices that relied on the wisdom of the ages, Lord Hardwicke's Act, with its insistence on documentation and standardization, seemed to many a new-fangled set of controls on personal choice.

Opie's novel (like Wollstonecraft's *The Wrongs of Woman: or, Maria* before it, which in many ways it echoes)[3] could be read as a commentary on the laws regarding marriage. Her characters include two bigamists (Sir Patrick and Berrendale) and a couple "married" in the eyes of God, though not according to the laws of church and state (Glenmurray and Adeline).[4]

---

1 The excerpt reprinted as Appendix D1 demonstrates the stringent control this Act intended to exert: tampering with the registry of marriages was a capital felony, a fact which makes Adeline's difficulty in establishing the legality of her marriage to Berrendale a very serious matter indeed.

2 Lawrence Stone, *Road to Divorce: England 1530-1987* (Oxford: Oxford UP, 1990), 100.

3 See the excerpt reprinted as Appendix D4. Opie's novel deserves to be read not only in relation to Wollstonecraft's writings but in conjunction with such eighteenth-century predecessors as Samuel Richardson's *Clarissa* (1747-48) and Jean-Jacques Rousseau's *La Nouvelle Héloïse, ou Julie* (1761), and with contemporary fictions by women, notably *Emma Courtney* (1796) and *The Victim of Prejudice* (1799) by Wollstonecraft's friend Mary Hays.

4 Adeline tells Mary Warner, "I look on myself as his wife in the sight of God; nor will I quit him till death shall separate us" (149).

Like Wollstonecraft, Opie appears to challenge the binary categorization of women as either respectable (i.e., either married or celibate) or disreputable (i.e., whores).[1] Opie, who had frequented assize trials during her early years in Norwich[2] and who was herself the wife of a divorced man, demonstrates an informed understanding of laws governing inheritance, the social and legal effects of illegitimacy, the sexual hypocrisy of both men and women, the function of marriage in fashionable society, and the crucial practical importance of documents proving the legality of a marriage. Her knowledge is as much a criticism of "things as they are" as it is an endorsement of legal order: marriage, the novel seems to argue, should certainly be *more than* a mere official act—yet a document is enough to make the difference between degradation and respectability. Whether for legal reasons or for moral ones—and this uncertain relationship of law and morality is central—love is simply not enough. Unlike Wollstonecraft's Maria, who fights a losing battle in court against the double standard,[3] most women (including Adeline after Glenmurray's death) may prudently settle for loveless respectability.

★ ★ ★

In taking on such large issues, Opie addresses much more than the personal lives and intellectual legacy of Godwin and Wollstonecraft. She invites us to consider the relationship between theory and practice, between principle and action—whether the particular context be revolution, women's rights, marriage, divorce, slavery, social class, family relations, or, significantly, religion. Whether the novel is radical, as some scholars have attempted to argue, or profoundly conservative, as some of Opie's nineteenth-century admirers believed, is less important than the range of questions it raises and reflects on. Opie might have substituted almost any "radical" writer for Godwin, in a strategy well understood by her contemporaries: Hume, Voltaire, Godwin, and Rousseau become almost interchangeable in the discourse of reaction to the French Revolution, their charms as balefully seductive as those of Glenmurray are to Adeline.

---

1  Wollstonecraft states the point as follows: "Highly as I respect marriage, as the foundation of almost every social virtue, I cannot avoid feeling the most lively compassion for those unfortunate females who are broken off from society, and by one error torn from all those affections and relationships that improve the heart and mind" (*A Vindication of the Rights of Woman*, in *The Vindications*, ed. D.L. Macdonald and Kathleen Scherf, 190).
2  See Brightwell 23-27.
3  See Appendix D4.

"[T]hese pernicious skepticisms and sophistical delusions," remarks an evidently conservative contemporary writer,

> from their fascinating stile, and animated diction, obtained many readers:—and those, unaccustomed to the higher pursuits of literature, in which Hume and Gibbon moved, were accessible through the medium of novels, in which were disseminated the most dangerous of principles:—principles which corrupt the heart and debase the understanding:—giving to vice the charms of virtue—to infidelity the specious colourings of superior intellectual attainment—to crimes, the shameful sophistry of irresistible necessity—and to self-destruction the delusive argument of a right in the creature to resign his existence when it ceases to afford him happiness, and the reasonableness of escaping misery.[1]

Adeline is never tempted by infidelity or by arguments in favour of suicide (though her willingness to die may seem very close to suicidal "self-destruction")—but Opie does, through Mrs. Pemberton, accuse her of intellectual and spiritual pride. Thus the novel constructs a laboratory in which to test Adeline's principles—at the same time as it undercuts those principles by drawing attention to their specious authority, their incompatibility with reality, and their delusive inversion of those moral categories which Opie increasingly trusts.

Imagine, Opie seems to be saying, a kind, generous, and attractive young woman from a wealthy family. Without the mitigating influence of a sensible mother (and without the guidance of even a surrogate father, for Dr. Norberry, who might have performed this role, is distracted by American politics and his own family problems), her mind is formed almost entirely by unmediated reading. From the works of Glenmurray (whose style is at least as persuasive as his ideas), she comes to believe that marriage is an absurd institution. Not content with theory, when she and Glenmurray fall in love she insists on living in accordance with her principles. Given the way the world is—its prejudices, traditions, and laws—she finds herself shunned, impoverished, and degraded by a choice made according to the highest principles of integrity and reason. While I agree with Eleanor Ty that Opie "seeks to develop a female subject position outside the stereotypical mistress or fallen woman,"[2] there is little doubt that Adeline eventually comes to the conclusion that no such subject posi-

---

1  Joseph Wildman, *The Force of Prejudice, A Moral Tale* (London: T. Barfield, 1799) 1: 66-67; qtd. in M.O. Grenby, *The Anti-Jacobin Novel: British Conservatism and the French Revolution* (Port Chester, NY: Cambridge UP, 2001), 225.

2  *Empowering the Feminine: The Narratives of Mary Robinson, Jane West, and Amelia Opie, 1796-1812* (Toronto: U of Toronto P, 1998), 157.

tion is possible for a respectable woman. Writing, teaching, and preaching may offer public roles for some women; a degree of eccentricity in dress, speech, and principles may be admirable (as Mrs. Pemberton illustrates). Yet in order to achieve a measure of respectable happiness, a woman must accommodate herself to the principles, conventions, or precepts of society in general. Daughters, wives, or widows, women are defined in relationship to men and, only secondarily, in relation to one another. Even a hopeful ending without men relies in large part on economic arrangements beyond the scope of women's legal power.

A crux of interpretation is whether the novel's focus of criticism is the social world that abuses and judges Adeline or Adeline herself, who—however much the modern reader may sympathize with her earlier principles—is at various times self-destructive, tedious, self-righteous, and downright deluded. There is no doubt that Opie is appalled by the hypocrisy of many of those who condemn Adeline. Mrs. Norberry's dislike of Adeline is based on jealousy: her husband (although his relation to Adeline is fatherly) has a reputation as a "gallant man" (129). Maynard's sisters, also jealous, are delighted to see a paragon of perfection reduced to the status of a "kept mistress" (111). Glenmurray's female relatives, without principle or virtue themselves, are wealthy and cunning enough to maintain their reputations and proud enough to look down on Adeline because her transgression is more public than theirs. Almost every woman who meets her or hears about her turns her into a joke or a stereotype. Almost every man who meets her during and after her relationship with Glenmurray makes a pass at her. The law (represented by its unsavoury representatives Langley and Drury) considers her claims beneath contempt. There is no doubt that *Adeline Mowbray* is far from a vindication of "things as they are" in its exposé of cruelty, intolerance, unkindness, and gallantry.

Neither is it a vindication of Adeline and her principles. To admit this is not to offer a simply conservative interpretation of the novel. While Mrs. Pemberton is clearly presented as a positive character, and while we can conclude that Opie shared Mrs. Pemberton's assessment of Adeline's spiritual pride, it would be simplistic to say that the novel condones Adeline's version of *any* principle—even after she changes her views of marriage. Even truth-telling, to which Opie was increasingly devoted, becomes in Adeline's practice remarkably unattractive: Savanna's willingness to tell benevolent fibs is endearingly human. When Adeline claims, late in the novel, that she "became a wife, after [her] idle declamations against marriage, from change of principle, on assurance of error, and not from interest, or necessity" (237), the reader may well be skeptical. Adeline is a problematic heroine whether she is right or wrong—and perhaps this, rather than her own tangled arguments, makes the reader wonder if she could ever have been a good mother to her own growing daughter.

Adeline's decision not to marry Glenmurray is surely much more principled than her decision to marry Berrendale, whom she does not love. She marries Berrendale not only because Glenmurray has urged her to do so, but also because life as an unmarried woman who has previously lived with a lover has become intolerable. The "principle" that informs this decision is unclear: we might be persuaded that Adeline's relationship with Berrendale is little better than legalized prostitution, doubtfully sanctioned by Glenmurray's deathbed bequest but in reality far from the "virtuous" relationship than she has had with Glenmurray. Yet Adeline's "principles" have a certain consistency from first to last: a stubborn dogmatism, a strong thread of egotism, a denial of passion even when passion, not reason, appears to drive her. If Adeline's love for Glenmurray is a response to his character and principles—a Wollstonecraftian ideal of love—her marriage to Berrendale arguably begins as a project of self-interest calculating the benefits of self-sacrifice. Bearing this in mind, one could certainly argue that the truth or falsehood of Adeline's principles is less significant—at least from the perspective of most modern readers—than the rigidity of character that attracts her so stubbornly to principle in the first place.

★ ★ ★

Such an argument leads to relativism, and it works better for the 1805 edition than it does for the revised editions of 1810 and 1844. In general, both the 1810 and 1844 editions show a tendency towards increasing conservatism and a strengthening of the religious message already prominent in the first edition. In the later editions Opie goes to some lengths to minimize ambiguities and to clarify the difference between principles derived from the exercise of reason alone and principles based on religious faith. The 1805 text, the copy-text for this edition, presents us with a radical (but not entirely sympathetic) heroine—at least up to the middle of the second volume, where, as we have seen, she changes her mind (without necessarily becoming more sympathetic). In 1810, Opie made an effort to remove ambiguity from even the first volume, and to make it quite clear that Adeline and Glenmurray should never have lived together outside marriage.

Chapter 10 ends on a positive note. Adeline's education has been improved by her association with Glenmurray: "their attachment was cemented by one of the strongest of all ties—the consciousness of mutual benefit and assistance" (103). But, lest this be interpreted as an endorsement of their relationship,[1] in 1810 Opie adds the following passage:

---

1   And perhaps in response to the reviews of the 1805 edition: see especially the excerpt from the *Critical Review*, Appendix A1.

But the connexion that is founded on a guilty disregard of sound and positive institutions cannot long be productive of happiness, even though the reasonings of perverted intellect and the persuasions of self-love have convinced the offending parties that such an union is wise and virtuous.

Adeline and Glenmurray, while secluded from society, might fancy themselves happy, and be so perhaps in some measure, although they had violated those sacred ties by which society's best interests are kept together: but as soon as society could resume in any way its power, and opportunity of operating on their happiness, that happiness must necessarily vanish; as a dead body which has been preserved from decay by being entirely excluded from the external air, moulders into dust immediately on being exposed to its influence. (See Textual Variants, 288.)

This, more than the deletion of Dr. Norberry's oaths, indicates the intention behind Opie's revisions. Adeline may think she is virtuous; she may raise her hands to heaven with all the fervency of faith; she may seem like an angel to those who meet her. But she is wrong—not just because she is blindly opinionated, or because Opie disagrees with her, or because society makes life difficult for her, but because religion (later embodied by Mrs. Pemberton) teaches that Adeline's virtue is vicious from a divine perspective. One might go so far as to suggest that Mrs. Pemberton is a kind of sanctified revision of Opie's memory of Wollstonecraft: both speak their mind with passion and eloquence; both are heroines of sensibility as well as intellect; both nurse sick and dying friends in Lisbon.[1] However, Mrs. Pemberton asserts the power of a law according to which Adeline and Glenmurray's happiness is merely the illusion of happiness: society's best interests are met not primarily through intellectual effort but through submission to eternal truth.

We could argue, against this conviction, that Opie was wrong to see early nineteenth-century marriage as an expression of the wisdom of the ages. The laws of marriage that exclude Adeline from society were, arguably, refined in the eighteenth century in response to economic interests rather than in accordance with moral or spiritual ones. We could argue that Opie ultimately fails to distinguish an idealized social order—which, she claims, benefits from marriage as a positive institution—from things as they are: oppressive, hypocritical, superficial. We could accuse her of subscribing to an entrenched but insupportable double standard whereby Mordaunt, a self-proclaimed libertine, is able to reform his ways and

---

1   Wollstonecraft went to Lisbon in 1785 to stay with her friend, Fanny Blood, who suffered from consumption and who died in childbirth shortly afterwards. Cf. Wollstonecraft's novella, *Mary, a Fiction* (1788).

marry a good woman, whereas Adeline, a lover of virtue, thinks she has no choice but to welcome death.

Such criticism is justified. Yet Glenmurray is surely right when he comes to think that reason alone may not be an adequate guide for human life. Even Godwin himself had come to a similar position by the time Opie published *Adeline Mowbray*. In his Preface to his own novel, *Fleetwood* (also published in 1805), Godwin makes the point as follows:

> Certain persons, who condescend to make my supposed inconsistencies the favourite object of their research, will perhaps remark with exultation on the respect expressed in this work for marriage; and exclaim, "It was not always thus!" referring to the pages in which their subject is treated in the Enquiry concerning Political Justice for the proof of their assertion. The answer to this remark is exceedingly simple. The production referred to in it, the first foundation of its author's claim to public distinction and favour, was a treatise, aiming to ascertain what new institutions in political society might be found more conducive to general happiness than those which at present prevail. In the course of this disquisition it was enquired, whether marriage, as it stands described and supported in the laws of England, might not with advantage admit of certain modifications? Can any thing be more distinct, than such a proposition on the one hand, and a recommendation on the other than each man for himself should supersede and trample upon the institutions of the country in which he lives? ... The author of Political Justice ... is the last man in the world to recommend a pitiful attempt, by scattered examples to renovate the face of society, instead of endeavouring by discussion and reasoning, to effect a grand and comprehensive improvement in the sentiments of its members.[1]

Opie implies a similar distinction between speculation and rational principle on the one hand and law and social institutions on the other. Perhaps Adeline's critics *are* prejudiced; perhaps her grandparents *should* read Locke and learn to think (as Mrs. Mowbray tells them to do in an amusing early episode). Perhaps—to extend this kind of prescriptive thinking outside the bounds of the novel—Parliament should instantly stop the slave-trade and emancipate the slaves, causes for which Amelia Opie worked throughout her life.[2] Yet change, she well understood, can be a slow process, a mat-

---

1  *Fleetwood: or, The New Man of Feeling*, ed. Gary Handwerk and A.A. Markley (Peterborough: Broadview P, 2001), 48–49.

2  Opie wrote an anti-slavery poem for children, *The Black Man's Lament; or, How to Make Sugar* (London: Harvey and Darton, 1826). She attended the Anti-Slavery Convention in 1840. Throughout her life, long after the emancipation of slaves in

ter not of sudden enlightenment but of struggle, intermittent failure, and uncertain success guided (and here she parts company with Godwin) by faith.

The ambiguity of *Adeline Mowbray* is also the ambiguity and complexity of Amelia Opie's life. Hostess, actress, poet, novelist, and friend of radicals, after her husband's death she became increasingly drawn to the Society of Friends.[1] Her life-long Norwich correspondent and friend, the Quaker Joseph John Gurney, was the brother of Elizabeth Fry (1780-1845), one of the most famous and outspoken Quaker women of her generation, who preached to prisoners and agitated for prison reform: Fry may have helped to inspire the character of Mrs. Pemberton. We can trace in the revisions Opie made to *Adeline Mowbray* not only Opie's slow movement towards the Quakers (she joined the Society in 1825), but also a generational shift away from Revolution-era radicalism and the dazzle of the late Enlightenment towards quieter values, belief in social consensus, and an emphasis on personal religious conviction as a motivation for reform. Opie's admiration for the slavery abolitionist Thomas Clarkson (1760-1846) and her later correspondence with Henry Peter Brougham (1778-1868, Lord Chancellor from 1830 to 1834) associate her with evangelical reformers at least as much as with radicals. Arguably, she came to have as much in common with Hannah More—a member of the Clapham Sect of Anglican evangelicals opposed to the slave trade—as she had once had with the radicals More explicitly opposed.[2]

We know that Opie had read Jean-Jacques Rousseau's *Julie, ou La Nouvelle Héloïse* (1761), an epistolary novel which, to some degree, provides an alternative version of Adeline's own story.[3] Rousseau's heroine has a passionate love affair with Saint-Preux, who is too poor and socially insignificant to qualify as a possible suitor. Eventually she marries, and her husband, Wolmar, befriends Saint-Preux and includes him in the life of their growing family. Saint-Preux continues to love Julie throughout

---

the British Empire (1833), she was still agitating for the emancipation of slaves in America: see MS letter to Lord Brougham, 1 September 1843 (University College London, Special Collections, 17.510).

1 Or Quakers, a religious community founded by George Fox in 1648-50.

2 See the excerpt from More's *Strictures on the Modern System of Female Education, with a View of the Principles and Conduct Prevalent among Women of Rank and Fortune*, 2 vols. (London: T. Cadell, 1799), reprinted as Appendix B2.

3 Opie had also associated Mary Wollstonecraft with Rousseau's Julie, asking her in a letter, "will you help me to account for the strong desire I always feel when with you, to say affectionate things to you? Perhaps it is because you, like Julie, appear so capable of feeling affection that you can not fail to excite it" (28 August [1796], Oxford, Bodleian Library, [Abinger] Dep. b. 210/6).

her life (she dies saving one of her children from drowning). But their relationship is chaste and virtuous, and—some contemporary readers argued—demonstrates that a "fallen woman" can be redeemed and reintegrated into respectable society through marriage, a controversial point in *Adeline Mowbray*. Others (notably More) disagreed, citing the seductive language of the first sections of Rousseau's novel, with their passionate account of illicit love. When Adeline stumbles across *La Nouvelle Héloïse*, she gets no further than the opening letters before her mother forbids her to read further. There is a strong implication in the 1805 and 1810 editions that Adeline might have been spared her own fate had she read to the end of Rousseau's novel. Yet by the time Opie revised her novel for the 1844 edition, she appears to have changed her mind about the possibly beneficial effects of reading Rousseau: the entire passage describing Adeline's encounter with *La Nouvelle Héloïse* is deleted.[1] One effect of this deletion is to intensify Adeline's own point, late in the novel, that death itself is preferable to the morally anomalous status of a woman, no matter how sincerely reformed, who has once fallen into "vice."

Tracing such changes in allusion and emphasis demonstrates that *Adeline Mowbray* is not merely a novel of 1805. In its context and resonance, it spans the whole period from the American and French Revolutions, through the death of Wollstonecraft, the agitation leading up to the Slave Trade Abolition Act of 1807, the Napoleonic period, the period of reaction that followed it, into the first years of Victoria's reign. As we have seen, it perhaps influenced Percy and Harriet Shelley. Dorothy Wordsworth, more conservative than Shelley in her social attitudes, claimed that it "made us quite sick before we got to the end of it."[2] Charlotte Brontë perhaps found in the description of Berrendale's Creole wife, who "might even attack Berrendale's life in the first moment of ungoverned passion" (246), a hint for the much more fully developed character of Bertha Rochester in *Jane Eyre* (1847). Thomas Hardy may well have been thinking about the portrayal of chastity and "purity" in such novels as *Adeline Mowbray* when he subtitled *Tess of the d'Urbervilles* (1891), "A Pure Woman."

The revisions of *Adeline Mowbray* through the period from 1805 to 1844 allow us to trace the passage of a highly intelligent and well-connected writer from her youth in fashionable and radical society in the late eighteenth century, through literary fame in the early nineteenth century, to

---

1  See 93, and Textual Variants 257.
2  Letter to William Wordsworth, 23 April 1812: "us" refers to Dorothy and Sara Hutchinson.

her abandonment of fiction after she joined the Society of Friends[1]—and they invite us to speculate on her changing attitude to her own story, to the story she was telling, and to the telling of stories in general. In 1805 *Adeline Mowbray* had been rather a controversial book—read favourably by its contemporary reviewers, but still with the power to shock, to disturb, and to inspire debate. In 1810, it still had the power to engage its writer with values that mattered to her. By 1844, however, it had become part of Opie's past, a moral tale with a religious message, rather hastily revised for a new edition (if one can judge from the relatively large number of errors in the 1844 text).[2] By 1844, Opie revises much more superficially than she did in 1810, targeting oaths, expletives, and sexual references; indeed, she appears to have forgotten about many of the more interesting changes that had engaged her in 1810. Sometimes she appears not to be paying specific attention to context (as for example, when she adds a phrase saying that Glenmurray had called a coach without removing the earlier edition's attribution of the same action to Dr. Norberry). Perhaps she has lost interest in this particular novel—and, as a Quaker, in the writing of fiction in general. "I must not write pure fiction; I must not *lye*, and say, 'so and so occurred,' or 'such and such a thing took place,' when it did not," she wrote in 1827, in response to a request for a short story for a literary annual.[3]

Through the variant readings of 1805, 1810, and 1844, the present edition undertakes to present this changing context and consciousness. The central questions are not fully resolved: I find it difficult to believe that Adeline's death contributes anything significant to the lives of the other characters—and the women around her deathbed, as Roxanne Eberle argues, seem to have retreated into "the claustrophobic space of the 'domestic sphere' later in the century."[4] The peripheral colonial journeys are forgotten: Savanna, on whose bosom Adeline expires, has been thoroughly

---

1 However, even in her *Illustrations of Lying, in All Its Branches*, 2 vols. (London: Longman, Hurst, Rees, Orme, Brown, and Green, 1825) Opie uses extended and evidently fictional examples to illustrate each kind of lie she condemns.

2 The passage quoted above from 1810 was omitted in 1844—evidence for my view that Opie probably worked from an 1805 text in making her revisions for the 1844 edition. In their edition of *Adeline Mowbray* (Oxford: Oxford UP, 1999), Shelley King and John B. Pierce perhaps underestimate how substantial the changes made in 1810 actually were: see the headnote to their Textual Notes, 269.

3 S.C. Hall, *A Book of Memories of Great Men and Women of the Age*, 2nd ed. (1877), 169 n., qtd. in Gary Kelly, "Amelia Opie," in the *Oxford Dictionary of National Biography*, <http://www.oxforddnb.com>. Opie's dislike of all kinds of untruth is one thing she has in common with her heroine.

4 "Amelia Opie's *Adeline Mowbray*: Diverting the Libertine Gaze; or, The Vindication of a Fallen Woman." *Studies in the Novel* 26 (1994): 146.

converted (and co-opted). The vexed relationship between law (social) and morality (personal) has been not so much resolved as evaded. Neither things as they are nor the fallen woman who challenges them is truly vindicated: both are anatomized and then sidelined. Yet women's work in the world seems to go on, regardless of the ideological debates. The *practice* of benevolence—whether it takes the form of Mrs. Mowbray's charitable work on her estate, or Mrs. Pemberton's preaching, or Opie's anti-slavery agitation, or Hannah More's evangelical good works—becomes an important context for reading this novel and for understanding the life of its author.

Opie's apparent abandonment of Wollstonecraftian feminism and of a consistent theoretical approach to political and social change may rankle with modern readers; but she succeeded to a considerable degree in reaching the goals she set herself. Unlike Wollstonecraft, who "died alas! before she could see the victory which she so well deserved to obtain—,"[1] Opie lived to see at least one of her lifelong goals accomplished: the emancipation of slaves in the British Empire. Her biographer Cecilia Brightwell describes her at the age of eighty, racing an old friend in their wheel-chairs at the Great Exhibition of 1851.[2] At that high moment of Victorian optimism and celebration of imperialism, when Opie's life as a poet, novelist, fashionable beauty, and wife was well behind her, she had good reason for high spirits, and good reason to feel at home in the world she had played a considerable role in bringing into being. She never had a daughter of her own, but—a child of Empire and Enlightenment—she was one of the mothers of the Victorian world.

---

1  See above 23, n. 1.
2  Brightwell 389.

# Amelia Alderson Opie: A Brief Chronology

| | |
|---|---|
| 1769 | Born 12 November, Amelia Alderson is baptized at St. George Parish, Norwich; she is the only child of James Alderson, physician, and Amelia (Briggs) Alderson, daughter of Mary Worrell Briggs and Joseph Briggs. |
| 1784 | Mother dies, 31 December; Amelia Alderson becomes her father's hostess and is befriended by Susannah Taylor, who becomes her confidante. |
| 1790 | *Dangers of Coquetry* (2 vols.) published anonymously by William Lane of Minerva Press. |
| 1791 | *Adelaide*, a tragedy by Amelia Alderson, staged at the private theatre of Robert Plumptre, Prebend of Norwich, 4 and 6 January, with Alderson in the title role and the Plumptre sisters (Anne and Bell) playing other parts. |
| 1794 | *The Cabinet*, a radical periodical, founded in September at Norwich; Amelia Alderson contributes fifteen poems to the first three issues, 1794-95. Thomas Holcroft and Horne Tooke are tried for treason in November; Amelia Alderson attends the trial. |
| 1798 | Marries John Opie, 8 May; they live in London at 8 Berners St. |
| 1799 | Publishes four poems in the *Annual Anthology*, ed. Robert Southey. |
| 1800 | Another poem published in the *Annual Anthology*. |
| 1801 | *The Father and Daughter: A Tale in Prose; with an Epistle from the Maid of Corinth to her Lover; and Other Poetical Pieces*, published by Longman, Hurst, Rees, Orme and Brown. |
| 1802 | August: the Opies visit Paris during the Peace of Amiens, meeting the painter Benjamin West, the Whig politician Charles James Fox, the Polish-Lithuanian nationalist Tadeusz Kosciuszko, the painter Jacques-Louis David, the actor François Joseph Talma, and the writer Helen Maria Williams; Opie also sees Napoleon. *An Elegy to the Memory of the Late Duke of Bedford* is published in March, and *Poems* is published in October. |
| 1805 | *Adeline Mowbray, or The Mother and Daughter; A Tale* (3 vols.) published in early January. |
| 1806 | *Simple Tales* (4 vols.) published in the spring. |
| 1807 | John Opie dies 9 April; Amelia Opie arranges an elaborate funeral at St. Paul's, London; returns to her father's house in Norwich and resumes her childhood friendship with the Gurney family. |

| 1808 | *The Warrior's Return, and other Poems* (two editions published this year). |
|---|---|
| 1809 | Preface to John Opie's *Lectures on Painting*; *L'Agnese*, an opera by Ferdinando Paer, based on *The Father and Daughter*. |
| 1810 | *Adeline Mowbray, or The Mother and Daughter; A Tale*, "3rd ed." (actually the second). |
| 1812 | *Temper, or, Domestic Scenes: a Tale* (3 vols.). |
| 1813 | *Tales of Real Life* published in June. |
| 1814 | *Duty: A Novel*, by "Mrs. Roberts," edited with an introductory memoir by Opie; Opie begins attending Quaker meetings. |
| 1815 | Opie edits Margaret Ward Roberts, *Duty: A Novel* (3 vols.). |
| 1816 | *Valentine's Eve* published. |
| 1817 | Visits William Hayley at Eartham. |
| 1818 | *New Tales* published in the spring; Hayley dies in November. |
| 1820 | *Tales of the Heart*; Anti-Slavery Society founded; *The Father and Daughter* adapted for the stage by W.T. Moncrieff as *The Lear of Private Life; or, The Father and Daughter*. |
| 1822 | *Madeline: A Tale* (Opie's last completed published novel). |
| 1823 | Verse letters in the persona of Mary, Queen of Scots ("Epistles from Mary Queen of Scots to her Uncles"), for the *European Magazine*; also two stories; for religious reasons, Opie abandons her unfinished novel, *The Painter and his Wife*. |
| 1825 | Admitted to the Society of Friends in August; Opie's father dies in October; publishes *Illustrations of Lying in All its Branches* and *Tales of the Pemberton Family* (a children's book). |
| 1826 | *The Black Man's Lament, or, How to Make Sugar* (an illustrated anti-slavery poem). |
| 1828 | *Detraction Displayed* published. |
| 1829 | Visits Paris; sees Lafayette. |
| 1830 | Visits Paris again following the July Revolution. |
| 1834 | *Lays for the Dead* published; Opie tours the Scottish Highlands. |
| 1835 | Travels from Belgium up the Rhine to Switzerland. |
| 1840 | Represents Norwich at the Anti-Slavery Convention. |
| 1844 | *Adeline Mowbray, or The Mother and Daughter; A Tale*, revised and illustrated edition. |
| 1851 | Visits the Great Exhibition in London. |
| 1853 | Dies 2 December; Opie is buried with her father in the Friends' Cemetery, Norwich. |

# A Note on the Text

*Adeline Mowbray, or The Mother and Daughter; A Tale* was first published early in 1805, in three volumes, in a first impression of 2,000 copies.[1] According to Peter Garside, Longman archives in December 1804 record £260.15.6 spent for production and £30.0.0 for advertising. Copies began to be distributed on 12 January 1805. By June, 1,070 copies had been sold; by March 1806, another 369. By 20 June 1807 another 216 copies had been sold. Three years later, a total of 1,983 copies of the first edition had been sold.

A "second edition" of 1805 proves to be not an edition at all, but simply a reprint with a new title page. (Opie perhaps remembers this when, in 1825, she gives as an example of lying "the author ... who makes his publisher put second and third editions before a work of which, perhaps, not even the first edition is sold."[2]) Five hundred copies of the "third edition" (the second true edition) appeared in 1810, with authorial corrections.[3] Finally, Longman published "A New and Illustrated Edition" in 1844, again corrected by Opie (and including two previously published short stories, "The Welcome Home" and "The Quaker and the Young Man of the World"). It seems probable that in revising *Adeline Mowbray* for the 1844 edition she went back to the 1805 text: as my list of Textual Variants demonstrates, most of the substantive changes made in 1810 appear not to have been retained in 1844, and many of the changes that appear in both 1810 and 1844 editions are relatively minor.

There were many American editions during Opie's lifetime, none of which had her approval. The first was *Adeline Mowbray; or, The Mother and Daughter. A Tale, in Two Volumes. By Mrs. Opie* (Georgetown: J. Milligan, 1808). As the title-page indicates, it appeared in two rather than three volumes, with some revision of spelling and punctuation. Otherwise the text appears to be identical with that of 1805.

---

1  The title-page of the 1805 edition reads, "London and Edinburgh," not just "London" (as in the 1810 edition). For more information about the publication history, see Peter Garside et al., "British Fiction, 1800-1829: Publishing Papers," <http://www.british-fiction.cf.ac.uk/publishing/adel05-57.html>, and the Note on the Text in the edition of *Adeline Mowbray* by Shelley King and John B. Pierce, xxxiii-iv.

2  *Illustrations of Lying, in All Its Branches* (1825), 2: 64.

3  The British Library copy on which Gina Luria's Garland ed. is based appears to be a composite of the 1805 and 1810 editions: vol. 1 is 1805; vol. 2, "1801" (a typographical mistake for 1810); vol. 3, 1810.

In preparing the present edition, I have used as my copy-text the 1805 edition held by the Thomas Fisher Rare Books Library, University of Toronto, checking it against the facsimile edited by Gina Luria (volume 1 only: see 37, note 3 above), the Woodstock facsimile edition (based on a copy of the 1805 edition in the Bodleian Library), and the incomplete copy in the University of Alberta Library (volumes 1 and 2 only). Variant readings, indicated by superscripts in the text of the novel, are based on the facsimile edited by Gina Luria (for volumes 2 and 3 of 1810), on the copy of the 1810 edition held by the University of Wisconsin Library,[1] and on the copy of the 1844 edition held by Princeton University Library.

I have used the 1805 edition as my copy-text in spite of the fact that Opie herself revised the novel as late as 1844. While the latest edition published in her lifetime might be assumed to represent her final intentions, it appears to have been hastily prepared;[2] there is reason to believe that by 1844 Opie was no longer keenly interested in this novel of almost forty years earlier. The 1810 "third" edition is far more carefully and thoroughly revised. Yet many of Opie's changes diminish its interest for the modern reader: Dr. Norberry's oaths, the discussion of Rousseau, and the vulgarity of Adeline's assailants in the street are all mitigated or deleted. While the 1810 and 1844 editions are probably better reflections of Opie's increasingly conservative and religious views, the colloquial language and topical references in the 1805 edition make it a lively product of the time for which and out of which it was written. As a novel that draws heavily on contemporary debates about marriage, duelling, revolution, religion, and women's education, the roots of *Adeline Mowbray* in the debates of the late eighteenth and early nineteenth centuries deserve emphasis. Since the present edition includes a full list of textual variants (identified in the text by asterisk and other symbols), the reader who is interested in learning how the novel changed in subsequent revisions has an opportunity of doing so—and of tracing changing tastes and attitudes through the first half the nineteenth century.

I have retained spelling and almost all original punctuation, occasionally substituting Opie's 1810 revisions in cases where they serve to clarify meaning. Very occasionally I have silently amended punctuation where the original renders a passage obscure. I have corrected only evident typographical errors (e.g., "daughters" for "daughter's") and have made occasional changes in the use of quotation marks to comply, for the sake of clarity, with modern conventions.

---

1  Pages 103-04 of volume 2 are missing from the University of Wisconsin copy.
2  See Introduction 32-33.

# ADELINE MOWBRAY,

## OR THE MOTHER AND DAUGHTER;

## A TALE

# CHAPTER 1

In an old family mansion, situated on an estate in Gloucestershire known by the name of Rosevalley, resided Mrs. Mowbray, and Adeline her only child.

Mrs. Mowbray's father, Mr. Woodville, a respectable country gentleman, married, in obedience to the will of his mother, the sole surviving daughter of an opulent merchant in London, whose large dower paid off some considerable mortgages on the Woodville estates, and whose mild and unoffending character soon gained that affection from her husband after marriage, which he denied her before it.

Nor was it long before their happiness was increased, and their union cemented, by the birth of a daughter; who continuing to be an only child, and the probable heiress of great possessions, became the idol of her parents, and the object of unremitted attention to those who surrounded her. Consequently, one of the first lessons which Editha Woodville learnt was that of egotism, and to consider it as the chief duty of all who approached her, to study the gratification of her whims and caprices.

But, though rendered indolent in some measure by the blind folly of her parents, and the homage of her dependents, she had a taste above the enjoyments which they offered her.

She had a decided passion for literature, which she had acquired from a sister of Mr. Woodville, who had been brought up amongst literary characters of various pursuits and opinions; and this lady had imbibed from them a love of free inquiry, which she had little difficulty in imparting to her young and enthusiastic relation.

But, alas! that inclination for study, which, had it been directed to proper objects, would have been the charm of miss Woodville's life, and the safeguard of her happiness, by giving her a constant source of amusement within herself, proved to her, from the unfortunate direction which it took, the abundant cause of misery and disappointment.

For her, history, biography, poetry, and discoveries in natural philosophy, had few attractions, while she pored with still unsatisfied delight over abstruse systems of morals and metaphysics, or new theories in politics; and scarcely a week elapsed in which she did not receive, from her aunt's bookseller in London, various tracts on these her favourite subjects.

Happy would it have been for miss Woodville, if the merits of the works which she so much admired could have been canvassed in her presence by rational and unprejudiced persons: but, her parents and friends being too ignorant to discuss philosophical opinions or political controversies, the young speculator was left to the decisions of her own inexperienced enthusiasm. To her, therefore, whatever was bold and uncommon seemed new and wise; and every succeeding theory held her imagination captive till its power was weakened by one of equal claims to singularity.

She soon, however, ceased to be contented with reading, and was eager to become a writer also. But, as she was strongly imbued with the prejudices of an antient family, she could not think of disgracing that family by turning professed author: she therefore confined her little effusions to a society of admiring friends, secretly lamenting the loss which the literary world sustained in her being born a gentlewoman.

Nor is it to be wondered at, that, as she was ambitious to be, and to be thought, a deep thinker, she should have acquired habits of abstraction, and absence, which imparted a look of wildness to a pair of dark eyes, that beamed with intelligence, and gave life to features of the most perfect regularity.

To reverie, indeed, she was from childhood inclined; and her life was long a life of reverie.[1] To her the present moment had scarcely ever existence; and this propensity to lose herself in a sort of ideal world, was considerably increased by the nature of her studies.

Fatal and unproductive studies! While, wrapt in philosophical abstraction, she was trying to understand a metaphysical question on the mechanism of the human mind, or what constituted the true nature of virtue, she suffered day after day to pass in the culpable neglect of positive duties; and while imagining systems for the good of society, and the furtherance of general philanthropy, she allowed individual suffering in her neighbourhood to pass unobserved and unrelieved. While professing her unbounded love for the great family of the world, she suffered her own family to pine under the consciousness of her neglect; and viciously devoted those hours to the vanity of abstruse and solitary study, which might have been better spent in amusing the declining age of her venerable parents, whom affection had led to take up their abode with her.

Let me observe, before I proceed further, that Mrs. Mowbray scrupulously confined herself to theory, even in her wisest speculations; and being too timid, and too indolent, to illustrate by her conduct the various and opposing doctrines which it was her pride to maintain by turns, her practice was ever in opposition to her opinions.

---

1  A dream-like state. Opie, like Wollstonecraft, uses the term both positively and negatively: Wollstonecraft refers to "the reveries of the stupid novelists" (*A Vindication of the Rights of Woman*, in *The Vindications*, ed. D.L. Macdonald and Kathleen Scherf, 330), but—perhaps influenced by Jean-Jacques Rousseau's *Reveries of the Solitary Walker* (1782)—herself indulges in melancholy day-dreams in *Letters Written During a Short Residence in Sweden, Norway, and Denmark* (1796).

Hence, after haranguing with all the violence of a true whig* on the natural rights of man,[1] or the blessings of freedom, she would "turn to a tory† in her elbow chair,"[2] and govern her household with despotic authority; and after embracing at some moments the doubts of the sceptic, she would often lie motionless in her bed, from apprehension of ghosts, a helpless prey to the most abject superstition.

Such was the mother of ADELINE MOWBRAY! such was the woman who, having married the heir of Rosevalley, merely to oblige her parents, saw herself in the prime of life a rich widow, with an only child, who was left by Mr. Mowbray, a fond husband, but an ill-judging parent, entirely dependent on her!

At the time of Mr. Mowbray's death, Adeline Mowbray was ten years old, and Mrs. Mowbray thirty; and like an animal in an exhausted receiver,[3] she had during her short existence been tormented by the experimental philosophy of her mother.

Now it was judged right that she should learn nothing, and now that she should learn every thing. Now, her graceful form and well-turned limbs were to be free from any bandage, and any clothing save what decency required,—and now they were to be tortured by stiff stays, and fettered by the stocks and the back-board.

All Mrs. Mowbray's ambition had settled in one point, one passion, and that was EDUCATION. For this purpose she turned over innumerable volumes in search of rules on the subject, on which she might improve, anticipating with great satisfaction the moment when she should be held

---

1   John Locke (1632-1704) understood natural rights to include the right to worship freely, to participate in government, and to own property. Jean-Jacques Rousseau (1712-78) developed this into his theory of a social contract to which people voluntarily subscribed. Such ideas were influential in the period of the American Revolution, when natural rights were used to justify revolution against Britain. Whigs and Tories were the political parties of Opie's day, roughly associated respectively with liberal (even sometimes radical) and conservative views.

2   William Hayley, *The Triumphs of Temper, A Poem. In Six Cantos* (1781; 10th ed. 1799): "Beneath a father's care SERENA grew; / The good SIR GILBERT, to his country true, / A faithful Whig, who, zealous for the state, / In freedom's service led the loud debate; / Yet every day, by transmutation rare, / Turn'd to a Tory in his elbow-chair, / And made his daughter pay, howe'er absurd, / Passive obedience to his sovereign word" (29-36). Opie regularly visited Hayley, a former patron of the poet and engraver William Blake, until Hayley's death in 1820. (Blake had lived near Hayley's house in Felpham from 1800-03.)

3   A bell-jar from which the air has been removed; Opie evidently knows about the experiments which the natural philosopher Robert Boyle (1627-91) conducted on animal respiration.

up as a pattern of imitation to mothers, and be prevailed upon, though with graceful reluctance, to publish her system, without a name, for the benefit of society.[1]

But, however good her intentions were, the execution of them was continually delayed by her habits of abstraction and reverie. After having over night arranged the tasks of Adeline for the next day,—lost in some new speculations for the good of her child, she would lie in bed all the morning, exposing that child to the dangers of idleness.

At one time Mrs. Mowbray had studied herself into great nicety with regard to the diet of her daughter; but, as she herself was too much used to the indulgencies of the palate to be able to set her in reality an example of temperance, she dined in appearance with Adeline at one o'clock on pudding without butter, and potatoes without salt; but while the child was taking her afternoon's walk, her own table was covered with viands fitted for the appetite of opulence.

Unfortunately, however, the servants conceived that the daughter as well as the mother had a right to regale clandestinely; and the little Adeline used to eat for her supper, with a charge not to tell her mamma, some of the good things set by from Mrs. Mowbray's dinner.

It happened that, as Mrs. Mowbray was one evening smoothing Adeline's flowing curls, and stroking her ruddy cheek, she exclaimed triumphantly, raising Adeline to the glass, "See the effect of temperance and low living! If you were accustomed to eat meat, and butter, and drink any thing but water, you would not look so healthy, my love, as you do now. O the excellent effects of a vegetable diet!"[2]

The artless girl, whose conscience smote her during the whole of this speech, hung her blushing head on her bosom:—it was the confusion of guilt; and Mrs. Mowbray perceiving it earnestly demanded what it meant, when Adeline, half crying, gave a full explanation.

Nothing could exceed the astonishment and mortification of Mrs. Mowbray; but, though usually tenacious of her opinions, she in this case profited by the lesson of experience. She no longer expected any advantage from clandestine measures:—but Adeline, her appetites regulated by a proper exertion of parental authority, was allowed to sit at the well-fur-

---

1 Mrs. Mowbray's proposed book would have supplemented John Locke (*Some Thoughts Concerning Education* [1693], see Appendix B1), Jean-Jacques Rousseau (*Emile* [1762]), Mary Wollstonecraft (*Thoughts on the Education of Daughters* [1787]), and a whole range of commentators on women's social roles, including Hannah More (*Strictures on the Modern System of Female Education* [1799]; see Appendix B2).

2 Cf. for example, John Locke, *Some Thoughts Concerning Education* (1693), sections 1.13 and 1.14 (in Appendix B1).

nished table of her mother, and was precluded, by a judicious and open indulgence, from wishing for a secret and improper one; while the judicious praises which Mrs. Mowbray bestowed on Adeline's ingenuous confession endeared to her the practice of truth, and laid the foundation of a habit of ingenuousness which formed through life one of the ornaments of her character.... Would that Mrs. Mowbray had always been equally judicious!

Another great object of anxiety to her was the method of clothing children; whether they should wear flannel, or no flannel; light shoes, to give agility to the motions of the limbs; or heavy shoes, in order to strengthen the muscles by exertion;—when one day, as she was turning over a voluminous author on this subject, the nursery-maid hastily entered the room, and claimed her attention, but in vain; Mrs. Mowbray went on reading aloud:—

"Some persons are of opinion that thin shoes are most beneficial to health; others, equally worthy of respect, think thick ones of most use: and the reasons for these different opinions we shall class under two heads...."

"Dear me, ma'am!" cried Bridget, "and in the mean time miss Adeline will go without any shoes at all."

"Do not interrupt me, Bridget," cried Mrs. Mowbray, and proceeded to read on. "In the first place, it is not clear, says a learned writer, whether children require any clothing at all for their feet."[1]

At this moment Adeline burst open the parlour door, and, crying bitterly, held up her bleeding toes to her mother.

"Mamma, mamma!" cried she, "you forget to send for a pair of new shoes for me; and see, how the stones in the gravel have cut me!"

This sight, this appeal, decided the question in dispute. The feet of Adeline bleeding on a new Turkey carpet proved that some clothing for the feet was necessary; and even Mrs. Mowbray for a moment began to suspect that a little experience is better than a great deal of theory.


CHAPTER 2

MEANWHILE, in spite of all Mrs. Mowbray's eccentricities and caprices, Adeline, as she grew up, continued to entertain for her the most perfect respect and affection.

---

1 Cf. Locke, *Some Thoughts Concerning Education* 1.7, in Appendix B1. Most writers, however, argue for proper shoes, e.g., J. Fothergell, *Rules for the Preservation of Health* (1770?), Lewis Mansey, *The Practical Physician* (1800), William Buchan, *Domestic Medicine* (1792).

Her respect was excited by the high idea which she had formed of her abilities,—an idea founded on the veneration which all the family seemed to feel for her on that account,—and her affection was excited even to an enthusiastic degree by the tenderness with which Mrs. Mowbray had watched over her during an alarming illness.

For twenty-one days Adeline had been in the utmost danger; nor is it probable that she would have been able to struggle against the force of the disease, but for the unremitting attention of her mother. It was then, perhaps, for the first time that Mrs. Mowbray felt herself a mother:—all her vanities, all her systems, were forgotten in the danger of Adeline,—she did not even hazard an opinion on the medical treatment to be observed. For once she was contented to obey instructions in silence; for once she was never caught in a reverie; but, like the most common-place woman of her acquaintance, she lived to the present moment:—and she was rewarded for her cares by the recovery of her daughter, and by that daughter's most devoted attachment.

Not even the parents of Mrs. Mowbray, who, because she talked on subjects which they could not understand, looked up to her as a superior being, could exceed Adeline in deference to her mother's abilities; and when, as she advanced in life, she was sometimes tempted to think her deficient in maternal fondness, the idea of Mrs. Mowbray bending with pale and speechless anxiety over her sleepless pillow used to recur to her remembrance, and in a moment the recent indifference was forgotten.

Nor could she entirely acquit herself of ingratitude in observing this seeming indifference: for, whence did the abstraction and apparent coldness of Mrs. Mowbray proceed? From her mind's being wholly engrossed in studies for the future benefit of Adeline. Why did she leave the concerns of her family to others? why did she allow her infirm but active mother to superintend all the household duties? and why did she seclude herself from all society, save that of her own family, and Dr. Norberry, her physician and friend, but that she might devote every hour to endeavours to perfect a system of education for her beloved and only daughter, to whom the work was to be dedicated?[*] "And yet," said Adeline mentally, "I am so ungrateful sometimes as to think she does not love me sufficiently."

But while Mrs. Mowbray was busying herself in plans for Adeline's education, she reached the age of fifteen, and was in a manner educated; not, however, by her,—though Mrs. Mowbray would, no doubt, have been surprised to have heard this assertion.

Mrs. Mowbray, as I have before said, was the spoiled child of rich parents; who, as geniuses were rarer in those days than they are now, spite of their own ignorance, rejoiced to find themselves the parents of a genius;

and as their daughter always disliked the usual occupations of her sex, the admiring father and mother contented themselves with allowing her to please herself; saying to each other, "She must not be managed in a common way; for you know, my dear, she is one of your geniuses,—and they are never like other folks."

Mrs. Woodville, the mother, had been brought up with all the ideas of œconomy and housewifery which at that time of day prevailed in the city, and influenced the education of the daughters of citizens.

"My dear," said she one day to Adeline, "as you are no genius, you know, like your mother, (and God forbid you should! for one is quite enough in a family,) I shall make bold to teach you every thing that young women in my young days used to learn, and my daughter may thank me for it some time or other: for you know, my dear, when I and my good man die, what in the world would come of my poor Edith, if so be she had no one to manage for her! for, Lord love you! she knows no more of managing a family, and such-like, than a new-born babe."

"And can you, dear grandmother, teach me to be of use to my mother?" said Adeline.

"To be sure, child; for, as you are no genius, no doubt you can learn all them there* sort of things that women commonly know:—so we will begin directly."

In a short time Adeline, stimulated by the ambition of being useful, (for she had often heard her mother assert that utility was the foundation of all virtue,)[1] became as expert in household affairs as Mrs. Woodville herself: even the department of making pastry was now given up to Adeline, and the servants always came to her for orders, saying, that "as their mistress was a learned lady, and that, and so could not be spoken with except here and there on occasion, they wished their young mistress, who was more easy spoken, would please to order":† and as Mr. and Mrs. Woodville's infirmities increased every day, Adeline soon thought it right to assume the entire management of the family.

She also took upon herself the office of almoner[2] to Mrs. Woodville, and performed it with an activity unknown to her;‡ for she herself carried the broth and wine that were to comfort the infirm cottager; she herself saw the medicine properly administered that was to preserve his suffering existence: the comforts the poor required she purchased herself; and in sickness she visited, in sorrow she wept with them. And though§ Adeline was almost unknown personally to the neighbouring gentry, she

---

1  A Godwinian idea; see also David Hume, *An Enquiry into the Principles of Morals* (1751), section 5, "Why Utility Pleases," part 1.
2  Someone employed to distribute alms.

was followed with blessings by the surrounding cottagers; while many a humble peasant watched at the gate of the park to catch a glimpse of his young benefactress, and pray God* to repay to the heiress of Rosevalley the kindness which she had shown to him and his offspring.

Thus happy, because usefully employed, and thus beloved and respected, because actively benevolent, passed the early years of Adeline Mowbray; and thus was she educated, before her mother had completed her system of education.

It was not long before Adeline took on herself a still more important office. Mrs. Mowbray's steward was detected in very dishonest practices; but, as she was too much devoted to her studies to like to look into her affairs with a view to dismiss him, she could not be prevailed upon† to discharge him from her service. Fortunately, however, her father on his death-bed made it his request that she would do so; and Mrs. Mowbray pledged herself to obey him.

"But what shall I do for a steward in Davison's place?" said she soon after her father died.

"Is one absolutely necessary?" returned Adeline modestly. "Surely farmer Jenkins would undertake to do all that is necessary for half the money; and, if he were properly overlooked—"

"And pray who can overlook him properly?" asked Mrs. Mowbray.

"My grandmother and I," replied Adeline timidly: "we both like business, and—"

"Like business! ... but what do you know of it?"

"Know!" cried Mrs. Woodville, "why, daughter, Lina is very clever at it, I assure you!"

"Astonishing! She knows nothing yet of accounts."

"Dear me! how mistaken you are, child! She knows accounts perfectly."‡

"Impossible!" replied Mrs. Mowbray: "who should have taught her? I have been inventing an easy method of learning arithmetic, by which I was going to teach her in a few months."

"Yes, child: but I, thinking it a pity that the poor girl should learn nothing, like, till she was to learn every thing, taught her according to the old way; and I cannot but say she took to it very kindly. Did not you, Lina?"

"Yes, grandmother," said Adeline; "and as I love arithmetic very much, I am quite anxious to keep all my mother's accounts, and overlook the accounts of the person whom she shall employ to manage her estates in future."

To this Mrs. Mowbray, half pleased and half mortified, at length consented; and Adeline and farmer Jenkins entered upon their occupations. Shortly after Mrs. Woodville was seized with her last illness; and Adeline neglected every other duty, and Mrs. Mowbray her studies, "to watch, and weep, beside a parent's bed."[1]

But watch and weep was all Mrs. Mowbray did: with every possible wish to be useful, she had so long given way to habits of abstraction, and neglect of everyday occupations, that she was rather a hindrance than a help in the sick-room.

During Adeline's illness, excessive fear of losing her only child had indeed awakened her to unusual exertion; and as all that she had to do was to get down, at stated times, a certain quantity of wine and nourishment, her task though wearisome was not difficult: but to sooth the declining hours of an aged parent, to please the capricious appetite of decay, to assist with ready and skilful alacrity the shaking hand of the invalid, jealous of waiting on herself and wanting to be cheated into being waited upon;—these trifling yet important details did not suit the habits of Mrs. Mowbray. But Adeline was versed in them all; and her mother, conscious of her superiority in these things, was at last contented to sit by inactive, though not unmoved.

One day, when Mrs. Mowbray had been prevailed upon to lie down for an hour or two in another apartment, and Adeline was administering to Mrs. Woodville some broth which she had made herself, the old lady pressed her hand affectionately, and cried, "Ah! child, in a lucky hour I made bold to interfere, and teach you what your mother was always* too clever to learn. Wise was I to think one genius enough in a family,—else, what should I have done now? Lord bless me! my† daughter, though the best child in the world, could never have made such nice broth as this to comfort me, so hot, and boiled to a minute like! Lord bless‡ her! she'd have tried, that she would, but ten to one but she'd have smoked it, overturned it, and scalt her fingers into the bargain.—Ah, Lina, Lina! mayhap the time will come, when you, should you have a sick husband or child§ to nurse, may bless your poor grandmother for having taught you to be useful."

"Dear grandmother," said Adeline tenderly, "the time is** come: I am, you see, useful to you; and therefore I bless you already for having taught me to be so."

"Good girl, good girl! just what I would have you! And God forgive me, and you too,†† Lina, when I own that I have often thanked God for not making you a genius! Not but what no child can behave better than mine; for, with all her wit and learning, she was always so respectful, and so kind to me and my dear good man, that I am sure I could not but

---

1    Anna Laetitia Barbauld, "To Miss R——, on her Attendance upon her Mother at Buxton," in *Poems* (1773).

rejoice in such a daughter; though, to be sure, I used to wish she was more conversible like; for, as to the matter of a bit of chat, Lord help us and save us!* we never gossiped together in our lives. And though, to be sure, the squires' ladies about are none of the brightest, and not to compare with my Edith, yet still they would have done very well† for me and my dear good man to gossip a bit with. So I was vexed when my daughter declared she wanted all her time for her studies, and would not visit any body, no, not even Mrs. Norberry, who is to be sure a very good sort of woman, though a little given to speak ill of her neighbours. But then so we are all, you know: and, as I say, why, if one spoke well of all alike, what would be the use of one person's being better than his neighbours, except for conscience's sake? But, as I was going to say, my daughter was pleased to compliment me, and declare she was sure I could amuse myself without visiting women so much inferior to me; and she advised my beginning a course of study, as she called it."

"And did you?" asked Adeline with surprise.

"Yes. To oblige her, my good man and I began to read one Mr. Locke on the conduct of the human understanding;‡¹ which my daughter said would teach us to think."

"To think?" said Adeline.

"Yes.—Now, you must know, my poor husband did not look upon it as very respectful like in Edith to say that, because it seemed to say that we had lived all these years without having thought at all; which was not true, to be sure, because we were never thoughtless like, and my husband was so staid when a boy that he was called a little old man."

"But I am sure," said Adeline, half smiling, "that my mother did not mean to insinuate that you wanted proper thought."

"No, I dare say not," resumed the old lady, "and so I told my husband, and so we set to study this book: but, dear me! it was Hebrew Greek to us—and so dull!"

"Then you did not get through it, I suppose?"

"Through it, bless your heart! No—not three pages! So my good man says to Edith, says he, 'You gave us this book, I think, child, to teach us to think?' 'Yes, sir,' says she. 'And it has taught us think,' says he:—'it has taught us to think that it is very dull and disagreeable.' So my daughter laughed, and said her father was witty; but, poor soul! he did not mean it.

"Well, then: as, to amuse us, we liked to look at the stars sometimes, she told us we had better learn their names, and study astronomy; and so

---

1 John Locke's *An Essay Concerning Human Understanding* (1689), a foundational text in the history of empiricism, argues that we come into the world without innate ideas, but that the mind is shaped and furnished by experience.

we began that: but that was just as bad as Mr. Locke; and we knew no more of the stars and planets, than the man in the moon. Yet that's not right to say, neither; for, as he is so much nearer the stars, he must know more about them than any one whosomever. So at last my daughter found out that learning was not our taste: so she left us to please ourselves, and play cribbage and draughts[1] in an evening as usual.".

Here the old lady paused, and Adeline said affectionately, "Dear grandmother, I doubt[2] you exert yourself too much: so much talking can't be good for you."

"O! yes, child!" replied Mrs. Woodville: "it is no trouble at all to me, I assure you, but quite natural and pleasant like: besides, you know I shall not be able to talk much longer, so let me make the most of my time now."

This speech brought tears into the eyes of Adeline; and seeing her mother re-enter the room, she withdrew to conceal the emotion which she felt, lest the cheerful loquacity of the invalid, which she was fond of indulging, should be checked by seeing her tears. But it had already received a check from the presence of Mrs. Mowbray, of whose superior abilities Mrs. Woodville was so much in awe, that, concluding her daughter could not bear to hear her nonsense, the old lady smiled kindly on her when with a look of tender anxiety she hastened to her bedside, and then, holding her hand, composed herself to sleep.

In a few days more, she breathed her last on the supporting arm of Adeline; and lamented in her dying moments, that she had nothing valuable in money to leave, in order to show Adeline how sensible she was of her affectionate attentions: "but you are an only child," she added, "and all your mother has will be yours."

"No doubt," observed Mrs. Mowbray eagerly; and her mother died contented.


CHAPTER 3

AT this period Adeline's ambition had led her to form new plans, which Mrs. Woodville's death left her at liberty to put in execution. Whenever the old lady reminded her that she was no genius, Adeline had felt as much degraded as if she had said that she was no conjurer;[3] and though she was

---

1  Cribbage is a card game which employs a board with sixty-one holes on which the points are scored with pegs. Draughts is another name for checkers.
2  Opie consistently uses this verb in the sense of "suspect" or "apprehend."
3  According to the *OED*, the word "conjurer" can be used ironically to refer to a person of superior cleverness.

too humble to suppose that she could ever equal her mother, she was resolved to try to make herself more worthy of her, by imitating her in those pursuits and studies on which were founded Mrs. Mowbray's pretensions to superior talents.

She therefore made it her business to inquire what those studies and pursuits were; and finding that Mrs. Mowbray's noted superiority was built on her passion for abstruse speculations, Adeline eagerly devoted her leisure hours to similar studies: but, unfortunately, these new theories, and these romantic reveries, which only served to amuse Mrs. Mowbray's fancy, her more enthusiastic daughter resolved to make conscientiously the rules of her practice. And while Mrs. Mowbray expended her eccentric philosophy in words, as Mr. Shandy did his grief,[1] Adeline carefully treasured up hers in her heart, to be manifested only by its fruits.

One author in particular, by a train of reasoning captivating though sophistical, and plausible though absurd, made her a delighted convert to his opinions, and prepared her young and impassioned heart for the practice of vice, by filling her mind, ardent in the love of virtue, with new and singular opinions on the subject of moral duty. On the works of this writer Adeline had often heard her mother descant in terms of the highest praise; but she did not feel herself so completely his convert on her own conviction, till she had experienced the fatal fascination of his style, and been conveyed by his bewitching pen from the world as it is, into a world as it *ought* to be.[2]

This writer, whose name was Glenmurray, amongst other institutions, attacked the institution of marriage;[3] and after having elaborately pointed out its folly and its wickedness, he drew so delightful a picture of the superior purity, as well as happiness, of an union cemented by no ties but those of love and honour, that Adeline, wrought to the highest pitch of enthusiasm for a new order of things, entered into a solemn compact with herself to act, when she was introduced into society, according to the rules laid down by this writer.*

Unfortunately for her, she had no opportunity of hearing these opinions combated by the good sense and sober experience of Dr. Norberry, then their sole visitant; for at this time the American war[4] was the object of at-

---

1  See Laurence Sterne, *Tristram Shandy* (1759-69), vol. 5, chap. 3, where the eloquence of Walter Shandy's grief makes him forget about the son he is mourning.

2  Godwin condemned acquiescence with the status quo: cf. the title of his novel, *Things As They Are, or, The Adventures of Caleb Williams* (1794).

3  As William Godwin does in *Enquiry Concerning Political Justice*, Appendix to Book 8, chap. 8; see Appendix D3.

4  The War of Independence against Britain, 1775-83.

tention to all Europe: and as Mrs. Mowbray, as well as Dr. Norberry, were deeply interested in this subject, they scarcely ever talked on any other; and even Glenmurray and his theories were driven from Mrs. Mowbray's remembrance by political tracts and the eager anxieties of a politician. Nor had she even leisure to observe, that while she was feeling all the generous anxiety of a citizen of the world for the sons and daughters of American independence, her own child was imbibing, through her means, opinions dangerous to her well-being as a member of any civilized society, and laying, perhaps, the foundation to herself and her mother of future misery and disgrace. Alas! the astrologer in the fable was but too like Mrs. Mowbray![1]

But even had Adeline had an opportunity of discussing her new opinions with Dr. Norberry, it is not at all certain that she would have had the power.

Mrs. Mowbray was, if I may be allowed the expression, a showing-off woman, and loved the information which she acquired, less for its own sake than for the supposed importance which it gave her amongst her acquaintance, and the means of displaying her superiority over other women. Before she secluded herself from society in order to study education, she had been the terror of the ladies in the neighbourhood; since, despising small talk, she would always insist on making the gentlemen of her acquaintance (as much terrified sometimes as their wives) engage with her in some literary or political conversation. She wanted to convert every drawing-room into an arena for the mind, and all her guests into intellectual gladiators. She was often heard to interrupt two grave matrons in an interesting discussion of an accouchement,[2] by asking them if they had read a new theological tract, or a pamphlet against the minister? If they softly expatiated on the lady-like fatigue of body which they had endured, she discoursed in choice terms on the energies of the mind; and she never received or paid visits without convincing the company that she was the most wise, most learned, and most disagreeable of companions.

But Adeline, on the contrary, studied merely from the love of study, and not with a view to shine in conversation; nor dared she venture to

---

1 See "An Astrologer and a Traveller," in Aesop's *Fables*, trans. Sir Roger L'Estrange, No. 76: "A Certain Star-Gazer had the Fortune, in the very Height of his celestial Observations, to stumble into a very deep Ditch; and while he was scrabbling to get out, Friend, says a sober Fellow passing by, make a right Use of your present Misfortunes; and, for the future, pray let the Stars go on quietly in their Courses, and do you look a little better to the Ditches, for is it not strange, that you should tell other People their Fortunes, and know nothing of your own?" (London: Osborn, 1740).

2 Delivery of a child (Fr.).

expatiate on subjects which she had often heard Mrs. Woodville say were very rarely canvassed, or even alluded to, by women. She remained silent, therefore, on the subject nearest her heart, from choice as well as necessity, in the presence of Dr. Norberry, till at length she imbibed the political mania herself, and soon found it impossible to conceal the interest which she took in the success of the infant republic. She therefore one day put into the doctor's hands some bouts rimes*[1] which she had written on some recent victory of the American arms; exclaiming with a smile, "I, too, am a politician!" and was rewarded by an exclamation of "Zounds!†[2] girl—I protest you are as clever as your mother!"

This unexpected declaration fixed her in the path of literary ambition: and though wisely resolved to fulfil, as usual, every feminine duty, Adeline was convinced that she, like her mother, had a right to be an author, a politician, and a philosopher; while Dr. Norberry's praises of her daughter convinced Mrs. Mowbray, that almost unconsciously she had educated her into a prodigy, and confirmed her in her intention of exhibiting herself and Adeline to the admiring world during the next season at Bath;[3] for at Bath she expected to receive that admiration which she had vainly sought in London.

Soon after their marriage, Mr. Mowbray had carried his lovely bride to the metropolis, where she expected to receive the same homage which had been paid to her charms at the assize-balls[4] in her neighbourhood. What then must have been her disappointment, when, instead of hearing as she passed, "That is miss Woodville, the rich heiress—or the great genius—or the great beauty"—or, "That is the beautiful Mrs. Mowbray," she walked unknown and unobserved in public and in private, and found herself of as little importance in the wide world of the metropolis, as the most humble of her acquaintance in a country ball-room. True, she had beauty, but then it was unset-off by fashion; nay, more, it was eclipsed by unfashionable and tasteless attire; and her manner, though stately and imposing in an assembly where she was known, was wholly unlike the manners of the world, and in a London party appeared arrogant and of-

---

1   "End-rhymed verses" (Fr.).
2   A euphemistic abbreviation of "by God's wounds." In the revised edition of 1844, Opie deletes even this mild expletive.
3   October to June was the Bath season, during which ladies and gentlemen visited this fashionable resort to meet, dance, take the waters, attend concerts and the theatre, and (possibly) meet their future partners.
4   It was customary to hold balls while judges and their entourages were in town for Courts of Assize, or criminal courts, held annually at various centres throughout the country (including Norwich, where Opie grew up).

fensive. Her remarks, too, wise as they appeared to her and Mr. Mowbray, excited little attention,—as the few persons to whom they were known in the metropolis were wholly ignorant of her high pretensions, and knew not that they were discoursing with a professed genius, and the oracle of a provincial circle. Some persons, indeed, surprised at hearing from the lips of eighteen, observations on morals, theology, and politics, listened to her with wonder, and even attention, but turned away, observing—

> "Such things, 'tis true, are neither new nor rare,
> The only wonder is, how they got there":[1]

till at length, disappointed, mortified, and disgusted, Mrs. Mowbray impatiently returned to Rosevalley, where in beauty, in learning, and in grandeur she was unrivalled, and where she might deal out her dogmas, sure of exciting respectful attention, however she might fail of calling forth a more flattering tribute from her auditors. But in the narrower field of Bath she expected to shine forth with greater éclat than in London, and to obtain admiration more worthy of her acceptance than any which a country circle could offer.*

To Bath, therefore, she prepared to go; and the young heart of Adeline beat high with pleasure at the idea of mixing with that busy world which her fancy had often clothed in the most winning attractions.

But her joy, and Mrs. Mowbray's, was a little overclouded at the moment of their departure, by the sight of Dr. Norberry's melancholy countenance. What was to be, as they fondly imagined, their gain, was his loss, and with a full heart he came to bid them adieu.

For Adeline he had conceived not only affection, but esteem amounting almost to veneration; for she appeared to him to unite various and opposing excellencies. Though possessed of taste and talents for literature, she was skilled in the minutest details of housewifery and feminine occupations; and at the same time she bore her faculties so meekly, that she never wounded the self-love of any one, by arrogating to herself any superiority.

Such Adeline appeared to her excellent old friend; and his affection for her was, perhaps, increased by the necessity which he was under of concealing it at home. The praises of Mrs. Mowbray and Adeline were odious to the ears of Mrs. Norberry and his† daughters,—but especially the praises of the latter,—as the merit of Adeline was so uniform, that even the eye of envy could not at that period discover any thing in her vulnerable to censure: and as the sound of her name excited in his family

---

1   Cf. Alexander Pope, "Epistle to Arbuthnot" (1735), 171-72.

a number of bad passions and corresponding expressions of countenance, the doctor wisely resolved to keep his feelings, with regard to her, locked up in his own bosom.

But he persisted in visiting at the Park daily; and it is no wonder, therefore, that the loss, even for a few months, of the society of its inhabitants should by him be anticipated as a serious calamity.

"Zounds!"* cried he, as Adeline, with an exulting bound, sprung after her mother into the carriage, "how gay and delighted you are! though my heart feels devilish† queer and heavy."

"My dear friend," cried Mrs. Mowbray, "I must miss your society wherever I go."—"I wish you were going too," said Adeline: "I shall often think of you." "Pshaw,¹ girl! don't lie," replied Dr. Norberry, swallowing a sigh as he spoke: "you will soon forget an old fellow like me."—"Then I conclude that you will soon forget us."—"He! how! what! think so at your peril."—"I must think so, as we usually judge of others by ourselves."—"Go to—go, miss mal-a-pert.²—Well, but, drive on, coachman—this taking leave is plaguy disagreeable, so shake hands and be off."

They gave him their hands, which he pressed very affectionately, and the carriage drove on.

"I am an old fool," cried the doctor, wiping his eyes as the carriage disappeared. "Well: God‡ grant, sweet innocent, that you may return to me as happy and spotless as you now are!"

Mrs. Mowbray had been married at a very early age, and had accepted in Mr. Mowbray the first man who addressed her: consequently, that passion for personal admiration, so natural to women, had in her never been gratified, nor even called forth. But seeing herself, at the age of thirty-eight,³ possessed of almost undiminished beauty, she recollected that her charms had never received that general homage for which Nature§ intended them; and she who at twenty had disregarded, even to a fault, the ornaments of dress, was now, at the age of thirty-eight, eager to indulge in the extremes of decoration, and to share in the delights of conquest and admiration with her youthful and attractive daughter.

Attractive, rather than handsome, was the epithet best suited to describe Adeline Mowbray. Her beauty was the beauty of expression of countenance, not regularity of feature, though the uncommon fairness and delicacy of her complexion, the lustre of her hazel eyes, her long dark eyelashes, and the profusion of soft light hair which curled over the ever-

---

1  An exclamation expressing contempt, impatience, or disgust.
2  Presumptuous, impudent, saucy.
3  Cf. Charlotte Smith, "Thirty-eight: Addressed to Mrs. H——y," in *Elegiac Sonnets and Other Poems*, 6th ed. (1792).

mantling colour of her cheek, gave her some pretensions to what is denominated beauty. But her own sex declared she was plain—and perhaps
they were right—though the other protested against the decision—and
probably they were right also: but women criticize in detail, men admire
in the aggregate. Women reason, and men feel, when passing judgment
on female beauty: and when a woman declares another to be plain, the
chances are that she is right in her opinion, as she cannot, from her being a woman, feel the charm of that power to please, that "something
than beauty dearer,"[1] which often throws a veil over the irregularity of
features, and obtains, for even a plain woman, from men at least, the appellation of pretty.

Whether Adeline's face were plain or not, her form could defy even
the severity of female criticism. She was indeed tall, almost to a masculine
degree; but such were the roundness and proportion of her limbs, such the
symmetry of her whole person, such the lightness and gracefulness of her
movements, and so truly feminine were her look and manner, that her*
superior height was forgotten in the superior loveliness of her figure.

It is not to be wondered at, then, that miss Mowbray was an object of
attention and admiration at Bath, as soon as she appeared, nor that her
mother had her share of flattery and followers. Indeed, when it was known
that Mrs. Mowbray was a rich widow, and Adeline dependent upon her,
the mother became, in the eyes of some people, much more attractive than
her† daughter.

It was impossible, however, that, in such a place as Bath, Mrs. Mowbray
and Adeline could make, or rather retain, a general acquaintance. Their
opinions on most subjects were so very different from those of the world,
and they were so little conscious, from the retirement in which they had‡
lived, that this difference existed, or was likely to make them enemies, that
not a day elapsed in which they did not shock the prejudices of some, and
excite the contemptuous pity of others; and they soon saw their acquaintance coolly dropped by those who, as persons of family and fortune, had
on their first arrival sought it with eagerness.

But this was not entirely owing to the freedom of their sentiments on
politics, or on other subjects; but, because they associated with a well-
known but obnoxious author;—a man whose speculations had delighted
the inquiring but ignorant lover of novelty, terrified the timid idolater of
antient usages, and excited the regret of the cool and rational observer:—
regret, that eloquence so overwhelming, powers of reasoning so acute,
activity of research so praise-worthy, and a love of investigation so ardent,
should be thrown away on the discussion§ of moral and political subjects,

---

1   James Thomson, *The Seasons* (1746), "Spring," 1141.

incapable of teaching the world to build up again with more beauty and propriety, a fabric, which they were, perhaps, calculated to pull down: in short, Mrs. Mowbray and Adeline associated with Glenmurray, that author over whose works they had long delighted to meditate, and who had completely led their imagination captive, before the fascination of his countenance and manners had come in aid of his eloquence.

## CHAPTER 4

FREDERIC GLENMURRAY was a man of family, and of a small independent estate, which, in case he died without children, was to go to the next male heir; and to that heir it was certain it would go, as Glenmurray on principle was an enemy to marriage, and consequently not likely to have a child born in wedlock.

It was an unfortunate circumstance for Glenmurray, that, with the ardour of a young and inexperienced mind, he had given his eccentric opinions to the world as soon as they were conceived and arranged,—as he, by so doing, prejudiced the world against him in so unconquerable a degree, that to him almost every door and every heart was shut;* and he by that means excluded from every chance of having the errors of his imagination corrected by the arguments of the experienced and enlightened—and corrected, no doubt, they would have been, for he had a mild and candid spirit, and a mind open to conviction.

"I consider myself," he used to say, "as a sceptic, not as a man really certain of the truth of any thing which he advances. I doubt of all things, because I look upon doubt as the road to truth; and do but convince me what is the truth, and at whatever† risk, whatever sacrifice, I am ready to embrace it."

But, alas! neither the blamelessness of his life, nor even his active virtue, assisted by the most courteous manners, were deemed sufficient to counteract the mischievous tendency of his works; or rather, it was supposed impossible that his life could be blameless and his seeming virtues sincere:—and unheard, unknown, this unfortunate young man was excluded from those circles which his talents would have adorned, and forced to lead a life of solitude, or associate with persons unlike to him in most things, except in a passion for the bold in theory, and the almost impossible in practice.

Of this description of persons he soon became the oracle—the head of a sect, as it were; and those tenets which at first he embraced, and put forth more for amusement than from conviction, as soon as he began to suffer on their account, became as dear to him as the cross to the christian martyr: and deeming persecution a test of truth, he considered the opposition made to him and his doctrines, not as the result of dispassionate reason striving to correct absurdity, but as selfishness and fear endeavouring to put out the light which showed the weakness of the foundation on which were built their claims to exclusive respect.

When Mrs. Mowbray and Adeline first arrived at Bath, the latter had attracted the attention and admiration of colonel Mordaunt, an Irishman of fortune, and an officer in the guards;[1] and Adeline had not been insensible to the charms of a* very fine person and engaging manners, united to powers of conversation which displayed an excellent understanding improved by education and reading. But colonel Mordaunt was not a *marrying man*, as it is called: therefore, as soon as he began to feel the influence of Adeline growing too powerful for his freedom, and to observe that his attentions were far from unpleasing to her,—too honourable to excite an attachment in her which he was† resolved to combat in himself, he resolved to fly from the danger, which he knew he could not face and overcome; and after a formal but embarrassed adieu to Mrs. Mowbray and Adeline, he suddenly left Bath.

This unexpected departure both surprised and grieved Adeline; but, as her feelings of delicacy were too strong to allow her to sigh for a man who, evidently, had no thoughts of sighing for her, she dismissed colonel Mordaunt from her remembrance, and tried to find as much interest still in the ball-rooms, and the promenades, as his presence had given them: nor was it long before she found in them an attraction and an interest stronger than any which she had yet felt.

It is naturally to be supposed that Adeline had often wished to know personally an author whose writings delighted her as much as Glenmurray's had done, and that her fancy had often portrayed him: but though it had clothed him in a form at once pleasing and respectable,—still, from an idea of his superior wisdom, she had imagined him past the meridian of life, and not likely to excite warmer feelings than those of esteem and veneration: and such continued to be Adeline's idea of Glenmurray, when he arrived at Bath, having been sent thither by his physicians for the benefit of his health.

Glenmurray, though a sense of his unpopularity had long banished him from scenes of public resort in general, was so pleased with the novelties of Bath, that, though he walked wholly unnoticed except by the lovers of genius in whatsoever shape it shows itself, he frequented daily the pump-

---

1  Also known as the life-guards: two regiments forming, together with the Horse Guards, the royal household cavalry.

room,[1] and the promenades; and Adeline had long admired the countenance and dignified person of this young and interesting invalid, without the slightest suspicion of his being the man of all others whom she the* most wished to see.

Nor had Glenmurray been slow to admire Adeline: and so strong, so irresistible was the feeling of admiration which she had excited in him, that, as soon as she appeared, all other objects vanished from his sight; and as women are generally quick-sighted to the effect of their charms, Adeline never beheld the stranger without a suffusion of pleasurable confusion on her cheek.

One morning at the pump-room,† when Glenmurray, unconscious that Adeline was near, was reading the newspaper with great attention, and Adeline for the first time was looking at him unobserved, she heard the name of Glenmurray pronounced, and turned her head towards the person who spoke, in hopes of seeing Glenmurray himself; when Mrs. Mowbray, turning round and looking at the invalid, said to a gentleman next her, "Did you say, sir, that that tall, pale, dark, interesting-looking young man is Mr. Glenmurray, the celebrated author?"

"Yes, ma'am," replied the gentleman with a sneer: "that is Mr. Glenmurray, the celebrated author."

"Oh! how I should like to speak to him!" cried Mrs. Mowbray.

"It will be no difficult matter," replied her informant: "the gentleman is always quite as much at leisure as you see him now; for *all* persons have not the same taste as Mrs. Mowbray."

So saying, he bowed and departed, leaving Mrs. Mowbray, to whom the sight of a great author was new, so lost in contemplating Glenmurray, that the sarcasm with which he spoke entirely escaped her observation.

Nor was Adeline less abstracted: she too was contemplating Glenmurray, and with mixed but delightful feelings.

"So then he is young and handsome too!" said she mentally: "it is a pity he looks so *ill*," added she *sighing*: but the sigh was caused rather by his looking so *well*—though Adeline was not conscious of it.

By this time Glenmurray had observed who were his neighbours, and the newspaper was immediately laid down.

"Is there any news to-day?" said Mrs. Mowbray to Glenmurray, resolved to make a bold effort to become acquainted with him. Glenmurray, with a bow and a blush of mingled surprise and pleasure, replied that there was a great deal,—and immediately presented to her the paper which he had relinquished, setting chairs at the same time for her and Adeline.

---

1   Opened in 1795, the Pump Room was where visitors to Bath went to drink the restorative mineral water.

Mrs. Mowbray, however, only slightly glanced her eye over the paper:—her desire was to talk to Glenmurray; and in order to accomplish this point, and prejudice him in her favour, she told him how much she rejoiced in seeing an author whose works were the delight and instruction of her life. "Speak, Adeline," cried she, turning to her blushing daughter; "do we not almost daily read and daily admire Mr. Glenmurray's writings?"—"Yes, certainly," replied Adeline, unable to articulate more, awed no doubt by the presence of so superior a being; while Glenmurray, more proud of being an author than ever, said internally, "Is it possible that that sweet creature should have read and admired my works?"

But in vain, encouraged by the smiles and even by the blushes of Adeline, did he endeavour to engage her in conversation. Adeline was unusually silent, unusually bashful. But Mrs. Mowbray made ample amends for her deficiency; and Mr. Glenmurray, flattered and amused, would have continued to converse with her and look at Adeline, had he not observed the impertinent sneers and rude laughter to which conversing so familiarly with him exposed Mrs. Mowbray. As soon as he observed this, he arose to depart; for Glenmurray was, according to Rochefoucault's maxim, so exquisitely selfish, that he always considered the welfare of others before his own;[1] and heroically sacrificing his own gratification to save Mrs. Mowbray and Adeline from further censure, he bowed with the greatest respect to Mrs. Mowbray, sighed as he paid the same compliment to Adeline, and, lamenting his being forced to quit them so soon, with evident reluctance left the room.

"What an elegant bow he makes!" exclaimed Mrs. Mowbray. Adeline had observed nothing but the sigh; and on that she did not choose to make any comment.

The next day Mrs. Mowbray, having learned Glenmurray's address, sent him a card for a party at her lodgings. Nothing but Glenmurray's delight could exceed his astonishment at this invitation. He had observed Mrs. Mowbray and Adeline, even before Adeline had observed him; and, as he gazed upon the fascinating Adeline, he had sighed to think that she too would be taught to avoid the dangerous and disreputable acquaintance of Glenmurray. To him, therefore, this mark of attention was a source both of consolation and joy. But, being well convinced that it was owing to her ignorance of the usual customs and opinions of those with whom

---

1  This kind of paradox is characteristic of François, duc de La Rochefoucauld (1613–80). See, for example, *Maxims and Moral Reflections* (trans. 1799), No. 172: "We love nothing but on our own account, and only follow our taste and inclination when we prefer our friends to ourselves: and yet it is this preference which alone constitutes true and perfect friendship."

she associated, he was too generous to accept the invitation, as he knew that his presence at a rout at Bath would cause general dismay, and expose the mistress to disagreeable remarks at least: but he endeavoured to make himself amends for his self-denial, by asking leave to wait on them when they were alone.

## CHAPTER 5

A DAY or two after, as Adeline was leaning on the arm of a young lady, Glenmurray passed them, and to his respectful bow she returned a most cordial salutation. "Gracious me! my dear," said her companion, "do you know who that man is?"

"Certainly:—it is Mr. Glenmurray."

"My good gracious! and* do you speak to him?"

"Yes:—why should I not?"

"Dear me! Why, I am sure! Why ... don't you know what he is?"

"Yes; a celebrated writer, and a man of genius."

"Oh, that may be, miss Mowbray: but they say one should not notice him, because he is——"

"He is what?" said Adeline eagerly.

"I do not exactly know what; but I believe it is a French spy, or a Jesuit."[1]

"Indeed?" replied Adeline laughing. "But I am used to have better evidence against a person than a *they say* before I neglect an acknowledged acquaintance: therefore, with your leave, I shall turn back and talk a little to poor Mr. Glenmurray."

It so happened that *poor Mr. Glenmurray* heard every word of this conversation; for he had turned round and followed Adeline and her fair companion, to present to the former the† glove which she had dropped; and as they were prevented from proceeding by the crowd on the parade, which

---

1 Adeline's companion has adopted the pro-government anxieties of the 1790s (when William Wordsworth and Samuel Taylor Coleridge, among many others, were suspected of spying for France, and when Roman Catholic émigrés were greeted with suspicion as well as sympathy). Cf. [T.J. Mathias,] *A Letter to the Lord Marquis of Buckingham ... Chiefly on the Subject of the Numerous French Priests and Others of the Church of Rome, Resident and Maintained in England at the Public Expence ...* (London, 1797): "Is there a county in which we are not elbowed by a French Priest or a French Spy?" (28). In 1794 Opie herself attended the treason trials of the radicals Horne Tooke, Thomas Holcroft, Thomas Hardy, and John Thelwall. The allusion to Jesuits and spies perhaps indicates that the historical framework of Opie's novel is not very stable: we seem no longer to be in the period of the American Revolution.

was assembled to see some unusual sight, he, being immediately behind them, could distinguish all that passed; so that Adeline turned round to go in search of him, before the blush of grateful admiration for her kindness had left his cheek.

"Then she seeks me because I am shunned by others!" said Glenmurray to himself. In a moment the world to him seemed to contain only two beings, Adeline Mowbray and Frederic Glenmurray; and that Adeline, starting and blushing with joyful surprise at seeing him so near her, was then coming in search of him!—of him, the neglected Glenmurray! Scarcely could he refrain catching the lovely and ungloved hand next him to his heart; but he contented himself with keeping the glove that he was before so eager to restore, and in a moment it was lodged in his bosom.

Nor could "I can't think what I have done with my glove," which every now and then escaped Adeline, prevail on him to own that he had found it. At last, indeed, it became unnecessary; for Adeline, as she glanced her eye towards Glenmurray, discovered it in the hiding-place: but, as delicacy forbade her to declare the discovery which she had made, he was suffered to retain his prize; though a deep and sudden blush which overspread his* cheek, and a sudden pause which she made in her conversation, convinced Glenmurray that she had detected his secret. Perhaps he was not sorry— nor Adeline;† but certain it is that Adeline was for the remainder of the morning more lost in reverie than ever her mother had been; and that from that day every one, but Adeline and Glenmurray, saw that they were mutually enamoured.

Glenmurray was the first of the two lovers to perceive that they were so; and he made the discovery with a mixture of pain and pleasure. For what could be the result of such an attachment? He was firmly resolved never to marry; and it was very unlikely that Adeline, though she had often expressed to him her approbation of his writings and opinions, should be willing to sacrifice every thing to love, and become his mistress. But a circumstance took place which completely removed his doubts on this subject.

Several weeks had elapsed since the first arrival of the Mowbrays at Bath, and in that time almost all their acquaintances had left them one by one; but neither Mrs. Mowbray nor Adeline had paid much attention to this circumstance. Mrs. Mowbray's habits of abstraction, as usual, made her regardless of common occurrences; and to these were added the more delightful reveries occasioned by the attentions of a very handsome and insinuating man, and the influence of a growing passion. Mrs. Mowbray, as we have before observed, married from duty, not inclination; and to the passion of love she had remained a total stranger, till she became acquainted at Bath with sir Patrick O'Carrol. Yes; Mrs. Mowbray was in love for the first time when she was approaching her fortieth year! and a woman is never so likely to be the fool of love, as when it assails her late in life, especially if a lover be as great a novelty to her as the passion itself. Though not, alas! restored to a second youth, the tender victim certainly enjoys a second childhood, and exhibits but too openly all the little tricks and *minauderies*[1] of a lovesick girl, without the youthful appearance that in a degree excuses them. This was the case with Mrs. Mowbray; and while, regardless of her daughter's interest and happiness, she was lost in the pleasing hopes of marrying the agreeable baronet,[2] no wonder the cold neglect of her Bath associates was not seen by her.

Adeline, engrossed also by the pleasing reveries of a first love, was as unconscious of it as herself. Indeed she thought of nothing but love and Glenmurray; else, she could not have failed to see, that, while sir Patrick's attentions and flatteries were addressed to her mother, his ardent looks and passionate sighs were all directed to herself.

Sir Patrick O'Carrol was a young Irishman, of an old family but an encumbered estate; and it was his wish to set his estate free by marrying a rich wife, and one as little disagreeable as possible. With this view he came to Bath; and in Mrs. Mowbray he not only beheld a woman of large independent fortune, but possessed of great personal beauty, and young enough to be attractive. Still, though much pleased with the wealth and appearance of the mother, he soon became enamoured of the daughter's person;* and had he not gone so far in his addresses to Mrs. Mowbray as to make it impossible she should willingly transfer him to Adeline, and give her a fortune at all adequate to his wants, he would have endeavoured honourably to gain her affections, and entered the lists against the favoured Glenmurray.

But, as he wanted the mother's wealth, he resolved to pursue his advantage with her, and trust to some future chance for giving him possession of the daughter's person.† In his dealings with men, sir Patrick was a man of honour; in his dealings with women, completely the reverse: he considered them as a race of subordinate beings, formed for the service and amusement of men;‡ and that if, like horses, they were well lodged, fed, and kept clean, they had no right to complain.

Constantly therefore did he besiege Mrs. Mowbray with his conversation, and Adeline with his eyes; and the very libertine[3] gaze with which he often beheld her, gave a pang to Glenmurray which was but too soon painfully increased.

---

1 "Self-conscious smiles" (Fr.).
2 The holder of a hereditary title awarded by the British Crown.
3 Licentious, dissolute.

Sir Patrick was the only man of fashion who did not object to visit at Mrs. Mowbray's on account of her intimacy with Glenmurray; but he had his own private reasons for going thither, and continued to visit at Mrs. Mowbray's though Glenmurray was generally there, and sometimes he and the latter gentleman were the whole of their company.

One evening they and two ladies were drinking tea at Mrs. Mowbray's lodgings, when Mrs. Mowbray was unusually silent and Adeline unusually talkative. Adeline scarcely ever spoke in her mother's presence, from deference to her abilities; and whatever might be Mrs. Mowbray's defects in other respects, her conversational talents and her uncommon command of words were indisputable. But this evening, as I before observed, Adeline, owing to her mother's tender abstractions, was obliged to exert herself for the entertainment of the guests.

It so happened, also, that something was said by one of the party which led to the subject of marriage, and Adeline was resolved not to let so good an opportunity pass of proving to Glenmurray how sincerely she approved his doctrine on that subject. Immediately, with an unreserve which nothing but her ignorance of the world, and the strange education which she had received, could at all excuse, she began to declaim against marriage, as an institution at once absurd, unjust, and immoral, and to declare that she would never submit to so contemptible a form, or profane the sacred ties of love by so odious and unnecessary a ceremony.

This extraordinary speech, though worded elegantly and delivered gracefully, was not received by any of her hearers, except sir Patrick, with any thing like admiration. The baronet, indeed, clapped his hands, and cried "Bravo! a fine spirited girl, upon my soul!"* in a manner so loud, and so offensive to the feelings of Adeline, that, like the orator of old, she was tempted to exclaim, "What foolish thing can I have said, that has drawn forth this applause?"[1]

But Mrs. Mowbray, though she could not help admiring the eloquence of her daughter,—eloquence† which she attributed to her example,—was shocked at hearing Adeline declare that her practice should be consonant to her theory; while Glenmurray, though Adeline had only expressed his sentiments, and his reason approved what she had uttered, felt his delicacy and his feelings wounded by so open and decided an avowal of her

---

1　See Plutarch, *Life of Phocion* (trans. Philip Fowke [London, 1685]): "Happening ... to speak his own opinion, to the general approbation of the Assembly, turning to some of his Friends, [Phocion] demanded of them, *What foolish thing had escaped him unawares to merit their Applause?*" *The Fourth Volume of Plutarch's Lives, Translated from the Greek, by Several Hands*. Phocion was an Athenian statesman who died in 317 BCE.

opinions, and intended conduct in consequence of them: and he was still more hurt when he saw how much it delighted sir Patrick, and offended the rest of the company; who, after a silence the result of surprise and disgust, suddenly rose,* and, coldly wishing Mrs. Mowbray good night, left the house.

By Mrs. Mowbray the cause of this abrupt departure was unsuspected: but Adeline, who had more observation, was convinced that she was the cause of it; and sighing deeply at the prejudices of the world, she sought to console herself by looking at Glenmurray, expecting to find in his eyes an expression of delight and approbation. To her great disappointment, however, his countenance was sad; while sir Patrick, on the contrary, had an expression of impudent triumph in his look, which made her turn blushing from his ardent gaze, and indignantly follow her mother, who was then leaving the room.

As she passed him, sir Patrick caught her hand rapturously to his lips (an action which made Glenmurray start from his chair), and exclaimed, "Upon my soul,† you are the only honest little woman I ever knew! I always was sure that what you just now said was the opinion of all your sex, though they were so confoundedly‡ coy they would not own it."

"Own what, sir?" asked the astonished Adeline.

"That they thought marriage a cursed bore, and preferred leading the life of honour, to be sure."

"The life of honour! What is that?" demanded Adeline, while Glenmurray paced the room in agitation.

"The life, my dear girl, which you mean to lead;—love and liberty with the man of your heart."

"Sir Patrick," cried Glenmurray impatiently, "this conversation is——"

"Prodigiously amusing to me," returned the baronet, "especially as I never could hold it to a modest woman before."

"Nor shall you now, sir," fiercely interrupted Glenmurray.

"Shall not, sir?" vociferated sir Patrick.

"Pray, gentlemen, be less violent," exclaimed the terrified and astonished Adeline. "I can't think what could offend you, Mr. Glenmurray, in sir Patrick's original observation: the life of honour appears to me a very excellent name for the pure and honourable union which it is my wish to form; and——"

"There; I told you so"; triumphantly interrupted sir Patrick: "and I never was better pleased in my life:—sweet creature! at once so lovely, so wise, and so liberal!"

"Sir," cried Glenmurray, "this is a mistake: your life of honour and miss Mowbray's are as different as possible; you are talking of what you are grossly ignorant of."

"Ignorant! I ignorant! Look you, Mr. Glenmurray, do you pretend to tell me I know not what the life of honour is, when I have led it so many times with so many different women?"

"How, sir!" replied Adeline: "many times? and with many different women? My life of honour can be led with one only."

"Well, my dear soul, I only led it with one at a time."

"O sir! you are indeed ignorant of my meaning," she rejoined: "it is the individuality of an attachment that constitutes its chastity;* and——"

"Ba-ba-bu, my lovely girl! what has chastity† to do in the business?"

"Indeed, sir Patrick," meekly returned Adeline, "I——"

"Miss Mowbray," angrily interrupted Glenmurray, "I beg, I conjure you to drop this conversation: your innocence is no match for——"

"For what, sir?" furiously demanded sir Patrick.

"Your licentiousness," replied Glenmurray.

"Sir, I wear a sword," cried the baronet—"And I a cane," said Glenmurray calmly, "either to defend myself or chastise insolence."

"Mr. Glenmurray! Sir Patrick!" exclaimed the agitated Adeline: "for my sake, for pity's sake, desist!"

"For the present I will, madam," faltered out sir Patrick;—"but I know Mr. Glenmurray's address, and he shall hear from me."

"Hear from you! Why, you do not mean to challenge him? you can't suppose Mr. Glenmurray would do so absurd a thing as fight a duel? Sir, he has written a volume to prove the absurdity of the custom.[1]—No, no, thank God!‡ you threaten his life in vain," she added, giving her hand to Glenmurray; who, in the tenderness of the action and the tone of her voice, forgot the displeasure which her inadvertency had caused, and, pressing her hand to his lips, secretly renewed his vows of unalterable attachment.

"Very well, madam," exclaimed sir Patrick in a tone of pique: "then, so as Mr. Glenmurray's life is safe, you care not what becomes of mine!"

"Sir," replied Adeline, "the safety of a fellow creature is always of importance in my eyes."

"Then you care for me as a fellow creature only," retorted sir Patrick, "not as sir Patrick O'Carrol?—Mighty fine, truly, you dear ungrateful—" seizing her hand; which he relinquished, as well as the rest of his speech, on the entrance of Mrs. Mowbray.

Soon after Adeline left the room, and Glenmurray bowed and retired; while sir Patrick, having first repeated his vows of admiration to the

---

[1] For Godwin's argument against duelling, see *Enquiry Concerning Political Justice*, Appendix to Book 2 (Appendix C, below). A duel was an illegal fight between gentlemen over a point of honour. The combatants were usually accompanied by "seconds" (companions who might also fight).

mother, returned home to muse on the charms of the daughter, and the necessity of challenging the moral Glenmurray.

Sir Patrick was a man of courage, and had fought several duels: but as life at this time had a great many charms for him, he resolved to defer at least putting himself in the way of getting rid of it; and after having slept late in the morning, to make up for the loss of sleep in the night, occasioned by his various cogitations, he rose, resolved go to Mrs. Mowbray's, and, if he had an opportunity, indulge himself in some practical comments on the singular declaration made the evening before by her lovely daughter.

Glenmurray meanwhile had passed the night in equal watchfulness and greater agitation. To fight a duel would be, as Adeline observed, contrary to his principles; and to decline one, irritated as he was against sir Patrick, was repugnant to his feelings. To no purpose did he peruse and re-peruse nearly the whole of his own book against duelling; he had few religious restraints to make him resolve on declining a challenge, and he felt moral ones of little avail: but in vain did he sit at home till the morning was far advanced, expecting a messenger from sir Patrick;—no messenger came:— he therefore left word with his servant, that, if wanted, he might be found at Mrs. Mowbray's, and went thither, in hopes of enjoying an hour's conversation with Adeline; resolving to hint to her, as delicately as he could, that the opinions which she had expressed were better confined, in the present dark state of the public mind, to a select and discriminating circle.

## CHAPTER 6

SIR PATRICK had reached Mrs. Mowbray's some time before him, and had, to his great satisfaction, found Adeline alone; nor did it escape his penetration that her cheeks glowed, and her eyes sparkled with pleasure, at his approach.

But he would not have rejoiced in this circumstance, had he known that Adeline was pleased to see him merely because she considered his appearance as a proof of Glenmurray's safety; for, in spite of his having written against duelling, and of her confidence in his firmness and consistency, she was not quite convinced that the reasoning philosopher would triumph over the feeling man.

"You are welcome, sir Patrick!" cried Adeline, as he entered, with a most winning smile: "I am very glad to see you: pray sit down."

The baronet, who, audacious as his hopes and intentions were, had not expected so kind a reception, was quite thrown off his guard by it, and, catching her suddenly in his arms, endeavoured to obtain a still kinder welcome. Adeline as suddenly disengaged herself from him, and, with the dignity of offended modesty, desired him to quit the room, as, after such an insolent attempt, she could not think herself justified in suffering him to remain with her.

But her anger was soon changed into pity, when she saw sir Patrick lay down his hat, seat himself, and burst into a long deliberate laugh.

"He is certainly mad!" she exclaimed; and, leaning against the chimney-piece, she began to contemplate him with a degree of fearful interest.

"Upon my soul! now," cried the baronet, when his laugh was over, "you do not suppose, my dear creature, that you and I do not understand one another! Telling a young fellow to leave the house on such occasions, means, in the pretty no meaning of your sex, 'Stay, and offend again,' to be sure."

"He is certainly mad!" said Adeline, more confirmed than before in her idea of his insanity, and* immediately endeavoured to reach the door: but in so doing she approached sir Patrick, who, rather roughly seizing her trembling hand, desired her to sit down, and hear what he had to say to her. Adeline, thinking it not right to irritate him, instantly obeyed.

"Now, then, to open my mind to you," said the baronet, drawing his chair close to hers: "From the very first moment I saw you, I felt that we were made for one another; though, being bothered by my debts, I made up to the old duchess, and she nibbled the bait directly,—deeming my clean inches (six feet one, without shoes) well worth her dirty acres."

"How dreadfully incoherent he is!" thought Adeline, not suspecting for a moment that, by the old duchess, he meant her still blooming mother.

"But, my lovely love!"† continued sir Patrick, most ardently pressing her hand, "so much have your sweet person, and your frank and liberal way of thinking, charmed me, that I here freely offer myself to you, and we will begin the life of honour together as soon as you please."

Still Adeline, who was unconscious how much her avowed opinions had exposed her to insult, continued to believe sir Patrick insane; a belief which the wildness of his eyes confirmed. "I really know not,—you surprise me, sir Patrick,—I——"

"Surprise you, my dear soul! How could you expect anything else from a man of my spirit, after your honest declaration last night?.... All I feared was, that Glenmurray should get the start of me."

Adeline, though alarmed, bewildered, and confounded, had still recollection enough to know that, whether sane or insane, the words and looks of sir Patrick were full of increasing insult. "I believe, I think I had better retire," faltered out Adeline.

"Retire!.... Aye, by all means,"‡ exclaimed the baronet, rudely seizing her.

This outrage restored Adeline to her usual spirit and self-possession; and bestowing on him the epithet of "mean-soul'd ruffian!" she had almost freed herself from his grasp, when a quick step was heard on the stairs, and the door was thrown open by Glenmurray. In a moment Adeline, bursting into tears, threw herself into his arms, as if in search of protection.

Glenmurray required no explanation of the scene before him: the appearance of the actors in it was explanation sufficient; and while with one arm he fondly held Adeline to his bosom, he raised the other in a threatening attitude against sir Patrick, exclaiming as he did it, "Base, unmanly villain!"

"Villain!" echoed sir Patrick.... "but it is very well—very well for the present—Good morning to you, sir!" So saying, he hastily withdrew.

As soon as he was gone, Glenmurray for the first time declared to Adeline the ardent passion with which she had inspired him; and she, with equal frankness, confessed that her heart was irrevocably his.

From this interesting tête-à-tête Adeline was summoned to attend a person on business to her mother; and during her absence Glenmurray received a challenge from the angry baronet, appointing him to meet him that afternoon at five o'clock, about two miles from Bath. To this note, for fear of alarming the suspicions of Adeline, Glenmurray returned only a verbal message, saying he would answer it in two hours: but as soon as she returned he pleaded indispensable business; and before she could mention any fears respecting the consequences of what had passed between him and sir Patrick, he had left the room, having, to prevent any alarm, requested leave to wait on her early the next day.

As soon as Glenmurray reached his lodgings, he again revolved in his mind the propriety of accepting the challenge. "How can I expect to influence others by my theories to act right, if my practice sets them a bad example?" But then again he exclaimed, "How can I expect to have any thing I say attended to, when, by refusing to fight, I put it in the power of my enemies to assert I am a poltroon,[1] and worthy only of neglect and contempt? No, no; I must fight:—even Adeline herself, especially as it is on her account, will despise me if I do not":—and then, without giving himself any more time to deliberate, he sent an answer to sir Patrick, promising to meet him at the time appointed.

But after he had sent it he found himself a prey to so much self-reproach, and after he had forfeited his claims to consistency of conduct, he felt himself so strongly aware of the value of it, that, had not the time of the meeting been near at hand, he would certainly have deliberated upon some means of retracting his consent to it.

---

1   A coward.

From Amelia Opie, *Adeline Mowbray, or The Mother and Daughter.*
A New and Illustrated Edition. London: Longman, 1844.
Reproduced with the permission of the
Princeton University Library.

Being resolved to do as little mischief as he could, he determined on having no second in the business; and accordingly repaired to the field accompanied only by a trusty servant, who had orders to wait his master's pleasure at a distance.

Contrary to Glenmurray's expectations, sir Patrick also came unattended by a second; while his servant, who was with him, was, like the other, desired to remain in the back ground.

"I wish, Mr. Glenmurray, to do every thing honourable," said the baronet, after they had exchanged salutations: "therefore, sir, as I concluded* you would find it difficult to get a second, I am come without one, and I *conclude* that I *concluded* right.—Aye, men of your principles† can have but few friends."

"And men of your practice ought to have none, sir Patrick," retorted Glenmurray: "but, as I don't think it worth while to explain to you my reasons for not having a second, as I fear that you are incapable of understanding them, I must desire you to take your ground."

"With all my heart," replied his antagonist; and then taking aim, they agreed to fire at the same moment.

They did so; and the servants, hearing the report of the pistols, ran to the scene of action, and saw sir Patrick bleeding in the sword-arm, and Glenmurray, also wounded, leaning against a tree.

"This is cursed unlucky," said sir Patrick coolly: "as you have disabled my right arm I can't go on with this business at present; but when I am well again, command me. Your wound, I believe, is as slight as mine; but as I can walk, and you cannot, and as I have a chaise, and you not, you shall use it to convey you and your servant home, and I and mine will go on foot."

To this obliging offer Glenmurray was incapable of giving a‡ denial; for he became insensible from loss of blood, and with the assistance of his antagonist was carried to the chaise, and, supported by his terrified servant, conveyed back to Bath.

It is not to be supposed that an event of this nature should be long unknown. It was soon told all over the city that sir Patrick O'Carrol and Mr. Glenmurray had fought a duel, and that the latter was dangerously wounded; the quarrel having originated in Mr. Glenmurray's scoffing at religion, king, and constitution, before the pious and loyal baronet.

This story soon reached the ears of Mrs. Mowbray, who, in an agony of tender sorrow, and in defiance of all decorum, went in person to call on her admired sir Patrick; and Adeline, who heard of the affair soon after, as regardless of appearances as her mother, and more alarmed, went in person to inquire concerning her wounded Glenmurray.

By the time that she had arrived at his lodgings, not only his own surgeon but sir Patrick's had seen him, as his antagonist thought it necessary to ascertain the true state of his wound, that he might know whether he ought to stay, or fly his country.[1]

The account of both the surgeons was, however, so favourable, and Glenmurray in all respects so well, that sir Patrick's alarms were soon quite at an end; and the wounded man was lying on a sopha, lost in no very pleasant reflections, when Adeline knocked at his door. Glenmurray at that very moment was saying to himself, "Well;—so much for principle and consistency! Now, my next step must be to marry, and then I shall have made myself a complete fool, and the worst of all fools,—a man presuming to instruct others by his precepts, when he finds them incapable even of influencing* his own actions."

At this moment his servant came up with "miss Mowbray's compliments, and, if he was well enough to see her, she would come up and speak to him."

In an instant all his self-reproaches were forgotten; and when Adeline hung weeping and silent on his shoulder, he could not but rejoice in an affair which had procured him a moment of such heartfelt delight. At first Adeline expressed nothing but terror at the consequences of his wound, and pity for his sufferings; but when she found that he was in no danger, and in very little pain, the tender mistress yielded to the severe monitress, and she began to upbraid Glenmurray for having acted not only in defiance of her wishes and principles, but of his own; of principles laid down by him to the world in the strongest point of view, and in a manner convincing to every mind.

"Dearest Adeline, consider the provocation," cried Glenmurray;—"a gross insult offered to the woman I love!"

"But who ever fought a duel without provocation, Glenmurray? If provocation be a justification, your book was unnecessary; and did not you offer an insult to the understanding of the woman you love, in supposing that she could be obliged to you for playing the fool on her account?"

"But I should have been called a coward had I declined the challenge; and though I can bear the world's hatred, I could not its contempt:—I could not endure the loss of what the world calls honour."

"Is it possible," rejoined Adeline, "that I hear the philosophical Glenmurray talking thus, in the silly jargon of a man of the world?"

"Alas! I am a man, not a philosopher, Adeline!"

"At least be a sensible one;—consistent I dare not now call you. But have you forgotten the distinction which, in your volume on the subject

---

[1] To avoid prosecution if his opponent died.

of duels, you so strongly lay down between real and apparent honour?[1] In which of the two classes do you put the honour of which, in this instance, you were so tenacious? What is there in common between the glory of risking the life of a fellow-creature, and the testimony of an approving conscience?"

"An excellent observation that of yours, indeed, my sweet monitress," said Glenmurray.

"An observation of mine! It is your own," replied Adeline: "but see, I have the book in my muff; and I will punish you for the badness of your practice, by giving you a dose of your theory."

"Cruel girl!" cried Glenmurray, "I am not ordered a sleeping draught!"

Adeline was however resolved; and, opening the book, she read argument after argument with unyielding perseverance, till Glenmurray, who, like the eagle in the song, saw on the dart that wounded him his own feathers, cried "Quarter!"[2]

"But tell me, dear Adeline," said Glenmurray, a little piqued at her too just reproofs, "you, who are so severe on my want of consistency, are you yourself capable of acting up in every respect to your precepts?"

"After your weakness," replied Adeline, smiling, "it becomes me to doubt my own strength; but I assure you that I make it a scruple of conscience, to show by my conduct my confidence in the truth of my opinions."

"Then, in defiance of the world's opinion, that opinion which I, you see, had not resolution to brave, you will be mine—not according to the ties of marriage, but with no other ties or sanction than those of love and reason?"

"I will," said Adeline: "and may that God* whom I worship" (raising her fine eyes and white arms to heaven) "desert me when I desert you!"

Who that had seen her countenance and gesture at that moment, could have imagined she was calling on heaven† to witness an engagement to

---

1   This distinction is made not only by radicals like Glenmurray, but by such writers as the clergyman William Davy, *A System of Divinity, in a Course of Sermons*, vol. 10 (1799): "Where Honour is a Support to virtuous Principles, & runs Parallel with the laws of God and our Country, it cannot be too much cherished and encouraged: but when the Dictates of Honour are contrary to those of Religion and Equity, they are the greatest Depravations of human Nature, by giving wrong, ambitious and false Ideas of what is good and laudable; and should therefore be exploded by all Governments, and driven out as the Bane and pest of human Society" (83).

2   To cry "quarter" is to cry for mercy when one surrenders to an adversary. The song is Edmund Waller's "To a Lady Singing a Song of his Composing": "That Eagles fate and mine are one / Which on that shaft that made him die, / Espy'd a feather of his own / Wherewith he meant to soar so high" (*Poems* [1645], lines 5-8).

From Amelia Opie, *Adeline Mowbray, or The Mother and Daughter.*
A New and Illustrated Edition. London: Longman, 1844.
Reproduced with the permission of the
Princeton University Library.

lead a life of infamy? Rather would they have thought her a sublime enthusiast breathing forth the worship of a grateful soul.

It may be supposed that Glenmurray's heart beat with exultation at this confession from Adeline, and that he forgot, in the promised indulgence of his passion, to confine himself within* those bounds which strict decorum required. But Glenmurray did her justice; he beheld her as she was—all purity of feeling and all delicacy; and, if possible, the slight favours by which true passion† is long contented to be fed, though granted by Adeline with more conscious emotion, were received by him with more devoted respect: besides, he again felt that mixture of pain with pleasure, on this assurance of her love, which he had experienced before. For he knew, though Adeline did not, the extent of the degradation into which the step which her conscience approved would necessarily precipitate her; and experience alone could convince him that her sensibility to shame, when she was for the first time exposed to it, would not overcome her supposed fortitude and boasted contempt of the world's opinion, and change all the roses of love into the thorns of regret and remorse.

And could he who doted on her;—he, too, who admired her as much for her consummate purity as for any other of her qualities;—could he bear to behold this fair creature, whose open eye beamed with the consciousness of virtue, casting her timid glances to the earth, and shrinking with horror from the conviction of having in the world's eye forfeited all pretensions to that virtue which alone was the end of her actions! Would the approbation of her own mind be sufficient to support her under such a trial, though she had with such sweet earnestness talked to him of its efficacy! These reflections had for some time past been continually occurring to him, and now they came across his mind blighting the triumphs of successful passion:—nay, but from the dread of incurring yet more ridicule, on account of the opposition of his practice to his theory, and perhaps the indignant contempt of Adeline, he could have thrown himself at her feet, conjuring her to submit to the degradation of being a wife.

But, unknown to Glenmurray, perhaps, another reason prompted him to desire this concession from Adeline. We are never more likely to be in reality the slaves of selfishness, than when we fancy ourselves acting with most heroic disinterestedness.—Egotism loves a becoming dress, and is always on the watch to hide her ugliness by the robe of benevolence. Glenmurray thought that he was willing to marry Adeline merely for *her* sake; but I suspect it was chiefly for *his*. The true and delicate lover is always a monopolizer,[1] always desirous of calling the woman of his affections his own: it is not only because he considers marriage as a holy institution that

---

[1] See Godwin's negative view of marriage as a monopoly, Appendix D3.

the lover leads his mistress to the altar; but because it gives him a right to appropriate the fair treasure to himself,—because it sanctions and perpetuates the dearest of all monopolies, and erects a sacred barrier to guard his rights,—around which, all that is respectable in society, all that is most powerful and effectual in its organization, is proud and eager to rally.

But while Glenmurray, in spite of his happiness, was sensible to an alloy of it, and Adeline was tenderly imputing to the pain of his wound the occasionally mournful expression of his countenance, Adeline took occasion to declare that she would live with Glenmurray only on condition that such a step met with her mother's approbation.

"Then are my hopes for ever at an end," said Glenmurray:—"or,—or" (and spite of himself his eyes sparkled as he spoke) "—or we must submit to the absurd ceremony of marriage."[1]

"Marriage!" replied the astonished Adeline: "can you think so meanly of my mother, as to suppose her practice so totally opposite to her principles, that she would require her daughter to submit to a ceremony which she herself regards with contempt?—Impossible. I am sure, when I solicit her consent to my being yours, she will be pleased to find that her sentiments and observations have not been thrown away on me."

Glenmurray thought otherwise: however, he bowed and was silent; and Adeline declared that, to put an end to all doubt on the subject, she would instantly go in search of Mrs. Mowbray and propose the question to her: and Glenmurray, feeling himself more weak and indisposed than he chose to own to her, allowed her, though reluctantly, to depart.

CHAPTER 7

Mrs. Mowbray was but just returned from her charitable visit when Adeline entered the room. "And pray, miss Mowbray, where have you been?" she exclaimed, seeing Adeline with her hat and cloak on.

"I have been visiting poor Mr. Glenmurray," she replied.

"Indeed!" cried Mrs. Mowbray: "and without my leave! and pray who went with you?"

"Nobody, ma'am."

"Nobody!—What! visit a man alone at his lodgings, after the education which you have received!"

"Indeed, madam," replied Adeline meekly, "my education never taught me that such conduct was improper; nor, as you did the same this afternoon, could I have dared to think it so."

---

1 Cf. Godwin's phrase, "absurd institution of marriage," in *Memoirs*: see Appendix E1.

"You are mistaken, miss Mowbray," replied her mother: "I did not do the same; for the terms which I am upon with sir Patrick made my visiting him no impropriety at all."

"If you think I have acted wrong," replied Adeline timidly, "no doubt I have done so; though you were quite right in visiting sir Patrick, as the respectability of your age and character, and sir Patrick's youth, warranted the propriety of the visit:—but, surely the terms which I am upon with Mr. Glenmurray——"

"The terms which you are upon with Mr. Glenmurray! and my age and character! what can you mean?" angrily exclaimed Mrs. Mowbray.

"I hoped,* my dear mother," said Adeline tenderly, "that you had long ere this guessed the attachment which subsists between Mr. Glenmurray and me;—an attachment cherished by your high opinion of him and his writings; but which respect has till now made me hesitate to mention to you."

"Would to heaven!" replied Mrs. Mowbray, "that respect had made you for ever silent on the subject! Do you suppose that I would marry my daughter to a man of small fortune,—but more especially to one who, as sir Patrick informs me, is shunned for his principles and profligacy by all the world?"

"To what sir Patrick says of Mr. Glenmurray I pay no attention," answered Adeline; "nor are you, my dear mother, capable, I am sure, of being influenced by the prejudices of the world.—But you are quite mistaken in supposing me so lost to consistency, and so regardless of your liberal opinions and the books which we have studied, as to think of *marrying* Mr. Glenmurray."

"Grant me patience!" cried Mrs. Mowbray: "why, to be sure you do not think of living with him *without* being married?"

"Certainly, madam; that you may have the pleasure of beholding one union founded on rational grounds and cemented by rational ties."

"How!" cried Mrs. Mowbray, turning pale. "I!—I have pleasure in seeing my daughter a kept mistress!—You are mad, quite mad.—*I* approve such unhallowed connections!"

"My dearest mother," replied Adeline, "your agitation terrifies me,—but indeed what I say is strictly true; and see here, in Mr. Glenmurray's book, the very passage which I so often have heard you admire."[1] As she

---

[1]  Since Godwin's attack on marriage is largely based on a rejection of binding ties between individuals, it seems unlikely that the romantic and idealistic Adeline would endorse the grounds of his argument. Possibly Opie has in mind the passage where he claims that "the positive laws which are made to restrain our vices, irritate and multiply them," and goes on to suggest that the "the same sentiments of justice

said this, Adeline pointed to the passage; but in an instant Mrs. Mowbray seized the book and threw it on the fire.

Before Adeline had recovered her consternation Mrs. Mowbray fell into a violent hysteric; and long was it before she was restored to composure. When she recovered she was so exhausted that Adeline dared not renew the conversation; but leaving her to rest, she made up a bed on the* floor in her mother's room, and passed a night of wretchedness and watchfulness,—the first of the kind which she had ever known.—Would it had been the last!

In the morning Mrs. Mowbray awoke, refreshed and calm; and, affected at seeing the pale cheek and sunk eye of Adeline, indicative of a sleepless and unhappy night, she held her hand out† to her with a look of kindness; Adeline pressed it to her lips, as she knelt by the bed side, and moistened it with tears of regret for the past and alarm for the future.

"Adeline, my dear child," said Mrs. Mowbray in a faint voice, "I hope you will no longer think of putting a design in execution so fraught with mischief to you, and horror to me. Little did I think that you were so romantic as to see no difference between amusing one's imagination with new theories and new systems, and acting upon them in defiance of common custom, and the received usages of society. I admire the convenient trowsers and graceful dress of the Turkish women; but I would not wear them myself, lest it should expose me to derision."

"Is there no difference," thought Adeline, "between the importance of a dress and an opinion!—Is the one to be taken up, and laid down again, with the same indifference as the other!" But she continued silent, and Mrs. Mowbray went on.

"The poetical philosophy which I have so much delighted to study, has served me to ornament my conversation, and make persons less enlightened than myself wonder at the superior boldness of my fancy, and the acuteness of my reasoning powers;—but I should as soon have thought of making this little gold chain round my neck fasten the hall-door, as act upon the precepts laid down in those delightful books. No; though I think all they say‡ true, I believe the purity they inculcate too much for this world."

Adeline listened in silent astonishment and consternation. Conscience, and the conviction of what is right, she then for the first time learned,

---

and happiness, which, in a state of equality, would destroy our relish for expensive gratifications, might be expected to decrease our inordinate appetites of every kind, and to lead us universally to prefer the pleasures of intellect to the pleasures of sense" (*Enquiry Concerning Political Justice*, Book 8, chapter 8, "Of Cooperation, Cohabitation and Marriage"). See also Appendix D3.

were not to be the rule of action; and though filial tenderness made her resolve never to be the mistress of Glenmurray, she also resolved never to be his wife, or that of any other man; while, in spite of herself, the great respect with which she had hitherto regarded her mother's conduct and opinions began to diminish.

"Would to heaven, my dear mother," said Adeline, when Mrs. Mowbray had done speaking, "that you had said all this to me ere my mind had been indelibly impressed with the truth of these forbidden doctrines; for now my conscience tells me that I ought to act up to them!"

"How!" exclaimed Mrs. Mowbray, starting up in her bed, and in a voice shrill with emotion, "are you then resolved to disobey me, and dishonour yourself?"

"Oh! never, never!" replied Adeline, alarmed at her mother's violence, and fearful of a relapse. "Be but the kind affectionate parent that you have ever been to me; and though I will never marry, out of regard to my own principles, I will also never contract any other union, out of respect to your wishes,—but will lead with you a quiet, if not a *happy*, life; for never, never can I forget Glenmurray."

"There speaks the excellent child I always thought you to be!" replied Mrs. Mowbray; "and I shall leave it to time and good counsels to convince you, that the opinions of a girl of eighteen, as they are not founded on long experience, may possibly be erroneous."

Mrs. Mowbray never made a truer observation; but Adeline was not in a frame of mind to assent to it.

"Besides," continued Mrs. Mowbray, "had I ever been disposed to accept of Mr. Glenmurray as a son-in-law, it is very unlikely that I should be so now; as the duel took place not only, I find, from the treasonable opinions which he put forth, but from some disrespectful language which he held concerning me."

"Who could dare to invent so infamous a calumny!" exclaimed Adeline.

"My authority is unquestionable, miss Mowbray: I speak from sir Patrick himself."

"Then he adds falsehood to his other villanies!" returned Adeline, almost inarticulate with rage:—"but what could be expected from a man who could dare to insult a young woman under the roof of her mother with his licentious addresses."*

"What mean you?" cried Mrs. Mowbray, turning pale.

"I mean that sir Patrick yesterday morning insulted me by the grossest familiarities, and——"

"My dear child," replied Mrs. Mowbray laughing, "that is only the usual freedom of his manner; a manner which your ignorance of the world led you to mistake. He did not mean to insult you, believe me. I am sure that, spite of his ardent passion for me, he never, even when alone with me, hazarded any improper liberty."

"The ardent passion which he feels for you, madam!" exclaimed Adeline, turning pale in her turn.

"Yes, miss Mowbray! What, I suppose you think me too old to inspire one!—But, I assure you, there are people who think the mother handsomer than the daughter!"

"No doubt, dear mother, every one ought to think so,—and would to heaven sir Patrick were one of those! But he, unfortunately——"

"Is of that opinion," interrupted Mrs. Mowbray angrily: "and to convince you—so tenderly does he love me, and so fondly do I return his passion, that in a few days I shall become his wife."

Adeline, on hearing this terrible information, fell insensible on the ground. When she recovered she saw Mrs. Mowbray anxiously watching by her, but not with that look of alarm and tenderness with which she had attended her during her long illness; that look which was always present to her grateful and affectionate remembrance. No; Mrs. Mowbray's eye was cast down with a half-mournful, half-reproachful, and half-fearful expression, when it met that of Adeline.

The emotion of anguish which her fainting had evinced was a reproach to the proud heart of Mrs. Mowbray, and Adeline felt that it was so; but when she recollected that her mother was going to marry a man who had so lately declared a criminal passion for herself, she was very near relapsing into insensibility. She however struggled with her feelings, in order to gain resolution to disclose to Mrs. Mowbray all that had passed between her and sir Patrick. But as soon as she offered to renew the conversation, Mrs. Mowbray sternly commanded her to be silent; and insisting on her going to bed, she left her to her own reflections, till wearied and exhausted she fell into a sound sleep: nor, as it was late in the evening when she awoke, did she rise again till the next morning.

Mrs. Mowbray entered her room as she was dressing, and inquired how she did, with some kindness.

"I shall be better, dear mother, if you will but hear what I have to say concerning sir Patrick," replied Adeline, bursting into tears.

"You can say nothing that will shake my opinion of him, miss Mowbray," replied her mother coldly: "so I advise you to reconcile yourself to a circumstance which it is not in your power to prevent." So saying, she left the room; and Adeline, convinced that all she could say would be vain, endeavoured to console herself, by thinking that, as soon as sir Patrick became the husband of her mother, his wicked designs on her would undoubtedly cease; and that, therefore, in one respect, this* ill-assorted union would be beneficial to her.

Sir Patrick, meanwhile, was no less sanguine in his expectations from his marriage. Unlike the innocent Adeline, he did not consider his union with the mother as a necessary check to his attempts on the daughter; but, emboldened by what to him appeared the libertine sentiments of Adeline, and relying on the opportunities of being with her, which he must infallibly enjoy under the same roof in the country, he looked on her as his certain prey. Though he believed Glenmurray to be at that moment preferred to himself, he thought it impossible that the superior beauty of his person should not, in the end, have its due weight; as a passion founded in esteem, and the admiration of intellectual beauty, could not, in his opinion, subsist: besides, Adeline appeared in his eyes not a deceived enthusiast, but a susceptible and forward girl, endeavouring to hide her frailty[1] under fine sentiments and high-sounding theories. Nor was sir Patrick's inference an unnatural one. Every man of the world would have thought the same; and on very plausible grounds.

## CHAPTER 8

As sir Patrick was not "punctual as lovers to the moment sworn,"[2] Mrs. Mowbray resolved to sit down and write immediately to Glenmurray; flattering herself at the same time, that the letter which was designed to confound Glenmurray would delight the tender baronet;—for Mrs. Mowbray piqued herself on her talents for letter-writing, and was not a little pleased with an opportunity of displaying them to a celebrated author. But never before did she find writing a letter so difficult a task. Her eager wish of excelling deprived her of the means; and she who, in a letter to a friend or relation, would have written in a style at once clear and elegant, after two hours' effort produced the following specimen of the obscure, the pedantic, and affected.

"Sir,

"The light which cheers and attracts, if we follow its guidance, often leads us into bogs and quagmires:—Verbum sapienti.[3] Your writings are the lights, and the practice to which you advise my deluded daughter is the bog and the* quagmire. I agree with you in all you have said against marriage;—I agree with the savage nations

---

1  In the sense of "moral weakness; instability of mind; liability to err or yield to temptation" (*OED*).

2  Edward Young, *Night Thoughts on Life, Death, and Immortality* (1741-45), 3.4.

3  "A word to the wise" (Latin).

in the total uselessness of clothing; still I condescend to wear clothes, though neither becoming nor useful, because I respect public opinion; and I submit to the institution of marriage for reasons equally cogent. Such being my sentiments, sir, I must desire you never to see my daughter more. Nor could you expect to be received with open arms by me, whom the shafts of your ridicule have pierced, though warded off by the shield of love and gallantry;—but for this I thank you! Now shall I possess, owing to your baseness, at once a declared lover and a tried avenger; and the chains of Hymen[1] will be rendered more charming by gratitude's having blown the flame, while love forged the fetters.

"But with your writings I continue to amuse my imagination.— Lovely is the flower of the nightshade, though its berry be poison. Still shall I admire and wonder at you as an author, though I avoid and detest you as a man.

"EDITHA MOWBRAY."

This letter was just finished when sir Patrick arrived, and to him it was immediately shown.

"Heh! what have we here?" cried he laughing violently as he perused it. "Here you talk of being pierced by shafts which were warded off. Now, had I* said that, it would have been called a bull.[2] As to the concluding paragraph——"†3

"O! that, I flatter myself," said Mrs Mowbray, "will tear him with remorse."

"He must first understand it," cried sir Patrick: "I can but just comprehend it, and am sure it will be all botheration to him."

"I am sorry to find such is your opinion," replied Mrs. Mowbray; "for I think that sentence the best written of any."

"I did not say it was not fine writing," replied the baronet, "I only said it was not to be understood.—But, with your leave, you shall send the letter, and we'll drop the subject."

So said, so done, to the great satisfaction of sir Patrick, who felt that it was for his interest to suffer the part of Mrs. Mowbray's letter which alluded to Glenmurray's supposed calumnies against her to remain obscurely worded, as he well knew that what he had asserted on this subject was wholly void of foundation.

---

1  The Roman god of marriage.

2  A self-contradictory proposition.

3  Opie's revision in the 1810 edition makes it clear that Sir Patrick is referring to the second-last (actually the first) paragraph of the letter.

Glenmurray did not receive it with equal satisfaction. He was indignant at the charge of having advised Adeline to become his mistress rather than his wife; and as so much of the concluding passage as he could understand seemed to imply that he had calumniated her mother, to remain silent a moment would have been to confess himself guilty: he therefore answered Mrs. Mowbray's letter immediately. The answer was as follows:

"MADAM,

"To clear myself from the charge of having advised miss Mowbray to a step contrary to the common customs, however erroneous, of society at this period, I appeal to the testimony of miss Mowbray herself; and I here repeat to you the assurance which I made to her, that I am willing to marry her when and where she chooses. I love my system and my opinions, but the respectability of the woman of my affections *more*. Allow me, therefore, to make you a little acquainted with my situation in life:

"To you it is well known, madam, that wealth, honours, and titles have no value in my eyes; and that I reverence talents and virtues, though they wear the garb of poverty, and are born in the most obscure stations. But you, or rather those who are so fortunate as to influence your determinations, may consider my sentiments on this subject as romantic and absurd. It is necessary, therefore, that I should tell you, as an excuse in their eyes for presuming to address your daughter, that, by the accident of birth, I am descended from an antient family, and nearly allied to a noble one; and that my paternal inheritance, though not large enough for splendour and luxury, is sufficient for all the purposes of comfort and genteel affluence. I would say more on this subject, but I am impatient to remove from your mind the prejudice which you seem to have imbibed against me. I do not perfectly understand the last paragraph* in your letter. If you will be so kind as to explain it to me, you may depend on my being perfectly ingenuous: indeed, I have no difficulty in declaring, that I have neither encouraged a feeling, nor uttered a word, capable of giving the lie to the declaration which I am now going to make—That I am,

"With respect and esteem,
"Your obedient servant,
F. GLENMURRAY."

This letter had an effect on Mrs. Mowbray's feelings so much in favour of Glenmurray, that she was almost determined to let him marry Adeline. She felt that she owed her some amends for contracting a marriage so suddenly, and without either her knowledge or approbation; and she thought

AMELIA ALDERSON OPIE

that, by marrying her to the man of her heart, she should make her peace both with Adeline and herself. But, unfortunately, this design, as soon as it began to be formed, was communicated to sir Patrick.

"So, then!" exclaimed he, "you have forgotten and forgiven the impertinent things which the puppy said!—things which obliged me to wear this little useless appendage in a sling thus" (pointing to his wounded arm).

"O! no, my dear sir Patrick! But though what Mr. Glenmurray said might alarm the scrupulous tenderness of a lover, perhaps it was a remark which might only suit the sincerity of a friend. Perhaps, if Mr. Glenmurray had made it to me, I should have heard it with thanks, and with candour have approved it."

"My sweet soul!" replied sir Patrick, "you may be as candid and amiable as ever you please, but, 'by St. Patrick!' never shall sir Patrick O'Carrol be father-in-law[1] to the notorious and infamous Glenmurray—that subverter of all religion and order, and that scourge of civilized society!"

So saying, he stalked about the room; and Mrs. Mowbray, as she gazed on his handsome person, thought it would be absurd for her to sacrifice her own happiness to her daughter's, and give up sir Patrick as her husband in order to make Glenmurray her son. She therefore wrote another letter to Glenmurray, forbidding him any further intercourse with Adeline, on any pretence whatever; and delayed not a moment to send him her final decision.

"That is acting like the sensible woman I took you for," said sir Patrick: "the fellow has now gotten his quietus,[2] I trust, and the dear little Adeline is reserved for a* happier fate. Sweet soul! you do not know how fond she will be of me! I protest that I shall be so kind to her, it will be difficult for people to decide which I love best, the daughter or the mother."

"But I hope *I* shall always know, sir Patrick," said Mrs. Mowbray gravely.

"You!—O yes, to be sure. But I mean that my fatherly attentions shall be of the warmest kind.† But now do me the favour of telling me at what hour to-morrow I may appoint the clergyman to bring the license?"

The conversation that followed, it were needless and tedious to describe. Suffice, that eight o'clock the next morning was fixed for the marriage; and Mrs. Mowbray, either from shame or compassion, resolved that Adeline should not accompany her to church, nor even know of the ceremony till it was over.

Nor was this a difficult matter. Adeline remained in her own apartment all the preceding day, endeavouring, but in vain, to reconcile herself to what she justly termed the degradation of her mother. She felt, alas!

---

1 Stepfather, a common usage in this period.
2 Death, release from life. Cf. *Hamlet* 3.1.75.

the most painful of all feelings, next to that of self-abasement,—the consciousness of the abasement of one to whom she had all her life looked up with love and veneration. To write to Glenmurray while oppressed by such contending emotions she knew to be impossible; she therefore contented herself with sending a verbal message, importing that he should hear from her the next day: and poor Glenmurray passed the rest of that day and the night in a state little better than her own.

The next morning Adeline, who had not closed her eyes till day-light, woke late, and from a sound but unrefreshing sleep. The first object she saw was her maid, smartly dressed, sitting by her bed-side; and she also saw that she had been crying.

"Is my mother ill, Evans?" she exclaimed.

"O! no, miss Adeline, quite well," replied the girl, sighing.

"Thank God!" replied Adeline. The girl sighed still more deeply.* "But why are you so much dressed?" demanded Adeline.

"I have been out," answered the maid.

"Not on unpleasant business?"

"That's as it may be," she cried, turning away; and Adeline, from delicacy, forbore to press her further.

"'Tis very late—is it not?" asked Adeline, "and time for me to rise?"

"Yes, miss—I believe you had better get up."

Adeline immediately rose.—"Give me the dark gown I wore yesterday," said she.

"I think, miss, you had better put on your new white one," returned the maid.

"My new white one!" exclaimed Adeline, astonished at an interference so new.

"Yes, miss—I think it will be taken kinder, and look better."

At these words Adeline's suspicions were awakened. "I see, Evans," she cried, "you have something extraordinary to tell me:—I partly guess; I,—my mother——" Here, unable to proceed, she lay down on the bed which she had just quitted.

"Yes, miss Adeline—'tis very true; but pray compose yourself. I am sure I have cried enough on your account, that I have."

"What is true, my good Evans?" said Adeline faintly.

"Why, miss, my lady was married this morning to sir Patrick O'Carrol!—Mercy on me, how pale you look! I am sure I wish the villain was at the bottom of the sea, so I do."

"Leave me," said Adeline faintly, struggling for utterance.

"No—that I will not," bluntly replied Evans; "you are not fit to be left; and they are rejoicing below with sir Pat's great staring servant. But, for my part, I had rather stay here and cry with you than laugh with them.

Adeline hid her face in the pillow, incapable of further resistance, and groaned aloud.

"Who should ever have thought my lady would have done so!" continued the maid.—"Only think, miss! they say, and I doubt it is too true, that there have been no writings, or settlements, I think they call them, drawn up; and so sir Pat have got all, and he is over head and ears in debt, and my lady is to pay him out on't!"

At this account, which Adeline feared was a just one, as she had seen no preparations for a wedding going on, and had observed no signs of deeds, or any thing of the kind, she started up in an agony of grief—"Then has my mother given me up, indeed!" she exclaimed, clasping her hands together, "and the once darling child may soon be a friendless outcast!"

"You want a friend, miss Adeline!" said the kind girl, bursting into tears.—"Never, while I live, or any of my fellow-servants." And Adeline, whose heart was bursting with a sense of forlornness and abandonment, felt consoled by the artless sympathy of her attendant; and, giving way to a violent flood of tears, she threw her arms round her neck, and sobbed upon her bosom.

Having thus eased her feelings, she recollected that it was incumbent on her to exert her fortitude; and that it was a duty which she owed her mother not to condemn her conduct openly herself, nor suffer any one else to do it in her presence: still, at that moment, she could not find in her heart to reprove the observations by which, in spite of her sense of propriety, she had been soothed and gratified, but she hastened to dress herself as became a bridal dinner, and dismissed, as soon as she could, the affectionate Evans from her presence. She then walked up and down her chamber, in order to summon courage to enter the drawing-room.—"But how strange, how cruel it was," said she, "that my mother did not come to inform me of this important event herself!"

In this respect, however, Mrs. Mowbray had acted kindly. Reluctant, even more than she was willing to confess to her own heart, to meet Adeline alone, she had chosen to conclude that she was still asleep, and had desired she might not be disturbed; but soon after her return from church, being assured that she was in a sound slumber, she had stolen to her bed-side and put a note under her pillow, acquainting her with what had passed: but this note Adeline in her restlessness had, with her pillow, pushed on the floor, and there unseen it had remained. But, as Adeline was pacing to and fro, she luckily observed it; and, by proving that her mother had not been so very neglectful of her, it tended to fortify her mind against the succeeding interview. The note began:—

"My *dearest*\* child! *to spare*† you, in your present weak state, the emotion which you would necessarily feel in attending me to the altar, I have resolved to let the ceremony be performed unknown to you. But, my beloved Adeline, I trust that your affection for me will make you rejoice in a step which you may, perhaps, at present disapprove, when convinced that it was absolutely necessary to my happiness, and can, in no way, be the means of diminishing yours.

"I remain

"Your ever affectionate mother."

"She loves me still then!" cried Adeline, shedding tears of tenderness, "and I accused her unjustly.—O my dear mother, if this event should indeed increase your happiness, never shall I repine at not having been able to prevent it." And then, after taking two or three hasty turns round the room, and bathing her eyes to remove in a degree the traces of her tears, she ventured into the drawing-room.

But the sight of her mother seated by sir Patrick, his arm encircling her waist, in that very room which had so lately witnessed his profligate attempts on herself, deprived her of the little resolution which she had been able to assume, and pale and trembling she sunk speechless with emotion on the first chair near her.

Mrs. Mowbray, or, as we must at present call her, lady O'Carrol, was affected by Adeline's distress, and, hastening to her, received the almost fainting girl in her arms; while even sir Patrick, feeling compassion for the unhappiness which he could more readily understand than his bride, was eager to hide his confusion by calling for water, drops, and servants.

"I want neither medicine nor assistance now," said Adeline, gently raising her head from her mother's shoulder: "the first shock is over, and I shall, I trust, behave in future with proper self-command."

"Better late than never," muttered lady O'Carrol, on whom the word *shock* had not made a pleasant impression; while sir Patrick, approaching Adeline, exclaimed, "If you have not self-command, miss Mowbray, it is the only command which you cannot boast; for your power of commanding others no one can dispute, who has ever had the happiness of beholding you."

So saying, he took her hand; and, as her mother's husband, claimed the privilege of saluting her,—a privilege which Adeline, though she almost shrunk with horror from his touch, had *self-command* enough not to deny him: immediately after he claimed the same favour from his bride; and they resumed their position on the sopha.

But so embarrassing was the situation of all parties that no conversation took place; and Adeline, unable any longer to endure the restraint to which she was obliged, rose, to return to her own room, in order to hide the sorrow which she was on the point of betraying, when her mother in a tone of reproach exclaimed, "It grieves me to the soul, miss Mowbray, to perceive that you appear to consider as a day of mourning the day which I consider as the happiest of my life."

"Oh! my dearest mother!" replied Adeline, returning and approaching her, "it is the dread of your deceiving yourself, only, that makes me sad at a time like this: if this day in its consequences prove a happy one——"

"And wherefore should you doubt that it will, miss Mowbray?"

"Miss Mowbray, do you doubt my honour?" cried sir Patrick hastily.

Adeline instantly fixed her fine eyes on his face with a look which he knew how to *interpret*,\* but not how to support; and he cast his to the ground with painful consciousness.

She saw her triumph, and it gave her courage to proceed:—"O sir!" she cried, "it is in your power to convert all my painful doubts into joyful certainties; make but my mother happy, and I will love and bless you ever.—Promise me, sir," she continued, her enthusiasm and affection kindling as she spoke, "promise me to be kind and indulgent to her;—she has never known contradiction; she has been through life the darling object of all who surrounded her; the pride of her parents, her husband, and her child: neglect, injury, and unkindness she would inevitably sink under: and I conjure you" (here she dropped on her knees and extended her arms in an attitude of entreaty), "by all your hopes of happiness hereafter, to give her reason to continue to name this the happiest day of her life."

Here she ceased, overcome by the violence of her emotions; but continued her look and attitude of entreaty, full of such sweet earnestness, that the baronet could hardly conceal the variety of feelings which assailed him; amongst which, passion for the lovely object before him predominated. To make a jest of Adeline's seriousness he conceived to be the best way to conceal what he felt; and while Mrs. Mowbray, overcome with Adeline's expressions of tenderness, was giving way to them by a flood of tears, and grasping in both hers the clasped hands of Adeline, he cried, in an ironical tone,—"You are the most extraordinary motherly young creature that I ever saw in my life, my dear girl! Instead of your mother giving the nuptial benediction to you, the order of nature is reversed, and you are giving it to her. Upon my soul† I begin to think, seeing you in that posture, that you are my bride begging a blessing of mamma on our union, and that I ought to be on my knees too."

So saying, he knelt beside Adeline at lady O'Carrol's feet, and in a tone of mock solemnity besought her to bless both her affectionate children: and as he did this, he threw his arm round the weeping girl, and pressed her to his bosom. This speech, and this action, at once banished all self-command from the indignant Adeline, and in an instant she sprung from his embrace; and forgetting how much her violence must surprise, if not alarm and offend, her mother, she rushed out of the room, and did not stop till she* reached her own chamber.

When there, she was alarmed lest her conduct should have occasioned both pain and resentment to lady O'Carrol; and it was with trembling reluctance that she obeyed the summons to dinner; but her fears were groundless. The bride had fallen into one of her reveries during sir Patrick's strange speech, from which she awakened only at the last words of it, viz. "affectionate children": and seeing sir Patrick at her feet, with a very tender expression on his face, and hearing the words "affectionate children," she conceived that he was expressing his hopes of their being blest with progeny, and that a selfish feeling of fear at such a prospect had hurried Adeline out of the room. She was therefore disposed to regard her daughter with pity, but not with resentment, when she entered the dinner-room, and Adeline's tranquillity in a degree returned: but when she retired for the night she could not help owning to herself, that that day, her mother's wedding-day, had been the most painful day† of her existence—and she literally sobbed herself to sleep.

The next morning a new trial awaited her; she had to write a final farewell to Glenmurray. Many letters did she begin, many did she finish, and many did she tear; but recollecting that the longer she delayed sending him one, the longer she kept him in a state of agitating suspense, she resolved to send the last written, even though it appeared to her not quite so strong a transcript of her feelings as the former ones. Whether it were‡ so or not, Glenmurray received it with alternate agony and transport;—with agony, because it destroyed every hope of Adeline's being his,—and with transport, because every line breathed the purest and yet most ardent attachment, and convinced him that, however long their separation, the love of Adeline would experience no change.

Many days elapsed before Glenmurray could bear any companion but the letter of Adeline; and during that time she was on the road with the bride and bridegroom to a beautiful seat in Berkshire, called the Pavilion, hired by sir Patrick, the week before his marriage, of one of his profligate friends. As the road lay through a very fine country, Adeline would have thought the journey a pleasant one, had not the idea of Glenmurray ill and dejected continually haunted her. Sir Patrick appeared to be engrossed by his bride, and she was really wholly wrapt up in him; and at times the beauties of the scenery around had power to engage Adeline's attention: but she immediately recollected how much Glenmurray§ would have participated in her delight, and the contemplation of the prospect ended in renewed recollections of him.**

# CHAPTER 9

At length they arrived at the place of their destination; and sir Patrick, warmly embracing his bride, bade her welcome to her new abode; and immediately approaching Adeline, he bestowed on her an embrace no less cordial:—or, to say the truth, so ardent seemed the welcome, even to the innocent Adeline, that she vainly endeavoured to persuade herself that, as her father-in-law, sir Patrick's tenderness was excusable.

Spite of her efforts to be cheerful she was angry and suspicious, and had an indistinct feeling of remote danger; which though she could not define even to herself, it was new and painful to her to experience. But as the elastic mind of eighteen soon rebounds from the pressure of sorrow, and forgets in present enjoyment the prospect of evil, Adeline gazed on the elegant apartment she was in with joyful surprise; while, through folding doors on either side of it, she beheld a suite of rooms, all furnished with a degree of tasteful simplicity such as she had never before beheld: and through the windows, which opened on a lawn that sloped to the banks of a rapid river, she saw an amphitheatre of wooded hills, which proved that, how great soever had been the efforts of art to decorate their new habitation, the hand of Nature had done still more to embellish it; and all fear of sir Patrick was lost in gratitude for his having chosen such a retirement.

With eager curiosity Adeline hurried from room to room; admired in the western apartments the fine effect of the declining sun shining through rose-coloured window-curtains; gazed with delight on the statues and pictures that every where met the eye, and reposed with unsuspecting gaiety on the couches of eider down which were in profusion around. Every thing in the house spoke it to be the temple of Pleasure: but the innocent Adeline and her unobservant mother saw nothing but elegant convenience in an abode in which the disciples of Epicurus[1] might have delighted; and while Æolian harps[2] in the windows, and perfumes of all kinds, added to the enchantment of the scene, the bride only beheld in the choice of the villa a proof of her husband's desire of making her happy; and Adeline sighed for virtuous love and Glenmurray, as all that was wanting to complete her fascination.

Sir Patrick, meanwhile, was not blind to the impressions made on Adeline by the beauty of the spot which he had chosen, though he was far

---

1   Epicurus (c. 341-271 BCE) taught that the purpose of life was happiness. His hedonism has been misunderstood as a mere pursuit of pleasure.
2   Stringed instruments named for Aeolus, god of the winds; they were placed in a window so that the wind would blow across them and make music.

from suspecting the companion* she had pictured to herself as most fitted to enjoy and embellish it; and pleased because she was pleased, and delighted to be regarded by her with such unusual looks of complacency, he gave himself up to his natural vivacity; and Adeline passed a merry, if not a happy, evening with the bride and bridegroom.

But the next morning she arose with the painful conviction as fresh as ever on her mind, that day would succeed to day, and yet she should not behold Glenmurray; and that day would succeed to day, and still should she see O'Carrol, still be exposed to his noisy mirth, to his odious familiarities, which, though she taught herself to believe they proceeded merely from the customs of his country, and the nearness of their relationship, it was to her most painful to endure.

Her only resource, therefore, from unpleasant thoughts was reading; and she eagerly opened the cases of books in the library, which were unlocked. But, on taking down some of the books, she was disappointed to find none of the kind to which she had been accustomed. Mrs. Mowbray's peculiar taste had led her, as we have before observed, to the perusal of nothing but political tracts, systems of philosophy, and Scuderi's[1] and other romances. Scarcely had the works of our best poets found their way to her library; and novels, plays, and works of a lighter kind she was never in the habit of reading herself, and consequently had not put in the hands of her daughter. Adeline had, therefore, read Rousseau's Contrat Social, but not his Julie; Montesquieu's Esprit des Lois, but not his Lettres Persannes; and had glowed with republican ardour over the scenes of Voltaire's Brutus, but had never had her pure† mind polluted by the pages of his Candide.‡[2]

---

1  Madeleine de Scudéry (1607-1701), French novelist, very popular in her own time and widely translated into English.

2  Adeline has read political theory, but not much fiction or other literature with an emotional appeal. Jean-Jacques Rousseau (1712-78) wrote *The Social Contract* (1762), but he also wrote the autobiographical *Confessions* (1782) and the epistolary novel *Julie, ou La Nouvelle Héloïse* (1761). In *La Nouvelle Héloïse,* Julie redeems herself through marriage to Wolmar following a passionate love affair with Saint-Preux, who continues to be in love with Julie after her marriage. Hannah More—like many other writers on women's education—was concerned about this novel's influence on impressionable girls (see Appendix B2). Charles-Louis de Secondat, Baron de la Brède et de Montesquieu (1689-1755) was the author of *Esprit des Loix* (*The Spirit of Laws*, 1748), an influential political treatise, and *Lettres Persannes* (*Persian Letters*, 1721), a satirical account of French society from the viewpoint of two Persian travellers. François-Marie Arouet, better known by his pseudonym, Voltaire (1694-1778), was a central writer of the French Enlightenment, whose tragedy *Brutus* (1730) was revived in Paris during the revolutionary 1790s. *Candide,* his satirical tale of 1759, takes a skeptical view of almost every contemporary idea and institution.

Different had been the circumstances, and consequently the practice, of the owner of sir Patrick's new abode. Of all Rousseau's works, he had in his library only the New Heloise and his Confessions; of Montesquieu, none but the glowing letters above mentioned; and while Voltaire's chaste and moral tragedies were excluded, his profligate tales attracted the eye by the peculiar elegance of their binding; while dangerous French novels of all descriptions met the view under the downy pillows of the inviting sofas around, calculated to inflame the fancy and corrupt the morals.

But Adeline, unprepared by any reading of the kind to receive and relish the poison contained in them, turned with disgust from pages so uncongenial to her feelings; nor did her eye dwell delighted on any of the stores which the shelves contained,* till she opened the Nouvelle Heloise; and as soon as she had read a few letters in that enchanting work, she seated herself in the apartment but the moment before become disgusting to her; and in a short time she forgot even Glenmurray himself,—or rather, she gave his form to the eloquent lover of Julie. But, unfortunately, the bride came in while her daughter was thus pleasantly engaged; and on being informed what her studies were, she peremptorily forbad her to read a book so pregnant with mischief; and though she had not read it, and consequently could not justly appreciate its character, she was sure, on the words of others, that such reading was improper for her daughter.

In vain did Adeline venture to say that Julie, like the works of Glenmurray, might be, perhaps, condemned by those who had never read a line of it. The book was prohibited; and Adeline, with a reluctant hand, restored it to its place.

Had she read it, the sacrifice which the guilty but penitent Julia makes to filial affection, and the respectable light in which the institution of marriage is held up to view, would have strengthened, no doubt, Adeline's resolution to obey her mother, and give up Glenmurray; and have led her to reconsider those opinions which taught her to think contemptible what ages and nations had been content to venerate. But it was decreed that every thing the mother of Adeline did should accelerate the fate of her devoted daughter.

Disappointed in her hopes of finding amusement in reading, Adeline had recourse to walking; and none of the beautiful scenes around remained long unexplored by her. In her rambles she but too frequently saw scenes of poverty and distress, which ill contrasted with the beauty of the house which she inhabited; scenes, which even a small portion of the money expended there in useless decoration would have entirely alleviated: and they were scenes, too, which Adeline had been accustomed to relieve. The extreme of poverty in the cottage did not disgrace, on the Mowbray estate, the well-furnished mansion-house; but Adeline, as we have observed before, was allowed to draw on her mother for money sufficient to prevent industrious labour from knowing the distresses of want.

"And why should I not draw on her here for money for the same purposes?" cried Adeline to herself, as she beheld one spectacle of peculiar hardships:—"Surely my mother is not dependent on her husband? and even if she were, sir Patrick has not a hard heart, and will not refuse my prayer": and therefore, promising the sufferers instant relief, she left them, saying she should soon reach the Pavilion and be back again; while the objects of her bounty were silent with surprise at hearing that their relief was to come from the Pavilion, a place hitherto closed to the solicitations of poverty, though ever open to the revels and the votaries of pleasure.

Adeline found her mother alone; and with a beating heart and a flushed cheek, she described the scene which she had witnessed, and begged to be restored to her old office of almoner on such occasions.

"A sad scene, indeed, my dear Adeline!" replied the bride in evident embarrassment, "and I will speak to sir Patrick about it."

"Speak to sir Patrick, madam! cannot you follow the impulse of humanity without consulting him?"

"I can't give the relief you ask without his assistance," replied her mother; "for, except a guinea or so, I have no loose cash about me for my own uses.—Sir Patrick's benevolence has long ago emptied his purse, and I gladly surrendered mine to him."

"And shall you in future have no money for the purposes of charity but that you must claim from sir Patrick?" asked Adeline mournfully.

"O dear! yes,—I have a very handsome allowance settled on me; but then at present he wants it himself" (Adeline involuntarily clasped her hands together in an agony, and sighed deeply). "But, however, child," added the bride, "as you seem to make such a point of it, take this guinea to the cottage you mention, *en attendant!*"[1]

Adeline took the guinea: but it was very insufficient to pay for medical attendance, to discharge the rent due to a clamorous landlord, and to purchase several things necessary for the relief of the poor sufferers: therefore she added another guinea to it, and, not liking to relate her disappointment, sent the money to them, desiring the servant to say that she would see them the next morning, when she resolved to apply to sir Patrick for the relief which her mother could not give; feeling at the same time the mournful conviction, that she herself, as well as her mother, would be in future dependent on his bounty.

Though disposed to give way to mournful reflections on her own account, Adeline roused herself from the melancholy abstraction into which

---

1 Literally, "while you wait" (Fr.); synonymous here with "in the meantime."

she was falling, by reflecting that she had still to plead the cause of the poor cottagers with sir Patrick; and hearing he was in the house, she hastened to prefer her petition.

Sir Patrick listened to her tone of voice, and gazed on her expressive countenance with delight: but when she had concluded her narration a solitary half-guinea was all he bestowed on her, saying, "I am never roused to charity by the descriptions of others; I must always see the distress which I am solicited to relieve."

"Then go with me to the cottage," exclaimed Adeline; but to her great mortification he only smiled, bowed, and disappeared: and when he returned to supper, Adeline could scarcely prevail on herself to look at him without displeasure, and could not endure the unfeeling vivacity of his manner.

Mortified and unhappy, she next morning went to the cottage, reluctant to impart to its expecting inhabitants the ill success which she had experienced. But what was her surprise when they came out joyfully to meet her, and told her that a gentleman had been there that morning very early, had discharged their debts, and given them a sum of money for their future wants!

"His name, his name?" eagerly inquired Adeline: but that they said he refused to give; and as he was in a horseman's large coat, and held a handkerchief to his face, they were sure they should not know him again.

A pleasing suspicion immediately came across Adeline's mind that this benevolent unknown might be Glenmurray; and the idea that he was perhaps unseen hovering round her, gave her one of the most exquisite feelings which she had ever known. But this agreeable delusion was soon dissipated by one of the children's giving her a card which the kind stranger had dropped from his pocket; and this card had on it "Sir Patrick O'Carrol."

At first it was natural for her to be hurt and disappointed at finding that her hopes concerning Glenmurray had no foundation in truth; but her benevolence, and indeed regard for her mother's happiness as well as her own, led her to rejoice in this unexpected proof of excellence in sir Patrick.—He had evidently proved that he loved to do good by stealth, and had withdrawn himself even from her thanks.

In a moment, therefore, she banished from her mind every trace of his unworthiness. She had done him injustice, and she sought refuge from the remorse which this consciousness inflicted on her, by going into the opposite extreme. From that hour, indeed, her complaisance to his opinions, and her attentions to him, were so unremitting and evident, that sir Patrick's passion became stronger than ever, and his hopes of a return to it seemed to be built on a very strong foundation.

Adeline had given all her former suspicions to the wind: daily instances of his benevolence came to her knowledge, and threw such a charm over all he said and did, that even the familiarity in his conduct, look, and manner towards her, appeared to her now nothing more than the result of the free manners of his countrymen;—and she sometimes could not help wishing sir Patrick to be known to, and intimate with, Glenmurray. But the moment was now at hand that was to unveil the real character of sir Patrick, and determine the destiny of Adeline.

One day sir Patrick proposed taking his bride to see a beautiful *ferme ornée*[1] at about twelve miles' distance; and if it answered the expectations which he had formed of it, they were determined to spend two or three days in the neighbourhood to enjoy the beauty of the grounds;—in that case he was to return in the evening to the Pavilion, and drive Adeline over the next morning to partake in their pleasure.

To this scheme both the ladies gladly consented, as it was impossible for them to suspect the villanous design which it was intended to aid.

The truth was, that sir Patrick, having, as he fondly imagined, gained Adeline's affections, resolved to defer no longer the profligate attempt which he had long meditated; and had contrived this excursion in order to insure his wife's absence from home, and a tête-a-tête with her daughter,—not doubting but that opportunity was alone wanting to enable him to succeed in his abandoned wishes.*

At an early hour the curricle[2] was at the door, and sir Patrick, having handed his lady in, took leave of Adeline. He told her that he should probably return early in the evening, pressed her hand more tenderly than usual, and, springing into the carriage, drove off with a countenance animated with expected triumph.

Adeline immediately set out on a long walk to the adjoining villages, visited the cottages near the Pavilion, and, having dined at an early hour, determined to pass the rest of the day in reading, provided it was possible for her to find any book in the house proper for her perusal.

With this intention she repaired to an apartment called the library, but what in these times would be denominated a *boudoir*;[3] and this, even in Paris, would have been admired for its voluptuous elegance.—On the table lay several costly volumes, which seemed have been very lately perused

---

1 Literally, "ornamented farm" (Fr.), a farm in which beauty and productivity were carefully balanced; an example of the eighteenth-century fashion for landscape gardening.

2 A light two-wheeled carriage.

3 A room in which a lady could be alone or receive her intimate friends; literally "a place to sulk in" (Fr.).

by sir Patrick, as some of them were open, some turned down at particular passages: but as soon as she glanced her eye over their contents, Adeline indignantly threw them down again; and, while her cheek glowed with the blush of offended modesty, she threw herself on a sofa, and fell into a long and mournful reverie on the misery which awaited her mother, in consequence of her having madly dared to unite herself for life to a young libertine, who could delight in no other reading but what was offensive to good morals and to delicacy. Nor could she dwell upon this subject without recurring to her former fears for herself; and so lost was she in agonising reflections, that it was some time before she recollected herself sufficiently to remember that she was guilty of an indecorum, in staying so long in an apartment which contained books that she ought not even to be suspected of having had an opportunity to peruse.

Having once entertained this consciousness, Adeline hastily arose, and had just reached the door when sir Patrick himself appeared at it. She started back in terror when she beheld him, on observing in his countenance and manner evident marks not only of determined profligacy, but of intoxication. Her suspicions were indeed just. Bold as he was in iniquity, he dared not in a cool and sober moment put his guilty purpose in execution; and he shrunk with temporary horror from an attempt on the honour of the daughter of his wife, though he believed that she would be a willing victim. He had therefore stopped on the road to fortify his courage with wine; and, luckily for Adeline, he had taken more than he was aware of; for when, after a vehement declaration of the ardour of his passion, and protestations that she should that moment be his,* he dared irreverently to approach her, Adeline, strong in innocence, aware of his intention, and presuming on his situation, disengaged herself from his grasp with ease; and pushing him with violence from her, he fell with such force against the brass edge of one of the sofas, that, stunned and wounded by the fall, he lay bleeding on the ground. Adeline involuntarily was hastening to his assistance: but recollecting how mischievous to her such an exertion of humanity might be, she contented herself with ringing the bell violently to call the servants to his aid. Then, in almost frantic haste, she rushed out of the house, ran across the park, and when she recovered her emotion she found herself, she scarcely knew how, sitting on a turf seat by the road side.

"Great God! what† will become of me!" she wildly exclaimed: "my mother's roof is no longer a protection to me;—I cannot absent myself from it without alleging a reason for my conduct, which will ruin her peace of mind for ever. Wretch that I am! whither can I go, and where can I seek for refuge?"

At this moment, as she looked around in wild dismay, and raised her streaming eyes to heaven, she saw a man's face peeping from between the branches of a tree opposite to her, and observed that he was gazing on her intently. Alarmed and fluttered, she instantly started from her seat, and was hastening away, when the man suddenly dropped from his hiding-place, and, running after her, called her by her name, and conjured her to stop; while, with an emotion of surprise and delight, she recognised in him Arthur, the servant of Glenmurray!

Instantly, scarcely knowing what she did, she pressed the astonished Arthur's rough hand in hers; and by this action confused and confounded the poor fellow so much, that the speech which he was going to make faltered on his tongue.

"Oh! where is your master?" eagerly inquired Adeline.

"My master have* sent you this, miss," replied Arthur, holding out a letter, which Adeline joyfully received; and, spite of her intended obedience to her mother's will, Glenmurray himself could not have met with a less† favourable reception, for the moment was a most propitious one to his love: nor, as it happened, was Glenmurray too far off to profit by it. On his way from Bath he went a few miles out of his road, in order, as he said, and perhaps as he thought, to pay a visit to an old servant of his mother's, who was married to a respectable farmer; but, fortunately, the farm commanded a view of the Pavilion, and Glenmurray could from his window gaze on the house that contained the woman of his affections.

But to return to Adeline, who, while hastily tearing open the letter, asked Arthur where his master was, and heard with indescribable emotion that he was in the neighbourhood.

"Here! so providentially!" she exclaimed, and proceeded to read the letter; but her emotion forbade her to read it entirely. She only saw that it contained bank-notes; that Glenmurray was going abroad for his health; and, in case he should die there, had sent her the money which he had meant to leave her in his will,—lest she should be, in the mean while, any way dependent on sir Patrick.

Numberless conflicting emotions took possession of Adeline's heart while this new proof of her lover's attentive tenderness met her view; and, as she contrasted his generous and delicate attachment with the licentious passion of her mother's libertine husband, a burst of uncontrollable affection for Glenmurray agitated her bosom; and, rendered superstitious by her fears, she looked on him as sent by Providence to save her from the dangers of her home.

"This is the second time," cried she, "that Glenmurray, as my guardian angel, has appeared at the moment when I was exposed to danger from the same guilty quarter! Ah! surely there is more than accident in this! and he is ordained to be my guide and my protector!"

When once a woman has associated with an amiable man the idea of protection, he can never again be indifferent to her; and when the protector happens to be the chosen object of her love, his power becomes fixed on a basis never to be shaken.

"It is enough," said Adeline in a faltering voice, pressing the letter to her lips, and bursting into tears of grateful tenderness as she spoke: "Lead me to your master directly."

"Bless my heart! will you see him then, miss?" cried Arthur.

"See him?" replied Adeline—"see the only friend I now can boast?— But let us be gone this moment, lest I should be seen and pursued."

Instantly, guided by Arthur, Adeline set off full speed for the farm-house, nor stopped till she found herself in the presence of Glenmurray!

"O! I am safe now!" exclaimed Adeline, throwing herself into his arms; while he was so overcome with surprise and joy that he could not speak the welcome which his heart gave her: and Adeline, happy to behold him again, was as silent as her lover. At length Glenmurray exclaimed:

"Do we then meet again, Adeline!"

"Yes," replied she; "and we meet to part no more."

"Do not mock me," cried Glenmurray starting from his seat, and seizing her extended hand; "my feelings must not be trifled with."

"Nor am I a woman to trifle with them. Glenmurray, I come to you for safety and protection;—I come to seek shelter in your arms from misery and dishonour. You are ill, you are going into a foreign country: and from this moment look on me as your nurse, your companion;—your home shall be my home, your country my country!"

Glenmurray, too much agitated, too happy to speak, could only press the agitated girl to his bosom, and fold his arms round her, as if to assure her of the protection which she claimed.

"But there is not a moment to be lost," cried Adeline: "I may be missed and pursued: let us be gone directly."

The first word was enough for Glenmurray: eager to secure the recovered treasure which he had thought for ever lost, his orders were given, and executed by the faithful Arthur with the utmost dispatch; and even before Adeline had explained to him the cause of her resolution to elope with him they were on their road to Cornwall, meaning to embark at Falmouth for Lisbon.[1]

---

1  Like the heroine of Wollstonecraft's *Mary, a Fiction* (1788)—and like Wollstonecraft herself in 1785. Falmouth is a seaport in Cornwall (in south-west England). Lisbon, in Portugal, was a popular destination for invalids: later in the novel Mrs. Pemberton travels to Lisbon with a sick friend (154, 187).

But Arthur, who was going to marry, and leave Glenmurray's service, received orders to stay at the farm till he had learned how sir Patrick was; and having obtained the necessary information, he was to send it to Glenmurray at Falmouth. The next morning he saw sir Patrick himself driving full speed past the farm; and having written immediately to his master, Adeline had the satisfaction of knowing that she had not purchased her own safety by the sufferings or danger of her persecutor, and the consequent misery of her mother.

## CHAPTER 10

BUT Glenmurray's heart needed no explanation of the cause of Adeline's elopement. She was with him—with him, as she said, for ever. True, she had talked of flying from misery and dishonour; but he knew they could not reach her in his arms,—not even dishonour according to the ideas of society,—for he meant to make Adeline legally his as soon as they were safe from pursuit, and his illness was forgotten in the fond transport of the present moment.

Adeline's joy was of a much shorter duration. Recollections of a most painful nature were continually recurring. True it was that it was no longer possible for her to reside under the roof of her mother:—but was it necessary for her to elope with Glenmurray? the man whom she had solemnly promised her mother to renounce! Then, on the other side, she argued that the appearance of love for Glenmurray was an excuse sufficient to conceal from her deluded parent the real cause of her elopement.

"It was my sole alternative," said she mentally:—"my mother must either suppose me an unworthy child, or know sir Patrick to be an unworthy husband; and it will be easier for her to support the knowledge of the one than of the other: then, when she forgives me, as no doubt she will in time, I shall be happy: but that I could never be, while convinced that I had made her miserable by revealing to her the wickedness of sir Patrick."

While this was passing in her mind, her countenance was full of such anxious and mournful expression, that Glenmurray, unable to keep silence any longer, conjured her to tell him what so evidently weighed upon her spirits.

"The difficulty that oppressed me is past," she replied, wiping from her eyes the tears which the thought of having left her mother so unexpectedly, and for the first time, produced. "I have convinced myself, that to leave home and commit myself to your protection was the most proper and virtuous step that I could take: I have not obeyed the dictates of love, but of reason."

"I am very sorry to hear it," said Glenmurray mournfully.

"It seems to me so very rational to love you," returned Adeline tenderly, shocked at the sad expression of his countenance, "that what seem to be the dictates of reason may be those of love only."

To a reply like this, Glenmurray could only answer by those incoherent yet intelligible expressions of fondness to the object of them, which are so delightful to lovers themselves, and so uninteresting to other people: nay, so entirely was Glenmurray again engrossed by the sense of present happiness, that his curiosity was still suspended, and Adeline's story remained untold. But Adeline's pleasure was damped by painful recollections, and still more by her not being able to hide from herself the mournful consciousness that the ravages of sickness were but too visible in Glenmurray's face and figure, and that the flush of unexpected delight could but ill conceal the hollow paleness of his cheek, and the sunk appearance of his eyes.

Meanwhile the chaise rolled on,—post succeeded to post; and though night was far advanced, Adeline, fearful of being pursued, would not consent to stop, and they travelled till morning. But Glenmurray, feeling himself exhausted, prevailed on her, for his sake, to alight at a small inn on the road side near Marlborough.[1]

There Adeline narrated the occurrences of the past day; but with difficulty could she prevail on herself to own to Glenmurray that she had been the object of such an outrage as she had experienced from sir Patrick.

A truly delicate woman feels degraded, not flattered, by being the object of libertine attempts; and, situated as Adeline and Glenmurray now were, to disclose the insult which had been offered to her was a still more difficult task: but to conceal it was impossible. She felt that, even to *him*,* some justification of her precipitate and unsolicited flight was necessary; and nothing but sir Patrick's attempt could justify it. She therefore, blushing and hesitating, revealed the disgraceful secret: but such was its effect on the weak spirits and delicate health of Glenmurray, that the violent emotions which he underwent brought on a return of his most alarming symptoms; and in a few hours Adeline, bending over the sick bed of her lover, experienced for the first time that most dreadful of feelings, fear for the life of the object of her affection.†

Two days, however, restored him to comparative safety, and they reached a small and obscure village within a short distance from Falmouth, most conveniently situated. There they took up their abode, and resolved to remain till the wind should change, and enable them to sail for Lisbon.

---

1   In Wiltshire, in the south of England.

In this retreat, situated in air as salubrious as that of the south of France, Glenmurray was soon restored to health, especially as happy love was now his, and brought back the health of which hopeless love had contributed to deprive him. The woman whom he loved was his companion and his nurse; and so dear had the quiet scene of their happiness become to them, that, forgetful there was still a danger of their being discovered, it was with considerable regret that they received a summons to embark, and saw themselves on their voyage to Portugal.

But before she left England Adeline wrote to her mother.

After a pleasant and short voyage the lovers found themselves at Lisbon; and Glenmurray, pursuant to his resolution, immediately proposed to Adeline to unite himself to her by the indissoluble ties of marriage.

Nothing could exceed Adeline's surprise at this proposal: at first she could not believe Glenmurray was in earnest; but seeing that he looked not only grave but anxious, and as if earnestly expecting an answer, she asked him whether he had convinced himself that what he had written against marriage was a tissue of mischievous absurdity.

Glenmurray, blushing, with the conceit of an author replied "that he still thought his arguments unanswerable."

"Then, if you still are convinced your theory is good, why let your practice be bad? It is incumbent on you to act up to the principles that you profess, in order to give them their proper weight in society—else you give the lie to your own declarations."

"But it is better for me to do that, than for you to be the sacrifice to my reputation."

"I," replied Adeline, "am entirely out of the question: you are to be governed by no other law but your desire to promote general utility, and are not to think at all of the interest of an individual."[1]

"How can I do so, when that individual is dearer to me than all the world beside?" cried Glenmurray passionately.

"And if you but once recollect that you are dearer to me than all the world beside, you will cease to suppose that my happiness can be affected by the opinion entertained of my conduct by others." As Adeline said this,

---

1   An important idea in Godwin, *Enquiry Concerning Political Justice*. Most famously, in Book 2, chapter 2 of the 3rd ed. (1798), "Of Justice," Godwin makes a case for choosing on rational grounds to rescue from a fire the writer François de Salignac de la Mothe Fénelon (1651-1715) rather than his valet. Even if the valet were a close relative, says Godwin, the principle of justice would be the same: saving Fénelon would promote the general good by allowing his work (specifically his pedagogical work, *Télémaque* [1699]) to benefit thousands of other people. (In the first edition of *Political Justice* [1793], the choice was between Fénelon and his chambermaid.)

she twisted both her hands in his* arms so affectionately, and looked up in his face with so satisfied and tender an expression, that Glenmurray could not bear to go on with a subject which evidently drew a cloud across her brow; and hours, days, weeks, and months passed rapidly over their heads before he had resolution to renew it.

Hours, days, weeks, and months spent in a manner most dear to the heart and most salutary to† the mind of Adeline!—Her taste for books, which had hitherto been cultivated in a partial manner, and had led her to one range of study only, was now directed by Glenmurray to the perusal of general literature; and the historian, the biographer, the poet, and the novelist, obtained alternately her attention and her praises.

In her knowledge of the French and Italian languages, too, she was now considerably improved by the instructions of her lover; and while his occasional illnesses were alleviated by her ever watchful attentions, their attachment was cemented by one of the strongest of all ties—the consciousness of mutual benefit and assistance.‡

CHAPTER 11

ONE evening, as they were sitting on a bench in one of the public walks, a gentleman approached them, whose appearance bespoke him to be an Englishman, though his sun-burnt complexion showed that he had been for years exposed to a more ardent climate than that of Britain.

As he came nearer, Glenmurray thought his features were familiar to him; and the stranger, starting with joyful surprise, seized his hand, and welcomed him as an old friend. Glenmurray returned his salutation with great cordiality, and recognised in the stranger a Mr. Maynard, an amiable man, who had gone to seek his fortune in India, and was returned a nabob,[1] but with an irreproachable character.

"So, then," cried Mr. Maynard gaily, "this is the elegant young English couple that my servant, and even the inn-keeper himself, was so loud in praise of! Little did I think the happy man was my old friend,—though no man is more deserving of being happy: but I beg you will introduce me to your lady."

Glenmurray, though conscious of the mistake he was under, had not resolution enough to avow that he was not married; and Adeline, unaware of the difficulty of Glenmurray's situation, received Mr. Maynard's salutation with the utmost ease, though the tremor of her lover's voice, and the

---

1    Someone who returned from India to Europe with a fortune, from the Urdu *nawab*: "a Muslim official or governor under the Mogul empire" (*OED*).

blush on his cheek as he said—"Adeline, give me leave to introduce to you Mr. Maynard, an old friend of mine,"—were sufficient indications that the rencontre[1] disturbed him.

In a few minutes Adeline and Mr. Maynard were no longer strangers. Mr. Maynard, who had not lived much in the society of well-informed women, and not at all in that of women accustomed to original thinking, was at once astonished and delighted at the variety of Adeline's remarks, at the playfulness of her imagination, and the eloquence of her expressions. But it was very evident, at length, to Mr. Maynard, that in proportion as Adeline and he became more acquainted and more satisfied with each other, Glenmurray grew more silent and more uneasy. The consequence was unavoidable: as most men would have done on a like occasion, Mr. Maynard thought Glenmurray was jealous of him.

But no thought so vexatious to himself, and so degrading to Adeline, had entered the confiding and discriminating mind of Glenmurray. The truth was, he knew that Mr. Maynard, whom he had seen in the walks, though he had not known him again, had ladies of his party; and he expected that the more Mr. Maynard admired his supposed wife, the more would he be eager to introduce her to his companions.

Nor was Glenmurray wrong in his conjectures.

"I have two sisters with me, madam," said Mr. Maynard, "whom I shall be happy and proud to introduce to you. One of them is a widow, and has lived several years in India, but returned with me in delicate health, and was ordered hither: she is not a woman of great reading, but has an excellent understanding, and will admire you. The other is several years younger; and I am sure she would be happy in an opportunity of profiting by the conversation of a lady, who, though not older than herself, seems to have had so many more opportunities of improvement."

Adeline bowed, and expressed her impatience to form this new acquaintance; and looked triumphantly at Glenmurray, meaning to express—"See, spite of the supposed prejudices of the world, here is a man who wants to introduce me to his sisters." Little did she know that Maynard concluded she was a wife: his absence from England had made him ignorant of the nature of Glenmurray's works, or even that he was an author; so that he was not at all likely to suppose that the moral, pious youth, whom he had always respected, was become a visionary philosopher, and, in defiance of the laws of society, was living openly with a mistress.

"But my sister will wonder what is become of me," suddenly cried Maynard; "and as Emily is so unwell as to keep her room to-day, I must

---

1  "Meeting" (Fr.).

not make her anxious. But for her illness, I should have requested your company to supper."

"And I should have liked to accept the invitation," replied Adeline; "but I will hope to see the ladies soon."

"Oh! without fail, to-morrow," cried Maynard: "if Emily be not well enough to call on you, perhaps you will come to her apartments."

"Undoubtedly: expect me at twelve o'clock."

Maynard then shook his grave and silent friend by the hand and, departed,—his vanity not a little flattered by the supposed jealousy of Glenmurray.

"There now," said Adeline, when he was out of hearing, "I hope some of your tender fears are done away.* You see there are liberal and unprejudiced persons in the world; and Mr. Maynard, instead of shunning me, courts my acquaintance for his sisters."

Glenmurray shook his head, and remained silent; and Adeline was distressed to feel by his burning hand that he was seriously uneasy.

"I shall certainly call on these ladies to-morrow," continued Adeline:— "I really pine for the society of amiable women."

Glenmurray sighed deeply: he dreaded to tell her that he could not allow her to call on them, and yet he knew that this painful task awaited him. Besides, she wished, she said, to know some amiable women; and, eager as he was to indulge all her wishes, he felt but too certainly that in this wish she could never be indulged. Even had he been capable of doing so dishonourable an action as introducing his mistress as his wife, he was sure that Adeline would have spurned at the deception; and silent and sad he grasped Adeline's hand as her arm rested within his, and, complaining of indisposition, slowly returned to the inn.

The next morning at breakfast, Adeline again expressed her eagerness to form an acquaintance with the sisters of Mr. Maynard; when Glenmurray, starting from his seat, paced the room in considerable agitation.

"What is the matter?" cried Adeline, hastily rising and laying her hand on his arm.

Glenmurray grasped her hand, and replied with assumed firmness: "Adeline, it is impossible for you to form an acquaintance with Mr. Maynard's sisters: propriety and honour both forbid me to allow it."

"Indeed!" exclaimed Adeline, "are they not as amiable, then, as he described them? are they improper acquaintances for me? Well then—I am disappointed: but you are the best judge of what is right, and I am contented to obey you."

The simple, ingenuous and acquiescent sweetness with which she said this, was a new pang to her lover:—had she repined, had she looked ill-humoured, his task would not have been so difficult.

"But what reason can you give for declining this acquaintance?" resumed Adeline.

"Aye! there's the difficulty," replied Glenmurray: "pure-minded and amiable as I know you to be, how can I bear to tell these children of prejudice that you are not my wife, but my mistress?"

Adeline started; and, turning pale, exclaimed, "Are you sure, then, that they do not know it already?"

"Quite sure—else Maynard would not have thought you a fit companion for his sisters."

"But surely he must know your principles;—he must have read your works?"

"I am certain he is ignorant of both, and does not even know that I am an author."

"Is it possible?" cried Adeline: "is there any one so unfortunate as to be unacquainted with your writings?"

Glenmurray at another time would have been elated at a compliment like this from the woman whom he idolized; but at this moment he heard it with a feeling of pain which he would not have liked to define to himself, and casting his eyes to the ground he said nothing.

"So then," said Adeline mournfully, "I am an improper companion for *them*, not they for *me!*"* and spite of herself her eyes filled with tears.———
At this moment a waiter brought in a note for Glenmurray;—it was from Maynard, and as follows:

MY DEAR FRIEND,

Emily is better to-day; and both my sisters are so impatient to see, and know, your charming wife, that they beg me to present their compliments to Mrs. Glenmurray and you; and request the honour of your company to a late breakfast:—at eleven o'clock we hope to see you.

Ever yours,
G.M.

"We will send an answer," said Glenmurray: but the waiter had been gone some minutes before either Adeline or Glenmurray spoke. At length Adeline, struggling with her feelings, observed, "Mr. Maynard seems so amiable a man, that I should think it would not be difficult to convince him of his errors: surely, therefore, it is your duty to call on him, state our real situation, and our reasons for it, and endeavour to convince him that our attachment is sanctioned both by reason and virtue."

"But not by the church," replied Glenmurray, "and Maynard is of the old school: besides, a man of forty-eight is not likely to be convinced by the arguments of a young man of twenty-eight, and the example of a girl of nineteen."

"If age be necessary to give weight to arguments," returned Adeline, "I wonder that you thought proper to publish four years ago."

"Would to God I never had published!" exclaimed Glenmurray, almost pettishly.

"If you had not, I probably should never have been yours," replied Adeline, fondly leaning her head on his shoulder, and then looking up in his face. Glenmurray clasped her to his bosom; but again the pleasure was mixed with pain. "All this time," rejoined Adeline, "your friends are expecting an answer: you had better carry it in person."

"I cannot," replied Glenmurray, "and there is only one way of getting out of this business to my satisfaction."

"Name it; and rest assured that I shall approve it."

"Then I wish to order horses immediately, and set off on our road to France."

"So soon,—though the air agrees with you so well?"

"O yes;—for when the mind is uneasy no air can be of use to the body."

"But why is your mind uneasy?"

"Here I should be exposed to see Maynard, and—and—he would see you too."

"And what then?"

"What then?—Why, I could not bear to see him look on you with an eye of disrespect."

"And wherefore should he?"

"O Adeline, the name of wife imposes restraint even on a libertine; but that of mistress——"

"Is Mr. Maynard then a libertine?" said Adeline gravely: and Glenmurray, afraid of wounding her feelings by entering into a further explanation, changed the subject, and again requested her consent to leave Lisbon.

"I have often told you," said Adeline sighing, "that my will is yours; and if you will give strict orders to have letters sent after us to the towns that we shall stop at, I am ready to set off immediately."

Glenmurray then gave his orders; wrote a letter explaining his situation to Maynard, and in an hour they were on their journey to France.


CHAPTER 12

IN the mean while Mr. Maynard, miss Maynard, and Mrs. Wallington his widowed sister, were impatiently expecting Glenmurray's answer, and earnestly hoping to see him and his lovely companion,—but from different motives. Maynard was impatient to see Adeline because he really admired her; his sisters, because they hoped to find her unworthy of such violent admiration.

Their vanity had been piqued, and their envy excited, by the extravagant praises of their brother; and they had interrupted him by the first questions which all women ask on such occasions,—"Is she pretty?"

And he had* answered, "Very pretty."

"Is she tall?"

"Very tall, taller than I am."

"I hate tall women," replied miss Maynard (a little round girl of nineteen).

"Is she fair?"

"Exquisitely fair."

"I like brown women," cried the widow: "fair people always look silly."

"But Mrs. Glenmurray's eyes are hazel, and her eye-lashes long and dark."

"Hazel eyes are always bold-looking," cried miss Maynard.

"Not Mrs. Glenmurray's; for her expression is the most pure and ingenuous that ever I† saw. Some girls, indecent in their dress and very licentious in their manner, passed us as we sat on the walk; and the comments which I made on them provoked from Mrs. Glenmurray some remarks on the behaviour and dress of women; and, as she commented on the disgusting expression of vice in women, and the charm of modest dignity both in dress and manners, her own dress, manners, and expression, were such an admirable comment on her words, and she shone so brightly, if I may use the expression, in the graceful awfulness of virtue, that I gazed with delight, and somewhat of apprehension lest this fair perfection should suddenly take flight to her native skies, toward which her fine eyes were occasionally turned."

"Bless me! if our brother is not quite poetical! This prodigy has inspired him," replied the widow with a sneer.

"For my part, I hate *prodigies*,"‡ said miss Maynard: "I feel myself unworthy to associate with them."

When one woman calls another a prodigy, and expresses herself as unworthy to associate with her, it is very certain that she means to insult rather than compliment her; and in this sense Mr. Maynard understood his sister's words: therefore, after having listened with tolerable patience to a few more sneers at the unconscious Adeline, he was provoked to say that, ill-disposed as he found they were towards his new acquaintance, he hoped that when they became acquainted with her they would still give him reason to say, as he always had done, that he was proud of his sisters; for, in his opinion, no woman ever looked so lovely as when she was doing justice to the merits and extenuating the faults of a rival.

"A rival!" exclaimed the sisters at once:—"And, pray, what rivalship could there be in this case?"

"My remark was a general one; but since you choose to make it a particular one, I will answer to it as such," continued Mr. Maynard. "All women are rivals in one sense—rivals for general esteem and admiration; and she* only shall have my suffrage in her favour, who can point out a beauty or a merit in another woman without insinuating at the same time a counterbalancing defect."

"But Mrs. Glenmurray, it seems, has no† defects!"

"At least I have not known her long enough to find them out; but you, no doubt, will, when you know her, very readily spare me that trouble."

How injudiciously had Maynard prepared the minds of his sisters to admire Adeline! It was a preparation to make them hate her; and they were very impatient to begin the task of depreciating both her *morale* and her *physique*, when Glenmurray's note arrived.

"It is not Glenmurray's hand," said Maynard—(indeed, from agitation of mind the writing was not recognisable). "It must be hers then," continued he, affecting to kiss the address with rapture.

"It is the hand of a sloven," observed Mrs. Wallington, studying the writing.

"But in dress she is as neat as a quaker," retorted the brother, eagerly snatching the letter back, "and her mind seems as pure as her dress."

He then broke the seal, and read out what follows:

"DEAR MAYNARD,
    "When you receive this, Adeline and I shall be on our road to France, and you,—start not!—are the occasion of our abrupt departure."

"So, so, jealous indeed," said Maynard to himself, and more impressed than ever with the charms of Adeline; for he concluded that Glenmurray had discovered in her an answering prepossession.

"You the occasion, brother!" cried both sisters.

"Have patience."

"You saw Adeline; you admired her; and wished to introduce her to your sisters—this, honour forbad me to allow"—(the sisters started from their seats) "for Adeline is not my wife, but my companion."

Here Maynard made a full pause—at once surprised and confounded. His sisters, pleased as well as astonished, looked triumphantly at each other; and Mrs. Wallington exclaimed, "So, then, this angel of purity turns out to be a kept lady!" At this remark miss Maynard laughed heartily; but Maynard, to hide his confusion, commanded silence, and went on with the letter:

"But, spite of her situation, strange as it may seem to you, believe me, no wife was ever more pure than Adeline."

At this passage the sisters could no longer contain themselves, and they gave way to loud bursts of laughter, which Maynard could hardly help joining in; but being angry at the same time he uttered nothing but an oath, which I shall not repeat, and retreated to his chamber to finish the letter alone.

During his absence the laughter redoubled;—but in the midst of it Maynard re-entered, and desired they would allow him to read the letter to the end. The sisters immediately begged that he would proceed, as it was so amusing that they wished to hear more.—Glenmurray continued thus:

"You have no doubt yet to learn that some few years ago I commenced author, and published opinions contrary to the established usage of society: amongst other things I proved the absurdity of the institution of marriage; and Adeline, who at an early age read my works, became one of my converts."

"The man is certainly mad," cried Maynard, "and how dreadful it is that this angelic creature should have been his victim."

"But perhaps this *fallen* angel, brother, for such you will allow she is, spite of her *purity*, was as wicked as he. I know people in general only blame the seducer, but I always blame the seduced equally."

"I do not doubt it," said her brother sneeringly, and going on with the letter.

"No wonder then, that, being forced to fly from her maternal roof, she took refuge in my arms."

"Lucky dog!"

"But though Adeline was the victim neither of her own weakness nor of my seductions, but was merely urged by circumstances to act up to the principles which she openly professed, I felt so conscious that she would be degraded in your eyes after you were acquainted with her situation, though in mine she appears as spotless as ever, that I could not bear to expose her even to a glance from you less respectful than those with which you beheld her last night. I therefore prevailed on her to leave Lisbon; nor had I any difficulty in so doing, when she found that your wish of introducing her to your sisters was founded on your supposition of her being my wife, and that all chance of your desiring her acquaintance for them would be over, when you knew the nature of her connection with me. I shall now bid you farewell. I write in haste and agitation, and have not time to say more than God bless you!

"F.G."

"Yes, yes, I see how it is," muttered Mr. Maynard to himself when he had finished the letter, "he was jealous of me. I wish" (raising his voice) "that he had not been in such a confounded* hurry to go away."

"Why, brother," replied Mrs. Wallington, "to be sure you would not have introduced us to this piece of angelic purity a little the worse for the wear!"

"No," replied he; "but I might have enjoyed her company myself."

"And perhaps, brother, you might have rivalled the philosophic author in time," observed miss Maynard.

"If I had not, it would have been from no want of good will on my part," returned Maynard.

"Well, then I rejoice that the creature is gone," replied Mrs. Wallington, drawing up.

"And I too," said miss Maynard disdainfully: "but I think we had better drop this subject; I have had quite enough of it."

"And so have I," cried Mrs. Wallington: "but I must observe, before we drop it entirely, that when next my brother comes home and wearies his sisters by exaggerated praises of another woman, I hope he will take care that his goddess, or rather his angel of purity, does not turn out to be a kept mistress."

So saying she left the room, and miss Maynard, tittering, followed her; while Maynard, too sore on this subject to bear to be laughed at, took his hat in a pet, and, flinging the door after him with great violence, walked out to muse on the erring but interesting companion of Glenmurray.

## CHAPTER 13

WHILE these conversations were passing at Lisbon, Glenmurray and Adeline were pursuing their journey to France; and insensibly did the charm of being together obliterate from the minds of each the rencontre which had so much disturbed them.

But Adeline began to be uneasy on a subject of much greater importance; she every day expected an answer from her mother, but no answer arrived; and they had been stationary at Perpignan[1] some days, to which

---

1   In southern France, near the Spanish border.

place they had desired their letters to be addressed, *poste restante*,[1] and still none were forwarded thither from Lisbon.

The idea that her mother had utterly renounced her now took possession of her imagination, and love had no charm to offer her capable of affording her consolation: the care which she had taken of her infancy, the affectionate attentions that had preserved her life, and the uninterrupted kindness which she had shown towards her till her attachment to sir Patrick took place,—all these pressed powerfully and painfully on her memory, till her elopement seemed wholly unjustifiable in her eyes, and she reprobated her conduct in terms of the most bitter self-reproach.

At these moments even Glenmurray seemed to become the object of her aversion. Her mother had forbidden her to think of him; yet, to make her flight more agonizing to her injured parent, she had eloped with *him*. But as soon as ever she beheld him he regained his wonted influence over her heart, and her self-reproaches became less poignant: she became sensible that sir Patrick's guilt and her mother's imprudent marriage were the causes* of her own fault, and not Glenmurray; and could she but receive a letter of pardon from England, she felt that her conscience would again be at peace.

But soon an idea of a still more harassing nature succeeded and overwhelmed her. Perhaps her desertion had injured her mother's health; perhaps she was too ill to write; perhaps she was dead:—and when this horrible supposition took possession of her mind she used to avoid even the presence of her lover; and as her spirits commonly sunk towards evening, when the still renewed expectations of the day had been deceived, she used to hasten to a neighbouring church when the bell called to vespers, and, prostrate on the steps of the altar, lift up her soul to heaven in the silent breathings of penitence and prayer.[2] Having thus relieved her heart she returned to Glenmurray, pensive but resigned.

One evening after she had unburthened her feelings in this manner, Glenmurray prevailed on her to walk with him to a public promenade; and being tired they sat down on a bench in a shady part of the mall. They had not sat long before a gentleman and two ladies seated themselves beside them.

Glenmurray instantly rose up to depart; but the gentleman also rose and exclaimed, "'Tis he indeed! Glenmurray, have you forgotten your old friend Willie Douglas?"

---

1  Held at the post office to be picked up.

2  Perhaps an echo of Mary's attraction to continental Roman Catholicism in Wollstonecraft's *Mary, a Fiction* (1788).

Glenmurray, pleased to see a friend whom he had once so highly valued, returned the salutation with marked cordiality; while the ladies with great kindness accosted Adeline, and begged she would allow them the honour of her acquaintance.

Taught by the rencontre at Lisbon, Adeline for a moment felt embarrassed; but there was something so truly benevolent in the countenance of both ladies, and she was so struck by the extreme beauty of the younger one, that she had not resolution to avoid, or even to receive their advances coldly; and while the gentlemen were commenting on each other's looks, and in an instant going over the occurrences of past years, the ladies, pleased with each other, had entered into conversation.

"But I expected to see you and your lady," said major Douglas; "for Maynard was writing to me from Lisbon when he laid by his pen and took the walk in which he met you; and on his return he filled up the rest of his letter with the praises of Mrs. Glenmurray, and expressions of envy at your happiness."

Glenmurray and Adeline both blushed deeply. "So!" said Adeline to herself, "here will be another letter to write when we get home"; for, though ingenuousness was one of her most striking qualities, she had not resolution enough to tell her new acquaintance that she was not married: besides, she flattered herself, that, could she once interest these charming women in her favour, they would not refuse her their society even when they knew her real situation; for she thought them too amiable to be prejudiced, as she called it, and was not yet aware how much the perfection of the female character depends on respect even to what may be called the prejudices of others.

The day began to close in; but major Douglas, though Glenmurray was too uneasy to answer him except by monosyllables, would not hear of going home, and continued to talk with cheerfulness and interest of the scenes of his and Glenmurray's early youth. He too was ignorant of his friend's notoriety as an author: he had lived chiefly at his estates in the Highlands; nor would he have left them, but because he was advised to travel for his health; and the lovely creature whom he had married, as well as his only sister, was anxious on his account to put the advice in execution. He therefore made no allusions to Glenmurray's opinions that could give him an opportunity of explaining his real situation; and he saw with confusion, that every moment increased the intimacy of Adeline and the wife and sister of his friend.

At length his feelings operated so powerfully on his weak frame, that a sudden faintness seized him, and supported by Adeline and the major, and followed by his two kind companions, he returned to the inn: there, to get rid of the Douglases and avoid the inquiries of Adeline, who suspected the cause of his illness, he immediately retired to bed.

His friends also returned home, lamenting the apparently declining health of Glenmurray, and expatiating with delight on the winning graces of his supposed wife: for these ladies were of a different class of women to the sisters of Maynard.—Mrs. Douglas was so confessedly a beauty, so rich in acknowledged attractions, that she could afford to do justice to the attractions of another; and miss Douglas was so decidedly devoid of all pretensions to the lovely in person, that the idea of competition with the beautiful never entered her mind, and she was always eager to admire what she knew that she was incapable of rivalling. Unexposed, therefore, to feel those petty jealousies, those paltry competitions which injure the character of women in general, Emma Douglas's mind was the seat of benevolence and candour,—as was her beautiful sister's from a different cause; and they were both warmer even than the major in praise of Adeline.

But a second letter from Mr. Maynard awaited major Douglas at the inn, which put a fatal stop to their self-congratulations at having met Glenmurray and his companion.

Mr. Maynard, full of Glenmurray's letter, and still more deeply impressed than ever with the image of Adeline, could not forbear writing to the major on the subject; giving as a reason, that he wished to let him know the true state of affairs, in order that he might avoid Glenmurray.... The letter came too late.

"And I have seen him, have welcomed him as a friend, and he has had the impudence to introduce his harlot to my wife and sister!"

So spoke the major in the language of passion,—and passion is never accurate.—Glenmurray had *not* introduced Adeline: and this was gently hinted by the kind and candid Emma Douglas; while the younger and more inexperienced wife sat silent with consternation, at having pressed with the utmost kindness the hand of a kept mistress.

Vain were the representations of his sister to sooth the wounded pride of major Douglas. Without considering the difficulty of such a proceeding, he insisted upon it that Glenmurray should have led Adeline away instantly, as unworthy to breathe the same air with his wife and sister.

"You find by that letter, brother," said miss Douglas, "that this unhappy Adeline is still an object of respect in his eyes, and he could not wound her feelings so publicly, especially as she seems to be more ill-judging than vicious."

She spoke in vain.—The major was a soldier, and so delicate in his ideas of the honour of women, that he thought his wife and sister polluted from having, though unconsciously, associated with Adeline: being violently irritated therefore at the supposed insult offered him by Glenmurray, he left the room, and, having dispatched a challenge to him, told the ladies he had letters to write to England till bed-time arrived: then, after having settled his affairs in case he should fall in the conflict, he sat brooding alone over the insolence of his former friend.

There was a consciousness too which aggravated his resentment. Calumny had been busy with his reputation; and, though he deserved it not, had once branded him with the name of coward. Besides, his elder sister had been seduced by a man of very high rank, and was then living with him as his mistress. Made still more susceptible therefore of affront by this distressing consciousness, he suspected that Glenmurray, from being acquainted with these circumstances, had presumed on them, and dared to take a liberty with him, situated as he then was, which in former times he would not have ventured to offer.

As Adeline and Glenmurray were both retired for the night when the major's note arrived, it was not delivered till morning,—nor then, luckily, till Adeline, supposing Glenmurray asleep, was gone to take her usual walk to the post-office: Glenmurray, little aware of its contents, opened it, and read as follows:

"SIR,
"For your conduct in introducing your mistress to my wife and sister, I demand immediate satisfaction. As you may possibly not have recovered your indisposition of last night, and I wish to take no unfair advantages, I do not desire you to meet me till evening; but at six o'clock, a mile out of the north side of the town, I shall expect you.—I can lend you pistols if you have none."

"There is only one step to be taken," said Glenmurray mentally, starting up and dressing himself: and in a few moments he was at major Douglas's lodgings.

The major had just finished dressing, when Glenmurray was announced. He started and turned pale at seeing him; then, dismissing his servant and taking up his hat and his pistols, he desired Glenmurray to walk out with him.

"With all my heart," replied Glenmurray. But, recollecting himself, "No no," said he: "I come hither now, merely to talk to you; and if, after what has passed, the ladies should see us go out together, they would be but too sure of what was going to happen, and might follow us."

"Well, then sir," cried the major, "we had better separate till evening."

"I shall not leave you, major Douglas," replied Glenmurray solemnly, "whatever harsh things you may say or do, till I have made you listen to me."

"How can I listen to you, when nothing you can say can be a justification of your conduct?"

"I do not mean to offer any.—I am only come to tell you my story, with that of my companion, and my resolutions in consequence of my situation; and I conjure you, by the recollections of our early days, of our past pleasures and fatigues, those days when fatigue itself was a pleasure, and I was not the weak emaciated being that I am now, unable to bear exertion, and overcome even to female weakness by agitation of mind such as I experienced last night—"

"For God's sake sit down," cried the major, glancing his eye over the faded form of Glenmurray.—Glenmurray sat down.

"I say, I conjure you by these recollections," he continued, "to hear me with candour and patience. Weakness will render me brief." Here he paused to wipe the damps from his forehead; and Douglas, in a voice of emotion, desired him to say whatever he chose, but to say it directly.

"I will," replied Glenmurray; "for indeed there is one at home who will be alarmed at my absence."

The major frowned; and, biting his lip, said, "Proceed, Mr. Glenmurray," in his usual tone.

Glenmurray obeyed. He related his commencing author,—the nature of his works,—his acquaintance with Adeline,—its consequences,—her mother's marriage,—sir Patrick's villany,—Adeline's elopement, her refusal to marry him, and the grounds on which it was founded. "And now," cried Glenmurray when his narration was ended, "hear my firm resolve. Let the consequences to my reputation be what they may, let your insults be what they may, I will not accept your challenge; I will not expose Adeline to the risk of being left without a protector in a foreign land, and probably without one in her own. I fear that, in the natural course of things, I shall not continue with her long; but, while I can watch over her* and contribute to her happiness, no dread of shame, no fear for what others may think of me, no selfish consideration whatever shall induce me to hazard a life which belongs to her, and on which at present her happiness depends. I think, Douglas, you are incapable of treating me with indignity; but even to that I will patiently submit, rather than expose my life; while, consoled by my motive, I will triumphantly exclaim—'See, Adeline, what I can endure for thy sake!'"

Here he paused; and the major, interested and affected, had involuntarily put out his hand to him; but, drawing it back, he said "Then I may be sure that you meant no affront to me by suffering my wife and sister to converse with miss Mowbray?"

Glenmurray having put an end to these suspicions entirely, by a candid avowal of his feelings, and of his wish to have escaped directly if possible, the major shook him affectionately by the hand, and told him that though he firmly believed too much learning had made him mad, yet, that he was as much his friend as ever. "But what vexes me is," said he, "that you should have turned the head of that sweet girl. The opinion of the world is every thing to a woman."

"Aye, it is indeed," replied Glenmurray; "and, spite of ridicule, I would marry Adeline directly, as I said before, to guaranty her against reproach.—I wish you would try to persuade her to be mine legally."

"That I will," eagerly replied the major; "I am sure I shall prevail with her. I am sure I shall soon convince her that the opinions she holds are nothing but nonsense."

"You will find," replied Glenmurray, blushing, "that her arguments are unanswerable notwithstanding."

"What, though taken from the cursed books you mentioned?"

"You forget that I wrote these books."

"So I did; and I wish she could forget it also: and then they would appear to her, as they must do no doubt to all people of common sense, and that is, abominable stuff."

Glenmurray bit his lips,—but the author did not long absorb the lover, and he urged the major to return with him to his lodgings.

"Aye, that I will," cried he: "and what is more, my sister Emma, who writes admirably, shall write her a letter to convince her that she had better be married directly."

"She had better converse with her," said Glenmurray.

The major looked grave, and observed that they would do well to go and consult the women on the subject, and tell them the whole story. So saying, he opened the door of a closet leading to their apartment: but there, to their great surprise, they found Mrs. Douglas and Emma, and as well informed of every thing as themselves;—for, expecting that a duel might be the consequence of the major's impetuosity, and hearing Mr. Glenmurray announced, they resolved to listen to the conversation, and, if it took the turn which they expected, to rush in and endeavour to mollify the disputants.

"So, ladies! this is very pretty indeed! Eaves-droppers, I protest," cried major Douglas: but he said no more; for his wife, affected by the recital which she had heard, and delighted to find that there would be no duel, threw her arms round his neck, and burst into tears. Emma, almost equally affected, gave her hand to Glenmurray, and told him nothing on her part should be omitted to prevail on Adeline to sacrifice her opinions to her welfare.

"I said so," cried the major. "You will write to her."

"No; I will see her, and argue with her."

"And so will I," cried the wife.

"That you shall not," bluntly replied the major.

"Why not? I think it my duty to do all I can to save a fellow creature from ruin; and words spoken from the heart are always more powerful than words written."

"But what will the world say, if I permit you to converse with a kept mistress?"

"The world here to us, as we associate with none and are known to none, is Mr. Glenmurray and miss Mowbray; and of their good word we are sure."

"Aye," cried Emma, "and sure of succeeding with this interesting Adeline too; for if she likes us, as I think she does——"

"She adores you," replied Glenmurray.

"So much the better:—then, when we shall tell her that we cannot associate with her, much as we admire her, unless she consents to become a wife, surely she will hear reason."

"No doubt," cried Mrs. Douglas; "and then we will go to church with her, and you, Emma, shall be bride's maid."

"I see no necessity for that," observed the major gravely.

"But I do," replied Emma. "She will repeat her vows with more heartfelt reverence, when two respectable women, deeply impressed themselves with their importance, shall be there to witness them."

"But there is no protestant church here," exclaimed Glenmurray: "however, we can go back to Lisbon, and you are already resolved to return thither."

This point being settled, it was agreed that Glenmurray should prepare Adeline for their visit; and with a lightened heart he went to execute his commission. But when he saw Adeline he forgot his commission and every thing but her distress; for he found her with an open letter in her hand, and an unopened one on the floor, in a state of mind almost bordering on phrensy.[1]

CHAPTER 14

As soon as Adeline beheld Glenmurray, "See!" she exclaimed in a hoarse and agitated tone, "there is my letter to my mother, returned unopened, and here is a letter from Dr. Norberry which has broken my heart:—however, we must go to England directly."

The letter was as follows:

---

1  Or "frenzy": delirium, temporary insanity. Vol. 1 ends here.

"You have made a pretty fool of me, deluded but still dear girl! for you have made me believe in forebodings, and be hanged to you.* You may remember with what a full heart I bade you adieu, and I recollect what a devilish queer sensation I had when the park-gates closed on your fleet carriage. I swore a good oath† at the postillions[1] for driving so fast, as I wished to see you as long as I could; and now I protest that I believe I was actuated by a foreboding that at that house, and on that spot, I should never behold you again." (Here a tear had fallen on the paper, and the word "*again*" was nearly blotted out.) "Dear, lost Adeline, I prayed for you too! I prayed that you might return as innocent and happy as you left me. Lord‡ have mercy on us! who should have thought it!—But this is nothing to the purpose, and I suppose you think you have done nought but what is right and clever."

He then proceeded to inform Adeline, who had written to him to implore his mediation between her and her mother, "that the latter had sent express for him on finding, by the hasty scrawl which came the day after Adeline's departure from the farm-house, that she had eloped, and who was the companion of her flight; that he found her in violent agitation, as sir Patrick, stung to madness at the success of his rival, had with an ingenuousness worthy a better cause avowed to her his ardent passion for her daughter, his resolution to follow the fugitives, and by every means possible separate Adeline from her lover; and that, after having thanked lady O'Carrol for her great generosity to him, he had taken his pistols, mounted his horse, attended by his groom also well armed, and vowed that he would never return unless accompanied by the woman whom he adored."

"No wonder therefore," continued the doctor, "that I was an unsuccessful advocate for you,—especially as I was not inclined to manage the old bride's self-love; for I was so provoked at her cursed§ folly in marrying the handsome profligate, that, if she had not been in distress, I never meant to see her again. But, poor silly soul! she suffers enough for her folly, and so do you;—for her affections and her self-love, being equally wounded by sir Patrick's confession, you are at present the object of her aversion. To you she attributes all the misery of having lost the man on whom she still dotes; (an old blockhead!)** and when she found from your last letter to me that

---

[1]  Men who rode one of each pair of horses pulling a carriage, so that a coachman was unnecessary.

you are not the wife but the mistress of Glenmurray, (by the bye, your letter to her from Lisbon she desires me to return unopened,) and that the child once her pride is become her disgrace, she declared her solemn resolution never to see you more, and to renounce you for ever— (Terrible words, Adeline, I tremble to write them). But a circumstance has since occurred which gives me hopes that she may yet forgive, and receive you on certain conditions. About a fortnight after sir Patrick's departure, a letter from Ireland, directed to him in a woman's hand, arrived at the Pavilion. Your mother opened it, and found it was from a wife of her amiable husband, whom he had left in the north of Ireland, and who, having heard of his second marriage, wrote to tell him that, unless he came quickly back to her, she would prosecute him for bigamy, as he knew very well that undoubted proofs of the marriage were in her possession. At first this new proof of her beautiful spouse's villany drove your mother almost to phrensy, and I was again sent for; but time, reflection, and perhaps my arguments, convinced her, that to be able to free herself from this rascal for ever, and consequently her fortune, losing only the ten thousand pounds which she had given him to pay his debts, was in reality a consoling circumstance. Accordingly, she wrote to the real lady O'Carrol, promising to accede quietly to her claim, and wishing that she would spare her and herself the disgrace of a public trial; especially as it must end in the conviction of sir Patrick. She then, on hearing from him that he had traced you to Falmouth, and was going to embark for Lisbon when the wind was favourable, enclosed him a copy of his wife's letter, and bade him an eternal farewell!—But be not alarmed lest this insane profligate should overtake and distress you. He is gone to his final account. In his hurry to get on board, overcome as he was with the great quantity of liquor which he had drunk to banish care, he sprung from the boat before it was near enough to reach the vessel; his foot slipped against the side, he fell into the water, and, going under the ship, never rose again. I leave you to imagine how the complicated distresses of the last three months, and this awful climax to them, have affected your mother's mind; even I cannot scold her, now, for the life of me: she is not yet, I believe, disposed in your favour; but were you here, and were you to meet, it is possible that, forlorn, lonely, and deserted as she now feels, the tie between you might be once more cemented; and much as I resent your conduct, you may depend on my exertions.—O Adeline, child of my affection, why must I blush to subscribe myself

> "Your sincere friend,
> "J.N.?"

Words cannot describe the feelings of anguish which this letter excited in Adeline: nor could she make known her sensations otherwise than by reiterated requests to be allowed to set off for England directly,—requests to which Glenmurray, alarmed for her intellects, immediately assented. Therefore, leaving a hasty note for the Douglases, they soon bade farewell to Perpignan; and after a long laborious journey, but a short passage, they landed at Brighton.[1]

It was a fine evening; and numbers of the gay and fashionable of both sexes were assembled on the beach, to see the passengers land. Adeline and Glenmurray were amongst the first: and, while heart-sick, fatigued, and melancholy, Adeline took the arm of her lover, and turned disgusted from the brilliant groups before her, she saw, walking along the shore, Dr. Norberry, his wife, and his two daughters.

Instantly, unmindful of every thing but the delight of seeing old acquaintances, and of being able to gain some immediate tidings of her mother, she ran up to them; and just as they turned round, she met them, extending her hand in friendship as she was wont to do.—But in vain;—no hand was stretched out to meet hers, nor tongue nor look proclaimed a welcome to her; Dr. Norberry himself coldly touched his hat, and passed on, while his wife and daughters looked scornfully at her, and, without deigning to notice her, pursued their walk.

Astonished and confounded, Adeline had not power to articulate a word; and, had not Glenmurray caught her in his arms, she would have fallen to the ground.

"Then now I am indeed an outcast! even my oldest and best friend renounces me," she exclaimed.

"But I am left to you," cried Glenmurray.

Adeline sighed. She could not say, as she had formerly done, "and you are all to me." The image of her mother, happy as the wife of a man she loved, could not long rival Glenmurray; but the image of her mother, disgraced and wretched, awoke all the habitual but dormant tenderness of years; every feeling of filial gratitude revived in all its force; and, even while leaning on the shoulder of her lover, she sighed to be once more clasped to the bosom of her mother.

Glenmurray felt the change, but, though grieved, was not offended:—"I shall die in peace," he cried, "if I can but see you restored to your mother's affection, even though the surrender of my happiness is to be the purchase."

---

1 Brighton, already a fashionable resort town when this novel was written, is across the English Channel from Normandy in France.

"You shall die in peace!" replied Adeline shuddering. The phrase was well-timed, though perhaps undesignedly so. Adeline clung close to his arm, her eyes filled with tears, and all the way to the inn she thought only of Glenmurray with an apprehension which she could not conquer.

"What do you mean to do now?" said Glenmurray.

"Write to Dr. Norberry. I think he will at least have humanity enough to let me know where to find my mother."

"No doubt; and you had better write directly."

Adeline took up her pen. A letter was written,—and as quickly torn. Letter succeeded to letter; but not one of them answered her wishes. The dark hour arrived, and the letter remained unwritten.

"It is too soon to ring for candles," said Glenmurray, putting his arm round her waist and leading her to the window. The sun was below the horizon, but the reflection of his beams still shone beautifully on the surrounding objects. Adeline, reclining her cheek on Glenmurray's arm, gazed in silence on the scene before her; when the door suddenly opened, and a gentleman was announced. It was now so dark that all objects were indistinctly seen, and the gentleman had advanced close to Adeline before she knew him to be Dr. Norberry: and, before she could decide how she should receive him, she felt herself clasped to his bosom with the affection of a father.

Surprised and affected, she could not speak; and Glenmurray had ordered candles before Adeline had recovered herself sufficiently to say these words, "After your conduct on the beach, I little expected this visit."

"Pshaw!" replied the doctor: "when a man out of regard to society has performed a painful task, surely he may be allowed, out of regard to himself, to follow the dictates of his heart.—I obeyed my head when I passed you so cavalierly, and I thought I should never have gone through my task as I did;—but then for the sake of my daughters, I gave a gulp, and called up a fierce look. But I told madam that I meant to call on you, and she insisted, very properly, that it should be in the dark hour."

"But what of my mother?"

"She is a miserable woman, as she deserves to be—an old fool."

"Pray do not call her so; to hear she is miserable is torment sufficient to me:—where is she?"

"Still at the Pavilion: but she is going to let Rosevalley, retire to her estate in Cumberland,[1] and live unknown and unseen."

"But will she not allow me to live with her?"

"What? as Mr. Glenmurray's mistress? receive under her roof the seducer of her daughter?"

---

1   One of the northernmost counties of England, now part of the county of Cumbria.

"Sir, I am no seducer."

"No," cried Adeline: "I became the mistress of Mr. Glenmurray from the dictates of my reason, not my weakness or his persuasions."

"Humph!" replied the doctor, "I should expect to find such reason in Moorfields:[1] besides, had not Mr. Glenmurray's books turned your head, you would not have thought it pretty and right to become the mistress of any man: so he is your seducer, after all."

"So far I plead guilty," replied Glenmurray; "but whatever my opinions are, I have ever been willing to sacrifice them to the welfare of miss Mowbray, and have, from the first moment that we were safe from pursuit, been urgent to marry her."

"Then why the devil* are you not married?"

"Because I would not consent," said Adeline coldly.

"Mad, certainly mad," exclaimed the doctor: "but you, faith, you are an honest fellow after all," turning to Glenmurray and shaking him by the hand; "weak o'† the head, not bad in the heart: burn your d——d‡ books, and I am your friend for ever."

"We will discuss that point another time," replied Glenmurray: "at present the most interesting subject to us is the question whether Mrs. Mowbray will forgive her daughter or not?"

"Zounds,§ man, if I may judge of Mrs. Mowbray by myself, one condition of her forgiveness will be your marrying her daughter."

"O blest condition!" cried Glenmurray.

"I should think," replied Adeline coldly, "my mother must have had too much of marriage to wish me to marry; but if she should insist on my marrying, I will comply, and on no other account."

"Strange infatuation! To me it appears only justice and duty. But your reasons, girl, your reasons?"

"They are few, but strong. Glenmurray, philanthropically bent on improving the state of society, puts forth opinions counteracting its received usages, backed by arguments which are in my opinion incontrovertible."

"In your opinion!—Pray, child, how old are you?"

"Nineteen."

"And at that age you set up for a reformer? Well,—go on."

"But though it be important to the success of his opinions, and indeed to the respectability of his character, that he should act according to his precepts, he, for the sake of preserving to me the notice of persons whose narrowness of mind I despise, would conform to an institution which

---

1 A district in central London, undeveloped until 1777. Dr. Norberry is probably referring to its proximity to Bethlehem Hospital ("Bedlam"), an asylum for the mentally ill.

both he and I think unworthy of regard from a rational being.—And shall not I be as generous as he is? shall I scruple to give up for his honour and fame the petty advantages which marriage would give me? Never—his honour and fame are too dear to me; but the claims which my mother has on me are in my eyes so sacred that, for her sake, though not for my own, I would accept the sacrifice which Glenmurray offers. If, then, she says that she will never see or pardon me till I am become a wife, I will follow him to the altar directly; but till then I must insist on remaining as I am. It is necessary that I should respect the man I love; and I should not respect Glenmurray were he not capable of supporting with fortitude the consequences of his opinions; and could he, for motives less strong than those he avows, cease to act up to what he believes to be right. For, never can I respect or believe firmly in the truth of those doctrines, the followers of which shrink from a sort of martyrdom in support of them."

"O Mr. Glenmurray!" cried the doctor shaking his head, "what have you to answer for! What a glorious champion would that creature have been in the support of truth, when even error in her looks so like to virtue!—And then the amiable disinterestedness of you both!—Zounds! what* a powerful thing must true love be, when it can make a speculative philosopher indifferent to the interests of his system, and ready to act in direct opposition to it, rather than injure the respectability of the woman he loves! Well, well, the Lord forgive you, young man, for having taken it into your head to set up for a great author."

Glenmurray answered by a deep-drawn sigh; and the doctor continued: "Then there is that girl again, with a heart so fond and true that her love comes in aid of her integrity, and makes her think no sacrifice too great, in order to prove her confidence in the wisdom of her lover,—urging her to disregard all personal inconveniences rather than let him forfeit, for her sake, his pretensions to independence and consistency of character! 'Sdeath,† girl! I can't help admiring you. But no more I could a Malabar widow, who with fond and pious enthusiasm, from an idea of duty, throws herself on the funeral pile of her husband.¹ But still I should think you a cursed‡ fool, notwithstanding, for professing the opinions that led to such an exertion of duty. And now here are you, possessed of every quality both of head and heart to bless others and to bless yourself—owing to the§

---

1  Dr. Norberry refers to *sati*, the practice of Hindu widows burning themselves to death on the funeral pyres of their husbands. Possible sources include David Humphrey's *The Widow of Malabar*, a play set in India and based on *La Veuve du Malabar*, by Antoine Le Mierre; references in Voltaire's *Philosophical Dictionary* (chapters 107 and 282); and Mariana Starke (1761/62-1838), *The Widow of Malabar. A tragedy in three acts* (also adapted from Le Mierre's play and produced in London in 1790).

foolish and pernicious opinions;—here you are, I say, blasted in reputation in the prime of your days, and doomed perhaps to pine through existence in——Pshaw! by the Lord* I can't support the idea!" added he, gulping down a sob as he spoke, and traversing the room in great emotion.

Adeline and Glenmurray were both of them deeply and painfully affected; and the latter was going to express what he felt, when the doctor, seizing Adeline's hand, affectionately exclaimed, "Well, my poor child! I will see your mother once more; I will go to London tomorrow—by this time she is there—and you had better follow me; you will hear of me at the Old Hummums;[1] and here is a card of address to an hotel near it, where I would advise you to take up your abode."

So saying, he shook Glenmurray by the hand; when, starting back, he exclaimed "Odzooks,†[2] man! here is a skin like fire, and a pulse like lightning. My dear fellow, you must take care of yourself."

Adeline burst into tears.

"Indeed, doctor, I am only nervous."

"Nervous!....What, I suppose you think you understand my profession better than I do. But don't cry, my child: when your mind is easier, perhaps, he will do very well; and, as one thing likely to give him immediate ease, I prescribe a visit to the altar of the next parish church."

So saying he departed; and all other considerations were again swallowed up in Adeline's mind by the idea of Glenmurray's danger.

"Is it possible that my marrying you would have such a blessed effect on your health?" cried Adeline after a pause.

"It certainly would make my mind easier than it now is," replied he.

"If I thought so," said Adeline: "but no—regard for my supposed interest merely makes you say so; and indeed I should not think so well of you as I now do, if I imagined that you could be made easy by an action by which you forfeited all pretensions to that consistency of character so requisite to the true dignity of a philosopher."

A deep sigh from Glenmurray, in answer, proved that he was no philosopher.

In the morning the lovers set off for London, Dr. Norberry having preceded them by a few hours. This blunt but benevolent man had returned the evening before slowly and pensively to his lodgings, his heart full of pity for the errors of the well-meaning enthusiasts whom he had left, and his head full of plans for their assistance, or rather for that of Adeline. But

---

1   A hotel in Covent Garden, the theatre district of London.

2   Another of Dr. Norberry's mild expletives: a compound of "God's" with another word. The *OED* suggests "God's sokings" (undefined), and relates this to "Gadzooks."

he entered his own doors again reluctantly—he knew but too well that no sympathy with his feelings awaited him there. His wife, a woman of narrow capacity and no talents or accomplishments, had, like all women of that sort, a great aversion to those of her sex who united to feminine graces and gentleness, the charms of a cultivated understanding and pretensions to accomplishments or literature.

Of Mrs. Mowbray, as we have before observed, she had always been peculiarly jealous, because Dr. Norberry spoke of her knowledge with wonder, and of her understanding with admiration; not that he entertained one moment a feeling of preference towards her, inconsistent with an almost idolatrous love of his wife, whose skill in all the domestic duties, and whose very pretty face and person, were the daily themes of his praise. But Mrs. Norberry wished to engross all his panegyrics to herself, and she never failed to expatiate on Mrs. Mowbray's foibles and flightiness as long as the doctor had expatiated on her charms.

Sometimes, indeed, this last subject was sooner exhausted than the one which she had chosen; but when Adeline grew up, and became as it were the rival of her daughters in the praises of her husband, she found it difficult, as we have said before, to bring faults in array against excellencies.

Mrs. Norberry could with propriety observe, when the doctor was exclaiming, "What a charming essay Mrs. Mowbray has just written!"

"Aye,—but I dare say she can't write a market bill."

When he said, "How well she comprehends the component parts of the animal system!"

She could with great justice reply, "But she knows nothing of the component parts of a plum pudding."

But when Adeline became the object of the husband's admiration and the wife's enmity, Mrs. Norberry could not make these pertinent remarks, as Adeline was as conversant with all branches of housewifery as herself; and, though as learned in all systems as her mother, was equally learned in the component parts of puddings and pies. She was therefore at a loss what to say when Adeline was praised by the doctor; and all she could observe on the occasion was, that the girl might be clever, but was certainly very ugly, very affected, and very conceited.

It is not to be wondered at, therefore, that Mrs. Mowbray's degrading and unhappy marriage, and Adeline's elopement, should have been sources of triumph to Mrs. Norberry and her daughters; who, though they liked Mrs. Mowbray very well, could not bear Adeline.

"So, Dr. Norberry, these are your uncommon folks!"—exclaimed Mrs. Norberry on hearing of the marriage and of the subsequent elopement;— "I suppose you are now well satisfied at not having a genius for your wife, or geniuses for your daughters?"

"I always was, my dear," meekly replied the mortified and afflicted doctor, and dropped the subject as soon as possible; nor had it been resumed for some time when Adeline accosted them on the beach at Brighton. But her appearance called forth their dormant enmity; and the whole way to their lodgings the good doctor heard her guilt expatiated upon with as much violence as ever: but just as they got home he coldly and firmly observed, "I shall certainly call on the poor deluded girl this evening."

And Mrs. Norberry, knowing by the tone and manner in which he spoke, that this was a point which he would not give up, contented herself with requiring only that he should go in the dark hour.

## CHAPTER 15

It was to a wife and daughters such as these that he was returning, with the benevolent wish of interesting them for the guilty Adeline.

"So, Dr. Norberry, you are come back at last!" was his first salutation, "and what does the creature say for herself?"

"The creature?—Your *fellow*-creature,* my dear, says very little—grief is not wordy."

"Grief!—So then she is unhappy, is she?" cried miss Norberry; "I am monstrous glad of it."

The doctor started; and an oath nearly escaped his lips. He did say, "Why, zounds, Jane!—" but then he added, in a softer tone, "Why do you rejoice in the poor girl's affliction?"

"Because I think it is for the good of her soul."

"Good girl!" replied the father:—"but God grant, Jane," (seizing her hand) "that your soul may not† need such a medicine!"

"It never will," said her mother proudly: "she has been differently brought up."

"She has been well brought up, you might have added," observed the doctor, "had modesty permitted it. Mrs. Mowbray, poor woman, had good intentions; but she was too flighty. Had Adeline, my children, had such a mother as yours, she would have been like you."

"But not half so handsome," interrupted the mother in a low voice.

"But as our faults and our virtues, my dear, depend so much on the care and instruction of others, we should look with pity as well as aversion on the faults of those less fortunate in instructors than we have been."

"Certainly;—very true," said Mrs. Norberry, flattered and affected by this compliment from her husband: "but you know, James Norberry," laying her hand on his, "I always told you you over-rated Mrs. Mowbray; and that she was but a dawdle,[1] after all."

---

1 Someone who wastes time or hangs around idly.

"You always did, my good woman," replied he, raising her hand to his lips.

"But you men think yourselves so much wiser than we are!"

"We do so," replied the doctor.

The tone was equivocal—Mrs. Norberry felt it to be so, and looked up in his face.—The doctor understood the look: it was one of doubt and inquiry; and, as it was his interest to sooth her in order to carry his point, he exclaimed, "We men are, indeed, too apt to pride ourselves in our supposed superior wisdom: but I, you will own, my dear, have always done your sex justice; and you in particular."

"You have been a good husband, indeed, James Norberry," replied his wife in a faltering voice; "and I believe you to be, to every one, a just and honourable man."

"And I dare say, dame, I do no more than justice to you, when I think you will approve and further a plan for Adeline Mowbray's good, which I am going to propose to you."

Mrs. Norberry withdrew her hand; but returning it again:—"To be sure, my dear," she cried. "Any thing you wish; that is, if I see right to——"

"I will explain myself," continued the doctor gently.

"I have promised this poor girl to endeavour to bring about a reconciliation between her and her mother: but though Adeline wishes to receive her pardon on any terms, and even, if it be required, to renounce her lover, I fear Mrs. Mowbray is too much incensed against her, to see or forgive her."

"Hard-hearted woman!" cried Mrs. Norberry.

"Cruel, indeed!" cried her daughters.

"But a mother ought to be severe, very severe, on such occasions, young ladies," hastily added Mrs. Norberry: "but go on, my dear."

"Now it is but too probable," continued the doctor, "that Glenmurray will not live long, and then this young creature will be left to struggle unprotected with the difficulties of her situation; and who knows but that she may, from poverty and the want of a protector, be tempted to continue in the paths of vice?"

"Well, Dr. Norberry, and what then?—Who or what is to prevent it?—You know we have three children to provide for; and I am a young woman as yet."

"True, Hannah," giving her a kiss, "and a very pretty woman too."

"Well, my dear love, any thing we can do with prudence I am ready to do; I can say no more."

"You have said enough," cried the doctor exultingly; "then hear my plan: Adeline shall, in the event of Glenmurray's death, which though not certain seems likely.... to be sure, I could[*] not inquire into the nature of his nocturnal perspirations, his expectoration, and so forth...."[1]

"Dear papa, you are so professional!" affectedly exclaimed his youngest daughter.

"Well, child, I have done; and to return to my subject:—if Glenmurray lives or dies, I think it advisable that Adeline should go into retirement to lie-in. And where can she be better than in my little cottage now empty, within a four miles ride of our house? If she wants protection, I can protect her; and if she wants money before her mother forgives her, you can give it to her."

"Indeed, papa," cried both the girls, "we shall not grudge it."

The doctor started from his chair, and embraced his daughters with joy mixed with wonder; for he knew they had always disliked Adeline.— True; but then she was prosperous, and their superior. Little minds love to bestow protection; and it was easy to be generous to the fallen Adeline Mowbray: had her happiness continued, so would their hatred.

"Then it is a settled point, is it not, dame?" asked the doctor, chucking his wife under the chin; when, to his great surprise and consternation, she threw his hand indignantly from her, and vociferated, "She shall never live within a ride of our house, I can assure you, Dr. Norberry."

The doctor was petrified into silence, and the girls could only articulate "La! mamma!" But what could produce this sudden and violent change? Nothing but a simple and natural operation of the human mind. Though a very kind husband, and an indulgent father, Dr. Norberry was suspected[†] of being a very gallant man: and some of Mrs. Norberry's good-natured friends had occasionally hinted to her their sorrow at hearing such and such reports; reports which were indeed destitute of foundation: but which served to excite suspicions in the mind of the tenacious Mrs. Norberry. And what more likely to re-awaken them than the young and frail[2] Adeline Mowbray living in a cottage of her husband's, protected, supported, and visited by him! The moment this idea occurred, its influence was unconquerable; and with a voice and manner of determined hostility she made known her resolves in consequence of it.

After a pause of dismay and astonishment the doctor cried, "Zounds,[‡] dame, what have you gotten in your head? What, all on a sudden, has had such a cursed[§] ugly effect on you?"

---

1    Symptoms of tuberculosis: Glenmurray's disease is never named, but contemporary readers would have known why he visited Bath and travelled to Portugal (both recommended treatments for "consumption").

2    Morally weak: cf. p. 82 above, and note.

"Second thoughts are best, doctor; and I now feel that it would be highly improper for you, with daughters grown up, to receive with such marked kindness a young[*] woman at a cottage of yours, who is going to lie-in of a bastard child."[†]

"But, sdeath,[‡] my dear, it is a different case, when I do it to keep her out of the way of having any more."[§]

"That is more than I know, Dr. Norberry," replied the wife bridling, and fanning herself.

"Whew!" whistled the doctor; and then addressing his daughters, "Girls, you had better go to bed; it grows late."

The young ladies obeyed; but first hung round their mother's neck, as they bade her good night, and hoped she would not be so *cruel*[**] to the poor deluded Adeline.

Mrs. Norberry angrily shook them off, with a peevish—"Get along, girls." The doctor cordially kissed, and bade God bless them; while the door closed and left the loving couple alone.

What passed it were tedious to repeat: suffice that after a long altercation, continued even after they were retired to rest, the doctor found his wife, on this subject, incapable of listening to reason, and that, as a finishing stroke, she exclaimed "It does not signify talking, Dr. Norberry," (pushing her pillow vehemently towards the valance as she spoke,) "while[††] I have my senses, and can see into a mill-stone[1] a little, the hussey[2] shall never come near us."

The doctor sighed deeply; turned himself round, not to sleep but to think, and rose unrefreshed[‡‡] the next morning to go in search of Mrs. Mowbray, dreading the interview which he was afterwards to have with Adeline; for he did not expect to succeed in his application to her mother, and he could not now soften his intelligence with a "but," as he intended. "True," he meant to have said to her, "your mother will not receive you; but if you ever want a home or a place of retirement, I have a cottage, and so forth."

"Pshaw!" cried the doctor to himself, as these thoughts came across him on the road, and made him hastily let down the front window of the post-chaise for air.

"Did your honour speak?" cries the post-boy.

"Not I. But can't you drive faster and be hanged to you?"

The boy whipped his horses.—The doctor then found that it was up hill—down went the glass again:—"Zounds,[§§] you brute, why, do you

---

1  An expression meaning to be extraordinarily acute, usually used ironically.
2  A form of the word "housewife," usually applied to a lower-class or disreputable woman; in country usage it may simply mean "woman."

not see it is up hill?"—For find fault he must; and with his wife he could not, or dared not, even in fancy.

"Dear me! Why, your honour bade me put* on."

"Devilishly obedient," muttered the doctor: "I wish every one was like you in that respect."—And in a state of mind not the pleasantest possible the doctor drove into town, and to the hotel where Mrs. Mowbray was to be found.

Dr. Norberry was certainly now not in a humour to sooth any woman whom he thought in the wrong, except his wife; and, whether from carelessness or design, he did not, unfortunately for Adeline, manage the self-love of her unhappy mother.

He found Mrs. Mowbray with her heart shut up, not softened by sorrow. The hands once stretched forth with kindness to welcome him, were now stiffly laid one upon the other; and "How are you, sir?" coldly articulated, was followed by as cold a "Pray sit down."

"Zounds!—† Why, how ill you look!" exclaimed the doctor bluntly.

"I attend more to my feelings than my looks," with a deep sigh answered Mrs. Mowbray.

"Your feelings are as bad as your looks, I dare say."

"They are worse, sir," said Mrs. Mowbray, piqued.

"There was no need of *that*,"‡ replied the doctor: "but I am come to point out to you one way of getting rid of some of your unpleasant feelings:—see, and forgive your daughter."

Mrs. Mowbray started, changed colour, and exclaimed with quickness, "Is she in England?" but added instantly, "I have no daughter:—she, who was my child, is my most inveterate foe; she has involved me in disgrace and misery."

"With a little of your own help she has," replied the doctor. "Come, come, my old friend, you have both of you something to forget and forgive; and the sooner you set about it the better. Now do write, and tell Adeline, who is by this time in London, that you forgive her."

"Never:—after having promised me not to hold converse with that villain without my consent? Had I no other cause of complaint against her;—had she not by her coquettish arts seduced the affections of the man I loved;—never, never would I forgive her having violated the sacred promise which she gave me."

"A promise," interrupted the doctor, "which she would never have violated, had not you first violated that sacred compact which you entered into at her birth."

"What mean you, sir?"

"I mean, that though a parent does not, at a child's birth, solemnly make a vow to do all in his or her power to promote the happiness of that child,—still, as he has given it birth, he has tacitly bound himself to make it happy. This tacit agreement you broke, when at the age of forty, you, regardless of your daughter's welfare, played the fool and married a pennyless profligate, merely because he had a fine person and a handsome leg."

Mrs. Mowbray was too angry and too agitated to interrupt him, and he went on:

"Well; what was the consequence? The young fellow very naturally preferred the daughter to the mother; and, as he could not have her by fair, was resolved to have her by foul means; and so he——"

"I beg, Dr. Norberry," interrupted Mrs. Mowbray in a faint voice, "that you would spare the disgusting recital."

"Well, well, I will. Now do consider the dilemma your child was in: she must either elope, or by her presence keep alive a criminal passion in her father-in-law, which you sooner or later must discover; and be besides exposed to fresh insults.—Well, Glenmurray by chance happened to be on the spot just as she escaped from that villanous fellow's clutches, and——"

"He is dead, Dr. Norberry," interrupted Mrs. Mowbray; "and you know the old adage, Do not speak ill of the dead."[1]

"And a devilish* silly adage it is. I had rather speak ill of the dead than the living, for my part: but let me go on.—Well, love taking the name and habit of prudence and filial piety, (for she thought she consulted your happiness, and not her own,) bade her fly to and with her lover; and now there she is, owing to the pretty books which you let her read, living with him as his mistress, and glorying in it, as if it was a notable praise-worthy action."

"And you would have me forgive her?"

"Certainly: a fault which both your precepts and conduct occasioned. Not but what the girl has been wrong—terribly wrong:—no one ought to do evil that good may come. You had forbidden her to have any intercourse with Glenmurray; and she therefore knew that disobeying you would make you unhappy—that was a certainty. That fellow's persevering in his attempts, after the fine rebuff which she had given him, was an uncertainty; and she ought to have run the risk of it, and not committed a positive fault to avoid a possible evil. But then hers was a fault which she could not have committed had not you married that d——d dog.† And as to her not being married to Glenmurray, that is no fault of his: the good lad looks as ashamed of what he has done as any modest miss in Christendom;‡ and, with your consent,§ will marry your daughter to-morrow

---

1   "De mortuis nil nisi bonum dicendum est" (Latin): literally, "Concerning the dead, nothing but what is good must be said."

morning. Lord! Lord! that* ever so good, cleanly-hearted a youth should have poked his nose into the filthy mess of eccentric philosophy!"

"Have you done, doctor?" cried Mrs. Mowbray haughtily: "have you said all that miss Mowbray and you have invented to insult me?"

"Your *child*† send me to insult you!—She!—Adeline!—Why, the poor soul came broken-hearted and post haste from France, when she heard of your misfortunes, to offer her services to console you."

"She console me?—she, the first occasion of them?—But for her, I might still have indulged the charming delusion, even if it were delusion, that love of me, not of my wealth, induced the man I doted upon to commit a crime to gain possession of me."

"Why, zounds!"‡ hastily interrupted the doctor, "every one saw that he loved her long before he married you."

The storm, long gathering, now burst forth; and rising, with the tears, high colour, and vehement voice of unbridled passion, Mrs. Mowbray exclaimed, raising her arm and clenching her fist as she spoke, "And it is being the object of that cruel preference, which I never, never will forgive her!"

The doctor, after ejaculating "Whew!" as much as to say "The murder is out," instantly took his hat and departed, convinced his labour was vain. "Zounds!"§ muttered he as he went down stairs, "two instances in one day! Ah, ah!—that jealousy is the devil." He then slowly walked to the hotel, where he expected to find Adeline and Glenmurray.

They had arrived about two hours before; and Adeline in a frame of mind but ill fitted to bear the disappointment which awaited her. For, with the sanguine expectations natural to her age, she had been castle-building as usual; and their journey to London had been rendered a very short one, by the delightful plans, for the future, which she had been forming and imparting to Glenmurray.

"When I consider," said she, "the love which my mother has always shown for me, I cannot think it possible that she can persist in renouncing me; and however her respect for the prejudices of the world, a world which she intended to live in at the time of her unfortunate connexion, might make her angry at my acting in defiance of its laws,—now that she herself, from a sense of injury and disgrace, is about to retire from it, she will no longer have a motive to act contrary to the dictates of reason herself, or to wish me to do so."

"But your ideas of reason and hers may be so different———"

"No. Our practice may be different, but our theory is the same, and I have no doubt but that my mother will now forgive and receive us; and that, living in a romantic solitude, being the whole world to each other, our days will glide away in uninterrupted felicity."

"And how shall we employ ourselves?" said Glenmurray smiling.

"You shall continue to write for the instruction of your fellow-creatures; while my mother and I shall be employed in endeavouring to improve the situation of the poor around us, and perhaps in educating our children."

Adeline, when animated by any prospect of happiness, was irresistible: she was really Hope herself, as described by Collins—

> "But thou, oh Hope! with eyes so fair,
> What was thy delighted measure!"[1]

and Glenmurray, as he listened to her, forgot his illness; forgot every thing, but what Adeline chose to imagine. The place of their retreat was fixed upon. It was to be a little village near Falmouth, the scene of their first happiness. The garden was laid out; Mrs. Mowbray's library planned; and so completely were they lost in their charming prospects for the future, that every turnpike-man[2] had to wait a longer time than he was accustomed to for his money; and the postillion had driven into London in the way to the hotel, before Adeline recollected that she was, for the first time, in a city which she had long wished most ardently to see.

They had scarcely taken up their abode at the hotel recommended to them by Dr. Norberry, when he knocked at the door. Adeline from the window had seen him coming; and sure as she thought herself to be of her mother's forgiveness, she turned sick and faint when the decisive moment was at hand; and, hurrying out of the room, she begged Glenmurray to receive the doctor, and apologize for her absence.

Glenmurray awaited him with a beating heart. He listened to his step on the stairs: it was slow and heavy; unlike that of a benevolent man coming to communicate good news. Glenmurray began immediately to tremble for the peace of Adeline; and, hastily pouring out a glass of wine, was on the point of drinking it when Dr. Norberry entered.

"Gadzooks, give* me a glass," cried he: "I want one, I am sure, to recruit my spirits." Glenmurray in silence complied with his desire. "Come, I'll give you a toast," cried the doctor: "Here is——"

At this moment Adeline entered. She had heard the doctor's last words, and she thought he was going to drink to the reconciliation of her mother and herself; and hastily opening the door she came to receive the good news which awaited her. But, at sight of her, the toast died unfinished on her old friend's lips; he swallowed down the wine in silence, and then taking her hand led her to the sofa.

---

1   William Collins, "The Passions: An Ode for Music" (1746), 29-30.

2   A man who operates a barrier placed across a road until the toll is paid.

Adeline's heart began to die within her; and before the doctor, after having taken a pinch of snuff, and blowed his nose full three times, was prepared to speak, she was convinced that she had nothing but unwelcome intelligence to receive; and she awaited in trembling expectation an answer to a "Well, sir," from Glenmurray spoken in a tone of fearful emotion.

"No, it is not well, sir," replied the doctor; "it is d——d* ill, sir."†

"You have seen my mother,"‡ said Adeline, catching hold of the arm of the sofa for support; and in an instant Glenmurray was by her side.

"I have seen Mrs. Mowbray, but not your mother: for I have seen a woman dead to every graceful impulse of maternal affection, and alive only to a selfish sense of rivalship and hatred. My poor child! God forgive the deluded woman! But I declare she detests you!"

"Detests me?" exclaimed Adeline.

"Yes; she swears that she can never forgive the preference which that vile fellow gave you, and I am convinced that she will keep her word; and—Lord have mercy upon us!" cried the doctor, turning round and seeing the situation into which his words had thrown Adeline, who was then§ lying immoveable in Glenmurray's arms. But she did not long remain so, and with a frantic scream kept repeating the words "She detests me!" till, unable to contend any longer with the acuteness of her feelings, she sunk, sobbing convulsively, exhausted on the bed to which they carried her.

"My good friend, my only friend," cried Glenmurray, "what is to be done? Will she scream again, think you, in that most dreadful and unheard-of manner? For, if she does, I must run out of the house."

"What, then, she never treated you in this pretty way before, heh?"

"Never, never. Her self-command has always been exemplary."

"Indeed?—Lucky fellow! My wife and daughters often scream just as loud, on very trifling occasions: but that scream went to my heart; for I well know how to distinguish between the shriek of agony and that of passion."

When Adeline recovered, she ardently conjured Dr. Norberry to procure her an interview with her mother; contending that it was absolutely impossible to suppose, that the sight of a child so long and tenderly loved should not renew a little of her now dormant affection.

"But you were her rival, as well as her child: remember that. However, you look so ill, that now, if ever, she will forgive you, I think: therefore I will go back to Mrs. Mowbray; and while I am there do you come, ask for me, and follow the servant into the room."

"I will," replied Adeline: and leaning on the arm of her lover, she slowly followed the doctor to her mother's hotel.

## CHAPTER 16

"This is the most awful moment of my life," said Adeline.

"And the most anxious one of mine," replied Glenmurray. "If Mrs. Mowbray forgives you, it will be probably on condition that——"

"Whatever be the conditions, I must accept them," said Adeline.

"True," returned Glenmurray, wiping the cold dews of weakness from his forehead: "but no matter—at any rate, I should not have been with you long."

Adeline, with a look of agony, pressed the arm she held to her bosom.

Glenmurray's heart smote him immediately—he felt he had been ungenerous; and, while the hectic of a moment passed across his cheek, he added, "But I do not do myself justice in saying so. I believe my best chance of recovery is the certainty of your being easy. Let me but see you happy, and so disinterested is my affection, as I have often told you, that I shall cheerfully assent to any thing that may ensure your happiness."

"And can you think," answered Adeline, "that my happiness can be independent of yours? Do you not see that I am only trying to prepare my mind for being called upon to surrender my inclinations to my duty?"

At this moment they found themselves at the door of the hotel. Neither of them spoke; the moment of trial was come; and both were unable to encounter it firmly. At last Adeline grasped her lover's hand, bade him wait for her at the end of the street, and with some degree of firmness she entered the vestibule, and asked for Dr. Norberry.

Dr. Norberry, meanwhile, with the best intentions in the world, had but ill prepared Mrs. Mowbray's mind for the intended visit. He had again talked to her of her daughter, and urged the propriety of forgiving her; but he had at the same time renewed his animadversions on her own conduct.

"You know not, Dr. Norberry," observed Mrs. Mowbray, "the pains I took with the education of that girl; and I expected to be repaid for it by being styled the happiest as well as best of mothers."

"And so you would, perhaps, had you not wished to be a wife as well as mother."

"No more on that subject, sir," haughtily returned Mrs. Mowbray.— "Yes,—Adeline was indeed my joy, my pride."

"Aye, and pride will have a fall; and a devilish* tumble yours has had, to be sure, my old friend. Zounds, it† has broke its knees—never to be sound again."

At this unpropitious moment "a lady to Dr. Norberry" was announced, and Adeline tottered into the room.

"What strange intrusion is this?" cried Mrs. Mowbray: "who is this woman?"

Adeline threw back her veil, and, falling on her knees, stretched out her arms in an attitude of entreaty: speak she could not, but her countenance was sufficiently expressive of her meaning; and her pale sunk cheek spoke forcibly to the heart of her mother.—At this moment, when a struggle which might have ended favourably for Adeline was taking place in the mind of Mrs. Mowbray, Dr. Norberry injudiciously exclaimed,

"There,—there she is! Look at her, poor soul! There is little fear, I think, of her ever rivalling you again."

At these words Mrs. Mowbray darted an angry look at the doctor, and desired him to take away that woman; who came, no doubt instigated by him, to insult her. "Take her away," she cried, "and never let me see her again."

"O my mother, hear me, in pity hear me!" exclaimed Adeline.

"As it is for the last time, I will hear you," replied Mrs. Mowbray; "for never, no never will I behold you more! Hear me vow——"

"Mother, for God's* sake, make not a vow so terrible!" cried Adeline, gathering courage from despair, and approaching her: "I have grievously erred, and will cheerfully devote the rest of my life to endeavour, by the most submissive obedience and attention, to atone for my past guilt."

"Atone for it! Impossible; for the misery which I owe to you, no submission, no future conduct can make me amends. Away! I say: your presence conjures up recollections which distract me, and I solemnly swear——"

"Hold, hold, if you have any mercy in your nature," cried Adeline almost frantic: "this is, I feel but too sensibly, the most awful and important moment of my life; on the result of this interview depends my future happiness or misery. Hear me, O my mother! You, who can so easily resolve to tear the heart of a child that adores you, hear me! reflect that, if you vow to abandon me for ever, you blast all the happiness and prospects of my life; and at nineteen 'tis hard to be deprived of happiness for ever. True, I may not long survive the anguish of being renounced by my mother, a mother whom I love with even enthusiastic fondness; but then could you ever know peace again with the conviction of having caused my death? Oh! no. Save then yourself and me from these miseries, by forgiving my past errors, and deigning sometimes to see and converse with me!"

The eager and animated volubility with which Adeline spoke made it impossible to interrupt her, even had Mrs. Mowbray been inclined to do so: but she was not; nor, when Adeline had done speaking, could she find in her heart to break silence.

It was evident to Dr. Norberry that Mrs. Mowbray's countenance expressed a degree of softness which augured well for her daughter; and, as if conscious that it did so, she covered her face suddenly with her handkerchief.

"Now then is the time," thought the doctor. "Go nearer her, my child," said he in a low voice to Adeline, "embrace her knees."

Adeline rose, and approached Mrs. Mowbray: she seized her hand, she pressed it to her lips. Mrs. Mowbray's bosom heaved violently: she almost returned the pressure of Adeline's hand.

"Victory, victory!" muttered the doctor to himself, cutting a caper behind Mrs. Mowbray's chair.

Mrs. Mowbray took the handkerchief from her face.

"My mother, my dear mother! look on me, look on me with kindness only one moment, and only say that you do not hate me!"

Mrs. Mowbray turned round and fixed her eyes on Adeline with a look of kindness, and Adeline's began to sparkle with delight; when, as she threw back her cloak, which, hanging over her arm, embarrassed her as she knelt to embrace her mother's knees, Mrs. Mowbray's eyes glanced from her face to her shape.

In an instant the fierceness of her look returned: "Shame to thy race, disgrace to thy family!" she exclaimed, spurning her kneeling child from her: "and canst thou, while conscious of carrying in thy bosom the proof of thy infamy, dare to solicit and expect my pardon?—Hence! ere I load thee with maledictions."

Adeline wrapped her cloak round her, and sunk terrified and desponding on the ground.

"Why, what a ridiculous caprice is this!" cried the doctor. "Is it a greater crime to be in a family way,[1] than to live with a man as his mistress?—You knew your daughter had done the last: therefore 'tis* nonsense to be so affected at the former.—Come, come, forget and forgive!"

"Never: and if you do not leave the house with her this moment, I will not stay in it. My injuries are so great that they cannot admit forgiveness."

"What a horrible, unforgiving spirit yours must be!" cried Dr. Norberry: "and after all, I tell you again, that Adeline has something to forgive and forget too; and she sets you an example of christian charity in coming hither to console and comfort you, poor forsaken woman as you are!"

"Forsaken!" exclaimed Mrs. Mowbray: "aye; why, and for *whom*, was I forsaken? There's the pang! and yet you wonder that I cannot instantly forgive and receive the woman who injured me where I was most vulnerable."

"O my mother!" cried Adeline, almost indignantly, "and can that wretch, though dead, still have power to influence my fate in this dreadful manner? and can you still regret the loss of the affection of that man, whose addresses were a disgrace to you?"

---

1  The earliest example in the *OED* of the expression used in this sense ("pregnant") is dated 1796.

At these unguarded words, and too just reproaches, Mrs. Mowbray lost all self-command; and, in a voice almost inarticulate with rage, exclaimed:—"I loved that wretch, as you are pleased to call him. I gloried in the addresses which you are pleased to call my disgrace. But he loved you—he left me for you—and on your account he made me endure the pangs of being forsaken and despised by the man whom I adored. Then mark my words: I solemnly swear," dropping on her knees as she spoke, "and I call on God to witness my oath,* by all my hopes of happiness hereafter, that until you shall have experienced the anguish of being forsaken and despised as I have been,† till you shall be‡ as wretched in love, and as disgraced in the eye of the world,§ I never will see you more, or pardon your many sins against me—No—not even were you on your death-bed. Yet, no; I am wrong there—Yes; on your death-bed," she added, her voice faltering as she spoke, and passion giving way in a degree to the dictates of returning nature,—"yes, there; there I should—I should forgive you."

"Then I feel that you will forgive me soon," faintly articulated Adeline sinking on the ground; while Mrs. Mowbray was leaving the room, and Dr. Norberry was standing motionless with horror, from the rash oath which he had just heard. But Adeline's fall aroused him from his stupor.

"For God's** sake, do not go and leave your daughter dying!" cried he: "your vow does not forbid you to continue to see her now." Mrs. Mowbray turned back, and started with horror at beholding the countenance of Adeline.

"Is she really dying?" cried she eagerly, "and have I killed her?" These words, spoken in a faltering tone, and with a look of anxiety, seemed to recall the fleeting spirit of Adeline. She looked up at her mother, a sort of smile quivered on her lip; and faintly articulating "I am better," she burst into a convulsive flood of tears, and laid her head on the bosom of her compassionate friend.

"She will do now," cried he exultingly to Mrs. Mowbray: "you need alarm yourself no longer."

But alarm was perhaps a feeling of enjoyment, to the sensations which then took possession of Mrs. Mowbray. The apparent danger of Adeline had awakened her long dormant tenderness: but she had just bound herself by an oath not to give way to it, except under circumstances the most unwelcome and affecting, and had therefore embittered her future days with remorse and unavailing regret.—For some minutes she stood looking wildly and mournfully on Adeline, longing to clasp her to her bosom, and pronounce her pardon, but not daring to violate her oath. At length, "I cannot bear this torment," she exclaimed, and rushed out of the room: and when in another apartment, she recollected, and uttered a scream of agony as she did so, that she had seen Adeline probably for the last time; for, voluntarily, she was now to see her no more.

The same recollection[*] occurred to Adeline; and as the door closed on her mother, she raised herself up, and looked eagerly to catch the last glimpse of her gown, as the door shut it from her sight. "Let us go away directly now," said she, "for the air of this room is not good for me."

The doctor, affected beyond measure at the expression of quiet despair with which she spoke, went out to order a coach; and Adeline instantly rose, and kissed with fond devotion the chair on which her mother had sat. Suddenly she heard a deep sigh—it came from the next room—perhaps it came from her mother; perhaps she could still see her again: and with cautious step she knelt down and looked through the key-hole of the door.

She did see her mother once more. Mrs. Mowbray was lying on the bed, beating the ground with her foot, and sighing as if her heart would break.

"O! that I dare go in to her!" said Adeline to herself: "but I can at least bid her farewell here." She then put her mouth to the aperture, and exclaimed, "Mother, dearest mother! since we meet now for the last time—" (Mrs. Mowbray started from the bed) "let me thank you for all the affection, all the kindness which you lavished on me during eighteen happy years. I shall never cease to love and pray for you." (Mrs. Mowbray sobbed aloud.) "Perhaps, you will some day or other think you have been harsh to me, and may wish that you had not taken so cruel a vow." (Mrs. Mowbray beat her breast in agony: the moment of repentance was already come.) "It may therefore be a comfort to you at such moments to know that I sincerely, and from the bottom of my heart, forgive this rash action:—and now, my dearest mother, hear my parting prayers for your happiness!"

At this moment a noise in the next room convinced Adeline that her mother had fallen down in a fainting fit, and the doctor entered the room.

"What have I done?" she exclaimed. "Go to her this instant."—He obeyed. Raising up Mrs. Mowbray in his arms, he laid her on the bed, while Adeline bent over her in silent anguish, with all the sorrow of filial anxiety. But when the remedies which Dr. Norberry administered began to take effect, she exclaimed, "For the last time! Cruel, but most dear mother!" and pressed her head to her bosom, and kissed her pale lips with almost frantic emotion.

Mrs. Mowbray opened her eyes: they met those of Adeline, and instantly closed again.

"She has looked at me for the last time," said Adeline; "and now this one kiss, my mother, and farewell for ever!" So saying she rushed out of the room, and did not stop till she reached the coach,[†] and, springing into it, was received into the arms of Glenmurray.

"You are my all now," said she. "You have long been mine," replied he: but respecting the anguish and disappointment depicted on her countenance, he forbore to ask for an explanation; and resting her pale cheek on his bosom, they reached the inn in silence.

Adeline had walked up and down the room a number of times, had as often looked out of the window, before Dr. Norberry, whom she had been anxiously expecting and looking for, made his appearance. "Thank God, you are come at last!" said she, seizing his hand as he entered.

"I left Mrs. Mowbray," replied he, "much better both in mind and body."

"A blessed hearing!" replied Adeline.

"And you, my child, how are you?" asked the doctor affectionately.

"I know not yet," answered Adeline mournfully: "as yet I am stunned by the blow which I have received: but pray tell me what has passed between you and my mother since we left the hotel."

"What has passed?" cried Dr. Norberry, starting from his chair, taking two hasty strides across the room, pulling up the cape of his coat, and muttering an oath between his shut teeth—"Why, this passed:—The deluded woman renounced her daughter; and her friend, her old and faithful friend, has renounced her."

"Oh! my poor mother!" exclaimed Adeline.

"Girl! girl! don't be foolish," replied the doctor; "keep your pity for more deserving objects; and, as the wisest thing you can do, endeavour to forget your mother."

"Forget her! Never."

"Well, well, you will be wiser in time; and now you shall hear all that passed. When she recovered entirely, and found that you were gone, she gave way to an agony of sorrow, such as I never before witnessed; for I believe that I never beheld before the agony of remorse."

"My poor mother!" cried Adeline, again bursting into tears.

"What! again!" exclaimed the doctor. (Adeline motioned to him to go on, and he continued.) "At sight of this, I was weak enough to pity her; and, with the greatest simplicity, I told her, that I was glad to see that she felt penitent for her conduct, since penitence paved the way to amendment; when, to my great surprise, all the vanished fierceness and haughtiness of her look returned, and she told me, that so far from repenting she approved of her conduct; and that remorse had no share in her sorrow; that she wept from consciousness of misery, but of misery inflicted* by the faults of others, not her own."

"Oh! Dr. Norberry," cried Adeline reproachfully, "I doubt, by awakening her pride, you destroyed the tenderness returning towards me."

"May be so. However, so much the better; for anger is a less painful state of mind to endure than that of remorse; and while she thinks herself only injured and aggrieved, she will be less unhappy."

"Then," continued Adeline in a faltering voice, "I care not how long she hates me."

Dr. Norberry looked at Adeline a moment with tears in his eyes, and evidently gulped down a rising sob. "Good child! good child!" he at length articulated. "Yet—no. Girl, girl, your virtue only heaps coals of fire on that devoted woman's head."[1]

"For pity's sake, Dr. Norberry!" cried Adeline.

"Well, well, I have done.* But she'll forget and forgive all in time, I do not doubt."

"Impossible: remember her oath."

"And do you really suppose that she will think herself bound to keep so silly and rash an oath; an oath made in the heat of passion?"

"Undoubtedly I do; and I know, that were she to break it, she would never be otherwise than wretched all her life after. Therefore, unless Glenmurray forsakes me" (she added, trying to smile archly as she spoke), "and this I am not happy enough to expect, I look on our separation in this world to be eternal."

"You do?—Then, poor devil, how miserable she will be, when her present resentment shall subside! Well; when that time comes I may perhaps see her again," added the doctor, gulping again.

"Heaven bless you for that intention!" cried Adeline. "But how could you ever have the heart to renounce her?"

"Zounds, girl!† you are almost as provoking as your mother. Why, how could I have the heart to do otherwise, when she whitewashed herself and blackened you? To be sure, it did cause me a twinge or two to do it; and had she been an iota less haughty, I should have turned back and said, 'Kiss and be friends again.' But she seemed so provokingly anxious to get rid of me, and waved me with her hand to the door in such a d——d‡ tragedy queen sort of a manner, that, having told her very civilly to go to the devil her own way, I gulped down a sort of a tender choking in my throat, and made as rapid an exit as possible. And now another trial awaits me. I came to town, at some inconvenience to myself, to try to do you service. I have failed, and I have now no further business here: so we must part, and God knows§ when we shall meet again. For I rarely leave home, and may not see you again for years."

"Indeed!" exclaimed Adeline. "Surely," looking at Glenmurray, "we might settle in Dr. Norberry's neighbourhood?"

Glenmurray said nothing, but looked at the doctor; who seemed confused, and was silent.

---

1  Cf. Proverbs 25.22.

"Look ye, my dear girl," said he at length: "the idea of your settling near me had* occurred to me, but—" here he took two hasty strides across the room—"in short, that's an impossible thing; so I beg you to think no more about it. If, indeed, you mean to marry Mr. Glenmurray—"

"Which I shall not do," replied Adeline coldly.

"There again, now!" cried the doctor pettishly: "you, in your way, are quite as obstinate and ridiculous as your mother. However, I hope you will know better in time. But it grows late—'tis time I should be in my chaise, and I hear it driving up. Mr. Glenmurray," continued he in an altered tone of voice, "to your care and your tenderness I leave this poor child: and, zounds, man! if you will but burn your books before her face, and swear they are d——d† stuff, why, 'sdeath, I say, I would come to town on purpose to do you homage.—Adeline, my child, God bless you! I have loved you from your infancy, and I wish, from my soul, that I left you in a better situation. But you will write to me, heh?"

"Undoubtedly."

"Well, one kiss:—don't be jealous, Glenmurray. Your hand, man.—Woons,[1] what a hand! My dear fellow, take care of yourself, for that poor child's sake: get the advice which I recommended, and good air." A rising sob interrupted him—he hemmed it off, and ran into his chaise.


CHAPTER 17

"Now, then," said Adeline, her tears dropping fast as she spoke, "now, then, we are alone in the world; henceforward we must be all to each other."

"Is the idea a painful one, Adeline?" replied Glenmurray reproachfully.

"Not so," returned Adeline. "Still I can't yet forget that I had a mother, and a kind one too."

"And may have again."

"Impossible:—there is a vow in heaven against it. No—My plans for future happiness must be laid unmindful and independent of her. They must have you and your happiness for their sole object; I must live for you alone: and you," added she in a faltering voice, "must live for me."

"I will live as long as I can," replied Glenmurray sighing, "and as one step towards it I shall keep early hours: so to rest, dear Adeline, and let us forget our sorrows as soon as possible."

---

1  Another of Dr. Norberry's expletives; probably a form of "wounds," i.e., the wounds of Christ.

The next morning Adeline's and Glenmurray's first care was to determine on their future residence. It was desirable that it should be at a sufficient distance from London, to deserve the name and have the conveniencies* of a country abode, yet sufficiently near it for Glenmurray to have the advice of a London physician if necessary.

"Suppose we fix at Richmond?"[1] said Glenmurray: and Adeline, to whom the idea of dwelling on a spot at once so classical and beautiful was most welcome, joyfully consented; and in a few days they were settled there in a pleasant but expensive lodging.

But here, as when abroad, Glenmurray occasionally saw old acquaintances, many of whom were willing to renew their intercourse with him for the sake of being introduced to Adeline; and who, from a knowledge of her situation, presumed to pay her that sort of homage, which, though not understood by her, gave pangs unutterable to the delicate mind of Glenmurray. "Were she my wife, they dared not pay her such marked attention," said he to himself; and again, as delicately as he could, he urged Adeline to sacrifice her principles to the prejudices of society.

"I thought," replied Adeline gravely, "that, as we lived for each other, we might act independent of society, and serve it by our example even against its will."

Glenmurray was silent.—He did not like to own how painful and mischievous he found in practice the principles which he admired in theory—and Adeline continued:

"Believe me, Glenmurray, ours is the very situation calculated to urge us on in the pursuit of truth. We are answerable to no one for our conduct; and we can make any experiments in morals that we choose. I am wholly at a loss to comprehend why you persist in urging me to marry you. Take care, my dear Glenmurray—the high respect I bear your character was shaken a little by your fighting a duel in defiance of your principles; and your eagerness to marry, in further defiance of them, may weaken my esteem, if not my love."

Adeline smiled as she said this: but Glenmurray thought she spoke more in earnest than she was willing to allow; and, alarmed at the threat, he only answered, "You know it is for your sake merely that I speak," and dropped the subject; secretly resolving, however, that he would not walk with Adeline in the fashionable promenades, at the hours commonly spent there by the beau monde.

But, in spite of this precaution, they could not escape the assiduities of some gay men of fashion, who knew Glenmurray and admired his com-

---

1 Richmond, on the Thames west of London, was (and still is) a fashionable residential suburb of London.

panion; and Adeline at length suspected that Glenmurray was jealous. But in this she wronged him; it was not the attention paid her, but the nature of it, that disturbed him. Nor is it to be wondered at that Adeline herself was eager to avoid the public walks, when it is known that one of her admirers at Richmond was the colonel Mordaunt whom she had become acquainted with at Bath.

Colonel Mordaunt, "curst with every granted prayer,"[1] was just beginning to feel the tedium of life, when he saw Adeline unexpectedly at Richmond; and though he felt shocked at first, at beholding her in so different a situation from that in which he had first beheld her, still that very situation, by holding forth to him a prospect of being favoured by her in his turn, revived his admiration with more than its original violence, and he resolved to be, if possible, the lover of Adeline, after Glenmurray should have fallen a victim, as he had no doubt but he would, to his dangerous illness.

But the opportunities which he had of seeing her suddenly ceased. She no longer frequented the public walks; and him, though he suspected it not, she most studiously avoided; for she could not bear to behold the alteration in his manner when he addressed her, an alteration perhaps unknown to himself. True, it was not insulting; but Adeline, who had admired him too much at Bath not to have examined with minute attention the almost timid expression of his countenance, and the respectfulness of his manner when he addressed her, shrunk abashed from the ardent and impassioned expression with which he now met her,—an expression which Adeline used to call "looking like sir Patrick"; and which indicated even to her inexperience, that the admiration which he then felt was of a nature less pure and flattering than the one which she excited before; and though in her own eyes she appeared as worthy of respect as ever, she was forced to own even to herself, that persons in general would be of a contrary opinion.

But in vain did she resolve to walk very early in a morning only, being fully persuaded that she should then meet with no one. Colonel Mordaunt was as wakeful as she was; and being convinced that she walked during some part of the day, and probably early in a morning, he resolved to watch near the door of her lodgings, in hopes to obtain an hour's conversation with her. The consequence was, that he saw Adeline one morning walk pensively and* alone, down the shady road that leads from the terrace to Petersham.[2]

---

1    Alexander Pope, "To a Lady: Of the Characters of Women," *Moral Essays* (1735), 2.147.

2    South of Richmond.

This opportunity was not to be overlooked; and he overtook and accosted her with such an expression of pleasure on his countenance, as was sufficient to alarm the now suspicious delicacy of Adeline; and, conscious as she was that Glenmurray beheld colonel Mordaunt's attentions with pain, a deep blush overspread her cheek at his approach, while her eyes were timidly cast down.

Colonel Mordaunt saw her emotion, and attributed it to a cause flattering to his vanity; it even encouraged him to seize her hand; and, while he openly congratulated himself on his good fortune in meeting her alone, he presumed to press her hand to his lips. Adeline indignantly withdrew it, and replied very coldly to his inquiries concerning her health.

"But where have you hidden yourself lately?" cried he,—"O miss Mowbray! loveliest and, I may add, most beloved of women, how have I longed to see you alone, and pour out my whole soul to you!"

Adeline answered this rhapsody by a look of astonishment only—being silent from disgust and consternation,—while involuntarily she quickened her pace, as if wishing to avoid him.

"O hear me, and hear me patiently!" he resumed. "You must have noticed the effect which your charms produced on me at Bath; and may I dare to add that my attentions then did not seem displeasing to you?"

"Sir!" interrupted Adeline, sighing deeply, "my situation is now changed; and——"

"It is so, I thank Fortune that it is so," replied colonel Mordaunt; "and I am happy to say, it is changed by no crime of mine." (Here Adeline started and turned pale.) "But I were unworthy all chance of happiness, were I to pass by the seeming opportunity of being blest, which the alteration to which you allude holds forth to me."

Here he paused, as if in embarrassment, but Adeline was unable to interrupt him.

"Miss Mowbray," he at length continued, "I am told that you are not on good terms with your mother; nay, I have heard that she has renounced you: may I presume to ask if this be true?"

"It is," answered Adeline trembling with emotion.

"Then, as before long it is probable that you will be without—without a protector——" (Adeline turned round and fixed her eyes wildly upon him.) "To be sure," continued he, avoiding her steadfast gaze, "I could wish to call you mine this moment; but, unhappy as you appear to be in your present situation, I know, unlike many women circumstanced as you are, you are too generous and noble-minded to be capable of forsaking in his last illness the man whom in his happier moments you* honoured with your love." As he said this, Adeline, her lips parched with agitation, and breathing short, caught hold of his arm; and pressing her cold hand, he went on: "Therefore, I will not venture even to wish to be honoured with a kind look from you till Mr. Glenmurray is removed to a happier world. But *then*, dearest of women, you whom I loved without hope of possessing you, and whom now I dote upon to madness, I conjure you to admit my visits, and let my attentions prevail on you to accept my protection, and allow me to devote the remainder of my days to love and you!"

"Merciful heaven!"* exclaimed Adeline clasping her hands together, "to what insults am I reserved!"

"Insults!" echoed colonel Mordaunt.

"Yes sir," replied Adeline: "you have insulted me, grossly insulted me, and know not the woman whom you have tortured to the very soul."

"Hear me, hear me, miss Mowbray!" exclaimed colonel Mordaunt, almost as much agitated as herself: "by heaven I meant not to insult you! and perhaps I—perhaps I have been misinformed—No!—Yes, yes, it must be so;—your indignation proves that I have—You are, no doubt—and on my knees I implore your pardon—you are the wife of Mr. Glenmurray."

"And suppose I am *not* his wife," cried Adeline, "is it then given to a wife only to be secure from being insulted by offers horrible to the delicacy, and wounding to the sensibility, like those which I have heard from you?" But before colonel Mordaunt could reply, Adeline's thoughts had reverted to what he had said of Glenmurray's certain danger; and, unable to bear this confirmation of her fears, with the speed of phrensy she ran towards home, and did not stop till she was in sight of her lodging, and the still closed curtain of her apartment met her view.

"He is still sleeping, then," she exclaimed, "and I have time to recover myself, and endeavour to hide from him the emotion of which I could not tell the reason." So saying, she softly entered the house, and by the time Glenmurray rose she had regained her composure. Still there was a look of anxiety on her fine countenance, which could not escape the penetrating eye of love.

"Why are you so grave this morning?" said Glenmurray, as Adeline seated herself at the breakfast table:—"I feel much better and more cheerful to-day."

"But are you, indeed, better?" replied Adeline, fixing her tearful eyes on him.

"Or I much deceive myself," said Glenmurray.

"Thank God!"† devoutly replied Adeline. "I thought—I thought—" Here tears choked her utterance, and Glenmurray drew from her a confession of her anxious fears for him, though she prudently resolved not to agitate him by telling him of the rencontre with colonel Mordaunt.

But when the continued assurances of Glenmurray that he was better, and the animation of his countenance, had in a degree removed her fears for his life, she had leisure to revert to another source of uneasiness, and to dwell on the insult which she had experienced from colonel Mordaunt's offer of protection.

"How strange and irrational," thought Adeline, "are the prejudices of society! Because an idle ceremony has not been muttered over me at the altar, I am liable to be thought a woman of vicious inclinations, and to be exposed to the most daring insults."

As these reflections occurred to her, she could scarcely help regretting that her principles would not allow her delicacy and virtue to be placed under the sacred shelter bestowed by that ceremony which she was pleased to call idle. And she was not long without experiencing still further hardships from the situation in which she had persisted so obstinately to remain. Their establishment consisted of a footman and a maid servant; but the latter had of late been so remiss in the performance of her duties, and so impertinent when reproved for her faults, that Adeline was obliged to give her warning.

"Warning, indeed!" replied the girl: "a mighty hardship, truly! I can promise you I did not mean to stay long; it is no such favour to live with a kept miss;—and if you come to that, I think I am as good as you."

Shocked, surprised, and unable to answer, Adeline took refuge in her room. Never before had she been accosted by her inferiors without respectful attention; and now, owing to her situation, even a servant-maid thought herself authorised to insult her, and to raise herself to her level!

"But surely," said Adeline mentally, "I ought to reason with her, and try to convince her that I am in reality as virtuous as if I were Glenmurray's wife, instead of his mistress."

Accordingly she went back into the kitchen; but her resolution failed her when she found the footman there, listening with a broad grin on his countenance to the relation which Mary was giving him of the "fine trimming" which she had given "madam."

Scarcely did the presence of Adeline interrupt or restrain her; but at last she turned round and said, "And, pray, have you got any thing to say to me?"

"Nothing more now," meekly replied Adeline, "unless you will follow me to my chamber."

"With all my heart," cried the girl; and Adeline returned to her own room.

"I wish, Mary, to set you right," said Adeline, "with respect to my situation. You called me, I think, a kept miss, and seemed to think ill of me."

"Why, to be sure, ma'am," replied Mary, a little alarmed—"every body say* you are a kept lady, and so I made no bones of saying so; but I am sure if so be you are not so, why I ax pardon."

"But what do you mean by the term kept lady?"

"Why, a lady who lives with a man without being married to him, I take it; and that I take to be your case, an't it, I pray?"

Adeline blushed and was silent:—it certainly was her case. However, she took courage and went on:

"But mistresses, or kept ladies in general, are women of bad character, and would live with any man; but I never loved, nor ever shall love, any man but Mr. Glenmurray. I look on myself as his wife in the sight of God; nor will I quit him till death shall separate us."[1]

"Then if so be that you don't want to change, I think you might as well be married to him."

Adeline was again silent for a moment, but continued—

"Mr. Glenmurray would marry me to-morrow, if I chose."

"Indeed! Well, if master is inclined to make an honest woman of you, you had better take him at his word, I think."

"Gracious heaven!" cried Adeline, "what an expression! Why will you persist to confound me with those deluded women who are victims of their own weakness?"

"As to that," replied Mary, "you talk too fine for me; but a fact is a fact—are you or are you not my master's wife?"

"I am not."

"Why then you are his mistress, and a kept lady to all intents and purposes: so what signifies argufying the matter? I lived with a kept madam before; and she was as good as you, for aught I know."

Adeline, shocked and disappointed, told her she might leave the room.

"I am going," pertly answered Mary, "and to seek for a place: but I must beg that you will not own you are no better than you should be, when a lady comes to ask my character; for then perhaps I should not get any one to take me. I shall call you Mrs. Glenmurray."

"But I shall not call *myself* so," replied Adeline. "I will not say what is not true, on any account."

"There now, there's spite! and yet you pertend* to call yourself a gentlewoman, and to be better than other kept ladies! Why, you are not worthy to tie the shoestrings of my last mistress[2]—she did not mind telling a lie rather than lose a poor servant a place; and she called herself a married woman rather than hurt me."

"Neither she nor you, then," replied Adeline gravely, "were sensible of what great importance a strict adherence to veracity is, to the interests of society. I am;—and for the sake of mankind I will always tell the truth."

---

1  Cf. the promise in the marriage service to remain faithful "till death do us part."
2  Cf. Mark 1.7.

"You had better tell one innocent lie for mine," replied the girl pertly. "I dare to say the world will neither know nor care any thing about it: and I can tell you I shall expect you will."

So saying she shut the door with violence, leaving Adeline mournfully musing on the distresses attending on her situation, and even disposed to question the propriety of remaining in it.

The inquietude of her mind, as usual, showed itself in her countenance, and involved her in another difficulty: to make Glenmurray uneasy by an avowal of what had passed between her and Mary was impossible; yet how could she conceal it from him? And while she was deliberating on this point, Glenmurray entered the room, and tenderly inquired what had so evidently disturbed her.

"Nothing of any consequence," she faltered out, and burst into tears.

"Could 'nothing of consequence' produce such emotion?" answered Glenmurray.

"But I am ashamed to own the cause of my uneasiness."

"Ashamed to own it to me, Adeline? To be sure, you have a great deal to fear from my severity!" said he, faintly smiling.

Adeline for a moment resolved to tell him the whole truth; but, fearful of throwing him into a degree of agitation hurtful to his weak frame, she, who had the moment before so nobly supported the necessity of a strict adherence to truth, condescended to equivocate and evade; and turning away her head, while a conscious blush overspread her cheek, she replied, "You know that I look forward with anxiety and uneasiness to the time of my approaching confinement."

Glenmurray believed her; and overcome by some painful feelings, which fears for himself and anxiety for her occasioned him, he silently pressed her to his bosom; and, choked with contending emotions, returned to his own apartment.

"And I have stooped to the meanness of disguising the truth!" cried Adeline, clasping her hands convulsively together: "surely, surely, there must be something radically wrong in a situation which exposes one to such a variety of degradations!"

Mary, meanwhile, had gone in search of a place; and having found the lady to whom she had been advised to offer herself, at home, she returned to tell Adeline that Mrs. Pemberton would call in half an hour to inquire her character. The half-hour, an anxious one to Adeline, having elapsed, a lady knocked at the door, and inquired, in Adeline's hearing, for Mrs. Glenmurray.

"Tell the lady," cried Adeline immediately from the top of the staircase, "that miss Mowbray will wait on her directly." The footman obeyed, and Mrs. Pemberton was ushered into the parlour: and now, for the first time in her life, Adeline trembled to approach a stranger; for the first time she felt that she was going to appear before a fellow-creature as an object of scorn, and, though an enthusiast for virtue, to be* considered as a votary of vice. But it was a mortification which she must submit to undergo; and hastily throwing a large shawl over her shoulders, to hide her figure as much as possible, with a trembling hand she opened the door, and found herself in the dreaded presence of Mrs. Pemberton.

Nor was she at all re-assured when she found that lady dressed in the neat, modest garb of a strict quaker[1]—a garb which creates an immediate idea in the mind, of more than common rigidness of principles and sanctity of conduct in the wearer of it. Adeline curtsied in silence.

Mrs. Pemberton bowed her head courteously; then, with a countenance of great sweetness, and a voice calculated to inspire confidence, said, "I believe thy name is Mowbray; but I came to see Mrs. Glenmurray: and as on these occasions I always wish to confer with the principal, wouldst thou, if it be not inconvenient, ask the mistress of Mary to let me see her."†

"I am myself the mistress of Mary," replied Adeline in a faint voice.

"I ask thine excuse," answered Mrs. Pemberton, re-seating herself: "as thou art Mrs. Glenmurray, thou art the person I wanted to see."

Here Adeline changed colour, overcome with the consciousness that she ought to undeceive her, and the sense of the difficulty of doing so.

"But thou art very pale, and seemest uneasy," continued the gentle quaker—"I hope thy husband is not worse."‡

"Mr. Glenmurray, but not my husband," said Adeline, "is better to-day."

"Art thou not married?" asked Mrs. Pemberton with quickness.

"I am not."

"And yet thou livest with the gentleman I named, and art the person whom Mary called Mrs. Glenmurray?"§

"I am," replied Adeline, her paleness yielding to a deep crimson, and her eyes filling with tears.

Mrs. Pemberton sat for a minute in silence; then rising with an air of cold dignity, "I fear thy servant is not likely to suit me," she observed, "and I will not detain thee any longer."

"She can be an excellent servant," faltered out Adeline.

---

1  A member of the Religious Society of Friends, founded by George Fox in 1648-50. A "strict quaker" or a "plain Quaker" is "a Quaker dressed according to the strictest rules of the society to which he belongs" (see Opie, "The Quaker, and the Young Man of the World," 367). Strict Quakers used simple speech in addressing others, without distinctions of rank: hence their use of the intimate form "thou" rather than the more formal "you."

"Very likely—but there are objections." So saying she reached the door: but as she passed Adeline she stopped, interested and affected by the mournful expression of her countenance, and the visible effort she made to retain her tears.

Adeline saw, and felt humbled at the compassion which her countenance expressed: to be an object of pity was as mortifying as to be an object of scorn, and she turned her eyes on Mrs. Pemberton with a look of proud indignation: but they met those of Mrs. Pemberton fixed on her with a look of such benevolence, that her anger was instantly subdued; and it occurred to her that she might make the benevolent compassion visible in Mrs. Pemberton's countenance serviceable to her discarded servant.

"Stay, madam," she cried, as Mrs. Pemberton was about to leave the room, "allow me a moment's conversation with you."

Mrs. Pemberton, with an eagerness which she suddenly endeavoured to check, returned to her seat.

"I suspect," said Adeline, (gathering courage from the conscious kindness of her motive,) "that your objection to take Mary Warner into your service proceeds wholly from the situation of her present mistress."

"Thou judgest rightly," was Mrs. Pemberton's answer.

"Nor do I wonder," continued Adeline, "that you make this objection, when I consider the present prejudices of society."

"Prejudices!" softly exclaimed the benevolent quaker.

Adeline faintly smiled, and went on—"But surely you will allow, that in a family quiet and secluded as ours, and in daily contemplation of an union uninterrupted, faithful, and virtuous, and possessing all the sacredness of marriage, though without the name, it is not likely that the young woman in question should have imbibed any vicious habits or principles."*

"But in contemplating thy union itself, she has lived in the contemplation of vice; and thou wilt own, that, by having given it an air of respectability, thou hast only made it more dangerous."

"On this point," cried Adeline, "I see we must disagree—I shall therefore, without further preamble, inform you, madam, that Mary, aware of the difficulty of procuring a service, if it were known that she had lived with a kept mistress, as the phrase is" (here an indignant blush overspread the face of Adeline), "desired me to call myself the wife of Glenmurray: but this, from my abhorrence of all falsehood, I peremptorily refused."

"And thou didst well," exclaimed Mrs. Pemberton, "and I respect thy resolution."

"But my sincerity will, I fear, prevent the poor girl's obtaining other reputable places; and I, alas! am not rich enough to make her amends for the injury which my conscience forces me to do her. But if you, madam, could be prevailed upon to take her into your family, even for a short time only, to wipe away the disgrace which her living with me has brought upon her—"

"Why can she not remain with thee?" asked Mrs. Pemberton hastily.

"Because she neglected her duty, and, when reproved for it, replied in very injurious language."

"Presuming probably on thy way of life?"

"I must confess that she has reproached me with it."

"And this was all her fault?"

"It was:—she can be an excellent servant."

"Thou hast said enough; thy conscience shall not have the additional burthen to bear, of having deprived a poor girl of her maintenance—I will take her."

"A thousand thanks to you," replied Adeline: "you have removed a weight off my mind; but my conscience, I bless God,* has none to bear."

"No?" returned Mrs. Pemberton: "dost thou deem thy conduct blameless in the eyes of that Being whom thou hast just blessed?"

"As far as my connexion with Mr. Glenmurray is concerned, I do."

"Indeed!"

"Nay, doubt me not—believe me that I never wantonly violate the truth; and that even an evasion, which I, for the first time in my life, was guilty of to-day, has given me a pang to which I will not again expose myself."

"And yet, inconsistent beings as we are," cried Mrs. Pemberton, "straining at a gnat, and swallowing a camel,[1] what is the guilt of the evasion which weighs on thy mind, compared to that of living, as thou dost, in an illicit commerce? Surely, surely, thine heart accuses thee; for thy face bespeaks uneasiness, and thou wilt listen to the whispers of penitence, and leave, ere long, the man who has betrayed thee."

"The man who has betrayed me! Mr. Glenmurray is no betrayer—he is one of the best of human beings. No, madam: if I had acceded to his wishes, I should long ago have been his wife; but, from a conviction of the folly of marriage, I have preferred living with him without the performance of a ceremony which, in the eye of reason, can confer neither honour nor happiness."

"Poor thing!" exclaimed Mrs. Pemberton, rising as she spoke, ."I understand thee now—Thou art one of the enlightened, as they call themselves—Thou art one of those wise in their own conceit,[2] who, disregarding the customs of ages, and the dictates of experience, set up their

---

1  See Matthew 23.24.
2  Proverbs 26.5, 28.11.

own opinions against the hallowed institutions of men and the will of the Most High."

"Can you blame me," interrupted Adeline, "for acting according to what I think right?"

"But hast thou well studied the subject on which thou hast decided? Yet, alas! to thee how vain must be the voice of admonition!" (she continued, her countenance kindling into strong expression as she spoke)—"From the poor victim of passion and persuasion, penitence and amendment might be rationally expected; and she, from the path of frailty, might turn again to that of virtue: but for one like thee, glorying in thine iniquity, and erring, not from the too tender heart, but the vain-glorious head,—for thee there is, I fear, no blessed return to the right way; and I, who would have tarried with thee even in the house of sin, to have reclaimed thee, penitent, now hasten from thee, and for ever—firm as thou art in guilt."

As she said this she reached the door; while Adeline, affected by her emotion, and distressed by her language, stood silent and almost abashed before her.

But with her hand on the lock she turned round, and in a gentler voice said, "Yet not even against a wilful offender like thee, should one gate that may lead to amendment be shut. Thy situation and thy fortunes may soon be greatly changed; affliction may subdue thy pride, and the counsel of a friend of thine own sex might then sound sweetly in thine ears. Should that time come, I will be that friend. I am now about to set off for Lisbon with a very dear friend,[1] about whom I feel as solicitous as thou about thy Glenmurray; and there I shall remain some time. Here then is my address; and if thou shouldest want my advice or assistance write to me, and be assured that Rachel Pemberton will try to forget thy errors in thy distresses."

So saying she left the room, but returned again, before Adeline had recovered herself from the various emotions which she had experienced during her address, to ask her christian[2] name. But when Adeline replied, "My name is Adeline Mowbray," Mrs. Pemberton started, and eagerly exclaimed, "Art thou Adeline Mowbray of Gloucestershire—the young heiress, as she was called, of Rosevalley?"

"I was once," replied Adeline, sinking back into a chair, "Adeline Mowbray of Rosevalley."

Mrs. Pemberton for a few minutes gazed on her in mournful silence: "And art thou," she cried, "Adeline Mowbray? Art thou that courteous, blooming, blessed being, (for every tongue that I heard name thee blessed

---

1   Cf. 29 and n.

2   I.e., her baptismal name, Adeline.

thee) whom I saw only three years ago bounding over thy native hills, all grace, and joy, and innocence?"

Adeline tried to speak, but her voice failed her.

"Art thou she," continued Mrs. Pemberton, "whom I saw also leaning from the window of her mother's mansion, and inquiring with the countenance of a pitying angel concerning the health of a wan labourer who limped past the door?"

Adeline hid her face with her hands.

Mrs. Pemberton went on in a lower tone of voice,—"I came with some companions to see thy mother's grounds, and to hear the nightingales in her groves; but—" (here Mrs. Pemberton's voice faltered) "I have seen a sight far beyond that of the proudest mansion, said I to those who asked me of thy mother's seat; I have heard what was sweeter to my ear than the voice of the nightingale; I have seen a blooming girl nursed in idleness and prosperity, yet active in the discharge of every christian duty; and I have heard her speak in the soothing accents of kindness and of pity, while her name was followed by blessings, and parents prayed to have a child like her.—O lost, unhappy girl! such *was* Adeline Mowbray: and often, very often, has thy graceful image recurred to my remembrance: but, how art thou changed! Where is the open eye of happiness? where is the bloom that spoke a heart at peace with itself? I repeat it, and I repeat it with agony.—Father of mercies! is this thy Adeline Mowbray?"

Here, overcome with emotion, Mrs. Pemberton paused; but Adeline could not break silence: she rose, she stretched out her hand as if going to speak, but her utterance failed her, and again she sunk on a chair.

"It was thine," resumed Mrs. Pemberton in a faint and broken voice, "to diffuse happiness around thee, and to enjoy wealth unhated, because thy hand dispensed nobly the riches which it had received bounteously: when the ear heard thee, then it blessed thee; when the eye saw thee, it gave witness to thee; and yet—"

Here again she paused, and raised her fine eyes to heaven for a few minutes, as if in prayer; then, pressing Adeline's hand with an almost convulsive grasp, she drew her bonnet over her face, as if eager to hide the emotion which she was unable to subdue, and suddenly left the house; while Adeline, stunned and overwhelmed by the striking contrast which Mrs. Pemberton had drawn between her past and present situation, remained for some minutes motionless on her seat, a prey to a variety of feelings which she dared not venture to analyse.

But, amidst the variety of her feelings, Adeline soon found that sorrow, sorrow of the bitterest kind, was uppermost. Mrs. Pemberton had said that she was about to be visited by affliction—alluding, there was no doubt, to the probable death of Glenmurray—And was his fate so certain that it was the theme of conversation at Richmond? Were only *her* eyes blind to the certainty of his danger?

On these ideas did Adeline chiefly dwell after the departure of her monitress; and in an agony unspeakable she entered the room where Glenmurray was sitting, in order to look at him, and form her own judgment on a subject of such importance. But, alas! she found him with the brilliant deceitful appearance that attends his complaint—a bloom resembling health on his cheek, and a brightness in his eye rivalling that of the undimmed lustre of youth. Surprised, delighted, and overcome by these appearances, which her inexperience rendered her incapable of appreciating justly, Adeline threw herself on the sofa by him; and, as she pressed her cold cheek to his glowing one, her tearful eye was raised to heaven with an expression of devout thankfulness.

"Mrs. Pemberton paid you a long visit," said Glenmurray, "and I thought once, by the elevated tone of her voice, that she was preaching to you."[1]

"I believe she was," cheerfully replied Adeline, "and now I have a confession to make; the season of reserve shall be over, and I will tell you all the adventures of this day without *evasion*."

"Aye, I thought you were not ingenuous with me this morning," replied Glenmurray: "but better late than never."

Adeline then told him all that had passed between her and Mary and Mrs. Pemberton, and concluded with saying, "But the surety of your better health, which your looks give me, has dissipated every uneasiness; and if you are but spared to me, sorrow cannot reach me, and I despise the censure of the ignorant and the prejudiced.—The world approve! What is the world to me?—

'The conscious mind is its own awful world!'"[2]

Glenmurray sighed deeply as she concluded her narration.

"I have only one request to make," said he—"Never let that Mary come into my presence again; and be sure to take care of Mrs. Pemberton's address."

Adeline promised that both his requests should be attended to. Mary was paid her wages, and dismissed immediately; and a girl being hired to supply her place, the ménage went on quietly again.

---

1 Female members of the Society of Friends were permitted to preach: Opie's friend Elizabeth Fry (1780-1845), a famous preacher, went into prisons to minister to women inmates.

2 James Thomson, *Tancred and Sigismunda. A Tragedy* (1745), 5.6.94-95.

But a new mortification awaited Glenmurray and Adeline. In spite of Glenmurray's eccentricities and opinions, he was still remembered with interest by some of the female part of his family; and two of his cousins, more remarkable for their beauty than their virtue, hearing that he was at Richmond, made known to him their intention of paying him a morning visit on their way to their country seat in the neighbourhood.

"Most unwelcome visiters, indeed!" cried Glenmurray, throwing the letter down; "I will write to them and forbid them to come."

"That's impossible," replied Adeline, "for by this time they must be on the road, if you look at the date of the letter: besides, I wish you to receive them; I should like to see any relations or friends of yours, especially those who have liberality of sentiment enough to esteem you as you deserve."

"You!—you see them!" exclaimed Glenmurray, pacing the room impatiently: "O Adeline, that is *impossible!*"

"I understand you," replied Adeline, changing colour: "they will not deem me worthy," forcing a smile, "to be introduced to them."

"And therefore would I forbid their coming. I cannot bear to *exclude* you from my presence in order that I may receive them. No: when they arrive, I will send them word that I am unable to see them."

"While they will attribute the refusal to the influence of the *creature* who lives with you! No, Glenmurray, for my sake I must insist on your not being denied to them; and, believe me, I should consider myself as unworthy to be the choice of your heart, if I were not able to bear with firmness a mortification like that which awaits me."

"But you allow it to be a mortification?"

"Yes; it is mortifying to a woman who knows herself to be virtuous, and is an idolater of virtue, to pay the penalty of vice, and be thought unworthy to associate with the relations of the man whom she loves."

"They shall not come, I protest," exclaimed Glenmurray.

But Adeline was resolute; and she carried her point. Soon after this conversation the ladies arrived, and Adeline shut herself up in her own apartment, where she gave way to no very pleasant reflections. Nor was she entirely satisfied with Glenmurray's conduct:—true, he had earnestly and sincerely wished to refuse to see his unexpected and unwelcome guests; but he had never once expressed a desire of combating their prejudices for Adeline's sake, and an intention of requesting that she might be introduced to them; but, as any common man would have done under similar circumstances, he was contented to do homage to "things as they are,"[1] without an effort to resist the prejudice to which he was superior.

---

1  Cf. the title of Godwin's *Things As They Are, or, Caleb Williams* (1794), which exposes the evil effects of the status quo.

"Alas!" cried Adeline, "when can we hope to see society enlightened and improved, when even those who see and strive to amend its faults in theory, in practice tamely submit to the trammels which it imposes?"

An hour, a tedious hour to Adeline, having elapsed, Glenmurray's visitors departed; and by the disappointment that Adeline experienced at hearing the door close on them, she felt that she had had a secret hope of being summoned to be presented to them; and, with a bitter feeling of mortification, she reflected, that she was probably to the man whom she adored a shame and a reproach.

"Yet I should like to see them," she said, running to the window as the carriage drove up, and the ladies entered it. At that moment they, whether from curiosity to see her, or accident, looked up at the window where she was. Adeline started back indignant and confused; for, thrusting their heads eagerly forward, they looked at her with the bold unfeeling stare of imagined superiority; and Adeline, spite of her reason, sunk abashed and conscious from their gaze.

"And this insult," exclaimed she, clasping her hands and bursting into tears, "I experience from Glenmurray's *relations*! I think I could have borne it better from any one else."

She had not recovered her disorder when Glenmurray entered the room, and, tenderly embracing her, exclaimed, "Never, never again, my love, will I submit to such a sacrifice as I have now made"; when seeing her in tears, too well aware of the cause, he gave way to such a passionate burst of tenderness and regret, that Adeline, terrified at his agitation, though soothed by his fondness, affected the cheerfulness which she did not feel, and promised to drive the intruders from her remembrance.

Had Glenmurray and Adeline known the real character of the unwelcome visitors, neither of them would have regretted that Adeline was not presented to them. One of them was married, and to so accommodating a husband, that his wife's known gallant was his intimate friend; and under the sanction of his protection she was received every where, and visited by every one, as the world did not think proper to be more clear-sighted than the husband himself chose to be. The other lady was a young and attractive widow, who coquetted with many men, but intrigued with only one at a time; for which self-denial she was rewarded by being allowed to pass unquestioned through the portals of fashionable society. But these ladies would have scorned to associate with Adeline; and Adeline, had she known their private history, would certainly have returned the compliment.

The peace of Adeline was soon after disturbed in another way. Glenmurray finding himself disposed to sleep in the middle of the day, his cough having kept him waking all night, Adeline took her usual walk, and returned by the church-yard. The bell was tolling; and as she passed she saw a funeral enter the church-yard, and instantly averted her head.

In so doing her eyes fell on a decent-looking woman, who with a sort of angry earnestness was watching the progress of the procession.

"Aye, there goes your body, you rogue!" she exclaimed indignantly, "but I wonder where your soul is now?—where I would not be for something."

Adeline was shocked, and gently observed, "What crime did the person of whom you are speaking, that you should suppose his soul so painfully disposed of?"

"What crime?" returned the woman: "crime enough, I think:—why, he ruined a poor girl here in the neighbourhood; and then, because he never chose to make a will, there is she lying-in of a little by-blow,[1] with not a farthing[2] of money to maintain her or the child, and the fellow's money is gone to the heir at law, scarce of kin to him, while his own flesh and blood is left to starve."

Adeline shuddered:—if Glenmurray were to die, she and the child* she bore would, she knew, be beggars.

"Well, miss, or madam, belike, by the look of you," continued the woman, glancing her eye over Adeline's person, "what say you? Don't you think the fellow's soul is where we should not like to be? However, he had his hell here too, to be sure! for, when speechless and unable to move his fingers, he seemed by signs to ask for pen and ink, and he looked in agonies; and there was the poor young woman crying over him, and holding in her arms her† poor destitute baby, who would as he grew up be taught, he must think, to curse the wicked father who begot him, and the naughty mother who bore him!"

Adeline turned very sick, and was forced to seat herself on a tombstone. "Curse the mother who bore him!" she inwardly repeated,—"and will my child curse me? Rather let me undergo the rites I have despised!" and instantly starting from her seat she ran down the road to her lodgings, resolving to propose to Glenmurray their immediate marriage.

"But is the possession of property, then," she said to herself as she stopped to take breath, "so supreme a good, that the want of it, through the means of his mother, should dispose a child to curse that mother?— No: my child shall be taught to consider nothing valuable but virtue, nothing disgraceful but *vice*.—Fool that I am! a bugbear[3] frightened me; and to my foolish fears I was about to sacrifice my own principles, and

---

1   An illegitimate child.

2   A quarter of a penny.

3   An imaginary monster invoked by nurses to frighten children.

the respectability of Glenmurray. No—Let his property go to the heir at law—let me be forced to labour to support my babe, when its father——"
Here a flood of tears put an end to her soliloquy, and slowly and pensively she returned home.

But the conversation of the woman in the church-yard haunted her while waking, and continued to distress her in her dreams that night; and she was resolved to do all she could to relieve the situation of the poor destitute girl and child, in whose fate she might possibly see an anticipation of her own: and as soon as breakfast was over, and Glenmurray was engaged in his studies, she walked out to make the projected inquiries.

The season of the year was uncommonly fine; and the varied scenery visible from the terrace was, at the moment of Adeline's approach to it, glowing with more than common beauty. Adeline stood for some minutes gazing on it in silent delight; when her reverie was interrupted by the sound of boyish merriment, and she saw, at one end of the terrace, some well-dressed boys at play.

> "Alas! regardless of their doom
> The little victims play!"[1]

immediately recurred to her: for, contemplating the probable evils of existence, she was darkly brooding over the imagined fate of her own offspring, should it live to see the light; and the children at their sport, having no care of ills to come, naturally engaged her attention.

But these happy children ceased to interest her, when she saw standing at a distance from the group, and apparently looking at it with an eye of envy, a little boy, even better dressed than the rest; who was sobbing violently, yet ardently* trying to conceal his grief. And while she was watching the young mourner attentively, he suddenly threw himself on a seat; and, taking out his handkerchief, indignantly and impatiently wiped away the tears that would no longer be restrained.

"Poor child!" thought Adeline, seating herself beside him; "and has affliction reached thee so soon!"

The child was beautiful: and his clustering locks seemed to have been combed with so much care; the frill of his shirt was so fine, and had been so very neatly plaited; and his sun-burnt neck and hands were so very very clean, that Adeline was certain he was the darling object of some fond mother's attention. "And yet he is unhappy!" she inwardly exclaimed. "When my fate resembled his, how happy I was!" But from recollections like these she always hastened; and checking the rising sigh, she resolved to enter into conversation with the little boy.

---

1    Thomas Gray, "Ode on a Distant Prospect of Eton College" (1747), 51-52.

"What is the matter?" she cried.—No answer.—"Why are you not playing with the young gentlemen yonder?"

She had touched the right string:—and bursting into tears, he sobbed out, "Because they won't let me."

"No? and why will they not let you?" To this he replied not; but sullenly hung his blushing face on his bosom.

"Perhaps you have made them angry?" gently asked Adeline. "Oh! no, no," cried the boy; "but——" "But what?" Here he turned from her, and with his nail began scratching the arm of the seat.

"Well; this is very strange, and seems very unkind," cried Adeline: "I will speak to them." So saying, she drew near the other children, who had interrupted their play to watch Adeline and their rejected playmate. "What can be the reason," said she, "that you will not let that little boy play with you?" The boys looked down, and said nothing.

"Is he ill-natured?"

"No."

"Does he not play fair?"

"Yes."

"Don't you like him?"

"Yes."

"Then why do you make him unhappy, by not letting him join in your sport?"

"Tell the lady, Jack," cries one; and Jack, the biggest boy of the party, said: "Because he is not a gentleman's son like us, and is only a little bastard."

"Yes," cried one of the other children; "and his mamma is so proud she dresses him finer than we are, for all he is base-born: and our papas and mammas don't think him fit company for us."

They might have gone on for an hour—Adeline could not interrupt them. The cause of the child's affliction was a dagger in her heart; and, while she listened to the now redoubled sobs of the disgraced and proudly afflicted boy, she was driven almost to phrensy: for "Such," she exclaimed, "may one time or other be the pangs of my child, and so to him may the hours of childhood be embittered!"—Again she seated herself by the little mourner—and her tears accompanied his.

"My dear child, you had better go home," said she, struggling with her feelings; "your mother will certainly be glad of your company."

"No, I won't go to her; I don't love her: they say she is a bad woman, and my papa a bad man, because they are not married."

Again Adeline's horrors returned.—"But my dear, they love you, no doubt; and you ought to love them," she replied with effort.

"There, there comes your papa," cried one of the boys; "go and cry to him;—go."

At these words Adeline looked up, and saw an elegant-looking man approaching with a look of anxiety.

"Charles, my dear boy, what has happened?" said he, taking his hand; which the boy sullenly withdrew. "Come home directly," continued his father, "and tell me what is the matter, as we go along." But again snatching his hand away, the proud and deeply wounded child resentfully pushed the shoulder next him forward, whenever his father tried to take his arm, and elbowed him angrily as he went.

Adeline felt the child's action to the bottom of her heart. It was a volume of reproach to the father; and she sighed to think what the parents, if they had hearts, must feel, when the afflicted boy told the cause of his grief. "But, unhappy boy, perhaps my child may live to bless you!" she exclaimed, clasping her hands together: "never, never will I expose my child to the pangs which you have experienced to-day." So saying, she returned instantly to her lodgings; and having just strength left to enter Glenmurray's room, she faintly exclaimed: "For pity's sake, make me your wife to-morrow!" and fell senseless on the floor.

On her recovery she saw Glenmurray pale with agitation, yet with an expression of satisfaction in his countenance, bending over her. "Adeline! my dearest life!"* he whispered as her head lay on his bosom, "blessed be the words you have spoken, whatever be their cause! To-morrow you shall be my wife."

"And then our child will be legitimate, will he not?" she eagerly replied.

"It will."

"Thank God!" cried Adeline, and relapsed into a fainting fit. For it was not decreed that the object of her maternal solicitude should ever be born to reward it. Anxiety and agitation had had a fatal effect on the health of Adeline; and the day after her rencounter on the terrace she brought forth a dead child.[1]

As soon as Adeline, languid and disappointed, was able to leave her room, Glenmurray, whom anxiety during her illness had rendered considerably weaker, urged her to let the marriage ceremony be performed immediately. But with her hopes of being a mother vanished her wishes to become a wife, and all her former reasons against marriage recurred in their full force.

---

1   In the first American edition of 1808 the first volume (of two) ends here. The one-volume 1843 edition (also American) sensibly begins a new chapter at this point (numbered chapter 17 in error). However, in subsequent British editions Opie consistently treats this very long chapter as a single unit.

In vain did Glenmurray entreat her to keep her lately formed resolution: she still attributed his persuasions to generosity, and the heroic resolve of sacrificing his principles, with the consistency of his character, to her supposed good, and it was a point of honour with her to be as generous in return: consequently the subject was again dropped; nor was it likely to be soon renewed; an* anxiety of a more pressing nature disturbed their peace and engrossed their attention. They had been three months at Richmond, and had incurred there a considerable debt; and Glenmurray, not having sufficient money with him to discharge it, drew upon his banker for half the half-year's rents from his estate, which he had just deposited in his hands; when to his unspeakable astonishment he found that the house had stopped payment, and that the principal partner was† gone off with the deposits!

Scarcely could the firm mind of Glenmurray support itself under this‡ stroke. He looked forward to the certainty of passing the little remainder of his life not only in pain but in poverty, and of seeing increase as fast as his wants the difficulty of supplying them; while the woman of his heart bent in increased agony over his restless couch; for he well knew that to raise money on his estate, or to anticipate the next half-year's rents, was impossible, as he had only a life interest in it; and, as he held the fatal letter in his hand, his frame shook with agitation.

"I could not have believed," cried Adeline, "that the loss of any sum of money could have so violently affected you."

"Not the loss of my all! my support during the tedious scenes of illness!"

"Your all!" faltered out Adeline; and when she heard the true state of the case she found her agitation equalled that of Glenmurray, and in hopeless anguish she leaned on the table beside him.

"What is to be done," said she, "till the next half-year's rents become due? Where can we procure money?"

"Till the next half-year's rents become due!" replied he, looking at her mournfully: "I shall not be distressed for money then."

"No?" answered Adeline (not understanding him): "our expenses have never yet been more than that sum can supply."

Glenmurray looked at her, and, seeing how unconscious she was of the certainty of the evil that awaited her, had not the courage to distress her by explaining his meaning; and she went on to ask him what steps he meant to take to raise money.

"My only resource," said he, "is dunning[1] a near relation of mine who owes me three hundred pounds: he is now, I believe, able to pay it. He is in Holland, indeed, at present; but he is daily expected in England, and

---

1  Importuning for debt.

will come to see me here.—I have named him to you before, I believe. His name is Berrendale."

It was then agreed that Glenmurray should write to Mr. Berrendale immediately; and that, to prevent the necessity of incurring a further debt for present provisions and necessaries, some of their books and linen should be sold:—but week after week elapsed, and no letter was received from Mr. Berrendale.

Glenmurray grew rapidly worse;—and their landlord was clamorous for his rent;—advice from London also became necessary to quiet Adeline's mind,—though Glenmurray knew that he was past cure: and after she had paid a small sum to quiet the demands of the landlord for a while, she had scarcely enough left to pay a physician: however, she sent for one, recommended by Dr. Norberry, and by selling a writing-desk inlaid with silver, which she valued because it was the gift of her father, she raised money sufficient for the occasion.

Dr. —— arrived, but not to speak peace to the mind of Adeline. She saw, though he did not absolutely say so, that all chance of Glenmurray's recovery was over: and though with the sanguine feelings of nineteen she could "hope though hope were lost,"[1] when she watched Dr. ——'s countenance as he turned from the bed-side of Glenmurray, she felt the coldness of despair thrill through her frame; and, scarcely able to stand, she followed him into the next room, and awaited his orders with a sort of desperate tranquillity.

After prescribing alleviations of the ill beyond his power to cure, Dr. —— added that terrible confirmation of the fears of anxious affection.— "Let him have whatever he likes; nothing can hurt him now; and all your endeavours must be to make the remaining hours of his existence as comfortable as you can, by every indulgence possible: and indeed, my dear madam," he continued, "you must be prepared for the trial that awaits you."

"Prepared! did you say?" cried Adeline in the broken voice of tearless and almost phrensied sorrow.—"O God! if he must die, in mercy let me die with him. If I have sinned," (here she fell on her knees,) "surely, surely the agony of this moment is atonement sufficient."

Dr. ——, greatly affected, raised her from the ground, and conjured her for the sake of Glenmurray, and that she might not make his last hours miserable, to bear her trial with more fortitude.

"And can you talk of his 'last hours,' and yet expect me to be composed?—O sir! say but that there is one little little gleam of hope for me, and I will be calm."

---

1   Anna Laetitia Barbauld, "Song 1" ["Come here, Fond Youth"], *Poems* (1773).

"Well," replied Dr. ——, "I* *may* be mistaken; Mr. Glenmurray is young, and—and—" here his voice faltered, and he was unable to proceed; for the expression of Adeline's countenance, changing as it instantly did from misery to joy,—joy of which he knew the fallacy,—while her eyes were intently fixed on him, was too much for a man of any feeling to support; and when she pressed his hand in the convulsive emotions of her gratitude, he was forced to turn away his head to conceal the starting tear.

"Well, I may be mistaken—Mr. Glenmurray is young," Adeline repeated again and again, as his carriage drove off; and she flew to Glenmurray's bed-side to impart to him the satisfaction which he rejoiced to see her feel, but in which he could not share.

Her recovered security did not, however, last long: the change in Glenmurray grew every day more visible; and to increase her distress, they were forced, to avoid disagreeable altercations, to give the landlord a draft on Mr. Berrendale for the sum due to him, and remove to very humble lodgings in a closer part of the town.

Here their misery was a little alleviated by the unexpected receipt of twenty pounds, sent to Glenmurray by a tenant who was in arrears to him, which enabled Adeline to procure Glenmurray every thing that his capricious appetite required; and at his earnest entreaty, in order that she might sometimes venture to leave him, lest her health should suffer, she hired a nurse to assist her in her attendance upon him.

A hasty letter too was at length received from Mr. Berrendale, saying, that he should very soon be in England, and should hasten to Richmond immediately on his landing. The terror of wanting money, therefore, began to subside: but day after day elapsed, and Mr. Berrendale came not; and Adeline, being obliged to deny herself almost necessary sustenance that Glenmurray's appetite might be tempted, and his nurse, by the indulgence of hers, kept in good humour, resolved, presuming on the arrival of Mr. Berrendale, to write to Dr. Norberry and solicit the loan of twenty pounds.

Having done so, she ceased to be alarmed, though she found herself in possession of only three guineas to defray the probable expenses of the ensuing week; and, in somewhat less misery than usual, she, at the earnest entreaty of Glenmurray, set out to take a walk.

Scarcely conscious what she did, she strolled through the town, and seeing some fine grapes at the window of a fruiterer, she went in to ask the price of them, knowing how welcome fruit was to the feverish palate of Glenmurray. While the shopman was weighing the grapes, she saw a pine-apple on the counter, and felt a strong wish to carry it home as a more welcome present; but with unspeakable disappointment she heard that the price of it was two guineas—a sum which she could not think herself justified in expending, in the present state of their finances, even to please Glenmurray, especially as he had not expressed a wish for such an indulgence: besides, he liked grapes; and, as medicine, neither of them could be effectual.

It was fortunate for Adeline's feelings that she had not overheard what the mistress of the shop said to her maid as she left it.

"I should have asked another person only a guinea; but as those sort of women never mind what they give, I asked two, and I dare say she will come back for it."

"I have brought you some grapes," cried Adeline as she entered Glenmurray's chamber, "and I would have brought you a pine-apple, but that it was too dear."

"A pine-apple!" said Glenmurray languidly turning over the grapes, and with a sort of distaste putting one of them in his mouth, "a pine-apple!—I wish you had bought* it with all my heart! I protest that I feel as if I could eat a whole one."

"Well," replied Adeline, "if you would enjoy it so much, you certainly ought to have it."

"But the price, my dear girl!—what was it?"

"Only two guineas," replied Adeline, forcing a smile.

"Two guineas!" exclaimed Glenmurray: "No,—that is too much to give—I will not indulge my appetite at such a rate—but, take away the grapes—I can't eat them."

Adeline, disappointed, removed them from his sight; and, to increase her vexation, Glenmurray was continually talking of pine-apples, and in a† way that showed how strongly his diseased appetite wished to enjoy the gratification of eating one. At last, unable to bear to see him struggling with an ungratified wish, she told him that she believed they could afford to buy the pine-apple, as she had written to borrow some money of Dr. Norberry, to be paid as soon as Mr. Berrendale arrived. In a moment the dull eye of Glenmurray lighted up with expectation; and he, who in health was remarkable for self-denial and temperance, scrupled not, overcome by the influence of the fever which consumed him, to gratify his palate at a rate the most extravagant.

Adeline sighed as she contemplated this change effected by illness; and, promising to be back as soon as possible, she proceeded to a shop to dispose of her lace veil, the only ornament which she had retained; and that not from vanity, but because it concealed from the eye of curiosity the sorrow marked on her countenance. But she knew a piece of muslin would do as well; and for two guineas she sold a veil worth treble the‡ sum; but it was to give a minute's pleasure to Glenmurray, and that was enough for Adeline.

In her way to the fruiterer's she saw a crowd at the door of a mean-looking house, and in the midst of it she beheld a mulatto[1] woman, the picture of sickness and despair, supporting a young man who seemed ready to faint every moment, but whom a rough-featured man, regardless of his weakness, was trying to force from the grasp of the unhappy woman; while a mulatto boy, known in Richmond by the name of the Tawny Boy, to whom Adeline had often given halfpence in her walks, was crying bitterly, and hiding his face in the poor woman's apron.

Adeline immediately pressed forward to inquire into the cause of a distress only too congenial to her feelings; and as she did so, the tawny boy looked up, and, knowing her immediately, ran eagerly forward to meet her, seeming, though he did not speak, to associate with her presence an idea of certain relief.

"Oh! it is only a poor man," replied an old woman in answer to Adeline's inquiries, "who can't pay his debts,—and so they are dragging him to prison—that's all." "They are dragging him to his death too," cried a younger woman in a gentle accent; "for he is only just recovering from a bad fever: and if he goes to jail the bad air will certainly kill him, poor soul!"

"Is that his wife?" said Adeline. "Yes, and my mammy," said the tawny boy, looking up in her face, "and she so ill and sorry."

"Yes, unhappy creatures," replied her informant, "and they have known great trouble; and now, just as they had got a little money together, William fell ill, and in doctor's stuff Savanna[2] (that's the mulatto's name) has spent all the money she had earned, as well as her husband's; and now she is ill herself, and I am sure William's going to jail will kill her. And a hard-hearted, wicked wretch Mr. Davis is, to arrest him—that he is—not but what it is his due, I cannot say but it is—but, poor souls! he'll die, and she'll die, and then what will become of their poor little boy?"

The tawny boy all this time was standing, crying, by Adeline's side, and had twisted his fingers in her gown, while her heart sympathized most painfully in the anguish of the mulatto woman. "What is the amount of the sum for which he is taken up?" said Adeline.

"Oh! trifling: but Mr. Davis owes him a grudge, and so will not wait any longer. It is in all only six* pounds; and he says if they will pay half†‡ he will wait for the rest; but then he knows they could as well pay all as half."‡

---

1   From Spanish *mulato*, "person of mixed race." Cf. Appendix G2.

2   Probably named after the black servant who had accompanied Opie's orphaned mother to England from India in 1749. See Introduction, 10.

Adeline, shocked at the knowledge of a distress which she was not able to remove, was turning away as the woman said this, when she felt that the little boy pulled her gown gently, as if appealing to her generosity; while a surly-looking man, who was the creditor himself, forcing a passage through the crowd, said, "Why, bring him along, and have done with it; here is a fuss to make indeed about that idle dog, and that ugly black b——h!"*

Adeline till then had not recollected that she was a mulatto; and this speech, reflecting so brutally on her colour,—a circumstance which made her an object of greater interest to Adeline,—urged her to step forward to their joint relief with an almost irresistible impulse; especially when another man reproached the fellow for his brutality, and added, that he knew them both to be hard-working, deserving persons. But to disappoint Glenmurray of his promised pleasure was impossible; and having put sixpence in the tawny boy's hand, she was hastening to the fruiterer's, when the crowd, who were following William and the mulatto to the jail, whither the bailiffs were dragging rather than leading him, fell back to give air to the poor man, who had fainted on Savanna's shoulder, and seemed on the point of expiring—while she, with an expression of fixed despair, was gazing on his wan cheek.

Adeline thought on Glenmurray's danger, and shuddered as she beheld the scene; she felt it but a too probable anticipation of the one in which she might soon be an actor.

At this moment a man observed, "If he goes to prison he will not live two days, that every one may see"; and the mulatto uttered a shriek of agony.

Adeline felt it to her very soul; and, rushing forward, "Sir, sir," she exclaimed to the unfeeling creditor, "if I were to give you a guinea now, and promise you two more a fortnight hence, would you release this poor man for the present?"

"No: I must have three guineas this moment," replied he. Adeline sighed, and withdrew her hand from her pocket. "But were Glenmurray here, he would give up his own† indulgence, I am sure, to save the lives of, probably, two fellow-creatures," thought Adeline; "and he would not forgive me if I were to sacrifice such an opportunity to the sole gratification of his palate."—But then again, Glenmurray eagerly expecting her with the promised treat, so gratifying to the feverish taste of sickness, seemed to appear before her, and she turned away: but the eyes of the mulatto, who had heard her words, and had hung on them breathless with expectation, followed her with a look of such sad reproach for the disappointment which she had occasioned her, and the little boy looked up so wistfully in her face, crying, "Poor fader, and poor mammy!" that Adeline could not withstand the force of the appeal; but almost exclaiming "Glenmurray would upbraid me if I did not act thus," she gave the creditor the three guineas, paid the bailiffs their demand, and then made her way through the crowd, who respectfully drew back to give her room to pass, saying, "God bless you, lady! God bless you!"

But William was too ill, and Savanna felt too much to speak; and the surly creditor said, sneeringly, "If I had been you, I would, at least, have thanked the lady." This reproach restored Savanna to the use of speech; and (but with a violent effort) she uttered in a hoarse and broken voice, "*I* tank her! God tank her! I never can": and Adeline, kindly pressing her hand, hurried away from her in silence, though scarcely able to refrain exclaiming, "You know not the sacrifice which you have cost me!" The tawny boy still followed her, as loth to leave her. "God bless you, my dear!" said she kindly to him: "there, go to your mother, and be good to her." His dark face glowed as she spoke to him, and holding up his chin, "Tiss me!" cried he, "poor tawny boy love you!" She did so; and then, reluctantly, he left her, nodding his head, and saying "Dood bye" till he was out of sight.

With him, and with the display of his grateful joy, vanished all that could give Adeline resolution to bear her own reflections at the idea of returning home, and of the trial that awaited her. In vain did she now try to believe that Glenmurray would applaud what she had done.—He was now the slave of disease, nor was it likely that even his self-denial and principled benevolence could endure with patience so cruel a disappointment—and from the woman whom he loved too!—and to whom the indulgence of his slightest wishes ought to have been the first object.

"What shall I do?" cried she: "what will he say?—No doubt he is impatiently expecting me; and, in his weak state, disappointment may——" Here, unable to bear her apprehensions, she wrung her hands in agony; and when she arrived in sight of her lodgings she dared not look up, lest she should see Glenmurray at the window watching for her return. Slowly and fearfully did she open the door; and the first sound she heard was Glenmurray's voice from the door of his room, saying, "So, you are come at last!—I have been so impatient!" And indeed he had risen and dressed himself, that he might enjoy his treat more than he could do in a sick-bed.

"How can I bear to look him in the face!" thought Adeline, lingering on the stairs.

"Adeline, my love! why do you make me wait so long?" cried Glenmurray. "Here are knives and plates ready; where is the treat I have been so long expecting?"

Adeline entered the room and threw herself on the first chair, avoiding the sight of Glenmurray, whose countenance, as she hastily glanced her eyes over it, was animated with the expectation of a pleasure which he was not to enjoy. "I have not brought the pine-apple," she faintly articulated. "No!" replied Glenmurray, "how hard upon me!—the only thing for weeks that I have wished for, or could have eaten with pleasure! I suppose you were so long going that it was disposed of before you got there?"

"No," replied Adeline, struggling with her tears at this first instance of pettishness in Glenmurray.

"Pardon me the supposition," replied Glenmurray, recovering himself: "more likely you met some dun on the road, and so the two guineas were disposed of another way—If so, I can't blame you. What say you? Am I right?"

"No." "Then how was it?" gravely asked Glenmurray. "You must have had a very powerful and* sufficient reason, to induce you to disappoint a poor invalid of the indulgence which you had yourself excited him to wish for."

"This is terrible, indeed!" thought Adeline, "and never was I so tempted to tell a falsehood."

"Still silent! You are very unkind, miss Mowbray," said Glenmurray; "I see that I have tired even *you* out."

These words, by the agony which they excited, restored to Adeline all her resolution. She ran to Glenmurray; she clasped his burning hands in hers; and as succinctly as possible she related what had passed. When she had finished, Glenmurray was silent; the fretfulness of disease prompted him to say, "So then, to the relief of strangers you sacrificed the gratification of the man whom you love, and deprived him of the only pleasure he may live to enjoy!" But the habitual sweetness and generosity of his temper struggled, and struggled effectually, with his malady; and while Adeline, pale and trembling, awaited her sentence, he caught her suddenly to his bosom, and held her there a few moments in silence.

"Then you forgive me?" faltered out Adeline.

"Forgive you! I love and admire you more than ever! I know your heart, Adeline; and I am convinced that depriving yourself of the delight of giving me the promised treat, in order to do a benevolent action, was an effort of virtue of the highest order; and never, I trust, have you known, or will you know again, such bitter feelings as you this moment experienced."

Adeline, gratified by his generous kindness, and charmed with his praise, could only weep her thanks. "And now," said Glenmurray, laughing, "you may bring back the grapes—I am not like Sterne's dear Jenny; if I cannot get pine-apple, I will not insist on eating crab."[1]

---

1   Laurence Sterne's Jenny selects cheap cloth when she cannot get expensive silk (*Tristram Shandy*, vol. 1, chap. 18). The pineapple and crab may come from Thomas Hol-

The grapes were brought; but in vain did he try to eat them. At this time, however, he did not send them away without highly commending their flavour, and wishing that he dared give way to his inclinations, and feast upon them.

"O God of mercy!" cried Adeline, bursting into an agony of grief as she reached her own apartment, and throwing herself on her knees by the bed-side, "Must that benevolent being be taken from me for ever, and must I, must I survive him!"

She continued for some minutes in this attitude, and with her heart devoutly raised to heaven; till every feeling yielded to resignation, and she arose calm, if not contented; when, on turning round, she saw Glenmurray leaning against the door, and gazing on her.

"Sweet enthusiast!" cried he smiling: "so, thus, when you are distressed, you seek consolation."

"I do," she replied: "Sceptic, wouldst thou wish to deprive me of it?"

"No, by heaven!" warmly exclaimed Glenmurray; and the evening passed more cheerfully than usual.

The next post brought a letter not from Dr. Norberry, but from his wife; it was as follows, and contained three pound-notes:

"Mrs. Norberry's compliments to miss Mowbray, having opened her letter, poor Dr. Norberry being dangerously ill of a fever, find her distress; of which shall not inform the Dr., as he feel* so much for his friend's misfortunes, specially when brought on by misconduct. But, out of respect for your mother, who is a good sort of woman, though rather particular, as all learned ladies are, have sent three pound-notes; the miss Norberrys giving one a-piece, not to lend, but a gift, and they join Mrs. Norberry in hoping miss Mowbray will soon see the error of her ways; and, if so be, no doubt Dr. Norberry will use his interest to get her into the Magdalen."[1]

This curious epistle would have excited in Glenmurray and Adeline no other feelings save those of contempt, but for the information it contained of the doctor's being dangerously ill; and, in fear for the worthy husband, they forgot the impertinence of the wife and daughters.

---

croft's *Duplicity: A Comedy* (1781), where Sir Hornet "began to fancy [his] fine-flavoured pineapple [Clara] a crab."

1 Abbreviation of Magdalen house, an institution for reformed prostitutes; such institutions were named for Mary Magdalen, traditionally identified with the woman taken in adultery of Luke 8.37.

The next day, fortunately, Mr. Berrendale arrived, and with him the 300*l*.* Consequently, all Glenmurray's debts were discharged, better lodgings procured, and the three pound notes returned in a blank cover to Mrs. Norberry. Charles Berrendale was first cousin to Glenmurray, and so like him in face, that they were, at first, mistaken for brothers: but to a physiognomist[1] they must always have been unlike; as Glenmurray was remarkable for the character and expression of his countenance, and Berrendale for the extreme beauty of his features and complexion. Glenmurray was pale and thin, and his eyes and hair dark. Berrendale's eyes were of a light blue; and though his eye-lashes were black, his hair was of a rich auburn: Glenmurray was thin and muscular; Berrendale, round and corpulent: still they were alike; and it was not ill observed of them, that Berrendale was Glenmurray in good health.

But Berrendale could not be flattered by the resemblance, as his face and person were so truly what is called handsome, that, partial as our sex is said to be to beauty, any woman would have been excused for falling in love with him. Whether his mind was equal to his person we shall show hereafter.

The meeting between Berrendale and Glenmurray was affectionate on both sides; but Berrendale could scarcely hide the pain he felt on seeing the situation of Glenmurray, whose virtues he had always loved, whose talents he had always respected, and to whose active friendship towards himself he owed eternal gratitude.

But he soon learnt to think Glenmurray, in one respect, an object of envy, when he beheld the constant, skilful, and tender attentions of his nurse, and saw in that nurse every gift of heart, mind, and person, which could make a woman amiable.

Berrendale had heard that his eccentric cousin was living with a girl as odd as himself; who thought herself a genius, and pretended to universal knowledge: great then was his astonishment to find this imagined pedant, and pretender, not only an adept in every useful and feminine pursuit, but modest in her demeanour, and gentle in her manners: little did he expect to see her capable of serving the table of Glenmurray with dishes made by herself, not only tempting to the now craving appetite of the invalid but to the palate of an epicure,—while all his wants were anticipated by her anxious attention, and many of the sufferings of sickness alleviated by her inventive care.

Adeline, mean while, was agreeably surprised to see the good effect produced on Glenmurray's spirits, and even his health, by the arrival of

---

1    Someone who reads faces or other physical features to discern character.

his cousin; and her manner became even affectionate to Berrendale, from gratitude for the change which his presence seemed to have occasioned.

Adeline had now a companion in her occasional walks;—Glenmurray insisted on her walking, and insisted on Berrendale's accompanying her. In these tête-à-têtes Adeline unburthened her heart, by telling Berrendale of the agony she felt at the idea of losing Glenmurray; and while drowned in tears she leaned on his arm, she unconsciously suffered him to press the hand that leaned against him; nor would she have felt it a freedom to be reproved, had she been conscious that he did so. But these trifling indulgences were fewel* to the flame that she had kindled in the heart of Berrendale; a flame which he saw no guilt in indulging, as he looked on Glenmurray's death as certain, and Adeline would then be free.

But though Adeline was perfectly unconscious of his attachment, Glenmurray had seen it even before Berrendale himself discovered it; and he only waited a favourable opportunity to make the discovery known to the parties. All he had as yet ventured to say was, "Charles, my Adeline is an excellent nurse!—You would like such an one during your fits of the gout"; and Berrendale had blushed deeply while he assented to Glenmurray's remarks, because he was conscious that, while enumerating Adeline's perfections, he had figured her to himself warming his flannels, and leaning tenderly over his gouty couch.

One day, while Adeline was reading to Glenmurray, and Berrendale was attending not to what she read, but to the beauty of her mouth while reading, the nurse came in, and said that "a mulatto woman wished to speak to miss Mowbray."

"Show her up," immediately cried Glenmurray; "and if her little boy is with her, let him come too."

In vain did Adeline expostulate—Glenmurray wished to enjoy the mulatto's expressions of gratitude; and, in spite of all she could say, the mother and child were introduced.

"So!" cried the mulatto, (whose looks were so improved that Adeline scarcely knew her again,) "So! me find you at last; and, please God! we not soon part more." As she said this, she pressed the hem of Adeline's gown to her lips with fervent emotion.

"Not part from her again!" cried Glenmurray: "What do you mean, my good woman?"

"Oh! when she gave tree guinea for me, metought† she mus be rich lady, but now dey say she be poor, and me mus work for her."

"And who told you I was poor?"

"Dat cross man where you live once—he say you could not pay him, and you go away—and he tell me dat your love be ill; and me so sorry, yet so glad! for my love be well aden, and he have got‡ good employ; and now I can come and serve you, and nurse dis poor gentleman, and all for noting* but my meat and drink; and I know dat great fat nurse have gold wages, and eat and drink fat beside,—I knowd her well."

All this was uttered with great volubility, and in a tone between laughing and crying.

"Well, Adeline," said Glenmurray when she had ended, "you did not throw away your kindness on an unworthy and ungrateful object; so I am quite reconciled to the loss of the pine-apple; and I will tell your honest friend here the story,—to show her, as she has a tender heart herself, the greatness of the sacrifice you made for her sake."

Adeline begged him to desist; but he went on; and the mulatto could not keep herself quiet on her† chair while he related the circumstance.

"And did she do dat to save me?" she passionately exclaimed; "Angel woman! I should have let poor man go to prison, before disappoint my William!"

"And did you forgive her immediately?" said Berrendale.

"Yes, certainly."

"Well, that was heroic too," returned he.

"And no one but Glenmurray would have been so heroic, I believe," said Adeline.

"But, lady, you break my heart," cried the mulatto, "if you not take my service. My William and me, too poor to live togedder of some year perhaps. Here, child, tawny boy, down on knees, and vow wid me to be faithful and grateful to this our mistress, till our last day; and never to forsake her in sickness or in sorrow! I swear dis to my great God:—and now say dat after me." She then clasped the little boy's hands, bade him raise his eyes to heaven, and made him repeat what she had said, ending it with "I swear dis, to my great God."

There was such an affecting solemnity in this action, and in the mulatto such a determined enthusiasm of manner incapable of being controled, that Adeline, Glenmurray, and Berrendale observed what passed in respectful silence: and when it was over, Glenmurray said, in a voice of emotion, "I think, Adeline, we must accept this good creature's offer; and as nurse grows lazy and saucy, we had better part with her: and as for your young knight there," (the tawny boy had by this time nestled himself close to Adeline, who, with no small emotion, was playing with his woolly curls,) "we must send him to school; for, my good woman, we are not so poor as you imagine."

"God be thanked!" cried the mulatto.

"But what is your name?"

"I was christened Savanna," replied she.

"Then, good Savanna," cried Adeline, "I hope we shall both have reason to bless the day when first we met; and to-morrow you shall come home to us." Savanna, on hearing this, almost screamed with joy, and as she took her leave Berrendale slipped a guinea into her hand: the tawny boy meanwhile slowly followed his mother, as if unwilling to leave Adeline, even though she gave him halfpence to spend in cakes: but on being told that she would let him come again the next day, he tripped gaily down after Savanna.

The quiet of the chamber being then restored, Glenmurray fell into a calm slumber; Adeline took up her work; and Berrendale, pretending to read, continued to feed his passion by gazing on the unconscious Adeline.

While they were thus engaged, Glenmurray, unobserved, awoke; and he soon guessed how Berrendale's eyes were employed, as the book which he held in his hand was upside down; and through the fingers of the hand which he held before his face, he saw his looks fixed on Adeline.

The moment was a favourable one for Glenmurray's purpose: and just as he raised himself from his pillow, Adeline had discovered the earnest gaze of Berrendale; and a suspicion of the truth that instant darting across her mind, disconcerted and blushing, she had cast her eyes on the ground.

"That is an interesting study which you are engaged in, Charles," cried Glenmurray smiling.

Berrendale started; and, deeply blushing, faltered out, "Yes."

Adeline looked at Glenmurray, and, seeing a very arch and meaning expression on his countenance, suspected that he had made the same discovery as herself: yet, if so, she wondered at his looking so pleasantly on Berrendale as he spoke.

"It is a book, Charles," continued Glenmurray, "which the more you study the more you will admire; and I wish to give you a clue to understand some passages in it better than you can now do."

This speech deceived Adeline, and made her suppose that Glenmurray really alluded to the book which lay before Berrendale: but it convinced *him* that Glenmurray spoke metaphorically; and as his manner was kind, it also made him think that he saw and did not disapprove his attachment.

For a few minutes, each of them being engrossed in different contemplations, there was a complete silence; but Glenmurray interrupted it by saying, "My dear Adeline, it is your hour for walking; but, as I am not disposed to sleep again, will you forgive me if I keep your walking companion to myself to-day?—I wish to converse with him alone."

"Oh! most cheerfully," she replied with quickness: "you know l love a solitary ramble of all things."

"Not very flattering that to my cousin," observed Glenmurray.

"I did not wish to flatter him," said Adeline gravely; and Berrendale, fluttered at the idea of the coming conversation with Glenmurray, and mortified by Adeline's words and manner, turned to the window to conceal his emotion.

Adeline, then, with more than usual tenderness, conjured Glenmurray not to talk too much, nor do any thing to destroy the hopes on which her only chance of happiness depended, viz. the now possible chance of his recovery, and then set out for her walk; while, with a restraint and coldness which she could not conquer, she bade Berrendale farewell for the present.

The walk was long, and her thoughts perturbed:—"What could Glenmurray want to say to Mr. Berrendale?"—"Why did Mr. Berrendale sit with his eyes so intently and clandestinely, as it were, fixed on me?" were thoughts perpetually recurring to her: and half impatient, and half reluctant, she at length returned to her lodgings.

When she entered the apartment, she saw signs of great emotion in the countenance of both the gentlemen; and in Berrendale's eyes the traces of recent tears. The tone of Glenmurray's voice too, when he addressed her, was even more tender than usual, and Berrendale's attentions more marked, yet more respectful; and Adeline observed that Glenmurray was unusually thoughtful and absent, and that the cough and other symptoms of his complaint were more troublesome than ever.

"I see you have exerted yourself and talked too much during my absence," cried Adeline, "and I will never leave you again for so long a time."

"You never shall," said Glenmurray. "I must leave *you* for so long a time at last, that I will be blessed with the sight of you as long as I can."

Adeline, whose hopes had been considerably revived during the last few days, looked mournfully and reproachfully in his face as he uttered these words.

"It is even so, my dearest girl," continued Glenmurray, "and I say this to guard you against a melancholy surprise:—I wish to prepare you for an event which to me seems unavoidable."

"Prepare me!" exclaimed Adeline wildly. "Can there be any preparation to enable one to bear such a calamity? Absurd idea! However, I shall derive consolation from the severity of the stroke: I feel that I shall not be able to survive it." So saying, her head fell on Glenmurray's pillow; and, for some time, her sorrow almost suspended the consciousness of suffering.

From this state she was aroused by Glenmurray's being attacked with a violent paroxysm of his complaint, and all selfish distress was lost in the consciousness of his sufferings: again he struggled through, and seemed so relieved by the effort, that again Adeline's hopes revived; and she could scarcely return, with temper, Berrendale's "good night," when Glenmurray expressed a wish to rest, because his spirits had not risen in any proportion to hers.

The nurse had been dismissed that afternoon; and Adeline, as Savanna was not to come home till the next morning, was to sit up alone with Glenmurray that night; and, contrary to his usual custom, he did not insist that she should have a companion.

For a few hours his exhausted frame was recruited by a sleep more than usually quiet, and but for a few hours only. He then became restless, and so wakeful and disturbed, that he professed to Adeline an utter inability to sleep, and therefore he wished to pass the rest of the night in serious conversation with her.

Adeline, alarmed at this intention, conjured him not to irritate his complaint by so dangerous an exertion.

"My mind will irritate it more," replied he, "if I refrain from it; for it is burthened, my Adeline, and it longs to throw off its burthen. Now then, ere my senses wander, hear what I wish to communicate to you, and interrupt me as little as possible."

Adeline, oppressed and awed beyond measure at the unusual solemnity of his manner, made no answer; but, leaning her cheek on his hand, awaited his communication in silence.

"I think," said Glenmurray, "I shall begin with telling you Berrendale's history: it is proper that you should know all that concerns him."

Adeline, raising her head, replied hastily,—"Not to satisfy any curiosity of mine; for I feel none, I assure you."

"Well then," returned Glenmurray, sighing, "to please me, be it.—Berrendale is the son of my mother's sister, by a merchant in* the neighbourhood of the 'Change,[1] who hurt the family pride so much by marrying a tradesman, that I am the only one of the clan who has noticed her since. He ran away, about four years ago, with the only child of a rich West Indian from a boarding-school. The consequence was, that her father renounced her; but, when, three years ago, she died in giving birth to a son, the unhappy parent repented of his displeasure, and offered to allow Berrendale, who from the bankruptcy and sudden death of both his parents had been left destitute, an annuity of 300*l.* for life, provided he would send the child over to Jamaica, and allow him to have all the care of his education. To this Berrendale consented."

"Reluctantly, I hope," said Adeline, "and merely out of pity for the feelings of the childless father."

"I hope so too," continued Glenmurray; "for I do not think the chance of inheriting all his grandfather's property a sufficient reason to lead him to give up to another, and in a foreign land too, the society and education of his child: but, whatever were his reasons, Berrendale acceded to the request, and the infant was sent to Jamaica; and ever since the 300*l.* has been regularly remitted to him: besides that, he has recovered two thousand and odd hundred pounds from the wreck of his father's property;

---

1   The Stock Exchange, in the City of London: Berrendale, unlike Glenmurray and Adeline (at least on her father's side), belongs to a mercantile family.

and with œconomy, and had he a good wife to manage his affairs for him, Berrendale might live very comfortably."

"My dear Glenmurray," cried Adeline impatiently, "what is this to me? and why do you weary yourself to tell me particulars so little interesting to me?"

Glenmurray bade her have patience, and continued thus: "And now, Adeline," (here his voice evidently faltered) "I must open my whole heart to you, and confess that the idea of leaving you friendless, unprotected, and poor, your reputation injured, and your peace of mind destroyed, is more than I am able to bear, and will give me, in my last moments, the torments of the damned." Here a violent burst of tears interrupted him; and Adeline, overcome with emotion and surprise at the sight of the agitation which his own sufferings could never occasion in him, hung over him in speechless woe.

"Besides," continued Glenmurray, recovering himself a little, "I—O Adeline!" seizing her cold hand, "can you forgive me for having been the means of blasting all your fair fame and prospects in life?"

"For the sake of justice, if not of mercy," exclaimed Adeline, "forbear thus cruelly to accuse yourself. You know that from my own free, unbiassed choice I gave myself to you, and in compliance with my own principles."

"But who taught you those principles?—who led you to a train of reasoning, so alluring in theory, so pernicious in practice? Had not I, with the heedless vanity of youth, given to the world the crude conceptions of four-and-twenty, you might at this moment have been the idol of a respectable society; and I, equally respected, have been the husband of your heart; while happiness would perhaps have kept that* fatal disease at bay, of which anxiety has facilitated the approach."[1]

He was going on: but Adeline, who had till now struggled successfully with her feelings, wound up almost to phrensy at the possibility that anxiety had shortened Glenmurray's life, gave way to a violent paroxysm of sorrow, which, for a while, deprived her of consciousness; and when she recovered she found Berrendale bending over her, while her head lay on Glenmurray's pillow.

The sight of Berrendale in a moment roused her to exertion;—his look was so full of anxious tenderness, and she was at that moment so ill disposed to regard it with complacency, that she eagerly declared she was quite recovered, and begged Mr. Berrendale would return to bed; and Glenmurray seconding her request, with a deep sigh he departed.

"Poor fellow!" said Glenmurray, "I wish you had seen his anxiety during your illness!"

---

1    Cf. 21, n. 1.

"I am glad I did *not*," replied Adeline: "but, how can you persist in talking to me of any other person's anxiety, when I am tortured with yours? Your conversation of to-night has made me even more miserable then[*] I was before. By what strange fatality do you blame yourself for the conduct worthy of admiration?—for giving to the world, as soon as produced, opinions which were calculated to enlighten it?"

"But," replied Glenmurray, "as those opinions militated against the experience and custom of ages, ought I not to have paused before I published, and kept them back till they had received the sanction of my maturer judgement?"

"And does your maturer judgement condemn them?"

"Four years cannot have added much to the maturity of my judgment," replied Glenmurray: "but I will own that some of my opinions are changed; and that, though I believe those which are unchanged are right in theory, I think, as the mass of society could never at[†] *once* adopt them, they had better remain unacted upon, than that a few lonely individuals should expose themselves to certain distress, by making them the rules of their conduct. You, for instance, you, my Adeline, what misery—!" Here his voice again faltered, and emotion impeded his utterance.

"Live—do but live," exclaimed Adeline passionately, "and I can know of misery but the name."

"But I cannot live, I cannot live," replied Glenmurray, "and the sooner I die the better;—for thus to waste your youth and health in the dreadful solitude of a sick-room is insupportable to me."

"O Glenmurray!" replied Adeline, fondly throwing herself on his neck, "could you but live free from any violent pain, and were neither you nor I ever to leave this room again, believe me, I should not have a wish beyond it. To see you, to hear you, to prove to you how much I love you, would, indeed it would, be happiness sufficient for me!" After this burst of true and heartfelt tenderness, there was a pause of some moments: Glenmurray felt too much to speak, and Adeline was sobbing on his pillow. At length she pathetically again exclaimed, "Live; only live! and I am blest!"

"But I *cannot* live, I *cannot* live," again replied Glenmurray; "and when I die, what will become of you?"

"I care not," cried Adeline: "if I lose you, may the same grave receive us!"

"But it *will* not, my dearest girl;[‡]—grief does not kill; and, entailed as my estate is,[1] I have nothing to leave you: and though richly qualified to

---

1  Entail is a fixed rule of inheritance, preventing the current owner of a landed estate from leaving his property as he might wish and often excluding women from inheriting.

undertake the care of children, in order to maintain yourself, your unfortunate connection, and singular opinions, will be an eternal bar to your being so employed. O Adeline! these cutting fears, these dreadful reflections, are indeed the bitterness of death: but there is one way of alleviating my pangs."

"Name it," replied Adeline with quickness.

"But you must promise then to hear me with patience.—Had I been able to live through my illness, I should have conjured you to let me endeavour to restore you to your place in society, and consequently to your usefulness, by making you my wife: and young, and I may add innocent and virtuous, as you are, I doubt not but the world would at length have received you into its favour again."

"But you must, you will, you shall live," interrupted Adeline, "and I shall be your happy wife."

"Not *mine*," replied Glenmurray, laying an emphasis on the last word.

Adeline started, and, fixing her eyes wildly on his, demanded what he meant.

"I mean," replied he, "to prevail on you to make my last moments happy, by promising, some time hence, to give yourself a tender, a respectable, and a legal protector."

"O Glenmurray!" exclaimed Adeline, "and can you insult my tenderness for you with such a proposal? If I can even survive you, do you think that I can bear to give you a successor in my affection? or, how can you bear to imagine that I shall?"

"Because my love for you is without selfishness, and I wish you to be happy even though another makes you so. The lover, or the husband, who wishes the woman of his affection to form no second attachment, is, in my opinion, a selfish, contemptible being. Perhaps I do not expect that you will ever feel, for another man, an attachment like that which has subsisted between us—the first affection of young and impassioned hearts; but I am sure that you may again feel love enough to make yourself and the man of your choice perfectly happy; and I hope and trust that you will be so."

"And forget you, I suppose?" interrupted Adeline reproachfully.

"Not so: I would have you remember me always, but with a chastized and even a pleasing sorrow; nay, I would wish you to imagine me a sort of guardian spirit, watching your actions, and enjoying your happiness."

"I have *listened* to you," cried Adeline in a tone of suppressed anguish, "and, I trust, with tolerable patience: there is one thing yet for me to learn—the *name* of the object whom you wish me to marry, for I suppose *he* is found."

"He is," returned Glenmurray. "Berrendale loves you; and he it is whom I wish you to choose."

"I thought so," exclaimed Adeline, rising and traversing the room hastily, and wringing her hands.

"But wherefore does his name," said Glenmurray, "excite such angry emotion? Perhaps self-love makes me recommend him," continued he, forcing a smile, "as he is reckoned like me, and I thought that likeness might make him more agreeable to you."

"Only the more odious," impatiently interrupted Adeline. "To look like you, and not *be* you, Oh! insupportable idea!" she exclaimed, throwing herself on Glenmurray's pillow, and pressing his burning temples to her cold cheek.

"Adeline," said Glenmurray solemnly, "this is, perhaps, the last moment of confidential and uninterrupted intercourse that we shall ever have together"; Adeline started, but spoke not; "allow me, therefore, to tell you it is my *dying request*, that you would endeavour to dispose your mind in favour of Berrendale, and to become in time his wife. Circumstanced as you are, your only chance for happiness is becoming a wife: but it is too certain that few men worthy of you, in the most essential points, will be likely to marry you after your connection with me."

"Strange prejudice!" cried Adeline, "to consider as my disgrace, what I deem my glory!"

Glenmurray continued thus: "Berrendale himself has a great deal of the old school about him, but I have convinced him that you are not to be classed with the frail of your sex; and that you are one of the purest as well as loveliest of human beings."

"And did he want to be convinced of this?" cried Adeline indignantly; "and *yet* you advise me to marry him?"

"My dearest love," replied Glenmurray, "in all cases the most we can expect is, to choose the best *possible* means of happiness. Berrendale is not perfect; but I am convinced that you would commit a fatal error in not making him your husband; and when I tell you it is my *dying request* that you should do so—"

"If you wish me to retain my senses," exclaimed Adeline, "repeat that dreadful phrase no more."

"I will not say any more at all now," faintly observed Glenmurray, "for I am exhausted:—still, as morning begins to dawn, I should like to sit up in my bed, and gaze on it, perhaps for—" Here Adeline put her hand to his mouth: Glenmurray kissed it, sighed, and did not finish the sentence. She then opened the shutters to let in the rising splendor of day, and, turning round towards Glenmurray, almost shrieked with terror at seeing the visible alteration a night had made in his appearance; while the yellow rays of the dawn played on his sallow cheek, and his dark curls, once crisped and glossy, hung faint and moist on his beating temples.

"It is strange, Adeline," said Glenmurray (but with great effort), "that, even in my situation, the sight of morning, and the revival as it were of nature, seems to invigorate my whole frame. I long to breathe the freshness of its breeze also."

Adeline, conscious for the first time that all hope was over, opened the window, and felt even her sick soul and languid frame revived by the chill but refreshing breeze. To Glenmurray it imparted a feeling of physical pleasure, to which he had long been a stranger: "I breathe freely," he exclaimed, "I feel alive again!"—and, strange as it may seem, Adeline's hopes began to revive also.—"I feel as if I could sleep now," said Glenmurray, "the feverish restlessness seems abated; but, lest my dreams be disturbed, promise me, ere I lie down again, that you will behave kindly to Berrendale."

"Impossible! The only tie that bound me to him is broken:—I thought he sincerely sympathized with me in my wishes for your recovery; but now that, as he loves me, his wishes must be in direct opposition to mine,—I cannot, indeed I cannot, endure the sight of him."

Glenmurray could not reply to this natural observation: he knew that, in a similar situation, his feelings would have been like Adeline's; and, pressing her hand with all the little strength left him, he said "Poor Berrendale!" and tried to compose himself to sleep; while Adeline, lost in sad contemplation, threw herself in a chair by his bed-side, and anxiously awaited the event of his re-awaking.

But it was not long before Adeline herself, exhausted both in body and mind, fell into a deep sleep; and it was mid-day before she awoke: for no careless, heavy-treading, and hired nurse now watched the slumbers of the unhappy lovers; but the mulatto, stepping light as air, and afraid even of breathing lest she should disturb their repose, had assumed her station at the bed-side, and taken every precaution lest any noise should awake them. Hers was the service of the heart; and there is none like it.

At twelve o'clock Adeline awoke; and her first glance met the dark eyes of Savanna kindly fixed upon her. Adeline started, not immediately recollecting who it could be; but in a moment the idea of the mulatto, and of the service which she had rendered her, recurred to her mind, and diffused a sensation of pleasure through her frame. "There is a being whom I have served," said Adeline to herself, and, extending her hand to Savanna, she started from her seat, invigorated by the thought: but she felt depressed again by the consciousness that she, who had been able to impart so much joy and help to another, was herself a wretch for ever; and in a moment her eyes filled with tears, while the mulatto gazed on her with a look of inquiring solicitude.

"Poor Savanna!" cried Adeline in a low and plaintive tone.

There are moments when the sound of one's own voice has a mournful effect on one's feelings—this was one of those moments to Adeline; the pathos of her own tone overcame her, and she burst into tears: but Glenmurray slept on; and Adeline hoped nothing would suddenly disturb his rest, when Berrendale opened the door with what appeared unnecessary noise, and Glenmurray hastily awoke.

Adeline immediately started from her seat, and, looking at him with great indignation, demanded why he came in in such a manner, when he knew Mr. Glenmurray was asleep.

Berrendale, shocked and alarmed at Adeline's words and expression, so unlike her usual manner, stammered out an excuse. "Another time, sir," replied Adeline coldly, "I hope you will be more *careful*."

"What is the matter?" said Glenmurray, raising himself in the bed. "Are you scolding, Adeline? If so, let me hear you: I like novelty."

Here Adeline and Berrendale both hastened to him, and Adeline almost looked with complacency on Berrendale; when Glenmurray, declaring himself wonderfully refreshed by his long sleep, expressed a great desire for his breakfast, and said he had a most voracious appetite.

But to all Berrendale's attentions she returned the most forbidding reserve; nor could she for a moment lose the painful idea, that the death of Glenmurray would be to him a source of joy, not of anguish. Berrendale was not slow to observe this change in her conduct; and he conceived that, as he knew Glenmurray had mentioned his pretensions to her, his absence would be of more service to his wishes than his presence; and he resolved to leave Richmond that afternoon,—especially as he had a dinner engagement at a tavern in London, which, in spite of love and friendship, he was desirous of keeping.

He was not mistaken in his ideas: the countenance of Adeline assumed less severity when he mentioned his intention of going away, nor could she express regret at his resolution, even though Glenmurray with anxious earnestness requested him to stay. But Glenmurray entreated in vain: used to consider his own interest and pleasure in preference to that of others, Berrendale resolved to go; and resisted the prayers of a man who had often obliged him with the greatest difficulty to himself.

"Well, then," said Glenmurray mournfully, "if you must go, God bless you! I wish you, Charles, all possible earthly happiness; nay, I have done all I can to ensure it to* you: but you have disappointed me. I hoped to have joined your hand, in my last moments, to that of this dear girl, and to have bequeathed her in the most solemn manner to your care and tenderness; but, no matter, farewell! we shall probably meet no more."

Here Berrendale's heart failed him, and he almost resolved to stay: but a look of angry repugnance which he saw on Adeline's countenance, even amidst her sorrow, got the better of his kind emotions, by wounding his self-love; and grasping Glenmurray's hand, and saying, "I shall be back in a day or two," he rushed out of the room.

"I am sorry Mr. Berrendale is forced to go," said Adeline involuntarily when the street-door closed after him.

"Had you condescended to tell him so, he would undoubtedly have staid," replied Glenmurray rather peevishly. Adeline instantly felt, and regretted, the selfishness of her conduct. To avoid the sight of a disagreeable object, she had given pain to Glenmurray; or, rather, she had not done her utmost to prevent his being exposed to it.

"Forgive me," said Adeline, bursting into tears: "I own I thought only of myself, when I forbore to urge his stay. Alas! with you, and you alone, I believe, is the gratification of self always a secondary consideration."

"You forget that I am a philanthropist," replied Glenmurray, "and cannot bear to be praised, even by you, at the expense of my fellow-creatures. But come, hasten dinner; my breakfast agreed with me so well, that I am impatient for another meal."

"You certainly are better to-day," exclaimed Adeline with unwonted cheerfulness.

"My feelings are more tolerable, at least," replied Glenmurray: and Adeline and the mulatto began to prepare the dinner immediately. How often during her attendance on Glenmurray had she recollected the words of her grandmother, and blessed her for having taught her to be *useful!*

As soon as dinner was over, Glenmurray complained of being drowsy: still he declared he would not go to bed till he had seen the sun set, as he had that day, for the second time since his illness, seen it rise; and therefore, when it was setting, Adeline and Savanna led him into a room adjoining, which had a western aspect. Glenmurray fixed his eyes on the crimson horizon with a peculiar expression; and his lips seemed to murmur, "For the last time! Let me breathe the evening air, too, once more," said he.

"It is too chill, dear Glenmurray."

"It will not hurt me," replied Glenmurray;* and Adeline complied with his request.

"The breeze of evening is not refreshing like that of morning," he observed; "but the beauty of the setting is, perhaps, superior to that of the rising sun:—they are both glorious sights, and I have enjoyed them both to-day, nor have I for years experienced so strong a feeling of devotion."

"Thank God!" cried Adeline. "O Glenmurray! there has been one thing only wanting to the completion of our union; and that was, that we should worship together."

"Perhaps, had I remained longer here," replied Glenmurray, "we might have done so; for, believe me, Adeline, though my feelings have continually hurried me into adoration of the Supreme Being, I have often wished my homage to be as regular and as founded on immutable conviction as it once was: but it is too late now for amendment, though, alas! not for *regret, deep* regret: yet He who reads the heart knows that my intentions were pure, and that I was not fixed in the stubbornness of error."

"Let us change this discourse," cried Adeline, seeing on Glenmurray's countenance an expression of uncommon sadness, which he, from a regard to her feelings, struggled to cover. He did indeed feel sadness—a sadness of the most painful nature; and while Adeline hung over him with all the anxious and soothing attention of unbounded love, he seemed to shrink from her embrace with horror, and, turning away his head, feebly murmured, "O Adeline! this faithful kindness wounds me to the very soul. Alas! alas! how little have I deserved it!"

If Glenmurray, who had been the means of injuring the woman he loved, merely by following the dictates of his conscience, and a love of what he imagined to be truth, without any view to* his own benefit or the gratification of his personal wishes, felt thus acutely the anguish of self-upbraiding,—what ought to be, and what must be, sooner or later, the agony and remorse of that man, who, merely for the gratification of his own illicit desires, has seduced the woman whom he loved from the path of virtue, and ruined for ever her reputation and her peace of mind!

"It is too late now for you to sit at an open window, indeed it is," cried Adeline, after having replied to Glenmurray's self-reproaches by the touching language of tears, and incoherent expressions of confiding and unchanged attachment; "and as you are evidently better to-day, do not, by breathing too much cold air, run the risk of making yourself worse again."

"Would I were really better! would I could live!" passionately exclaimed Glenmurray: "but indeed I do feel stronger to-night than I have felt for many months." In a moment the fine eyes of Adeline were raised to heaven with an expression of devout thankfulness; and, eager to make the most of a change so favourable, she hurried Glenmurray back to his chamber, and, with a feeling of renewed hope, sat by to watch his slumbers. She had not sat long before the door opened, and the little tawny boy entered. He had watched all day to see the good lady, as he called Adeline; but, as she had not left Glenmurray's chamber except to prepare dinner, he had been disappointed: so he was resolved to seek her in her own apartment. He had bought some cakes with the penny which Adeline had given him, and he was eager to give her a piece of them.

"Hush!" cried Adeline, as she held out her hand to him; and he in a whisper crying "Bite," held his purchase to her lips. Adeline tasted it, said it was very good, and, giving him a halfpenny, the tawny boy disappeared again: the noise he made as he bounded down the stairs woke Glenmurray.

Adeline was sitting on the side of the bed; and as he turned round to sleep again he grasped her hand in his, and its feverish touch damped her hopes, and re-awakened her fears. For a short time she mournfully gazed on his flushed cheek, and then, gently sliding off the bed, and dropping on one knee, she addressed the Deity in the language of humble supplication.

Insensibly she ceased to pray in thought only, and the lowly-murmured prayer became audible. Again Glenmurray awoke, and Adeline reproached herself as the cause.

"My rest was uneasy," cried he, "and I rejoice that you woke me: besides, I like to hear you—Go on, my dearest girl; there is a something in the breathings of your pious fondness that soothes me," added he, pressing the hand he held to his parched lips.

Adeline obeyed: and as she continued, she felt ever and anon, by the pressure of Glenmurray's hand, how much he was affected by what she uttered.

"But must he be taken from me!" she exclaimed in one part of her prayer. "Father, if it be possible, permit this cup to pass by me untasted."[1] Here she felt the hand of Glenmurray grasp hers most vehemently; and, delighted to think that he had pleasure in hearing her, she went on to breathe forth all the wishes of a trembling yet confiding spirit, till overcome with her own emotions she ceased and arose, and leaning over Glenmurray's pillow was going to take his hand:—but the hand which she pressed returned not her pressure; the eyes were fixed whose approving glance she sought; and the horrid truth rushed at once on her mind, that the last convulsive grasp had been an eternal farewell, and that he had in that grasp expired.

Alas! what preparation however long, what anticipation however sure, can enable the mind to bear a shock like this! It came on Adeline like a thunder-stroke: she screamed not; she moved not; but, fixing a dim and glassy eye on the pale countenance of her lover, she seemed as insensible as poor Glenmurray himself; and hours might have elapsed—hours immediately fatal both to her senses and existence—ere any one had entered the room, since she had given orders to be disturbed by no one, had not the tawny boy, encouraged by his past success, stolen in again, unperceived, to give her a piece of the apple which he had bought with her last bounty.

The delighted boy tripped gaily to the bed-side, holding up his treasure; but he started back, and screamed in all the agony of terror, at the sight which he beheld—the face of Glenmurray ghastly, and the mouth distorted as if in the last agony, and Adeline in the stupor of despair.

---

1 Cf. Matthew 26.39.

The affectionate boy's repeated screams soon summoned the whole family into the room, while he, vainly hanging on Adeline's arm, begged her to speak to him: But nothing could at first rouse Adeline, not even Savanna's loud and extravagant grief. When, however, they tried to force her from the body, she recovered her recollection and her strength; and it was with great difficulty she could be carried out of the room, and kept out when they had accomplished their purpose.

But Savanna was sure that looking at such a sad sight would kill her mistress; for she should die herself if she saw William dead, she declared; and the people of the house agreed with her. They knew not that grief is the best medicine for itself; and that the overcharged heart is often relieved by the sight which standers-by conceive likely to snap the very threads of existence.

As Adeline and Glenmurray had both of them excited some interest in Richmond, the news of the death of the latter was immediately abroad; and it was told to Mrs. Pemberton, with a pathetic account of Adeline's distress, just as the carriage was preparing to convey her and her sick friend on their way to Lisbon. It was a relation to call forth all the humanity of Mrs. Pemberton's nature. She forgot Adeline's crime in her distress; and knowing she had no female friend with her, she hastened on the errand of pity to the abode of vice. Alas! Mrs. Pemberton had learnt but too well to sympathize in grief like that of Adeline. She had seen a beloved husband expire in her arms, and had afterwards followed two children to the grave. But she had taken refuge from sorrow in the active duties of her religion, and in becoming* a teacher of those truths to others, by which she had so much benefited herself.

Mrs. Pemberton entered the room just as Adeline, on her knees, was conjuring the persons with her to allow her to see Glenmurray once more.

Adeline did not at all observe the entrance of Mrs. Pemberton, who, in spite of the self-command which her principles and habits gave her, was visibly affected when she beheld the mourner's tearless affliction: and the hands which, on her entrance, were quietly crossed on each other, confining the modest folds of her simple cloke, were suddenly and involuntarily separated by the irresistible impulse of pity; while, catching hold of the wall for support, she leaned against it, covering her face with her hands. "Let me see him! only let me see him once more!" cried Adeline, gazing on Mrs. Pemberton, but unconscious who she was.

"Thou shalt see him," replied Mrs. Pemberton with considerable effort; "give me thy hand, and I will go with thee to the chamber of death." Adeline gave a scream of mournful joy at this permission, and suffered herself to be led into Glenmurray's apartment. As soon as she entered it she sprang to the bed, and, throwing herself beside the corpse, began to contemplate it with an earnestness and firmness which surprised every one. Mrs. Pemberton also fixedly gazed on the wan face of Glenmurray: "And art thou fallen!" she exclaimed, "thou, wise in thine own conceit,[1] who presumedst, perhaps, sometimes to question even the existence of the Most High, and to set up thy vain chimeras[2] of yesterday against the wisdom and experience of centuries? Child of the dust![3] child of error! what art thou now, and whither is thy guilty spirit fled? But balmy is the hand of affliction; and she, thy mourning victim, may learn to bless the hand that chastizes her, nor add to the offences which will weigh down thy soul, a dread responsibility for hers!"

Here she was interrupted by the voice of Adeline; who, in a deep and hollow tone, was addressing the unconscious corpse. "For God's sake, speak! for this silence is dreadful—it looks so like death."

"Poor thing!" said Mrs. Pemberton, kneeling beside her, "and is it even thus with thee? Would thou couldst shed tears, afflicted one!"

"It is very strange," continued Adeline: "he loved me so tenderly, and he used to speak and look so tenderly, and now, see how he neglects me! Glenmurray, my love! for mercy's sake, speak to me!" As she said this, she laid her lips to his: but, feeling on them the icy coldness of death, she started back, screaming in all the violence of phrensy; and, recovered to the full consciousness of her misfortune, she was carried back to her room in violent convulsions.

"Would I could stay and watch over thee!" said Mrs. Pemberton, as she gazed on Adeline's distorted countenance; "for thou, young as thou art, wert well known in the chambers of sorrow and of sickness; and I should rejoice to pay back to thee part of the debt of those whom thy presence so often soothed: but I must leave thee to the care of others."

"You leave her to my care," cried Savanna reproachfully,—who felt even her violent sorrow suspended while Mrs. Pemberton spoke in accents at once sad yet soothing,—"you leave her to my care, and who watch, who love her more than me?"

"Good Savanna!" replied Mrs. Pemberton, pressing the mulatto's hand as she returned to her station beside Adeline, who was fallen into a calm slumber, "to thy care, with confidence, I commit her. But perhaps there may be an immediate necessity for money, and I had better leave this with thee," she added, taking out her purse: but Savanna assured her that Mr. Berrendale was sent for, and to him all those concerns were to be left. Mrs.

---

1  Cf. Romans 11.25, 12.16.

2  An imaginary creature (originally a terrible fire-breathing monster in Greek mythology).

3  I.e., mortal creature; cf. Ecclesiastes 3.20.

Pemberton stood for a few moments looking at Adeline in silence, then slowly left the house.

When Adeline awoke, she seemed so calm and resigned, that her earnest request of being allowed to pass the night alone was granted, especially as Mrs. Pemberton had desired that her wish, even to see Glenmurray again, should be complied with: but the faithful mulatto watched till morning at the door. No bed that night received the weary limbs of Adeline. She threw herself on the ground, and in alternate prayer and phrensy passed the first night of her woe: towards morning, however, she fell into a per-turbed sleep. But when the light of day darting into the room awakened her to consciousness; and when she recollected that he to whom it usually summoned her existed no longer; that the eyes which but the preceding morning had opened with enthusiastic ardour to hail its beams, were now for ever closed; and that the voice which used to welcome her so tenderly, she should never, never hear again; the forlornness of her situation, the hopelessness of her sorrow burst upon her with a violence too powerful for her reason: and when Berrendale arrived, he found Glenmurray in his shroud, and Adeline in a state of insanity. For six months her phrensy resisted all the efforts of medicine, and the united care which Berrendale's love and Savanna's grateful attachment could bestow; while with Adeline's want of their care seemed to increase their desire of bestowing it, and their affection gathered new strength from the duration of her helpless malady. So true is it, that we become attached more from the aid which we give than that which we receive;[1] and that the love of the obliger is more apt to increase than that of the obliged by the obligation conferred. At length, however, Adeline's reason slowly yet surely returned; and she, by degrees, learnt to contemplate with firmness, and even calmness, the loss which she had sustained. She even looked on Berrendale and his attentions not with anger, but gratitude and complacency; she had even pleasure in observing the likeness he bore Glenmurray; she felt that it endeared him to her. In the first paroxysms of her phrensy, the sight of him threw her into fits of raving; but as she grew better she had pleasure in seeing him: and when, on her recovery, she heard how much she was indebted to his persevering tenderness, she felt for him a decided regard, which Berrendale tried to flatter himself might be ripened into love.

But he was mistaken; the heart of Adeline was formed to feel violent and lasting attachments only. She had always loved her mother with a tenderness of a most uncommon nature; she had felt for Glenmurray the fondest enthusiasm of passion: she was now separated from them both. But her mother still lived; and though almost hopeless of ever being restored to

---

1  Cf. Acts 20.35.

her society, all her love for her returned; and she pined for that consoling fondness, those soothing attentions, which, in a time of such affliction, a mother on a widowed daughter can alone bestow.

"Yet, surely," cried she in the solitude of her own room, "her oath cannot now forbid her to forgive me; for, am I not as WRETCHED IN LOVE, nay more, far more so, than *she* has been? Yes—yes; I will write to her: besides, HE wished me to do so" (meaning Glenmurray, whom she never named); and she did write to her, according to the address which Dr. Norberry sent soon after he returned to his own house. Still week after week elapsed, and month after month, but no answer came.

Again she wrote, and again she was disappointed; though her loss, her illness in consequence of it, her pecuniary distress, and the large debt which she had incurred to Berrendale, were all detailed in a manner calculated to move the most obdurate heart. What then could Adeline suppose? Perhaps her mother was ill; perhaps she was dead: and her reason was again on the point of yielding to this horrible supposition, when she received her two letters in a cover, directed in her mother's hand-writing.

At first she was overwhelmed by this dreadful proof of the continuance of Mrs. Mowbray's deep resentment; but, ever sanguine, the circumstance of Mrs. Mowbray's having written the address herself appeared to Adeline a favourable symptom; and with renewed hope she wrote to Dr. Norberry to become her mediator once more: but to this letter no answer was returned; and Adeline concluded her only friend had died of the fever which Mrs. Norberry had mentioned in her letter.

"Then I have lost my only friend!" cried Adeline, wringing her hands in agony, as this idea recurred to her. "Your only friend?" repeated Berrendale, who happened to be present, "O Adeline!"

Her heart smote her as he said this. "My oldest friend I should have said," she replied, holding out her hand to him; and Berrendale thought himself supremely happy.

But Adeline was far from meaning to give the encouragement which this action seemed to bestow: wholly occupied by her affliction, her mind had lost its energy, and she would not have made an effort to dissipate her grief by employment and exertion, had not that virtuous pride and delicacy, which in happier hours had been the ornament of her character, rebelled against the consciousness of owing pecuniary obligations to the lover whose suit she was determined to reject, and urged her to make some vigorous attempt to maintain herself.

Many were the schemes which occurred to her; but none seemed so practicable as that of keeping a day-school in some village near the metropolis.—True, Glenmurray had said, that her having been his mistress would prevent her obtaining scholars; but his fears, perhaps, were stronger than his justice in this case. These fears, however, she found existed in Berrendale's mind also, though he ventured only to hint them with great caution.

"You think, then, no prudent parents, if my story should be known to them, would send their children to me?" said Adeline to Berrendale.

"I fear—I—that is to say, I am sure they would not."

"Under such circumstances," said Adeline, "you yourself would not send a child to my school?"

"Why—really—I—as the world goes,"—replied Berrendale.

"I am answered," said Adeline with a look and tone of displeasure; and retired to her chamber, intending not to return till Berrendale was gone to his own lodging. But her heart soon reproached her with unjust resentment; and, coming back, she apologized to Berrendale for being angry at his laudable resolution of acting according to those principles which he thought most virtuous, especially as she claimed for herself a similar right.

Berrendale, gratified by her apology, replied, "that he saw no objection to her plan, if she chose to deny him the happiness of sharing his income with her, provided she would settle in a village where she was not likely to be known, and change her name."

"Change my name! Never. Concealment of any kind almost always implies the consciousness of guilt; and while my heart does not condemn me, my conduct shall not seem to accuse me. I will go to whatever place you shall recommend; but I beg your other request may be mentioned no more."

Berrendale, glad to be forgiven on any terms, promised to comply with her wishes; and he having recommended to her to settle at a village some few miles north of London, Adeline hired there a small but commodious lodging, and issued immediately cards of advertisement, stating what she meant to teach, and on what terms; while Berrendale took lodgings within a mile of her, and the faithful mulatto attended her as a servant of all-work.

Fortunately, at this time, a lady at Richmond, who had a son the age of the tawny boy, became so attached to him, that she was desirous of bringing him up to be the play-fellow and future attendant on her son; and the mulatto, pleased to have him so well disposed of, resisted the poor little boy's tears and reluctance at the idea of being separated from her and Adeline: and before she left Richmond she had the satisfaction of seeing him comfortably settled in the house of his patroness.

Adeline succeeded in her undertaking even beyond her utmost wishes. Though unknown and unrecommended, there was in her countenance and manner a something so engaging, so strongly inviting confidence, and so decisively bespeaking the gentlewoman, that she soon excited in the village general respect and attention: and no sooner were scholars intrusted to her care, than she became the idol of her pupils; and their improvement was rapid in proportion to the love which they bore her.

This fortunate circumstance proved a balm to the wounded mind of Adeline. She felt that she had recovered her usefulness;— that desideratum[1] in morals; and life,* spite of her misfortunes, acquired a charm in her eyes. True it was, that she was restored to her capability of being useful, by being where she was unknown; and because the mulatto, unknown to her, had described her as reduced to earn her living, on account of the death of the man to whom she was about to be married: but she did not revert to the reasons of her being so generally esteemed; she contented herself with the consciousness of being so; and for some months she was tranquil, though not happy. But her tranquillity was destined to be of short duration.[2]

## CHAPTER 18

THE village in which Adeline resided happened to be the native place of Mary Warner, the servant whom she had been forced to dismiss at Richmond; and who having gone from Mrs. Pemberton to another situation, which she had also quitted, came to visit her friends.

The wish of saying lessening things of those of whom one hears extravagant commendations, is, I fear, common to almost every one, even where the object praised comes in no competition with oneself:—and when Mary Warner heard from every quarter of the grace and elegance, affability and active benevolence of the new comer, it was no doubt infinitely gratifying to her to be able to exclaim,—"Mowbray! did you say her name is? La! I dares to say it is my old mistress, who was kept by one Mr. Glenmurray!" But so greatly were her auditors prepossessed in favour of Adeline, that very few of them could be prevailed upon to believe Mary's supposition was just; and so much was she piqued at the disbelief which she met with, that she declared she would go to church the next Sunday to shame the hussey, and go up and speak to her in the church-yard before all the people.

"Ah! do so, if you ever saw our miss Mowbray before," was the answer: and Mary eagerly looked forward to the approaching Sunday. Mean while, as we are all of us but too apt to repeat stories to the prejudice of others, even though we do not believe them, this strange assertion of

1 Something to be desired (Latin).
2 In 1805 and 1810, volume 2 ends here.

Mary was circulated through the village even by Adeline's admirers; and the next Sunday was expected by the unconscious Adeline alone with no unusual eagerness.

Sunday came; and Adeline, as she was wont to do, attended the service: but, from the situation of her pew, she could neither see Mary nor be seen by her till church was over. Adeline then, as usual, was walking down the broad walk of the church-yard, surrounded by the parents of the children who came to her school, and receiving from them the customary marks of respect, when Mary, bustling through the crowd, accosted her with,—"So!—your sarvant, miss Mowbray, I am glad to see you here in such a respectable situation."

Adeline, though in the gaily-dressed lady who accosted her she had some difficulty in recognising her quondam[1] servant, recollected the pert shrill voice and insolent manner of Mary immediately; and involuntarily starting when she addressed her, from painful associations and fear of impending evil, she replied, "How are you, Mary?" in a faltering tone.

"Then it is Mary's miss Mowbray," whispered Mary's auditors of the day before to each other; while Mary, proud of her success, looked triumphantly at them, and was resolved to pursue the advantage which she had gained.

"So you have lost Mr. Glenmurray, I find!" continued Mary.

Adeline spoke not, but walked hastily on:—but Mary kept pace with her, speaking as loud as she could.

"And did the little one live, pray?"

Still Adeline spoke not.

"What sort of a getting-up[2] had you, miss Mowbray?"

At this mischievously-intended question Adeline's other sensations were lost in strong indignation; and resuming all the modest but collected dignity of her manner, she turned round, and, fixing her eyes steadily on the insulting girl, exclaimed aloud, "Woman, I never injured you either in thought, word or deed:[3]—whence comes it, then, that you endeavour to make the finger of scorn point at me, and make me shrink with shame and confusion from the eye of observation?"

"Woman! indeed!" replied Mary—but she was not allowed to proceed; for a gentleman hastily stepped forward, crying, "It is impossible for us to suffer such insults to be offered to miss Mowbray;—I desire, therefore, that you will take your daughter away" (turning to Mary's father); "and,

---

1 "Formerly" (Latin); used in English as an adjective, "former."

2 I.e., after childbirth.

3 The General Confession in the Book of Common Prayer of the Church of England asks God's pardon for sins committed in "thought, word and deed."

if possible, teach her better manners." Having said this, he overtook the agitated Adeline; and, offering her his arm, saw her home to her lodgings: while those who had heard with surprise and suspicion the strange and impertinent questions and insolent tone of Mary, resumed in a degree their confidence in Adeline, and turned a disgusted and deaf ear to the hysterical vehemence with which the half-sobbing Mary defended herself, and vilified Adeline, as her father and brother-in-law, almost by force, led her out of the church-yard.

The gentleman who had so kindly stepped forward to the assistance of Adeline was Mr. Beauclerc, the surgeon of the village, a man of considerable abilities and liberal principles; and when he bade Adeline farewell, he said, "My wife will do herself the pleasure of calling on you this evening": then, kindly pressing her hand, he with a respectful bow took his leave.

Luckily for Adeline, Berrendale was detained in town that day; and she was spared the mortification of showing herself to him, writhing as she then* was under the agonies of public shame, for such it seemed to her. Convinced as she then† was of the light in which she must have appeared to the persons around her from the malicious interrogatories of Mary;—convinced too, as she was more than beginning to be, of the fallacy of the reasoning which had led her to deserve, and even to glory in, the situation which she now blushed to hear disclosed;—and conscious as she was, that to remain in the village, and expect to retain her school, was now impossible—she gave herself up to a burst of sorrow and despondence; during which her only consolation was, that it was not witnessed by Berrendale.

It never for a moment entered into the ingenuous mind of Adeline, that her declaration would have more weight than that of Mary Warner; and that she might, with almost a certainty of being believed, deny her charge entirely: on the contrary, she had no doubt but that Mrs. Beauclerc was coming to inquire into the grounds for Mary's gross address; and she was resolved to confess to her all the circumstances of her story.

After church in the afternoon Mrs. Beauclerc arrived, and Adeline observed, with pleasure, that her manner was even kinder than usual; it was such as to ensure the innocent of the most strenuous support, and to invite the guilty to confidence and penitence.

"Never, my dear miss Mowbray," said Mrs. Beauclerc, "did I call on you with more readiness than now; as I come assured that you will give me not only the most ample authority to contradict, but the fullest means to confute, the vile calumnies which that malicious girl, Mary Warner, has, ever since she entered the village, been propagating against you: but, indeed, she is so little respected in her rank of life, and you so highly in yours, that your mere denial of the truth of her statement will, to every candid mind, be sufficient to clear your character."

Adeline never before was so strongly tempted to violate the truth; and there was a friendly earnestness in Mrs. Beauclerc's manner, which proved that it would be almost cruel to destroy the opinion which she entertained of her virtue. For a moment Adeline felt disposed to yield to the temptation, but it was only for a moment,—and in a hurried and broken voice she replied, "Mary Warner has asserted of me nothing but——" Here her voice faltered.

"Nothing but falsehoods, no doubt," interrupted Mrs. Beauclerc triumphantly,—"I thought so."

"Nothing but the TRUTH!" resumed Adeline.

"Impossible!" cried Mrs. Beauclerc, dropping the cold hand which she held: and Adeline, covering her face, and throwing herself back in the chair, sobbed aloud.

Mrs. Beauclerc was herself for some time unable to speak; but at length she faintly said—"So sensible, so pious, so well-informed, and so pure-minded as you seem!—to what strange arts, what wicked seductions, did you fall a victim?"

"To no arts—to no seductions"—replied Adeline, recovering all her energy at this insinuation against Glenmurray. "My fall from virtue, as you would call it, was, I may say, from love of what I thought virtue; and if there be any blame, it attaches merely to my confidence in my lover's wisdom and my own too obstinate self-conceit. But you, dear madam, deserve to hear my whole story; and, if you can favour me with an hour's attention, I hope, at least, to convince you that I was worthy of a better fate than to be publicly disgraced by a malicious and ignorant girl."

Mrs. Beauclerc promised the most patient attention; and Adeline related the eventful history of her life, slightly dwelling on those parts of it which in any degree reflected on her mother, and extolling most highly her sense, her accomplishments, and her maternal tenderness. When she came to the period of Glenmurray's illness and death, she broke abruptly off, and rushed into her own chamber; and it was some minutes before she could return to Mrs. Beauclerc, or before her visitor could wish her to return, as she was herself agitated and affected by the relation which she had heard:—and when Adeline came in she threw her arms round her neck, and pressed her to her heart with a feeling of affection that spoke consolation to the wounded spirit of the mourner.

She then resumed her narration;—and, having concluded it, Mrs. Beauclerc, seizing her hand, exclaimed, "For God's sake, marry Mr. Berrendale immediately; and abjure for ever, at the foot of the altar, those errors in opinion to which all your misery has been owing!"

"Would I could atone for them some other way!" she replied.

"Impossible! and if you have any regard for me you will become the wife of your generous lover; for then, and not till then, can I venture to associate with you."

"I thought so," cried Adeline; "I thought all idea of remaining here, with any chance of keeping my scholars, was now impossible."

"It would not be so," replied Mrs. Beauclerc, "if every one thought like me: I should consider your example as a warning to all young people; and to preserve my children from evil I should only wish them to hear your story, as it inculcates most powerfully how vain are personal graces, talents, sweetness of temper, and even active benevolence, to ensure respectability and confer happiness, without a strict regard to the long-established rules for conduct, and a continuance in those paths of virtue and decorum which the wisdom of ages has pointed out to the steps of every one.—But others will, no doubt, consider, that continuing to patronise you, would be patronizing vice; and my rank in life is not high enough to enable me to countenance you with any chance of leading others to follow my example; while I should not be able to serve you, but should infallibly lose myself. But some time hence, as the wife of Mr. Berrendale, I might receive you as your merits deserve: till then—" here Mrs. Beauclerc paused, and she hesitated to add, "we meet no more."

Indeed it was long before the parting took place. Mrs. Beauclerc had justly appreciated the merits of Adeline, and thought she had found in her a friend and companion for years to come: besides, her children were most fondly attached to her; and Mrs. Beauclerc, while she contemplated their daily improvement under her care, felt grateful to Adeline for the unfolding excellencies of her daughters. Still, to part with her was unavoidable; but the pang of separation was in a degree soothed to Adeline by the certainty which Mrs. Beauclerc's sorrow gave her, that, spite of her errors, she had inspired a real friendship in the bosom of a truly virtuous and respectable woman; and this idea gave a sensation of joy to her heart to which it had long been a stranger.

The next morning some of the parents, whom Mary's tale had not yet reached, sent their children as usual. But Adeline refused to enter upon any school duties, bidding them affectionately farewell, and telling them that she was going to write to their parents, as she was obliged to leave her present situation, and, declining keeping school, meant to reside, she believed, in London.

The children on hearing this looked at each other with almost tearful consternation; and Adeline observed, with pleasure, the interest which she had made to herself in their young hearts. After they were gone she sent a circular letter to her friends in the village, importing that she was under the necessity of leaving her present residence; but that, whatever her future situation might be, she should always remember, with gratitude, the favours which she had received at ——.

The necessity that drove her away was, by this time, very well understood by every one; but Mrs. Beauclerc took care to tell those who mentioned the subject to her, the heads of Adeline's story; and to add always, "and I have reason to believe that, as soon as she is settled in town, she will be extremely well married."

To the mulatto the change in Adeline's plans was particularly pleasing, as it would bring her nearer her son, and nearer William, from whom nothing but a sense of grateful duty to Adeline would so long have divided her. But Savanna imagined that Adeline's removal was owing to her having at last determined to marry Mr. Berrendale; an event which she, for Adeline's sake, earnestly wished to take place, though for her own she was undecided whether to desire it or not, as Mr. Berrendale might not, perhaps, be as contented with her services as Adeline was.

While these thoughts were passing in Savanna's mind, and her warm and varying feelings were expressed by alternate smiles and tears, Mr. Berrendale arrived from town: and as Savanna opened the door to him, she, half whimpering half smiling, dropped him a very respectful curtsey, and looked at him with eyes full of unusual significance.

"Well, Savanna, what has happened?—Any thing new or extraordinary since my absence?" said Berrendale.

"Me tink not of wat have appen, but wat will appen,"* replied Savanna.

"And what is going to happen?" returned Berrendale, seating himself in the parlour, "and where is your mistress?"

"She dress herself, that dear missess," replied Savanna, lingering with the door in her hand, "and I,—I ope to ave† a dear massa too."

"What!" cried Berrendale, starting wildly from his seat, "what did you say?"

"Why, me ope my missess be married soon."

"Married! to whom?" cried Berrendale, seizing her hand, and almost breathless with alarm.

"Why, to you, sure," exclaimed Savanna, "and den me hope you will not turn away poor Savanna!"‡

"What reason you have, my dear Savanna, for talking thus, I cannot tell; nor dare I give way to the sweet hopes which you excite: but, if it be true that I may hope, depend on it you shall cook my wedding dinner, and then I am sure it will be a good one."

"Can full joy eat?" asked the mulatto thoughtfully.

"A good dinner is a good thing, Savanna," replied Berrendale, "and ought never to be slighted."

"Me good dinner day I marry, but I not eat it.—O sir, pity people look best in dere wedding clothes, but my William look well all day and every day, and perhaps you will too, sir; and den I ope to cook your wedding dinner, next day dinner, and all your dinners."

"And so you shall, Savanna," cried Berrendale, grasping her hand, "and I—" Here the door opened, and Adeline appeared; who, surprised at Berrendale's familiarity with her servant, looked gravely, and stopped at the door with a look of cold surprise. Berrendale, awed into immediate respect—for what is so timid and respectful as a man truly in love?—bowed low, and lost in an instant all the hopes which had elevated his spirits to such an unusual degree.

Adeline with an air of pique observed, that she feared she interrupted them unpleasantly, as something unusually agreeable and enlivening seemed to occupy them as she came in, over which her entrance seemed to have cast a cloud.

The mulatto had by this time retreated to the door, and was on the point of closing it, when Berrendale stammered out, as well as he could, "Savanna was, indeed, raising my hopes to such an unexpected height, that I felt almost bewildered with joy; but the coldness of your manner, miss Mowbray, has sobered me again."

"And what did Savanna say to you?" cried Adeline.

"I—I say," cried Savanna returning, "dat is, he say, I should be let cook de wedding dinner."

Adeline, turning even paler than she was before, desired her coldly to leave the room; and, seating herself at the greatest possible distance from Berrendale, leaned for some time in silence on her hand—he not daring to interrupt her meditations. But at last she said, "What could give rise to this singular conversation between you and Savanna I am wholly at a loss to imagine: still I—I must own that it is not so ill-timed as it would have been some weeks ago. I will own, that since yesterday I have been considering your generous proposals with the serious attention which they deserve."

On hearing this, which Adeline uttered with considerable effort, Berrendale in a moment was at her side, and almost at her feet.

"I—I wish you to return to your seat," said Adeline coldly: but hope had emboldened him, and he chose to stay where he was.

"But, before I require you to renew your promises, or make any on my side, it is proper that I should tell you what passed yesterday; and if the additional load of obloquy which I have acquired does not frighten you from continuing your addresses—" Here Adeline paused:—and Berrendale, rather drawing back, then pushing his chair nearer her as he spoke, gravely answered, that his affection was proof against all trials.

Adeline then briefly related the scene in the church-yard, and her conversation with Mrs. Beauclerc, and concluded thus:—"In consequence of this, and of the recollection* of HIS advice, and HIS decided opinion, that by becoming the wife of a respectable man, I could alone expect to recover my rank in society, and, consequently, my usefulness, I offer you my hand; and promise, in the course of a few months, to become yours in the sight of God and man."

"And from no other reason?—from no preference, no regard for me?" demanded Berrendale reproachfully.

"Oh! pardon me; from decided preference; there is not another being in the creation whom I could bear to call husband."

Berrendale, gratified and surprised, attempted to take her hand; but, withdrawing it, she continued thus:—"Still I almost scruple to let you, unblasted as your prospects are, take to wife a beggar, blasted in reputation, broken in spirits, with a heart whose best affections lie buried in the grave, and which can offer you in return for your faithful tenderness nothing but cold respect and esteem; one too who is not only despicable to others, but also self-condemned."

While Adeline said this, Berrendale, almost shuddering at the picture which she drew, paced the room in great agitation; and even the gratification of his passion, used as he was to the indulgence of every wish, seemed, for a moment, a motive not sufficiently powerful to enable him to unite his fate to that of a woman so degraded as Adeline appeared to be; and he would, perhaps, have hesitated to accept the hand she offered, had she not added, as a contrast to the picture which she had drawn—"But if, in spite of all these unwelcome considerations, you persist in your resolution of making me yours, and I have resolution enough to conquer the repugnance that I feel to make a second connection, you may depend on possessing in me one who will study your happiness and wishes in the minutest particulars;—one who will cherish you in sickness and in sorrow;[1]—" (here a twinge of the gout assisted Adeline's appeal very powerfully;) "and who, conscious of the generosity of your attachment, and her own unworthiness, will strive, by every possible effort, not to remain your debtor even in affection."

Saying this, she put out her hand to Berrendale; and that hand, and the arm belonging to it, were so beautiful, and he had so often envied Glenmurray while he saw them tenderly supporting his head, that while a vision of approaching gout, and Adeline bending over his restless couch,

---

1   Cf. the marriage service in the Book of Common Prayer of the Church of England, where the couple promise to love, comfort, honour and keep each other "in sickness and in health."

floated before him, all his prudent considerations vanished; and, eagerly pressing the proffered hand to his lips, he thanked her most ardently for her kind promise; and, putting his arm round her waist, would have pressed her to his bosom.

But the familiarity was ill-timed;—Adeline was already surprised, and even shocked, at the lengths which she had gone; and starting almost with loathing from his embrace, she told him it grew late, and it was time for him to go to his lodgings. She then retired to her own room, and spent half the night at least in weeping over the remembrance of Glenmurray, and in loudly apostrophizing his departed spirit.

The next day Adeline, out of the money which she had earned, discharged her lodgings; and having written a farewell note to Mrs. Beauclerc, begging to hear of her now and then, she and the mulatto proceeded to town, with Berrendale, in search of apartments; and having procured them, Adeline began to consider by what means, till she could resolve to marry Berrendale, she should help to maintain herself, and also contrive to increase their income if she became his wife.

The success which she had met with in instructing children, led her to believe that she might succeed in writing little hymns and tales for their benefit; a method of getting money which she looked upon to be more rapid and more lucrative than working plain or fancy works: and, in a short time, a little volume was ready to be offered to a bookseller;—nor was it offered in vain. Glenmurray's bookseller accepted it; and the sum which he gave, though trifling, imparted a balsam to the wounded mind of Adeline: it seemed to open to her the path of independence; and to give her, in spite of her past errors, the means of serving her fellow-creatures.

But month after month elapsed, and Glenmurray had been dead two years, yet still Adeline could not prevail on herself to fix a time for her marriage.

But next to the aversion she felt to marrying at all, was that[*] she experienced at the idea of having no fortune to bestow on the disinterested Berrendale; and so desirous was she of his acquiring some little property by his union with her, that she resolved to ask counsel's opinion on the possibility of her claiming a sum of money which Glenmurray had bequeathed her,[†] but without, as Berrendale had assured her, the customary formalities.

The money was near 300*l.*; but Berrendale had allowed it to go to Glenmurray's legal heir, because he was sure that the writing which bequeathed it would not hold good in law. Still Adeline was so unwilling to be under so many pecuniary obligations to a man whom she did not love, that she resolved to take advice on the subject, much against the will of Berrendale, who thought the money[‡] might as well be saved; but as a chance for saving the fee he resolved to let Adeline go to the lawyer's chambers alone, thinking it likely that no fee would be accepted from so fine a woman. Accordingly, more alive to œconomy than to delicacy or decorum, Berrendale, when Adeline, desiring a coach to be called, summoned him to accompany her to the Temple,[1] pleaded terror of an impending fit of the gout, and begged her to excuse his attendance; and Adeline, unsuspicious of the real cause of his refusal, kindly expressing her sorrow for the one he feigned, took the counsellor's address, and got into the coach, Berrendale taking care to tell her, as she got in, that the fare was but a shilling.

The gentleman, Mr. Langley, to whom Adeline was going, was celebrated for his abilities as a chamber counsellor,[2] and no less remarkable for his gallantries: but Berrendale was not acquainted with this part of his history; else he would not, even to save a lawyer's fee, have exposed his intended wife to a situation of such extreme impropriety; and Adeline was too much a stranger to the rules of general society, to feel any great repugnance to go alone on an errand so interesting to her feelings.

The coach having stopped near the entrance of the court to which she was directed, Adeline, resolving to walk home, discharged the coach, and knocked at the door of Mr. Langley's chambers. A very smart servant out of livery answered the knock; and Mr. Langley being at home, Adeline was introduced into his apartment.

Mr. Langley, though surprised at seeing a lady of a deportment so correct and of so dignified an appearance enter his room unattended, was inspired with so much respect at sight* of Adeline, whose mourning habit added to the interest which her countenance never failed to excite, that he received her with bows down to the ground, and leading her to a chair, begged she would do him the honour to be seated, and impart her commands.

Adeline embarrassed, she scarcely knew why, at the novelty of her situation, drew the paper from her pocket, and presented it to him.

"Mr. Berrendale recommended me to you, sir," said Adeline faintly.

"Berrendale, Berrendale, O, aye,—I remember—the cousin of Mr. Glenmurray: you know Mr. Glenmurray too, ma'am, I presume; pray how is he?"—Adeline, unprepared for this question, could not speak; and the voluble counsellor went on—"Oh!—I ask your pardon, madam, I see;—

---

1 An area of London named for the Knights Templar, who devoted themselves in the twelfth century to capturing the Temple in Jerusalem. The Inner Temple and Middle Temple housed law offices.

2 A lawyer who gives his opinion at his chambers, but who does not plead cases in court.

pray, might I presume so far, how long has that extraordinarily clever man been lost to the world?"

"More than two years, sir," replied Adeline faintly.

"You are,—may I presume so far,—you are his widow?"—Adeline bowed. There was a something in Mr. Langley's manner and look so like sir Patrick's, that she could not bear to let him know she was only Glenmurray's mistress.*

"Gone more than two years, and you still in deep mourning!—Amiable susceptibility!—How unlike the wives of the present day! But I beg pardon.—Now to business." So saying, he perused the paper which Adeline had given him, in which Glenmurray simply stated, that he bequeathed to Adeline Mowbray the sum of 260*l.* in the 5 per cents,[1] but it was signed by only one witness.

"What do you wish to know, madam?" asked the counsellor.

"Whether this will be valid, as it is not signed by two witnesses, sir?"

"Why,—really not," replied Langley; "though the heir at law, if he have either equity or gallantry, could certainly not refuse to fulfil what evidently was the intention of the testator:—but then, it is very surprising to me that Mr. Glenmurray should have wished to leave any thing from the lady whom I have the honour to behold. Pray, madam,—if I may presume to ask,—Who is Adeline Mowbray?"

"I—I am Adeline Mowbray," replied Adeline in great confusion.

"You, madam! Bless me, I presumed;—and pray, madam,—if I may make so bold,—what was your relationship to that wonderfully clever man?—his niece,—his cousin,—or—?"

"I was no relation of his," said Adeline still more confused; and this confusion confirmed the suspicions which Langley entertained, and also brought to his recollection something which he had heard of Glenmurray's having a very elegant and accomplished mistress.

"Pardon me, dear madam," said Mr. Langley, "I perceive now my mistake; and I now perceive why Mr. Glenmurray was so much the envy of those who had the honour of visiting at his house. 'Pon my soul," taking her hand, which Adeline indignantly withdrew, "I am grieved beyond words at being unable to give you a more favourable opinion."

"But you said, sir," said Adeline, "that the heir at law, if he had any equity, would certainly be guided by the evident intention of the testator."

"I did, madam," replied the lawyer, evidently piqued by the proud and cold air which Adeline assumed;—"but then,—excuse me,—the applicant would not stand much chance of being attended to, who is neither the *widow* nor *relation* of Mr. Glenmurray."

---

1  I.e., invested in government bonds.

"I understand you, sir," replied Adeline, "and need trouble you no longer."

"Trouble! my sweet girl!" returned Mr. Langley, "call it not trouble; I—" Here his gallant effusions were interrupted by the sudden entrance of a very showy woman, highly rouged, and dressed in the extremity of the fashion; and who in no very pleasant tone of voice exclaimed,—"I fear I interrupt you."

"Oh! not in the least," replied Langley, blushing even more than Adeline, "my fair client was just going. Allow me, madam, to see you to the door," continued he, attempting to take Adeline's hand, and accompanying her to the bottom of the first flight of stairs.

"Charming fine woman upon my soul!" cried he, speaking through his shut teeth, and forcibly squeezing her fingers as he spoke; "and if you ever want advice I should be proud to see you here; at present I am particularly engaged," (with a significant smile;) "but—"* Here Adeline, too angry to speak, put the fee in his hand, which he insisted on returning, and, in the struggle, he forcibly kissed the ungloved hand which was held out, praising its beauty at the same time, and endeavouring to close her fingers on the money: but Adeline indignantly threw it on the ground, and rushed down the remaining staircase; over-hearing the lady, as she did so, exclaim, "Langley! is not that black mawkin[1] gone yet? Come up this moment, you devil!" while Langley obsequiously replied, "Coming this moment, my angel!"

Adeline felt so disappointed, so ashamed, and so degraded, that she walked on some way without knowing whither she was going; and when she recollected herself, she found that she was wandering from court to court, and unable to find the avenue to the street down which the coach had come: while her very tall figure, heightened colour, and graceful carriage, made her an object of attention to every one whom she met.

At last she saw herself followed by two young men; and as she walked very fast to avoid them, she by accident turned into the very lane which she had been seeking: but her pursuers kept pace with her; and she overheard one of them say to the other, "A devilish fine girl! moves well too,—I cannot help thinking that I have seen her before."

"And so do I.—† O zounds! by‡ her height, it must be that sweet creature who lived at Richmond with that crazy fellow, Glenmurray."

Here Adeline relaxed in her pace: the name of Glenmurray—that name which no one since his death had ventured to pronounce in her presence,—had, during the last half-hour, been pronounced several times;

---

1  Or "malkin," a lower-class, untidy woman. "Black" here refers to Adeline's mourning dress.

and, unable to support herself from a variety of emotions, she stopped, and leaned for support against the wall.

"How do you do, my fleet and sweet girl?" said one of the gentlemen, patting her on the back as he spoke:*— and Adeline, roused at the insult, looked at him proudly and angrily, and walked on. "What! angry! If I may be so bold, (with a sneering smile,) fair creature, may I ask where you live now?"

"No, sir," replied Adeline; "you are wholly unknown to me."

"But were you to tell me where you live, we might cease to be strangers; but, perhaps your favours are all bespoken.—Pray† who is your friend now?"

"Oh! I have but few friends," cried Adeline mournfully.

"Few! the devil!" replied the young templar;[1] "and how many would you have?" Here he put his arm around her waist: and his companion giving way to a loud fit of laughter,‡ Adeline clearly understood what he meant by the term "friend"; and summoning up all her spirit, she called a coach which luckily was passing; and, turning round to her tormentor, with great dignity said,—"Though the situation, sir, in which I once was, may, in the eyes of the world and in yours, authorise and excuse your present insulting address, yet, when I tell you that I am on the eve of marriage with a most respectable man, I trust that you will feel the impropriety of your conduct, and be convinced of the fruitlessness and impertinence of the questions which you have put to me."

"If this be the case, madam," cried the gentleman, "I beg your pardon, and shall take my leave, wishing you all possible happiness, and begging you to attribute my impertinence wholly to my ignorance." So saying, he bowed and left her, and Adeline was driven to her lodgings.

"Now," said Adeline, "the die is cast;—I have used the sacred name of wife to shield me from insult; and I am therefore pledged to assume it directly. Yes, HE was right—I find I must have a legal protector."

She found Berrendale rather alarmed at her long absence; and, with a beating heart, she related her adventures to him: but when she said that Langley was not willing to take the fee, he exclaimed, "Very genteel in him, indeed! I suppose you took him at his word?"

"Good Heavens!" replied Adeline, "Do you think I would deign to owe such a man a pecuniary obligation?—No, indeed; I threw it with proud indignation on the floor."

"What madness!" returned Berrendale: "you had much better have put it in your pocket."

---

1  In the sense of "barrister," with ironic overtones of chivalry based on the association of the law offices in the Temple with the Knights Templar (see 201, n. 1).

"Mr. Berrendale," cried Adeline gravely, and with a look bordering on contempt, "I trust that you are not in earnest: for if these are your sentiments,—if this is your delicacy, sir—"

"Say no more, dearest of women," replied Berrendale pretending to laugh, alarmed at the seriousness with which she spoke: "how could you for one moment suppose me in earnest? Insolent coxcomb!—I wish I had been there."

"I wish you had," said Adeline, "for then no one would have dared to insult me": and Berrendale, delighted at this observation, listened to the rest of her story with a spirit of indignant knight-errantry which he never experienced before; and at the end of her narration he felt supremely happy; for Adeline assured him that the next week she would make him her protector for life:—and this assurance opened his heart so much, that he vowed he would not condescend to claim of the heir at law the pitiful sum which he might think proper to withhold.

To be brief.—Adeline kept her word; and resolutely struggling with her feelings, she became the next week the wife of Berrendale.

For the first six months the union promised well. Adeline was so assiduous to anticipate her husband's wishes, and contrived so many dainties for his table, which she cooked with her own hands, that Berrendale, declaring himself completely happy for the first time in his life, had not a thought or a wish beyond his own fire-side; while Adeline, happy because she conferred happiness, and proud of the name of wife, which she had before despised, began to hope that her days would glide on in humble tranquillity.

It was natural enough that Adeline should be desirous of imparting this change in her situation to Mrs. Pemberton, whose esteem she was eager to recover, and whose kind intentions towards her, at a moment when she was incapable of appreciating them, Savanna had, with great feeling, expatiated upon. She therefore wrote to her according to the address which Mrs. Pemberton had left for her, and received a most friendly letter in return. In a short time Adeline had again an expectation of being a mother; and though she could not yet entertain for her husband more than cold esteem, she felt that as the father of her child he would insensibly become more dear to her.

But Berrendale awoke from his dream of bliss, on finding to what a large sum the bills for the half-year's house-keeping amounted. Nor was he surprised without reason. Adeline, more eager to gratify Berrendale's palate than considerate as to the means, had forgotten that she was no longer at the head of a liberal establishment like her mother's, and had bought for the supply of the table many expensive articles.

In consequence of this terrible discovery Berrendale remonstrated very seriously with Adeline; who meekly answered, "My dear friend, good dinners cannot be had without good ingredients, and good ingredients cannot be had without money."

"But, madam," cried Berrendale, knitting his brows, but not elevating his voice, for he was one of those soft-speaking beings who in the sweetest tones possible can say the most heart-wounding things, and give a mortal stab to your self-love in the same gentle manner in which they flatter it:—"there must have been great waste, great mismanagement here, or these expenses could not have been incurred."

"There may have been both," returned Adeline, "for I have not been used to œconomize, but I will try to learn;—but, I doubt, my dear Berrendale, you must endeavour to be contented with plainer food; for not all the œconomy in the world can make rich gravies and high sauces cheap things."

"Oh! care and skill can do much," said Berrendale;—"and I find a certain person deceived me very much when he said you were a good manager."

"He only said," replied Adeline sighing deeply, "that I was a good cook, and you yourself allow that: but I hope in time to please your appetite at less expense: as to myself, a little suffices me, and I care not how plain that food is."

"Still, I think I have seen you eat with a most excellent appetite," said Berrendale, with a very significant expression.

Adeline, shocked at the manner more than at the words, replied in a faltering voice, "As a proof of my being in health, no doubt you rejoiced in the sight."

"Certainly; but less robust health would suit our finances better."

Adeline looked up, wishing, though not expecting, to see by his face that he was joking: but such serious displeasure appeared on it, that the sordid selfishness of his character was at once unveiled to her view; and clasping her hands in agony, she exclaimed, "Oh, Glenmurray!" and ran into her own room.

It was the first time that she had pronounced his name since the hour of his death, and now it was wrung from her by a sensation of acute anguish; no wonder, then, that the feelings which followed completely overcame her, and that Berrendale had undisputed and solitary possession of his supper.

But he, on his side, was deeply irritated. The "Oh, Glenmurray!" was capable of being interpreted two ways:—either it showed how much she regretted Glenmurray, and preferred him to his successor in spite of the superior beauty of his person, of which he was very vain; or it reproached Glenmurray for having recommended her to marry him. In either case it was an unpardonable fault; and this unhappy conversation laid the foundation of future discontent.

Adeline rose the next day dejected, pensive, and resolved that her appetite should never again, if possible, force a reproach from the lips of her
husband. She therefore took care that whatever she provided for the table,
besides the simplest fare, should be for Berrendale alone; and she flattered
herself that he would be shamed into repentance of what he had observed,
by seeing her scrupulous self-denial:—she even resolved, if he pressed her
to partake of his dainties, that she would, to show that she forgave him,
accept what he offered.

But Berrendale gave her no such opportunity of showing her generosity;—busy in the gratification of his own appetite, he never observed
whether any other persons ate or not, except when by eating they curtailed
his share of good things:—besides, to have an exclusive dish to himself was
to him *tout simple*;*[1] he had been a pampered child; and, being no advocate
for the equality of the sexes, he thought it only a matter of course that he
should fare better than his wife.

Adeline, though more surprised and more shocked than ever, could
not help laughing internally, at her not being able to put her projected
generosity in practice; but her laughter and indignation soon yielding to
contempt, she ate her simple meal in silence: and while her pampered husband sought to lose the fumes of indigestion in sleep, she blessed God that
temperance, industry and health went hand in hand; and, retiring to her
own room, sat down to write, in order to increase, if possible, her means
of living, and consequently her power of being generous to others.

But though Adeline resolved to forget, if possible, the petty conduct
of Berrendale,—the mulatto, who, from the door's being open, had heard
every word of the conversation which had so disturbed Adeline, neither
could nor would forget it; and though she did not vow eternal hatred to
her master, she felt herself very capable of indulging it, and from that moment it was her resolution to thwart him.

Whenever he was present she was always urging Adeline to eat some
refreshments between meals, and drink wine or lemonade, and tempting her weak appetite with some pleasant but expensive sweetmeats. In
vain did Adeline refuse them; sometimes they were bought, sometimes
only threatened to be bought; and once when Adeline had accepted some,
rather than mortify Savanna by a refusal, and Berrendale, by his accent and
expression, showed how much he grudged the supposed expense,—the
mulatto, snapping her fingers in his face, and looking at him with an expression of indignant contempt, exclaimed, "I buy dem, and pay for dem
wid mine nown money; and my angel lady sall no be oblige to you!"

---

1   "Quite simple or ordinary" (Fr.).

This was a declaration of war against Berrendale, which Adeline heard with anger and sorrow, and her husband with rage. In vain did Adeline promise that she would seriously reprove Savanna (who had disappeared) for her impertinence; Berrendale insisted on her being discharged immediately; and nothing but Adeline's assurances that she, for slender wages, did more work than two other servants would do for enormous ones, could pacify his displeasure: but at length he was appeased. And as Berrendale, from a principle of œconomy, resumed his old habit of dining out amongst his friends, getting good dinners by that means without paying for them, family expenses ceased to disturb the quiet of their marriage; and after she had been ten months a wife Adeline gave birth to a daughter.

That moment, the moment when she heard her infant's first cry, seemed to repay her for all she had suffered; every feeling was lost in the maternal one; and she almost fancied that she loved, fondly loved, the father of her child: but this idea vanished when she saw the languid pleasure, if pleasure it could be called, with which Berrendale congratulated her on her pain and danger being past, and received his child in his arms.

The mulatto was wild with joy: she almost stifled the babe with her kisses, and talked even the next day of sending for the tawny boy to come and see his new mistress, and vow to her, as he had done to her mother, eternal fealty and allegiance.

But Adeline saw on Berrendale's countenance a mixed expression,— and he had mixed feelings. True, he rejoiced in Adeline's safety; but he said within himself, "Children are expensive things, and we may have a large family"; and, leaving the bed-side as soon as he could, he retired, to endeavour to lose in an afternoon's nap his unpleasant reflections.

"How different," thought Adeline, "would have been HIS feelings and HIS expressions of them at such a time! Oh!—" but the name of Glenmurray died away on her lips; and hastily turning to gaze on her sleeping babe, she tried to forget the disappointed emotions of the wife in the gratified feelings of the mother.

Still Adeline, who had been used to attentions, could not but feel the neglect of Berrendale. Even while she kept her room he passed only a few hours in her society, but* dined out; and when she was well enough to have accompanied him on his visits, she found that he never even wished her to go with him, though the friends whom he visited were married; and he met, from his own confession,† other ladies at their tables. She therefore began to suspect that Berrendale did not mean to introduce her as his wife; nay, she doubted whether he avowed her to be such; and at last she brought him to own that, ashamed of having married what the world must consider as a kept mistress, he resolved to keep her still in the retirement to which she was habituated.

This was a severe disappointment indeed to Adeline: she longed for the society of the amiable and accomplished of her own sex; and hoped that, as Mr. Berrendale's wife, that intercourse with her own sex might be restored to her which she had forfeited as the mistress of Glenmurray. Nor could she help reproaching Berrendale for the selfish ease and indifference with which he saw her deprived of those social enjoyments which he daily enjoyed himself, convinced as she was that he might, if he chose, have introduced her at least to his intimate friends.

But she pleaded and reasoned in vain. Contented with the access which he had to the tables of his friends, it was of little importance to him that his wife ate her humble meal alone. His habits of enjoyment had ever been solitary: the pampered* school-boy, who had at school eaten his tart and cake by stealth in a corner, that he might not be asked to share them with another, had grown up with the same dispositions to manhood: and as his parents, though opulent, were vulgar in their manners and low in their origin, he had never been taught those graceful self-denials inculcated into the children of polished life, which, though taught from factitious and not real benevolence, have certainly a tendency, by long habit, to make that benevolence real which at first was only artificial.

Adeline had both sorts of kindness and affection, those untaught of the heart, and those of education;—she was polite from the situation into which the accident of birth had thrown her, and also from the generous impulse of her nature. To her, therefore, the uncultivated and unblushing *personnalité*, as the French call it, of Berrendale, was a source of constant wonder and distress: and often, very often did she feel the utmost surprise at Berrendale's having appeared to Glenmurray a man likely to make her happy. Often did she wonder how the defects of Berrendale's character could have escaped his penetrating eyes.

Adeline forgot that the faults of her husband were such as could be known only by an intimate connection, and which cohabitation could alone call forth;—faults, the existence of which such a man as Glenmurray, who never considered himself in any transaction whatever, could not suppose possible;—and which, though they inflicted the most bitter pangs on Adeline, and gradually untwisted the slender thread which had begun to unite her heart with Berrendale's, were of so slight a fabric as almost to elude the touch, and of a nature to appear almost too trivial to be mentioned in the narration of a biographer.

But though it has been long said that trifles make the sum of human things,[1] inattention to trifles continues to be the vice of every one; and

---

[1] Notably by Hannah More, "Sensibility: A Poetical Epistle to the Hon. Mrs. Boscawen" (1782), 306.

many a conjugal union which has never been assailed by the battery of crime, has fallen a victim to the slowly undermining power of petty quarrels, trivial unkindnesses and thoughtless neglect;—like the gallant officer, who, after escaping unhurt all the rage of battle by land and water, tempest on sea and earthquake on shore, returns perhaps to his native country, and perishes by the power of a slow fever.

But Adeline, who, amidst all the chimaeras of her fancy and singularities of her opinions, had happily held fast her religion, began at this moment to entertain a belief that soothed in some measure the sorrows which it could not cure. She fancied that all the sufferings she underwent were trials which she was doomed to undergo, as punishments for the crime she had committed in leaving her mother and living with Glenmurray; and as expiations also.* She therefore welcomed her afflictions, and lifted up her meek eyes to heaven† in every hour of her trials, with the look of tearful but grateful resignation.

Meanwhile her child, whom, after her mother, she called Editha, was nursed at her own bosom,[1] and thrived even beyond her expectations. Even Berrendale beheld its growing beauty with delight, and the mulatto was wild in praise of it; while Adeline, wholly taken up all day in nursing and in working for it, and every evening in writing stories and hymns to publish, which would, she hoped, one day be useful to her own child as well as to the children of others, soon ceased to regret her seclusion from society; and by the time Editha was a year old she had learnt to bear with patience the disappointment she had experienced in Berrendale.‡

Soon after she became a mother she again wrote to Mrs. Pemberton, as she longed to impart to her sympathizing bosom those feelings of parental delight which Berrendale could not understand, and the expression of which he witnessed with contemptuous and chilling gravity. To this letter she anticipated a most gratifying return; but month after month passed away, and no letter from Lisbon arrived. "No doubt my letter miscarried," said Adeline to Savanna, "and I will write again": but she never had resolution to do so; for she felt that her prospects of conjugal happiness were obscured, and she shrunk equally from the task of expressing the comfort which she did not feel, or unveiling to another the errors of her husband. The little regard, mean while, which she had endeavoured to return for Berrendale soon vanished, being unable to withstand a new violence offered to it.

Editha was seized with the hooping-cough: and as Adeline had sold her last little volume to advantage, Berrendale allowed her to take a lodging at a short distance from town, as change of air was good for the complaint.

---

1  Instead of by a hired wet-nurse.

She did so, and remained there two months. At her return she had the mortification to find that her husband, during her absence, had intrigued with the servant of the house:—a circumstance of which she would probably have remained ignorant, but for the indiscreet affection of Savanna, who, in the first transports of her indignation on discovering the connection, had been unable to conceal from her mistress what drove her almost frantic with indignation.

But Adeline, though she felt disgust and aversion swallowing up the few remaining sparks of regard for Berrendale which she felt, had one great consolation under this new calamity.—Berrendale had not been the choice of her heart: "But, thank God!* I never loved this man," escaped her lips as she ran into her own room; and pressing her child to her bosom, she shed on its unconscious cheeks the tears which resentment and a deep sense of injury wrung from her.—"Oh! had I loved him," she exclaimed, "this blow would have been mortal!"

She, however, found herself in one respect the better for Berrendale's guilt. Conscious that the mulatto was aware of what had passed, and afraid lest she should have mentioned her discovery to Adeline, Berrendale endeavoured to make amends for his infidelity by attention such as he had never shown her since the first weeks of his marriage; and had she not been aware of the motive, the change in his behaviour would have re-awakened her tenderness. However, it claimed at least complaisance and gentleness from her while it lasted: which was not long; for Berrendale, fancying from the apparent tranquillity of Adeline (the result of indifference, not ignorance) that she was not informed of his fault, and that the mulatto was too prudent to betray him, began to relapse into his old habits; and one day, forgetting his assumed liberality, he ventured, when alone with Savanna, who was airing one of Editha's caps, to expatiate on the needless extravagance of his wife in trimming her child's caps with lace.

This was enough to rouse the quick feelings of the mulatto, and she poured forth all her long concealed wrath in a torrent of broken English, but plain enough to be well understood.—"You man!" she cried at last, "you will kill her; she pine at your no kindness;—and if she die, mind me, man! never you marry aden.—You marry, forsoot! you marry a lady! true bred lady like mine! No, man!—You best get a cheap miss from de street and be content——"

As she said this, and in an accent so provoking that Berrendale was pale and speechless with rage, Adeline entered the room; and Savanna, self-condemned already for what she had uttered, was terrified when Adeline, in a tone of voice unusually severe, said, "Leave the room; you have offended me past forgiveness."

These words, in a great measure, softened the angry feelings of Berrendale, as they proved that Adeline resented the insult offered to him as deeply as he could wish; and with some calmness he exclaimed, "Then I conclude, Mrs. Berrendale, that you will have no objection to discharge your mulatto directly."*

This conclusion, though a very natural one, was both a shock and a surprise to Adeline; nor could she at first reply.

"You are *silent*, madam," said Berrendale; "what is your answer? Yes, or No?"

"Ye,†—yes,—certainly," faltered out Adeline; "she—she ought to go—I mean that she has used very improper language to you."

"And, therefore, a wife who resents as she ought to do, injuries offered to her husband, cannot hesitate for a moment to discharge her."

"True, very true in some measure," replied Adeline; "but——"

"But what?" demanded Berrendale.‡

"O Berrendale!" cried Adeline, bursting into an agony of frantic sorrow, "if she leaves me what will become of me! I shall lose the only person now in the world, perhaps, who loves me with sincere and faithful affection!"

Berrendale was wholly unprepared for an appeal like this; and, speechless from surprise not unmixed with confusion, staggered into the next chair. He was conscious, indeed, that his fidelity to his wife had not been proof against a few weeks' absence; but then, being, like most men, not over delicate in his ideas on such subjects, as soon as Adeline returned he had given up the connection which he had formed, and therefore he thought she had not much reason to complain. In all other respects he was sure that he was an exemplary husband, and she had no just grounds for doubting his affection. He was sure that she had no reason to accuse him of unkindness; and, unless she wished him to be always tied to her apron-string, he was certain he had never omitted to pay her all proper attention.

Alas! he felt not the many wounds he had inflicted by

> "The word whose meaning kills; yet, told,
> The speaker wonders that you thought it cold":[1]

and he had yet to learn, that in order to excite or testify affection, it is necessary to seem to derive exclusive enjoyment from the society of the object avowed to be beloved, and to seek its gratification in preference to one's own, even in the most trivial things. He knew not that opportuni-

---

1 Cf. Hannah More, "Sensibility," 336-37.

ties of conferring large benefits, like bank bills for 1000*l.*, rarely come into use; but little attentions, friendly participations and kindnesses, are wanted daily, and, like small change, are necessary to carry on the business of life and happiness.

A minute, and more perhaps,* elapsed, before Berrendale recovered himself sufficiently to speak; and the silence was made still more awful to Adeline, by her hearing from the adjoining room the sobs of the mulatto. At length, "I cannot find words to express my surprise at what you have just uttered," exclaimed Berrendale. "My conscience does not reproach me with deserving the reproof it contained."

"Indeed!" replied Adeline, fixing her penetrating eyes on his, which shrunk downcast and abashed from her gaze. Adeline saw her advantage, and pursued it.† "Mr. Berrendale," continued she, "it is indeed true, that the mulatto has offended both of us; for in offending *you* she has offended *me*; but, have you committed no fault, nothing for *me* to forgive? I know that you are too great a lover of truth, too honourable a man, to declare that you have not deserved the just anger of your wife: but you know that I have never reproached you, nor should you ever have been aware that I was privy to the distressing circumstance to which I allude, but for what has just passed: and, now, do but forgive the poor mulatto, who sinned only from regard for me, and from supposed slight offered to her mistress, and I will not only assure you of my forgiveness, but, from this moment, will strenuously endeavour to blot from my remembrance every trace of what has passed."

Berrendale, conscious and self-condemned, scarcely knew what to answer; but, thinking that it was better to accept Adeline's offer even on her own conditions, he said, that if Savanna would make a proper apology, and Adeline would convince her that she was seriously displeased with her, he would allow her to stay; and Adeline having promised every thing which he asked, peace was again restored.

"But what can you mean, Adeline," said Berrendale, "by doubting my affection? I think I gave a sufficient proof of that, when, disregarding the opinion of the world, I married you, though you had been the mistress of another: and I really think that, by accusing me of unkindness, you make me a very ungrateful return." To this indelicate and unfeeling remark Adeline vainly endeavoured to reply; but, starting from her chair, she paced the room in violent agitation.—"Answer me," continued Berrendale, "name one instance in which I have been unkind to you." Adeline suddenly stopped, and, looking steadfastly at him, smiled with a sort of contemptuous pity, and was on the point of saying, "Is not what you have now said an instance of unkindness?" But she saw that the same want of delicacy, and of that fine moral *tact* which led him to commit this and similar assaults on her feelings, made him unconscious of the violence which he offered.

Finding, therefore, that he could not understand her causes of complaint, even if it were possible for her to define them, she replied, "Well, perhaps I was too hasty, and in a degree unjust: so let us drop the subject; and, indeed, my dear Berrendale, you must bear with my weakness: remember, I have always been a spoiled child."

Here the image of Glenmurray and that of *home*, the home which she once knew, the home of her childhood, and of her *earliest* youth, pressed on her recollection. She thought of her mother, of the indulgences* which she had once known, of the advantages of opulence, the value of which she had never felt till deprived of them; and, struck with the comparative forlornness of her situation—united for life to a being whose sluggish sensibilities could not understand, and consequently not sooth, the quick feelings and jealous susceptibility of her nature—she could hardly forbear falling at the feet of her husband, and conjuring him to behave, at least, with forbearance to her, and to speak and look at her with kindness.

She did stretch out her hand to him with a look of mournful entreaty, which, though not understood by Berrendale, was not lost upon him entirely. He thought it was a confession of her weakness and his superiority; and, flattered by the thought into unusual softness, he caught her fondly to his bosom, and gave up an engagement to sup at an oyster club, in order to spend the evening tête-à-tête with his wife. Nay, he allowed the little Editha to remain in the room for a whole hour, though she cried when he attempted to take her in his arms, and, observing that it was a cold evening, allowed Adeline her due share of the fire-side.

These circumstances, trivial as they were, had more than their due effect on Adeline, whose heart was more alive to kindness than unkindness; and those paltry attentions of which happy wives would not have been conscious, were to her a source of unfeigned pleasure——As sailors are grateful, after a voyage unexpectedly long, for the muddy water which at their first embarking they would have turned from with disgust.

That very night Adeline remonstrated with the mulatto on the impropriety of her conduct; and, having convinced her that in insulting her husband she failed in respect to her, Savanna was prevailed upon the next morning to ask pardon of Berrendale; and, out of love for her mistress, she took care in future to do nothing that required forgiveness.

As Adeline's way of life admitted of but little variety, Berrendale having persisted in not introducing her to his friends, on the plea of not being rich enough to receive company in return, I shall pass over in silence what occurred to her till Editha was two years old; premising that a series of little injuries on the part of Berrendale, and a quick resentment of them on the part of Adeline, which not even her habitual good humour could prevent, had, during that time, nearly eradicated every trace of love for each other from their hearts.

One evening Adeline as usual, in the absence of her husband, undressed Editha by the parlour fire, and, playing with the laughing child, was enjoying the rapturous praises which Savanna put forth of its growing beauty; while the tawny boy, who had spent the day with them, built houses with cards on the table, which Editha threw down as soon as they were built, and he with good-humoured perseverance raised up again.

Adeline, alive only to the maternal feeling, at this moment had forgotten all her cares; she saw nothing but the happy group around her, and her countenance wore the expression of recovered serenity.

At this moment a loud knock was heard at the door, and Adeline, starting up, exclaimed, "It is my husband's knock!"

"O! no:—he never come so soon," replied the mulatto running to the door; but she was mistaken—it was Berrendale: and Adeline, hearing his voice, began instantly to snatch up Editha's clothes, and to knock down the tawny boy's newly-raised edifice: but order was not restored when Berrendale entered; and, with a look and tone of impatience, he said, "So! fine confusion indeed! Here's a fire-side to come to! Pretty amusement too, for a literary lady—building houses of card!* Shame on your extravagance, Mrs. Berrendale, to let that brat spoil cards in that way!"

The sunshine of Adeline's countenance on hearing this vanished: to be sure, she was accustomed to such speeches; but the moment before she had felt happy, for the first time, perhaps,† for years. She, however, replied not: but, hurrying Editha to bed, ordering the reluctant tawny boy into the kitchen, and setting Berrendale's chair, as usual, in the warmest place, she ventured in a faint voice to ask, what had brought him home so early.

"More early than welcome," replied Berrendale, "if I may judge from the bustle I have occasioned."

"It is very true," replied Adeline, "that, had I expected you, I should have been better prepared for your reception; and then you, perhaps, would have spoken more kindly to me."

"There—there you go again.—If I say but a word to you, then I am called unkind, though, God knows, I never speak‡ without just provocation: and, I declare, I came home in the best humour possible, to tell you what may turn out of great benefit to us both:—but when a man has an uncomfortable home to come to, it is enough to put him out of humour."

The mulatto, who was staying to gather up the cards which had fallen, turned herself round on hearing this, and exclaimed, "Home was very comfortable till you come"; and then with a look of the most angry contempt she left the room, and threw the door to with great violence.

"But what is this good news, my dear?" said Adeline, eager to turn Berrendale's attention from Savanna's insolent reply.

"I have received a letter," he replied, "which, by the by, I ought to have had some weeks ago, from my father-in-law in Jamaica, authorising me to draw on his banker for 900*l.*, and inviting me to come over to him; as he feels himself declining, and wishes to give me the care of his estate, and of my son, to whom all his fortune will descend; and of whose interest, he properly thinks, no one can be so likely to take good care as his own father."

"And do you mean that I and Editha should go with you?" said Adeline turning pale.

"No, to be sure not," eagerly replied Berrendale; "I must first see how the land lies. But if I go—as the old man no doubt will make a hand-some settlement on me—I shall be able to remit* you a very respectable annuity."

Adeline's heart, spite of herself, bounded with joy at this discovery; but she had resolution to add—and if duplicity can ever be pardonable, this was,—"So then the good news which you had to impart to me was, that we were going to be separated!" But as she said this, the consciousness that she was artfully trying to impress Berrendale with an idea of her feeling a sorrow which was foreign to her heart, overcame her; and affected also at being under the necessity of rejoicing at the departure of that being who ought to be the source of her comfort, she vainly struggled to regain composure, and burst into an agony of tears.

But her consternation cannot be expressed, when she found that Berrendale imputed her tears to tender anguish at the idea of parting with him: and when, his vanity being delighted by this homage to his attractions, he felt all his fondness for her revive, and, overwhelming her with caresses, he declared that he would reject the offer entirely if by accepting it he should give her a moment's uneasiness; Adeline, shocked at his error, yet not daring to set him right, could only weep on his shoulder in silence: but, in order to make real the distress which he only fancied so, she enumerated to herself all the diseases incident to the climate, and the danger of the voyage. Still the idea of Berrendale's departure was so full of comfort to her, that, though her tears continued to flow, they flowed not for his approaching absence. At length, ashamed of fortifying him in so gross an error, she made an effort to regain her calmness, and found words to assure him, that she would no longer give way to such unpardonable weakness, as she could assure him that she wished his acceptance of his father-in-law's offer, and had no desire to oppose a scheme so just and so profitable.

But Berrendale, to whose vanity she had never before offered such a tribute as her tears seemed to be, imputed these assurances to disinterested love and female delicacy, afraid to own the fondness which it felt; and the rest of the evening was spent in professions of love on his part, which, on Adeline's, called forth at least some grateful and kind expressions in return.

Still, however, she persisted in urging Berrendale to go to Jamaica: but, at the same time, she earnestly begged him to remember, that temperance could alone preserve his health in such a climate:—"or the use of pepper in great quantities," replied he, "to counteract the effects of good living?"[1]— and Adeline, though convinced temperance was the *best* preservative,* was forced to give up the point, especially as Berrendale began to enumerate the number of delicious things for the table which Jamaica afforded.

To be brief: Berrendale, after taking a most affectionate leave of his wife and child, a leave which almost made the mulatto his friend, and promising to allow them 200*l.* a year till he should be able to send over for them, set sail for Jamaica; while Adeline, the night of his departure, endeavoured, by conjuring up all the horrors of a tempest at sea on his passage, and of a hurricane and an earthquake on shore when he arrived, to force herself to feel such sorrow as the tenderness which he had expressed at the moment of parting seemed to make it her duty to feel.

But morning came, and with it a feeling of liberty and independence so delightful, that she no longer tried to grieve on speculation as it were; but giving up her whole soul to the joys of maternal fondness, she looked forward with pious gratitude to days of tranquil repose, save when she thought with bitter regret of the obdurate anger of her mother, and with tender regret of the lost and ever lamented Glenmurray.

Berrendale had been arrived at Jamaica some months, when Adeline observed a most alarming change in Savanna. She became thin, her appetite entirely failed, and she looked the image of despondence. In vain did Adeline ask the reason of a change so apparent: the only answer she could obtain was, "Me better soon"; and, continuing every day to give this answer, she in a short time became so languid as to be obliged to lie down half the day.

Adeline then found that it was necessary to be more serious in her interrogatories; but the mulatto at first only answered, "No, me die, but me never break my duty vow to you: no, me die, but never leave you."

---

1    Physicians prescribing a regimen for gout generally suggested temperance and moderation: e.g., *The Compleat Family Physician* (Newcastle upon Tyne, 1800-01): "Spices and seasoning should be very sparingly used; the habitual use of pepper, vinegar, mustard, and other stimulatives, blunts the palate so much, as in time to render large quantities of these incentives necessary to produce any effect at all, and by this means, these articles contribute largely to the production of disease" (444).

These words implying a wish to leave her, with a resolution not to do so how much soever it might cost her, alarmed in a moment the ever disinterested sensibility of Adeline; and she at length wrung from her a confession that her dear William, who was gone to Jamaica as* servant to a gentleman, was, she was credibly informed, very ill and like to die.

"You therefore wish to go and nurse him, I suppose, Savanna?"

"Oh! me no wish; me only tink dat me like to go to Jamaica, see if be true dat he be so bad; and if he die I den return, and die wid you."

"Live with me, you mean, Savanna; for, indeed, I cannot spare you. Remember, you have given me a right to claim your life as mine; nor can I allow you to throw away my property in fruitless lamentations, and the indolent indulgence of regret. You shall go to Jamaica, Savanna: God† forbid that I should keep a wife from her duty! You shall see and try to re-cover William if he be really ill," (Savanna here threw herself on Adeline's neck,) "and then you shall return to me, who will either warmly share in your satisfaction or fondly sooth your distress."

"Den you do love poor Savanna?"

"Love you! Indeed I do, next to my child, and, and my mother," replied Adeline, her voice faltering.

"Name not dat woman," cried Savanna hastily; "me will never see, never speak to her even in heaven."

"Savanna, remember, she is my mother."

"Yes, and Mr. Berrendale be your husban; and yet, who dat love you can love dem?"

"Savanna," replied Adeline, "these proofs of your regard, though rep-rehensible, are not likely to reconcile me to your departure; and I already feel that in losing you——" here she paused, unable to proceed.

"Den me no go—me no go:—yet, dearest lady, you have love yourself."

"Aye, Savanna, and can feel for you: so say no more. The only difficulty will be to raise money enough to pay for your passage, and expenses while there."

"Oh! me once nurse the captain's wife who now going to Jamaica, and she love me very much; and he tell me yesterday that he let me go for not-ing,‡ because I am good nurse to his wife, if me wish to see William."

"Enough," replied Adeline: "then all I have to do is to provide you with money for your maintenance when you arrive; and I have no doubt but that what I cannot supply the tawny boy's generous patroness will."

Adeline was not mistaken. Savanna obtained from her son's benefac-tress a sum equal to her wants; and almost instantly restored to her wonted health, by her mind's being lightened of the load which oppressed it, she took her passage on board her friend's vessel, and set sail for Jamaica, car-rying with her letters from Adeline to Berrendale; while Adeline felt the want of Savanna in various ways, so forcibly, that not even Editha could, for a time at least, console her for her loss. It had been so grateful to her feelings to meet every day the eyes of one being fixed with never-varying affection on hers, that, when she beheld those eyes no longer, she felt alone in the universe,—nor had she a single female friend to whom she could turn for relief or consolation.

Mrs. Beauclerc, to whose society she had expected to be restored by her marriage, had been forced to give up all intercourse with her, in compliance with the peremptory wishes of a rich old maid, from whom her children had great expectations, and who threatened to leave her fortune away from them, if Mrs. Beauclerc persisted in corresponding with a woman so bad in principle, and so wicked in practice, as Adeline appeared to her to be.

But, at length, from a mother's employments, from writing, and, above all, from the idea that by suffering she was making atonement* for her past sins, she derived consolation, and became resigned to every evil that had befallen, and to every evil that might still befall her.

Perhaps she did not consider as an evil what now took place: increasing coldness in the letters of Berrendale, till he said openly at last, that as they were, he was forced to confess, far from happy together, and as the air of Jamaica agreed with him, and as he was resolved to stay there, he thought she had better remain in England, and he would remit her as much money occasionally as his circumstances would admit of.

But she thought this a greater evil than it at first appeared; when an agent of Berrendale's father-in-law in England, and a friend of Berrendale himself, called on her, pretending that he came to inquire concerning her health, and raised in her mind suspicions of a very painful nature.

After the usual compliments:—"I find, madam," said Mr. Drury, "that our friend is very much admired by the ladies in Jamaica."

"I am glad to hear it, sir," coolly answered Adeline.

"Well, that's kind and generous now," replied Drury, "and very disinterested."

"I see no virtue, sir, in my rejoicing at† what must make Mr. Berrendale's abode in Jamaica pleasant to him."

"May be so; but most women, I believe, would be apt to be jealous on the occasion."

"But it has been the study of my life, sir, to endeavour to consider my own interest, when it comes in competition with another's, as little as possible;—I doubt I have not always succeeded in my endeavours: but, on this occasion I am certain that I have expressed no sentiment which I do not feel."

"Then, madam, if my friend should have an opportunity, as indeed I believe he has, of forming a most agreeable and advantageous marriage, you would not try to prevent it?"

"Good heavens! sir," replied Adeline; "What can you mean? Mr. Berrendale form an advantageous marriage when he is already married to me?"

"Married to you, ma'am!" answered Mr. Drury with a look of incredulity. "Excuse me, but I know that such marriages as yours may be easily dissolved."

At first Adeline was startled at this assertion; but recollecting that it was impossible any form or ceremony should have been wanting at the marriage, she recovered herself, and demanded, with an air of severity, what Mr. Drury meant by so alarming and ill-founded a speech.

"My meaning, ma'am," replied he, "must be pretty evident to you: I mean that I do not look upon you, though you bear Mr. Berrendale's name, to be his lawful wife; but that you live with him on the same terms on which you lived with Mr. Glenmurray."

"And on what, sir, could you build such an erroneous supposition?"

"On Mr. Berrendale's own words, madam; who always spoke of his connection with you, as of a connection which he had formed in compliance with love and in defiance of prudence."

"And is it possible that he could be such a villain?" exclaimed Adeline. "Oh my child! and does thy father brand thee with the stain of illegitimacy?—But, sir, whatever appellation Mr. Berrendale might choose to give his union with me to his friends in England, I am sure he will not dare to incur the penalty attendant on a man's marrying one wife while he has another living; for, that I am his wife, I can bring pretty sufficient evidence to prove."

"Indeed, madam! You can produce a witness of the ceremony, then, I presume?"

"No, sir; the woman who attended me to the altar, and the clergyman who married us, are dead; and the only witness is a child now only ten years old."

"That is unfortunate!" (with a look of incredulity) "but, no doubt, when you hear that Mr. Berrendale is married to a West Indian heiress, you will come forward with incontrovertible proofs of your prior claims; and if you do that, madam, you may command my good offices:—but, till then, I humbly take my leave." Saying this, with a very visible sneer on his countenance he departed, leaving Adeline in a state of distress—the more painful to endure from her having none to participate in it,—no one to whom she could impart the cause of it.

That Mr. Drury did not speak of the possible marriage of Berrendale from mere conjecture, was very apparent; and Adeline resolved not to delay writing to her husband immediately, to inform him of what had passed, and to* put before his eyes, in the strongest possible manner, the guilt of what he was about to do; and also the utter impossibility of its being successful guilt, as she was resolved to assert her claims for the sake of her child, if not for her own. This letter she concluded, and with truth too, with protestations of believing all Mr. Drury said to be false: for, indeed, the more she considered Berrendale's character, the more she was convinced that, however selfish and defective his disposition might be, it was more likely Mr. Drury should be mistaken, than Berrendale be a villain.

But, where a man's conduct is not founded on virtuous motives and immutable principles, he may not err while temptation is absent; but once expose him to her presence, and he is capable of falling into the very vices the most abhorrent to his nature: and though Adeline knew it not, such a man was Berrendale.

Adeline, having relieved her mind by this appeal to her husband, and being assured that Berrendale could not be married before her letter could reach him, as it was impossible that he should dare to marry while the mulatto was in the very town near which he resided, felt herself capable of attending to her usual employments again, and had recovered her tranquillity, when an answer to her letter arrived; and Adeline, being certain that the letter itself would be a proof of the marriage, had resolved to show it, in justification of her claims, to Mr. Drury.

What then must have been her surprise, to find it exactly such a letter as would be evidence against a marriage between her and Berrendale having ever taken place! He thanked her for the expressions of fond regret which her letter contained, and for the many happy hours which he owed to her society; but hoped that, as Fate had now separated their destinies, she could be as happy without him as she had been with him; and assuring her that he should, according to his promise, regularly remit her 150*l.* a year if possible, but that he could at present only inclose a draft for 50*l.*

Adeline was absolutely stupefied with horror at reading this apparent confirmation of the villany of her husband and the father of her child; but roused to indignant exertion by the sense of Berrendale's baseness, and of what she owed her daughter, she resolved to take counsel's opinion in what manner she should proceed to prove her marriage, as soon as she was assured that Berrendale's (which she had no doubt was fixed upon) should have taken place; and this intelligence she received a short time after from the mulatto herself, who, worn out with sorrow, sickness and hardship, one day tottered into the house, seeming as if she indeed only returned to die with her mistress.

At first the joy of seeing Savanna restored to her swallowed up every other feeling; but tender apprehension for the poor creature's health soon took possession of her mind, and Adeline drew from her a narrative, which exhibited Berrendale to her eyes as capable of most atrocious actions.

# CHAPTER 19

It is very certain that when Berrendale left England, though he meant to conceal his marriage entirely, he had not even the slightest wish to contract another; and had any one told him that he was capable of such wicked conduct, he would have answered like Hazael, "Is thy servant a dog that he should do this thing?"[1] But he was then unassailed by temptations:—and habituated as he was to selfish indulgence, it was impossible that to strong temptation he should not fall an immediate victim.

This strong temptation assailed him soon after his arrival, in the person of a very lovely and rich widow, a relation of his first wife, who, having no children of her own, had long been very fond of his child, then a very fine boy, and with great readiness transferred to the father the affection which she bore the son. For some time conscience and Adeline stood their ground against this new mistress and her immense property; but at length, being pressed by his father-in-law, who wished the match, to assign a sufficient reason for his coldness to so fine a woman, and not daring to give the true one, he returned the lady's fondness; and though he had not yet courage enough to name the marriage day, it was known that it would some time or other take place.

But all his scruples soon yielded to the dominion which the attractions of the lady, who was well versed in the arts of seduction, obtained over his senses, and to the strong power which the sight of the splendor in which she lived, acquired over his avarice; when, just as every thing was on the point of being concluded, the poor mulatto, who had found her husband dead, arrived almost broken-hearted at the place of Berrendale's abode, and delivered to him letters from Adeline.

Terrified and confounded at her presence, he received her with such evident marks of guilty confusion in his face, that Savanna's apprehensive and suspicious attachment to her mistress took the alarm; and, as she had seen a very fine woman leave the room as she entered, she, on pretence of leaving Berrendale alone to read his letters, repaired to the servants' apartments, where she learnt the intended marriage. Immediately forgetting her own distresses in those of Adeline, she returned to Berrendale, not with the languid, mournful pace with which she had first entered, but with the firm, impetuous and intrepid step of conscious integrity going to confound vice in the moment of its triumph.

Berrendale read his doom, the moment he beheld her, in her dark and fiery eye, and awaited in trembling silence the torrent of reproaches that trembled on her lip. But I shall not repeat what passed. Suffice that Ber-

---

1 See 2 Kings 8.13.

rendale pretended to be moved by what she said, and promised to break off the marriage,—only exacting from Savanna, in return, a promise of not imparting to the servants, or to any one, that he had a wife in England.

In the mean while he commended her most affectionately to the care of the steward; and confessing to his intended bride that he had a mistress in England, who had sent the mulatto over to prevent the match if possible, by persuading her he was already married, he conjured her to consent to a private marriage; and to prevent some dreadful scene, occasioned by the revenge of disappointed passion, should his mistress, as she had threatened, come over in person, he entreated her to let every splendid preparation for their nuptials be laid aside, in order to deceive Savanna, and induce her to return quietly to England.

The credulous woman, too much in love to believe what she did not wish, consented to all he proposed: but Berrendale, still fearful of the watchful jealousy of Savanna, contrived to find out the master to whom she belonged before she had escaped, early in life, with her first husband to England; and as she had never been made free, as soon as he arrived, he, on a summons from Berrendale, seized her as his property; and poor Savanna, in spite of her cries and struggles, was conveyed some miles up the country.

At length, however, she found means to escape to the coast; and, having discovered an old acquaintance in an English sailor on board a vessel then ready to sail, and who had great influence with the captain, she was by him concealed on board, with the approbation of the commander, and was on her way to England before Berrendale was informed of her escape.

I will not endeavour to describe Adeline's feelings on hearing this narration, and on finding also that Savanna before she left the island had been assured that Berrendale was really married, though privately, but that the marriage could not long be attempted to be concealed, as the lady even before it took place was likely to become a mother; and, that as a large estate depended on her giving birth to a son, the event of her confinement was looked for with great anxiety.

Still, in the midst of her distress, a sudden thought struck Adeline, which converted her anger into joy, and her sorrow into exultation. "Yes, my mother may now forgive me without violating any part of her oath," she exclaimed.—"I am now forsaken, despised and disgraced!"—and instantly she wrote to Mrs. Mowbray a letter, calculated to call forth all her sympathy and affection. Then, with a mind relieved beyond expression, she sat down to deliberate in what manner she should act to do herself justice as a wife and a mother, cruelly aggrieved in both these intimate relations. Nor could she persuade herself that she should act properly by her child, if she did not proceed vigorously to prove herself Berrendale's wife, and substantiate Editha's claim to his property; and as Mr. Langley was, she knew, a very great lawyer, she resolved, in spite of his improper conduct to her, to apply to him again.

Indeed she could not divest herself of a wish to let him know that she was become a wife, and no longer liable to be treated with that freedom with which, as a mistress, he had thought himself at liberty to address her. However, she wished that she had not been obliged to go to him alone: but, as the mulatto was in too weak a state of health to allow of her going out, and she could not speak of business like hers before any one else, she was forced to proceed unaccompanied to the Temple; and on the evening of the day after Savanna's return, she, with a beating heart, repaired once more to Mr. Langley's chambers.

Luckily, however, she met the tawny boy on her way, and took him for her escort. "Tell your master," said she to the servant, "that Mrs. Berrendale wishes to speak to him": and in a few minutes she was introduced.

"Mrs. Berrendale!" cried Langley with a sarcastic smile; "pray be seated, madam! I hope Mr. Berrendale is well."

"He is in Jamaica, sir," replied Adeline.

"Indeed!" returned Langley. "May I presume so far as to ask,—hem, hem,—whether your visit to me be merely of a professional nature?"

"Certainly, sir," replied Adeline: "of what other nature should it be?"

Langley replied to this only by a significant smile. At this moment the tawny boy asked leave to walk in the Temple gardens; and Adeline, though reluctantly, granted his request.

"Oh! à propos,[1] John," cried Langley to the servant, "let Mrs. Montgomery know that her friend miss Mowbray, Mrs. Berrendale I mean, is here—she is walking in the garden."

"My friend Mrs. Montgomery, sir! I have no friend of that name."

"No, my sweet soul? You may not know her by that name; but names change, you know. You, for instance, are Mrs. Berrendale now, but when I see you again you may be Mrs. somebody else."

"Never, sir," cried Adeline indignantly; "but, though I do not exactly understand your meaning, I feel as if you meant to insult me, and therefore—"

"Oh no—sit down again, my angel; you are mistaken, and so apt to fly off in a tangent! But—so—that wonderfully handsome man, Berrendale, is off—heh? Your friend and mine, heh! pretty one!"

"If, sir, Mr. Berrendale ever considered you as his friend, it is very strange that you should presume to insult his wife."

---

1 "By the way" (Fr.).

"Madam," replied Langley with a most provoking sneer, "Mr. Berrendale's wife shall always be treated by me with proper respect."

"Gracious Heaven!" cried Adeline, clasping her hands and looking upwards with tearful eyes, "when shall my persecutions cease! and how much greater must my offences be than even my remorse paints them, when their consequences still torment me so long after the crime which occasioned them has ceased to exist! But it is Thy will, and I will submit even to indignity with patience."

There was a touching solemnity in this appeal to heaven,* an expression of truth, which it was so impossible for art to imitate, that Langley felt in a moment the injustice of which he had been guilty, and an apology was on his lips, when the door opened, and a lady, rouged like a French countess of the ancien régime,[1] her hair covered with a profusion of brown powder, and dressed in the height of the fashion, ambled into the room; and saying, "How d'ye do, miss Mowbray?" threw herself carelessly on the sofa, to the astonishment of Adeline, who did not recollect her, and to the confusion of Langley, who now, impressed with involuntary respect for Adeline, repented of having exposed her to the scene that awaited her: but to prevent it was impossible; he was formed to be the slave of women,† and had not courage to protect another from the insolence to which he tamely yielded himself.

Adeline at first did not answer this soi-disant[2] acquaintance of hers; but, in looking at her more attentively, she exclaimed, "What do I see? Is it possible that this can be Mary Warner!"

"Yes, it is, my dear, indeed," replied she with a loud laugh, "Mary Warner, alias Mrs. Montgomery; as you, you know, are miss Mowbray, alias Mrs. Berrendale."

Adeline, incapable of speaking, only gazed at her in silence, but with a countenance more in sorrow than in anger.‡[3]

"But, come, sit down, my dear," cried Mary; "no ceremony, you know, among friends and equals, you know; and you and I have been mighty familiar, you know, before now. The last time we met you called me *woman*, you know—yes, 'woman!' says you—and I have not forgotten it, I assure you," she added with a sort of loud hysterical laugh, and a look of the most determined malice.

---

1  "Old regime" (Fr.), the aristocracy before the French Revolution. Mary Warner has (at least in her own eyes) risen in the world.
2  "So-called," "supposed" (Fr.).
3  See Shakespeare, *Hamlet* 1.2.231.

"Come, come, my dear Montgomery," said Langley, "you must forget and forgive;—I dare say miss Mowbray, that is to say Mrs. Berrendale, did not mean—"

"What should you know about the matter, Lang?" replied Mary; "I wish you would mind your own business, and let me talk to my dumb friend here. Well, I suppose you are quite surprised to see how smart I am!—seeing as how I once over-hard you say to Glenthingymy, 'How very plain Mary is!' though, to be sure, it was never a barrel the better herring, and 'twas the kettle in my mind calling the pot[1]—heh, Lang.?"

Here was the clue to the inveterate dislike which this unhappy girl had conceived against Adeline. So true is it that little wounds inflicted on the self-love are never forgotten or forgiven, and that it is safer to censure the morals of acquaintances than to ridicule them on their dress, or laugh at a defect in their person. Adeline, indeed, did not mean that her observation should be over-heard by the object of it,—still she was hated: but many persons make mortifying remarks purposely, and yet wonder that they have enemies!

Motionless and almost lifeless Adeline continued to stand and to listen, and Mary went on—

"Well, but I thank you for one thing. You taught me that marriage was all nonsense, you know; and so thought I, miss Mowbray is a learned lady, she must know best, and so I followed your example—that's all you know."

This dreadful information roused the feelings of Adeline even to phrensy, and with a shriek of anguish she seized her hand, and conjured her by all her hopes of mercy to retract what she had said, and not to let her depart with the horrible consciousness of having been the means of plunging a fellow-being into vice and ignominy.[*]

A loud unfeeling laugh, and an exclamation of "the woman is mad," was all the answer to this.

"This then is the completion of my sufferings," cried Adeline,—"this only was wanted to complete the misery of my remorse."

"Good God! this[†] is too much," exclaimed Langley. "Mary, you know very well that—"

"Hold your tongue, Lang.; you know nothing about the matter: it is all nothing, but that miss Mowbray, like a lawyer, can change sides, you see, and attack one day what she defended the day before, you know; and she have made you believe that she think[‡] now being kept a shameful thing."

---

1 A proverbial expression; cf. Henry Fielding, *The Covent Garden Tragedy* (1732): "Dares thus the kettle to rebuke our sin! / Dares thus the kettle say the pot is black!" (2.5).

"I do believe so," hastily replied Adeline; "and if it be true that my sentiments and my example led you to adopt your present guilty mode of life,—oh! save me from the pangs of remorse which I now feel, by letting my present example recall you from the paths of error to those of virtue."

"Well pleaded," cried the cold-hearted Mary—"Lang., you could not have done't so well—not up to that."

"Mrs. Montgomery," said Langley with great severity, "if you cannot treat Mrs. Berrendale with more propriety and respect, I must beg you to leave the room; she is come to speak to me on business, and—"

"I sha'n't stir, for all that: and mark me, Lang., if you turn me out of the room, you know, curse* me if ever I enter it again!"

"But your little boy may want you; you have left him now some time."

"Aye, that may be true, to be sure, poor little dear! Have you any family, miss Mowbray?"—when, without waiting for an answer, she added, "My little boy have got the small-pox very bad, and has been likely to die from convulsion fits, you know. Poor dear! I had been nursing it so long that I could not bear the stench of the room,[1] and so I was glad, you know, to come and get a little fresh air in the gardens."

At this speech Adeline's fortitude entirely gave way. *Her* child had not had the small-pox, and she had been for some minutes in reach of the infection; and with a look of horror, forgetting her business, and every thing but Editha, she was on the point of leaving the room, when a servant hastily entered, and told Mary that her little boy was dead.

At hearing this, even her cold heart was moved, and throwing herself back on the sofa she fell into a strong hysteric; while Adeline, losing all remembrance of her insolence in her distress, flew to her assistance; and, in pity for a mother weeping the loss of her infant, forgot for a moment that she was endangering the life of her own child.

Mr. Langley, mean time, though grieved for the death of the infant, was alive to the generous forgiving disposition which Adeline evinced; and could not help exclaiming, "Oh, Mrs. Berrendale! forgive us! we deserved not such kindness at your hands": and Adeline, wanting to loosen the tight stays of Mary, and not choosing to undress her before such a witness, coldly begged him to withdraw, advising him at the same time to go and see whether the child was really dead, as it might possibly only appear so.

Revived by this possibility, Mr. Langley left Mary to the care of Adeline, and left the room. But whether it was that Mary had a mind to impress her lover and the father of her child with an idea of her sensibility, or whether she had overheard Adeline's supposition, certain it is, that as soon as Langley went away, and Adeline began to unlace her stays, she hastily

---

1  Smallpox was associated with a distinctive and unpleasant odour.

recovered, and declared her stays should remain as they were: but still exclaiming about her poor dear Benny, she kept her arms closely clasped round Adeline's waist, and reposed her head on her bosom.

Adeline's fears and pity for her being thus allayed, she began to have leisure to feel and fear for herself; and the idea, that, by being in such close contact with Mary, she was imbibing so much of the disease as must inevitably communicate it to Editha, recurred so forcibly to her mind, that, begging for God's* sake she would loose her hold, she endeavoured to break from the arms of her tormentor.

But in vain.—As soon as Mary saw that Adeline wished to leave her, she was the more eager to hold her fast; and protesting she should die if she had the barbarity to leave her alone, she only hugged her the closer. "Well, then, I'll try to stay till Mr. Langley returns," cried Adeline: but some minutes elapsed, and Mr. Langley did not return; and then Adeline, recollecting that when he did return he would come fresh fraught with the pestilence from the dead body of his infant, could no longer master her feelings, but screaming wildly,—"I shall be the death of my child; for God's sake† let me go,"—she struggled with the determined Mary. "You will drive me mad if you detain me," cried Adeline.

"You will drive me mad if you go," replied Mary, giving way to a violent hysterical scream, while with successful strength she parried all Adeline's endeavours to break from her. But what can resist the strength of phrensy and despair? Adeline, at length worked up to madness by the fatal control exercised over her, by one great effort threw the sobbing Mary from her, and, darting down stairs with the rapidity of phrensy, nearly knocked down Mr. Langley in her passage, who was coming to announce the restoration of the little boy.

She soon reached Fleet-street, and was on her road home before Langley and Mary had recovered their consternation: but she suddenly recollected that homewards she must not proceed; that she carried death about her; and wholly bewildered by this insupportable idea, she ran along the Strand, muttering the incoherencies of phrensy as she went, till she was intercepted in her passage by some young men of *ton*,[1] who had been dining together, and, being half intoxicated, were on their way to the theatre.

Two of these gentlemen, with extended arms, prevented her further progress.

"Where are you going, my pretty girl," cried one, "in this hurry? shall I see you home? heh!"

"Home!" replied Adeline; "name it not. My child! my child! thy mother has destroyed thee."

---

1 "Manner" (Fr.): i.e., young men of fashionable manners.

"So!" cried another, "an actress, by all that's tragical!"

"Unhand me!" exclaimed Adeline wildly. "Do not you know, poor babe, that I carry death and pollution* about with me!"

"The devil you do!" returned the gentleman; "then the sooner you take yourself off the better."

"I believe the poor soul is mad," said a third, making way for Adeline to pass.

"But," cried the first who spoke, catching hold of her, "if so, there is method and meaning in her madness; for she called Jaby here a poor babe, and we all know he is little better."

By this time Adeline was in a state of complete phrensy, and was again darting down the street in spite of the gentleman's efforts to hold her, when another gentleman, whom curiosity had induced to stop and listen to what passed, suddenly seized hold of her arm, and exclaimed, "Good Heavens! what can this mean? It is—it can be no other than miss Mowbray."

At the sound of her own name Adeline started: but in a moment her senses were quite lost again; and the gentleman, who was no other than colonel Mordaunt, being fully aware of her situation, after reproving the young men for sporting with distress so apparent, called a coach which happened to be passing, and desired to know whither he should have the honour of conducting her.

But she was too lost to be able to answer the question: he therefore, lifting her into the coach, desired the man to drive towards Dover-street; and when there, he ordered him to drive to Margaret-street Oxford-street;[1] when, not being able to obtain one coherent word from Adeline, and nothing but expressions of agony, terror, and self-condemnation, he desired him to stop at such a house, and, conducting Adeline up stairs, desired the first assistance to be procured immediately.

It was not to his own lodgings that colonel Mordaunt had conducted Adeline, but to the house of a convenient friend of his, who, though not generally known as such, and bearing a tolerably good character in the world, was very kind to the tender distresses of her friends, and had no objection to assist the meetings of two fond lovers.

It is to be supposed, then, that she was surprised at seeing colonel Mordaunt with a companion, who was an object of pity and horror rather than of love: but she did not want humanity; and when the colonel recommended Adeline to her tenderest care, she with great readiness ordered a bed to be prepared, and assisted in prevailing on Adeline to lie down on

---

1  Adeline has walked north from the Temple to Fleet St.; Colonel Mordaunt takes her by coach west to Dover St. in Mayfair, and then to Margaret St., about a mile further north, running parallel to Oxford St.

it. In a short time a physician and a surgeon arrived; and Adeline, having been bled and made to swallow strong opiates, was undressed by her attentive landlady; and though still in a state of unconsciousness, she fell into a sound sleep, which lasted till morning.

But colonel Mordaunt passed a sleepless night. The sight of Adeline, even frantic and wretched as she appeared, had revived the passion which he had conceived for her; and if on her awaking the next morning she should appear perfectly rational, and her phrensy merely the result of some great fright which she had received, he resolved to renew his addresses, and take advantage of the opportunity now offered him, while she was as it were in his power.

But to return to the Temple. Soon after Mr. Langley had entered his own room, and while Mary and he were commenting on the frantic behaviour of Adeline, the tawny boy came back from his walk, and heard with marks of emotion, apparently beyond his age, (for though near twelve he did not look above eight years old,) of the sudden and frantic disappearance of Adeline.

"Oh! my dear friend," cried he, "if you are not gone home you will break my poor mother's heart!"

"And who is your mother?"

"Her name is Savanna; and she lives with Mrs. Berrendale."

"Mrs. Berrendale!" cried Mary, "miss Mowbray you mean."

"No, I do not;—her name was Mowbray, but is now Berrendale."

"What! is she really married?" asked Langley.

"Yes, to be sure."

"But how do you know that she is?"

"Oh! because I went to church with them, and my mother cooked the wedding-dinner, and I ate plum-pudding and drank punch, and we were very merry,—only my mother cried, because my father could not come."

"Very circumstantial evidence, indeed!" cried Langley, "and I am very sorry that I did not know so much before. So you and your mother love this extraordinary fine woman, Mrs. Berrendale, heh?"

"Love her! To be sure—we should be very wicked if we did not. Did you never hear the story of the pine-apple?" said the tawny boy.

"Not I. What was it?" and the tawny boy, delighted to tell the story, with sparkling eyes sat down to relate it.

"You must know, Mr. Glenmurray longed for a pine-apple."

"Mrs. Glenmurray you mean," said Mary laughing immoderately.[1]

---

[1] Remembering that Adeline had been pregnant at the time, Mary is joking about food cravings.

"I know what I say," replied the tawny boy angrily; "and so miss Adeline, as she was then called, went out to buy one;—well, and so she met my poor father going to prison, and I was crying after her, and so—" Here he paused, and bursting into tears exclaimed, "And perhaps she is crying herself now, and I must go and see for her directly."

"Do so, my fine fellow," cried Langley: "you had better go home, tell your mother what has passed, and to-morrow (accompanying him down stairs, and speaking in a low voice) I will either write a note of apology or call on Mrs. Berrendale myself."

The tawny boy instantly set off, running as fast as he could, telling Langley first, that if any harm had happened to his friend, both he and his mother should lie down and die. And this further proof of Adeline's merit did not tend to calm Langley's remorse for having exposed her to the various distresses which she had undergone at his chambers.

CHAPTER 20

ADELINE awoke early the next morning perfectly sane, though weakened by the exertions which she had experienced the night before, and saw with surprise and alarm that she was not in her own lodging.

But she had scarcely convinced herself that she was awake, when Mrs. Selby, the mistress of the house, appeared at her bed-side, and, seeing what was passing in her mind by her countenance, explained to her as delicately as she could the situation in which she had been brought there.

"And who brought me hither?" replied Adeline, dreadfully agitated, as the remembrance of what had passed by degrees burst upon her.

"Colonel Mordaunt of the life-guards,"* was the answer; and Adeline was shocked to find that he was the person to whom she was under so essential an obligation. She then hastily arose, being eager to return home; and in a short time she was ready to enter the drawing-room, and to express her thanks to colonel Mordaunt.

But in vain did she insist on going home directly, to ease the fears of her family. The physician, who arrived at the moment, forbade her going out without having first taken both medicine and refreshment; and by the time that, after the most earnest entreaties, she obtained leave to depart, she recollected that, as her clothes were the same, she might still impart disease to her child, and therefore must on no account think of returning to Editha.

"Whither, whither then can I go?" cried she, forgetting she was not alone.

"Why not stay here?" said the colonel, who had been purposely left alone with her. "O dearest of women! that you would but accept the protection of a man who adores you; who has long loved you; who has been so fortunate as to rescue you from a situation of misery and danger, and the study of whose life it shall be to make you happy."

He uttered this with such volubility, that Adeline could not find an opportunity to interrupt him; but when he concluded, she calmly replied, "I am willing to believe, colonel Mordaunt, from a conversation which I once had with you, that you are not aware of the extent of the insult which you are now offering to me. You probably do not know that I have been for years a married woman?"

Colonel Mordaunt started and turned pale at this intelligence; and in a faltering voice replied, that he was indeed a stranger to her present situation;—for that, libertine as he confessed himself to be, he had never yet allowed himself to address the wife of another.

This speech restored him immediately to the confidence of Adeline. "Then I hope," cried she, holding out her hand to him, which in spite of his virtue he passionately kissed, "that, as a friend, you will have the kindness to procure me a coach to take me to a lodging a few miles out of town, where I once was before; and that you will be so good as to drive directly to my lodgings, and let my poor maid know what is become of me. I dread to think," added she bursting into tears, "of the agony that my unaccountable absence must have occasioned her."

The colonel, too seriously attached to Adeline to know yet what he wished, or what he hoped on this discovery of her situation, promised to obey her, provided she would allow him to call on her now and then; and Adeline was too full of gratitude to him for the service which he had rendered her, to have resolution enough to deny his request. He then called a coach for himself, and for Adeline, as she insisted on his going immediately to her lodgings; and also begged that he would tell the mulatto to send for advice, and prepare her little girl for inoculation[1] directly.

Adeline drove directly to her old lodgings in the country, where she was most gladly received; and the colonel went to deliver his commission to the mulatto.

He found her in strong hysterics; the tawny boy crying over her, and the women of the house holding her down on the bed by force, while the little Editha had been conveyed to a neighbour's house, that she might not hear the screams which had surprised and terrified her.

Colonel Mordaunt had opened the door, and was witnessing this distressing scene, before any one was conscious of his presence; but the tawny boy soon discovered him, and crying out—

---

1 Intentional infection with a mild case of smallpox, in order to develop immunity. The practice became less common after 1796, when Edward Jenner introduced the safer practice of vaccination with cowpox.

"Oh! sir, do you bring us news of our friend?" sprang to him, and hung almost breathless on his arm.

Savanna, who was conscious enough to know what passed, though too much weakened from her own sufferings and anxieties to be able to struggle with this new affliction, started up on hearing these words, and screamed out "Does she live? Blessed man! but say so, dat's all," in a tone so affecting, and with an expression of agonized curiosity so overwhelming to the feelings, that colonel Mordaunt, whose spirits were not very high, was so choked that he could not immediately answer her; and when at last he faltered out, "She lives, and is quite well," the frantic joy of the mulatto overcame him still more. She jumped about his neck, she hugged the tawny boy; and her delight was as extravagant as her grief had been; till exhausted and silent she sunk upon the bed, and was unable for some minutes to listen quietly to the story which colonel Mordaunt came to relate.

When she was composed enough to listen to it, she did not long remain so; for as soon as she heard that colonel Mordaunt had met Adeline in her phrensy, and conveyed her to a place of safety, she fell at his feet, embraced his knees, and, making the tawny boy kneel down by her, invoked the blessing of God on him so fervently and so eloquently, that colonel Mordaunt wept like a child, and, exclaiming, "Upon my soul, my good woman, I cannot bear this," was forced to run out of the house to recover his emotion.

When he returned, Savanna said, "Well—now, blessed sir, take me to my dear lady."

"Indeed," replied he, "I must not; you are forbidden to see her."

"Forbidden!" replied she, her eyes flashing fire; "and who dare to keep Savanna from her own missess?*—I will see her."

"Not if she forbids it, Savanna; and if her child's life should be endangered by it?"

"O, no, to be sure not," cried the tawny boy, who doted upon Editha, and, having fetched her back from the next house, was lulling her to sleep in his arms.

Colonel Mordaunt started at sight of the child, and, stooping down to kiss its rosy cheek, sighed deeply as he turned away again.

"Well," cried Savanna, "you talk very strange—me no understand."

"But you shall, my excellent creature," replied the colonel, "immediately." He then entered on a full explanation to Savanna; who had no sooner heard that her mistress feared that she had been so much exposed to the infection of the small-pox, as to make her certain of giving it to her child, than she exclaimed, "Oh, my good God! save and protect her own self! She never have it, and she may get it and die!"

"Surely you must be mistaken," replied the colonel, "Mrs. Berrendale must have recollected and mentioned her own danger if this be the case."

"She!" hastily interrupted the mulatto, "she tink of herself! Never— she only mind others' good.—Do you tink, if she be one selfish beast like her husban, Savanna love her so dear? No, Mr. colonel, me know her, and me know though we may save the child we may lose the mother." Here she began to weep bitterly; while the colonel, more in love than ever with Adeline from these proofs of her goodness, resolved to lose no time in urging her to undergo herself the operation which she desired for Editha.

Then, begging the mulatto to send for a surgeon directly, in spite of the tears of the tawny boy, who thought it cruel to run the risk of spoiling miss Editha's pretty face, he took his leave, saying to himself, "What a heart has this Adeline! how capable of feeling affection! for no one can inspire it who is not able to feel it: and this creature is thrown away on a man undeserving her, it seems!"

On this intelligence he continued to muse till he arrived at Adeline's lodgings, to whom he communicated all that had passed; and from whom he learned, with great anxiety, that it was but too true that she had never had the small-pox; and that, therefore, she should probably show symptoms of the disease in a few days: consequently, as she considered it too late for her to be inoculated, she should do all that now remained to be done for her security, by low living and good air.

That same evening colonel Mordaunt returned to Savanna, in hopes of learning from her some further particulars respecting Adeline's husband; as he felt that his conscience would not be much hurt by inducing Adeline to leave the protection of a man who was unworthy of possessing her. Fortunately for his wishes, he could not wish to hear more than Savanna wished to tell every thing relating to her adored lady: and colonel Mordaunt heard with generous indignation of the perfidious conduct of Berrendale; vowing, at the same time, that his time, his interest, and his fortune, should all be devoted to bring such a villain to justice, and to secure to the injured Editha her rightful inheritance.

The mulatto was in raptures:—she told colonel Mordaunt that he was a charming man, and infinitely handsomer than Berrendale, though she must own he was very good to look at; and she wished with all her soul that colonel Mordaunt was married to her lady; for then she believed she would have never known sorrow, but been as happy as the day was long.

Colonel Mordaunt could not hear this without a secret pang. "Had I followed," said he mentally, "the dictates of my heart when I saw Adeline at Bath, I might now, perhaps, instead of being a forlorn unattached being, have been a happy husband and father; and Adeline, instead of having been the mistress of one man, and the disowned wife of another, might have been happy and beloved, and as respectable in the eyes of the world as she is now* in those of her grateful mulatto."

However, there was some hope left for him yet.—Adeline, he thought, was not a woman likely to be over-scrupulous in her ideas; and might very naturally think herself at liberty to accept the protection of a lover, when, from no fault of hers, she had lost that of her husband.

It is natural to suppose that, while elevated with these hopes, he did not fail to be very constant in his visits to Adeline; and that at length, more led by passion than policy, he abruptly, at the end of ten days, informed Adeline that he knew her situation, and that he trusted that she would allow him to hope that in due time his love, which had been proof against time, absence and disdain, would meet with reward; and that, on his settling a handsome income on her and her child for their joint lives, she would allow him to endeavour to make her as happy as she, and she only, could make him.

To this proposal, which was in form of a letter, colonel Mordaunt did not receive an immediate answer; nor was it at first likely that he should ever receive an answer to it at all, as Adeline was at the moment of its arrival confined to her bed, according to her expectations, with the disease which she had been but too fearfully† imbibing: while the half-distracted mulatto was forced to give up to others the care of the sickening Editha, to watch over the delirious and unconscious Adeline.

But the tawny boy's generous benefactress gave him leave to remain at Adeline's lodgings, in order to calm his fears for Editha, and assist in amusing and keeping her quiet; and if attention had any share in preserving the life and beauty of Editha, it was to the affectionate tawny boy that she owed them; and he was soon rewarded for all his care and anxiety by seeing his little charge able to play about as usual.

Colonel Mordaunt and the mulatto meanwhile did not obtain so speedy a termination to their anxieties; Adeline's recovery was for a long time a matter of doubt; and her weakness so great after the crisis of the disorder was past, that none ventured to pronounce her, even then, out of danger.

But at length she was in a great measure restored to health, and able to determine what line of conduct it was necessary for her to pursue.—To return an answer to colonel Mordaunt's proposals was certainly her first business; but as she felt that the situation in which he had once known her made his offer less affronting than it would have been under other circumstances, she resolved to speak to him on the subject with gentleness, not severity; especially as during her illness, to amuse the anxiety that had preyed upon him, he had taken every possible step to procure evidence of the marriage, and gave into Savanna's hands, the first day that he was permitted to see her, an attested certificate of it.

## CHAPTER 21

THE first question which Adeline asked on her recovery was, Whether any letter had come by the general post during her illness; and Savanna gave one to her immediately.

It was the letter so ardently desired; for the direction was in her mother's hand-writing! and she opened it full of eager expectation, while her whole existence seemed to depend on the nature of its contents. What then must have been her agony on finding that the *enveloppe*[1] contained nothing but her own letter returned! For some time she spoke not, she breathed not; while Savanna mixed with expressions of terror, at sight of her mistress's distress,* execrations on the unnatural parent who had so cruelly occasioned it.

After a few days' incessant struggle to overcome the violence of her sorrow, Adeline recovered the shock, in appearance at least: yet to Savanna's self-congratulations she could not help answering (laying her hand on her heart), "The blow is here, Savanna, and the wound incurable."

Soon after she thought herself well enough to see colonel Mordaunt, and to thank him for the recent proof of his attention to her and her interest. But no obligation, however great, could shut the now vigilant eyes of Adeline to the impropriety of receiving further visits from him, or to the guilt of welcoming to her house a man who made open professions to her of illicit love.

She however thought it her duty to see him once more, in order to try to reconcile him to the necessity of the rule of conduct which she was going to lay down for herself; nor was she without hope that the yet recent traces of the disease, to which she had so nearly fallen a victim, would make her appearance so unpleasing to the eyes of her lover, that he would be very willing to absent himself from the house, for some time at least, and probably give up all thoughts of her.

But she did neither herself nor colonel Mordaunt justice.—She was formed to inspire a real and lasting passion—a passion that no external change could destroy—since it was founded on the unchanging qualities of the heart and mind: and colonel Mordaunt felt for her such an attachment in all its force. He had always admired the attractive person and winning graces of Adeline, and felt for her what he denominated love; but that rational though enthusiastic preference, which is deserving of the name of true love, he never felt till he had an opportunity to appreciate justly the real character of Adeline: still there were times when he felt almost grati-

---

1   In the late eighteenth century "envelope" was customarily given French pronunciation (*OED*).

fied to reflect that she could not legally be his; for, whatever might have been the cause and excuse of her errors, she had erred, and the delicacy of his mind revolted at the idea of marrying the mistress of another.

But when he saw and heard Adeline this repugnance vanished; and he knew that, could he at those moments lead her to the altar, he should not have hesitated to bind himself to her for ever by the sacred ties which the early errors of her judgment had made her* in his opinion almost unworthy to form.

At length a day was fixed for his interview with Adeline, and with a beating heart he entered the apartment; nor was his emotion diminished when he beheld not only the usual vestiges of her complaint, but symptoms of debility, and a death-like meagreness of aspect, which made him fear that though one malady was conquered, another, even more dangerous, remained. The idea overcame him; and he was forced to turn to the window to hide his emotion: and his manner was so indicative of ardent yet respectful attachment, that Adeline began to feel in spite of herself that her projected task was difficult of execution.

For some minutes neither of them spoke: Mordaunt held the hand which she gave him to his heart, kissed it as she withdrew it, and again turned away his head to conceal a starting tear; while Adeline was not sorry to have a few moments in which to recover herself, before she addressed him on the subject at that time nearest to the heart of both. At length she summoned resolution enough to say:—

"Much as I have been mortified and degraded, colonel Mordaunt, by the letter which I have received from you, still I rejoice that I did receive it:—in the first place, I rejoice, because I look on all the sufferings and mortifications which I meet with as latent blessings,† as expiations required of‡ me in mercy by the Being whom I adore, for the sins of which I have been guilty; and, in the second place, because it gives me an opportunity of proving, incontrovertibly, my full conviction of the fallacy of my past opinions, and that I became a wife, after my idle declamations against marriage, from change of principle, on assurance of error, and not from interest, or necessity."

Here she paused, overcome with the effort which she had made; and colonel Mordaunt would have interrupted her, but, earnestly conjuring him to give her a patient hearing, she proceeded thus:—

"Had the change in my practice been the result of any thing but rational conviction, I should now, unfortunate as I have been in the choice of a husband, regret that ever I formed so foolish a tie, and perhaps be induced to enter into a less sacred connection, from an idea that that state which forced me to drag out existence in hopeless misery was contrary to reason, justice, and the benefit of society; and that the sooner its ties were dissolved, the better it would be for individual happiness and for the world at large."

"And do you not think so?" cried colonel Mordaunt; "cannot your own individual experience convince you of it?"

"Far from it," replied Adeline; "and I bless God that it does not: for thence, and thence only, do I begin to be reconciled to myself. I have no doubt that there is a great deal of individual suffering in the marriage state, from* contrariety of temper and other causes; but I believe that the mass of happiness and virtue is certainly increased by it. Individual suffering, therefore, is no more an† argument for the abolition of marriage, than the accidental bursting of a musquet‡¹ would be for the total abolition of fire-arms."

"But, surely, dear Mrs. Berrendale, you would wish divorce to be made easier than it is?"

"By no means," interrupted Adeline, understanding what he was going to say: "to BEAR and FORBEAR² I believe to be the grand secret of happiness, and§ ought to be the great study of life: therefore, whatever would enable married persons to separate on the slightest quarrel or disgust, would make it so much the less necessary for us to learn this important lesson; a lesson so needful in order to perfect the human character, that I believe the difficulty of divorce to be one of the greatest blessings of society."

"What can have so completely changed your opinions on this subject?" replied colonel Mordaunt.

"Not my own experience," returned Adeline; "for the painful situations in which I have been placed, I might attribute, not to the *fallacy*** of the system on which I have acted, but to those existing prejudices in society which I wish to see destroyed."

"Then, to what else is the change in your sentiments to be attributed?"

"To a more serious, unimpassioned, and unprejudiced view of the subject than I had before taken: at present I am not equal to expatiate on matters so important: however, some time or other, perhaps, I may make known to you my sentiments on them in a more ample manner: but I have, I trust, said enough to lead you to conclude, that though Mr. Berrendale's conduct to me has been atrocious, and that you are in many respects entitled to my gratitude and thanks, you and I must henceforward be strangers to each other."

Colonel Mordaunt, little expecting such a total overthrow to his hopes, was, on receiving it, choked with contending emotions; and his broken

---

1   Or musket; a long-barrelled gun.
2   A common proverbial expression; for one of many literary uses, see "Paris—Dwarf" in Laurence Sterne, *A Sentimental Journey* (1768).

sentences and pale cheek were sufficiently expressive of the distress which he endured. But I shall not enter into a detail of all he urged in favour of his passion; nor the calm, dignified, and feeling manner in which Adeline replied. Suffice that, at last, from a sort of intuitive knowledge of the human heart, as it were, which persons of quick talents and sensibilities possess, however defective their experience, Adeline resolved to try to sooth the self-love which she had wounded, knowing that self-love is scarcely to be distinguished in its effects from love itself; and that the agony of disappointed passion is always greater when it is inflicted by the coldness or falsehood of the beloved object, than when it proceeds from parental prohibition, or the cruel separation enjoined by conscious poverty. She therefore told colonel Mordaunt that he was once very near being the first choice of her heart: when she first saw him, she said, his person, and manners, and attentions, had so strongly prepossessed her in his favour, that he himself, by ceasing to see and converse with her, could alone have saved her from the pain of a hopeless attachment.

"For God's sake,* spare me," cried Mordaunt, "the contemplation of the happiness I might have enjoyed!"

"But you know you were not a marrying-man, as it is called; and forgive me if I say, that men who can on system suppress the best feelings of their nature, and prefer a course of libertine indulgence to a virtuous connection, at that time of life when they might become happy husbands and fathers, with the reasonable expectation of living to see their children grown up to manhood, and superintending their education themselves—such men, colonel Mordaunt, deserve, in the decline of life, to feel that regret and that self-condemnation which you this moment anticipate."

"True—too true!" replied the colonel; "but, for mercy's sake, torture me no more."

"I would not probe where I did not intend to make a cure," replied Adeline.

"A cure!—what mean you?"

"I mean to induce you, ere it be yet too late, to endeavour to form a virtuous attachment, and to unite yourself for life with some amiable young woman who will make you as happy as I would have endeavoured to make you, had it been my fortunate lot to be yours: for, believe me, colonel Mordaunt," and her voice faltered as she said it, "had *he*, whom I still continue to love with unabated tenderness, though years have elapsed since he was taken from me,—had he bequeathed me to you on his death-bed, the reluctance with which I went to the altar would have been more easily overcome."

Saying this, she suddenly left the room, leaving colonel Mordaunt surprised, gratified, and his mind struggling between hopes and fears; for

Adeline was not conscious that she imparted hope as well as consolation by the method which she pursued; and though she sent Savanna to tell the colonel she could see him no more that evening, he departed in firm expectation that Adeline would not have resolution to forbid him to see her again.

In this, however, he was mistaken: Adeline had learnt the best of all lessons,—distrust of her own strength;—and she resolved to put it out of her power to receive visits which a regard to propriety forbade, and which might injure her reputation, if not her peace of mind. Therefore, as soon as colonel Mordaunt was gone, she summoned Savanna, and desired her to proceed to business.

"What!" cried the delighted mulatto, "are we going to prosecu massa?"[1]

"No," replied Adeline, "we are going into the country: I am come to a determination to take no legal steps in this affair, but leave Mr. Berrendale to the reproaches of his own conscience."

"A fiddle's-end!" replied Savanna, "he have no conscience, or he no leave you: better get him hang; if you can* den you marry de colonel."

"I had better hang the father of my child, had I, Savanna?"

"Oh! no, no, no, no,—me forget dat."

"But I do not, nor can I even bear to disgrace the father of Editha: therefore, trusting that I can dispose of her, and secure her interest better than by forcing her father to do her justice, and bastardize the poor innocent whom his wife will soon bring into the world, I am going to bury myself in retirement, and live the short remainder of my days unknowing and unknown."[2]


## CHAPTER 22

SAVANNA was going to remonstrate, but the words "short remainder of my days" distressed her so much, that tears choked her words; and she obeyed in silence her mistress's orders to pack up, except when she indulged in a few exclamations against her lady's cruelty in going away without taking leave of colonel Mordaunt, who, sweet gentleman, would break his heart at her departure, especially as he was not to know whither she was going. A post-chaise[3] was at the door the next morning at six o'clock; and as Adeline had not much luggage, having left the chief part of her furniture to be divided between the mistresses of her two lodgings, in return for their

---

1  For bigamy.
2  Cf. Robert Burns, "Lament for James, Earl of Glencairn" (1791), 36.
3  A four-wheeled horse-drawn carriage for carrying mail and passengers.

kind attention to her and her child, she took an affectionate leave of her landlady, and desired the post-boy to drive a mile on the road before him; and when he had done so, she ordered him to go on to Barnet;[1] while the disappointed mulatto thanked God that the tawny boy was gone to Scotland with his protectress, as it prevented her having the mortification of leaving him behind her, as well as the colonel.—"Oh! had I had such* a lover," cried she, (her eyes filling with tears,) "me never leave him, nor he me!" and for the first time she thought her angel-lady hard-hearted.

For some miles they proceeded in silence, for Adeline was too much engrossed to speak; and the little Editha, being fast asleep in the mulatto's arms, did not draw her mother out of the reverie into which she had fallen.

"And where now?" said the mulatto, when the chaise stopped.

"To the next stage on the high north road." And on they went again: nor did they stop, except for refreshments, till they had travelled thirty miles; when Adeline, worn out with fatigue, staid all night at the inn where the chaise stopped, and the next morning they resumed their journey, but not their silence. The mulatto could no longer restrain her curiosity; and she begged to know whither they were going, and why they were to be buried in the country?

Adeline, sighing deeply, answered, that they were going to live in Cumberland; and then sunk into silence again, as she could not give the mulatto her true reasons for the plan that she was pursuing without wounding her affectionate heart in a manner wholly incurable. The truth was, that Adeline supposed herself to be declining: she thought that she experienced those dreadful languors, those sensations of internal weakness, which, however veiled to the eye of the observer, speak in forcible language to the heart of the conscious sufferer. Indeed, Adeline had long struggled, but in vain, against feelings of a most overwhelming nature; amongst which, remorse and horror, for having led by her example and precepts an innocent girl into a life of infamy, were the most painfully predominant: for, believing Mary Warner's assertion when she saw her at Mr. Langley's chambers, she looked upon that unhappy girl's guilt as the consequence of her own; and mourned, incessantly mourned, over the fatal errors of her early judgment, which had made her, though an idolater of virtue, a practical assistant to the cause of vice. When Adeline imagined the term of her existence to be drawing nigh, her mother, her obdurate but still dear mother, regained her wonted ascendancy over her affections; and to her, the approach of death seemed fraught with satisfaction. For that parent, so long, so repeatedly deaf to her prayers, and to the detail of those sufferings which she had made one of the conditions of her forgive-

1   Northwest of London (now in Greater London).

ness, had promised to see and to forgive her on her *death-bed*; and her heart yearned, fondly yearned, for the moment when she should be pressed to the bosom of a relenting parent.

To Cumberland, therefore, she was resolved to hasten, and into the very neighbourhood of Mrs. Mowbray; while, as the chaise wheeled them along to the place of their destination, even the prattle of her child could not always withdraw her from the abstraction into which she was plunged, as the scenes of her early years thronged upon her memory, and with them the recollection of those proofs of a mother's fondness, for a renewal of which, even in the society of Glenmurray, she had constantly and despondingly sighed.

As they approached Penrith,[1] her emotion redoubled, and she involuntarily exclaimed—"Cruel, but still dear, mother, you little think your child is so near!"

"Heaven save me!" cried Savanna; "are we to go and be near dat woman?"

"Yes," replied Adeline. "Did she not say she would forgive me on my death-bed?"

"But you not there yet, dear missess," sobbed Savanna; "you not there of long years!"

"Savanna," returned Adeline, "I should die contented to purchase my mother's blessing and forgiveness."

Savanna, speechless with contending emotions, could not express by words the feeling of mixed sorrow and indignation which overwhelmed her; but she replied by putting Editha in Adeline's arms; then articulating with effort, "Look there!" she sobbed aloud.

"I understand you," said Adeline, kissing away the tears gathering in Editha's eyes, at sight of Savanna's distress: "but perhaps I think my death would be of more service to my child than my life."

"And to me too, I suppose," replied Savanna reproachfully. "Well,— me go to Scotland; for no one love me but the tawny boy."

"You first will stay and close my eyes,* I hope!" observed Adeline mournfully.

In a moment Savanna's resentment vanished. "Me will live and die vid you," she replied, her tears redoubling, while Adeline again sunk into thoughtful silence.

As soon as they reached Penrith, Adeline inquired for lodgings out of the town, on that side nearest to her mother's abode; and was so fortunate, as she esteemed herself, to procure two apartments at a small house within two miles of Mrs. Mowbray's.

---

1   A town in the Lake District, on the route to and from Scotland.

"Then I breathe once more the same air with my mother!" exclaimed Adeline as she took possession of her lodging. "Savanna, methinks I breathe freer already!"

"Me more choked," replied the mulatto, and turned sullenly away.

"Nay, I—I feel so much better, that to-morrow I will—I will take a walk," said Adeline hesitatingly.

"And where?" asked Savanna eagerly.

"Oh, to-night I shall only walk to bed," replied Adeline smiling, and with unusual cheerfulness she retired to rest.

The next morning she arose early; and being informed that a stile near a peasant's cottage commanded a view of Mrs. Mowbray's house, she hired a man and cart to convey her to the bottom of the hill, and with Editha by her side, she set out to indulge her feelings by gazing on the house which contained her mother.

When they alighted, Editha gaily endeavoured to climb the hill, and urged her mother to follow her; but Adeline, rendered weak by illness and breathless by emotion, felt the ascent so difficult, that no motive less powerful than the one which actuated her could have enabled her to reach the summit.

At length, however, she did reach it:—and the lawn before Mrs. Mowbray's white house, her hay-fields, and the running stream at the bottom of it, burst in all their beauty on her view.—"And this is my mother's dwelling!" exclaimed Adeline; "and there was I born: and near here—" shall I die, she would have added but her voice failed her.

"Oh! what a pretty house and garden!" cried Editha in the unformed accents of childhood;—"how I should like to live there!"

This artless remark awakened a thousand mixed and overpowering feelings in the bosom of Adeline; and, after a pause of strong emotion, she exclaimed, catching the little prattler to her heart—"You *shall* live there, my child! —yes, yes, you *shall* live there!"

"But when?" resumed Editha.

"When I am in my grave," answered Adeline.

"And when shall you be there?" replied the unconscious child, fondly caressing her: "pray, mamma—pray be there soon!"

Adeline turned away, unable to answer her.

"Look—look, mamma!" resumed Editha: "there are ladies.—Oh! do let us go there now!—why can't we?"

"Would to God we could!" replied Adeline; as in one of the ladies she recognised Mrs. Mowbray, and stood gazing on her till her eyes ached again: but what she felt on seeing her she will herself describe in the succeeding pages; and I shall only add, that, as soon as Mrs. Mowbray returned into the house, Adeline, wrapped in a long and mournful reverie, returned, full of a new plan, to her lodgings.

There is no love so disinterested as parental love; and Adeline had all the keen sensibilities of a parent. To make, therefore, "assurance doubly sure"[1] that Mrs. Mowbray should receive and should love her orphan when she was no more, she resolved to give up the gratification to which she had looked forward, the hope, before she died, of obtaining her forgiveness—that she might not weaken, by directing any part of them to herself, those feelings of remorse, fruitless tenderness, and useless regret in her mother's bosom, which she wished should be concentrated in[*] her child.

"No," said Adeline to herself, "I am sure that she will not refuse to receive my orphan to her love and protection when I am no more, and am become alike insensible of reproaches and of blessings; and I think that she will love my child the more tenderly, because to me she will be unable to express the compunction which, sooner or later, she will feel from the recollection of her conduct towards me: therefore, I will make no demands on her love for myself; but, in a letter to be given her after my decease, bequeath my orphan to her care";—and with this determination she returned from her ride.

"Have you see her?" said Savanna, running out to meet her.

"Yes—but not spoken to her; nor shall I see her again."

"What—I suppose she see you, and not speak?"

"Oh, no; she did not see me, nor shall I urge her to see me: my plans are altered," replied Adeline.

"And we go back to town and colonel Mordaunt?"

"No," resumed Adeline, sighing deeply, and preparing to write to Mrs. Mowbray.

But it is necessary that we should for a short time go back to Berrendale, and relate that, while Adeline and Editha were confined with the small-pox, Mr. Drury received a summons from his employer in Jamaica to go over thither, to be intrusted with some particular business: in consequence of this he resolved to call again on Adeline, and inquire whether she still persisted in styling herself Mrs. Berrendale; as he concluded that Berrendale would be very glad of all the information relative to her and her child which he could possibly procure, whether his curiosity on the subject proceeded from fear or love.

It so happened, that as soon as Editha, as well as her mother, was in the height of the disorder, Mr. Drury called; and finding that they were both very bad, he thought that his friend Berrendale was likely to get rid of both his incumbrances at once; and being eager to communicate good news to a man whose influence in the island might be of benefit to him, he every day called to inquire concerning their health.

---

1   Cf. Shakespeare, *Macbeth* 4.1.83.

The second floor in the house where Adeline lodged was then occupied by a young woman in indigent circumstances, who, as well as her child, had sickened with the distemper the very day that Editha was inoculated: and when Drury, just as he was setting off for Portsmouth,[1] ran to gain the latest intelligence of the invalids, a char-woman, who attended to the door, not being acquainted with the name of the poor young woman and her little girl, concluding that Mr. Drury, by Mrs. Berrendale and miss who were ill with the small-pox, meant them, replied to his inquiries,— "Ah, poor things! it is all over with them, they died last night."

On which, not staying for any further intelligence, Drury set off for Portsmouth, and arrived at Jamaica just as Berrendale was going to remit to Adeline a draft for a hundred pounds. For Adeline, and the injury which he had done her, had been for some days constantly present to his thoughts. He had been ill; and as indigestion, the cause of his complaints, is apt to occasion disturbed dreams, he had in his dreams been haunted by the image of Glenmurray, who, with a threatening aspect, had reproached him with cruelty and base ingratitude to him, in deserting in such a manner the wife whom he had bequeathed to him.

The constant recurrence of these dreams had depressed his spirits and excited his remorse so much, that he could calm his feelings in no other way than by writing a kind letter to Adeline, and inclosing her a draft on his banker. This letter was on the point of being sent when Drury arrived, and, with very little ceremony, informed him that Adeline was dead.

"Dead!" exclaimed Berrendale, falling almost senseless on his couch:— "Dead!—Oh! for God's sake, tell me of what she died!—Surely, surely, she—" Here his voice failed him.

Drury coolly replied, that she and her child both died of the small-pox.

"But *when?* my dear fellow!—when? Say that they died nine months ago" (that was previous to his marriage), "and you make me your friend for life!"

Drury, so *bribed*, would have said *any thing*; and, with all the coolness possible, he replied, "Then be my friend for life:—they died rather better than nine months ago."

Berrendale, being then convinced that bigamy was not likely be proved against him, soon forgot, in the joy which this thought occasioned him, remorse for his conduct to Adeline, and regret for her early fate: besides, he concluded that he saved 100*l.* by the means; for he knew not that the delicate mind of Adeline would have scorned to owe pecuniary obligations to the husband who had basely and unwarrantably deserted her.

---

1   A port in the south of England.

But he was soon undeceived on this subject, by a letter which colonel Mordaunt wrote in confidence to a friend in Jamaica, begging him to inquire concerning Mr. Berrendale's second marriage; and to inform him privately that his injured wife had zealous and powerful friends in England, who were continually urging her to prosecute him for bigamy.

This intelligence had a fatal effect on the health of Berrendale; for though the violent temper and overbearing disposition of his second wife had often made him regret the gentle and compliant Adeline, and a separation from her, consequently, would be a blessing, still he feared to encounter the disgrace of a prosecution, and still more the anger of his West Indian wife; who, it was not improbable, might even attack his life in the first moment of ungoverned passion.

And to these fears he soon fell a sacrifice: for a frame debilitated by intemperance could not support the assaults made on it by the continued apprehensions which colonel Mordaunt's friend had excited in him; and he died in that gentleman's presence, whom in his last moments he had summoned to his apartment to witness a will, by which he owned Adeline Mowbray to be his lawful wife, and left Editha, his acknowledged and only heir, a very considerable fortune.

But this circumstance, an account of which, with the will, was transmitted to colonel Mordaunt, did not take place till long after Adeline took up her abode in Cumberland.


CHAPTER 23

BUT to return to colonel Mordaunt. Though Adeline had said that he must discontinue his visits, he resolved to disobey her; and the next morning, as soon as he thought she had breakfasted, he repaired to her lodgings; where he heard, with mixed sorrow and indignation, that she had set off in a post-chaise at six o'clock, and was gone no one knew whither.

"But, surely she has left some note or message for me!" exclaimed colonel Mordaunt.

"Neither the one nor the other," was the answer; and he returned home in no very enviable state of mind.

Various, indeed, and contradictory were his feelings: yet still affection was uppermost; and he could not but respect in Adeline the conduct which drove him to despair. Nor was self-love backward to suggest to him, that had not Adeline felt his presence and attentions to be dangerous, she would not so suddenly have withdrawn from them; and this idea was the only one on which he could at all bear to dwell: for, when he reflected that day after day might pass without his either seeing or hearing from her, existence seemed to become suddenly a burthen, and he wandered from place to place with joyless and unceasing restlessness.

At one time he resolved to pursue her; but the next, piqued at not having received from her even a note of farewell, he determined to endeavour to forget her: and this was certainly the wiser plan of the two: but the succeeding moment he determined to let a week pass, in hopes of receiving a letter from her, and, in case he did not, to set off in search of her, being assured of succeeding in his search,* because the singularity of Savanna's appearance, and the traces of the small-pox visible in the face of Adeline, made them liable to be observed, and easy for him to describe.

But before the week elapsed, from agitation of mind, and from having exposed himself unnecessarily to cold, by lying on damp grass at midnight, after having heated himself by immoderate walking, colonel Mordaunt became ill of a fever; and when, after a confinement of several weeks, he was restored to health, he despaired of being able to learn tidings of the fugitives; and disappointed and dejected, he sought in the gayest scenes of the metropolis and its environs to drown the remembrances, from which in solitude he had vainly endeavoured to fly. At this time a faded but attractive woman of quality, with whom he had formerly been intimate, returned from abroad, and, meeting colonel Mordaunt at the house of a mutual friend, endeavoured to revive in him his former attachment: but it was a difficult task for a woman, who, though capable of charming the senses,† had never been able to touch the heart, to excite an attachment in a man already sentimentally devoted to another.

Her advances, however, flattered colonel Mordaunt, and her society amused him, till, at length, their intimacy was renewed on its former footing: but soon disgusted with an intercourse in which the heart had no share,‡ tired of his mistress, and displeased with himself, he took an abrupt leave of her, and, throwing himself into his post-chaise, retired to the seat of a relation in Herefordshire.[1]

Near this gentleman's house lived Mr. Maynard and his two sisters, who had taken up their abode there immediately on their return from Portugal. Major Douglas, his wife, and Emma Douglas, were then on a visit to them. Mordaunt had known major Douglas in early life; and as soon as he found that he was in the neighbourhood, he rode over to renew his acquaintance with him; and received so cordial a welcome, not only from the major, but the master of the house and his sisters, that he was strongly induced to repeat his visits, and not a day passed in which he was not, during some part of it, a guest at Mr. Maynard's.

---

1   A county near the Welsh border.

Mrs. Wallington and miss Maynard, indeed, received him with such pointed marks of distinction and preference, as to make it visible to every observer that it was not as a friend only they were desirous of considering colonel Mordaunt; while, by spiteful looks and acrimonious remarks directed to each other, the sisters expressed the jealousy which rankled in their hearts, whenever he seemed by design or inadvertency to make one of them a* particular object of his attention.

Of Emma Douglas's chance for his favour, they were not at all fearful:—they thought her too plain, and too unattractive, to be capable of rivalling them; especially in the favour of an officer, a man of fashion; and therefore they beheld without emotion the attention which colonel Mordaunt paid to her whenever she spoke, and the deference which he evidently felt for her opinion, as her remarks on whatever subject she conversed were formed always to interest, and often to instruct.

One evening, while major Douglas was amusing himself in looking over some magazines which had lately been bound up together, and had not yet been deposited in Mr. Maynard's library, he suddenly started, laid down the book, and turning to the window, with an exclamation of— "Poor fellow!"—passed his hand across his eyes, as if meaning to disperse an involuntary tear.

"What makes you exclaim 'Poor fellow?'" asked his lovely wife: "have you met with an affecting story in those magazines?"

"No, Louisa," replied he, "but I met in the obituary with a confirmation of the death of an old friend, which I suspected must have happened by this time, though I never knew it before; I see by this magazine that poor Glenmurray died a very few months after we saw him at Perpignan."

"Poor fellow!" exclaimed Mrs. Douglas.

"I wish I knew what is become of his interesting companion, miss Mowbray," said Emma Douglas.

"I wish I did too," secretly sighed colonel Mordaunt: but his heart palpitated so violently at this unexpected mention of the woman for whom he still pined in secret, that he had not resolution to say that he knew her.

"Become of her!" cried miss Maynard sneeringly: "you need not wonder,† I think, what her fate is: no doubt Mr. Glenmurray's *interesting companion* has not lost her companionable qualities, and is a companion still."

"Yes," observed Mrs. Wallington; "or, rather, I dare say that angel of purity is gone upon the town."

It was the dark hour, else colonel Mordaunt's agitation, on hearing these gross and unjust remarks, must have betrayed his secret to every eye; while indignation now impeded his utterance as much as confusion had done before.

"Surely, surely," cried the kind and candid Emma Douglas, "I must grossly have mistaken miss Mowbray's character, if she was capable of the conduct which you attribute to her!"

"My dear creature!" replied Mrs. Wallington, "how should you know any thing of her character, when it was gone long before you knew her?—*Character*, indeed! you remind me of my brother.... Mr. Davenport," continued she to a gentleman present, "did you ever hear the story of my brother and an angel of purity whom he met with abroad?"

"No—never."

"Be quiet," said Maynard; "I will not be laughed at."

However, Mrs. Wallington and miss Maynard, who had not yet forgiven the deep impression which Adeline's graces had made on their brother, insisted on telling the story; to which colonel Mordaunt listened with eager and anxious curiosity. It received all the embellishments which female malice could give it; and if it amused any one, certainly that person was neither Mordaunt, nor Emma Douglas, nor her gentle sister.

"But how fortunate it was," added miss Maynard, "that we were not with my brother! as we should unavoidably have walked and talked with this angel."

Mordaunt longed to say, "I think the good fortune was all on miss Mowbray's side."

But Adeline and her cause were in good hands: Emma Douglas stood forth as her champion.—"We feel very differently on that subject," she replied. "I shall ever regret, not that I saw and conversed with miss Mowbray, but that I did not see and converse with her again and again."

At this moment Emma was standing by colonel Mordaunt, who involuntarily caught her hand and pressed it eagerly; but tried to disguise his motive* by suddenly seating her in a chair behind her, saying, "You had better sit down; I am sure you must be tired with standing so long."

"No; really, Emma," cried major Douglas, "you go too far there; though to be sure, if by seeing and conversing with miss Mowbray you could have convinced her of her errors, I should not have objected to your seeing her once more or so."

"Surely," said Mrs. Douglas timidly, "we ought, my love, to have repeated our visits till we had made a convert of her."

"A *convert* of her!" exclaimed Mr. Maynard's sisters, "a convert of a kept mistress!" bursting into a violent laugh, which had a most painful effect on the irritable nerves of colonel Mordaunt, whose tongue, parched with emotion, cleaved to the roof of his mouth[1] whenever he attempted to speak.

---

1  Cf. Psalm 137.6.

"Pray, to what other circumstance, yet untold, do you allude?" said Mr. Davenport.

"Oh, we too had a rencontre with the philosopher and his charming friend," said major Douglas, "and—but, Emma, do you tell the story.— 'Sdeath!—Poor fellow!—Well, but we parted good friends," added the kind-hearted Caledonian,[1] dispersing a tear; while Emma, in simple but impressive language, related all that passed at Perpignan between themselves, Adeline, and Glenmurray; and concluded with saying, that, "from the almost idolatrous respect with which Glenmurray spoke and apparently thought of Adeline, and from the account of her conduct and its motives, which he so fully detailed, she was convinced that, so far from being influenced by depravity in connecting herself with Glenmurray, Adeline was the victim of a romantic, absurd, and false conception of virtue; and she should have thought it her duty to have endeavoured, assisted by her sister, to have prevailed on her to renounce her opinions, and, by becoming the wife of Glenmurray, to restore to the society of her own sex, a woman formed to be its ornament and its example. Poor thing!" she added in a faltering voice, "would that I knew her fate!"

"I can guess it, I tell you," said Mrs. Wallington.

"We had better drop the subject, madam," replied Emma Douglas indignantly, "as it is one that we shall never agree upon. If I supposed miss Mowbray happy, I should feel for her, and feel interest sufficient in her fate to make me combat your prejudices concerning her; but now that she is perhaps afflicted, poor, friendless, and scorned, though unjustly, by every 'virtuous she that knows her story,'[2] I cannot command my feelings when she is named with sarcastic disrespect,* nor can I bear to hear an unhappy woman supposed to be plunged in the lowest depths of vice, whom I, on the contrary, believe to be at this moment atoning for the error of her judgment by a life of lonely penitence, or sunk perhaps already in the grave, the victim of a broken heart."

Colonel Mordaunt, affected and delighted, hung on Emma Douglas's words with breathless attention, resolving when she had ended her narration to begin his, and clear Adeline from the calumnies of Mrs. Wallington and miss Maynard; but after articulating with some difficulty—"Ladies,— I—miss Douglas,—I—" he found that his feelings would not allow him to proceed: therefore, suddenly raising Emma's hand to his lips, he† imprinted on it a kiss, at once fervent and respectful, and, making a hasty bow, ran out of the house.

Every one was astonished; but none so much as Emma Douglas.

---

1 Scotsman: from the Roman name for part of northern Britain.
2 Unidentified.

"Why, Emma!" cried the major, "who should have thought it? I verily believe you have turned Mordaunt's head;—I protest that he kissed your hand:—I suppose he will be here tomorrow, making proposals in form."

"I wish he may!" exclaimed Mrs. Douglas.

"It is not very likely, I think," cried miss Maynard.

Mrs. Wallington said nothing; but she fanned herself violently.

"How do you know that?" said Maynard. "He kissed your hand very tenderly—did he not, miss Douglas? and took advantage of the dark hour: that looks very lover-like."

Emma Douglas, who, in spite of her reason, was both embarrassed and flattered by colonel Mordaunt's unexpected mode of taking leave, said not a word; but Mrs. Wallington, in a voice hoarse with angry emotion, cried:

"It was very free in him, I think, and very unlike colonel Mordaunt; for he was not a sort of man to take liberties but where he met with encouragement."

"Then I am sure he would be free with *you*,* sister, sometimes," sarcastically observed miss Maynard.

"Nay, with both of you, I think," replied Maynard, who had not forgiven the laugh at his expense which they had tried to excite; on which an angry dialogue took place between the brother and sisters: and the Douglases, disgusted and provoked, retired to their apartment.

"There was something very strange and uncommon," said Mrs. Douglas, detaining Emma in her dressing-room, "in colonel Mordaunt's behaviour—Do you not think so, Emma?—If it should have any meaning!"

"Meaning!" cried the major: "what meaning should it have? Why, my dear, do you think Mordaunt never kissed a woman's hand before?"

"But it was so *particular.*—Well, Emma, if it should lead to consequences!"

"Consequences!" cried the major: "my dear girl, what can you mean?"

"Why, if he should *really love* our Emma?"

"Why then I hope our Emma will love him.—What say you, Emma?"

"I say?—I—" she replied: "really I never thought it possible that colonel Mordaunt should have any thoughts of me, nor do I now; but it is very strange that he should kiss my hand!"

The major† could not help laughing at the *naïveté* of this reply, and in a mutual whisper they agreed how much they wished to see their sister so happily disposed of; while Emma paced up and down her own apartment some time before she undressed herself; and after seeming to convince herself, by recollecting all colonel Mordaunt's conduct towards her, that he could not possibly *mean* anything by his unusual adieu, she went to sleep, exclaiming, "But it is very strange that he should kiss my hand!"

# CHAPTER 24

THE next morning explained the mystery: for breakfast was scarcely over, when colonel Mordaunt appeared; and his presence occasioned a blush, from different causes, on the cheeks of all the ladies, and a smile on the countenances of both the gentlemen.

"You left us very abruptly last night," said major Douglas.

"I did so," replied Mordaunt with a sort of grave smile.

"Were you taken ill?" asked Maynard.

"I—I was not quite easy," answered he: "but, miss Douglas, may I request the honour of seeing you alone for a few minutes?"

Again the ladies blushed, and the gentlemen smiled. But Emma's weakness had been temporary; she had convinced herself that colonel Mordaunt's action had been nothing more than a tribute to what he fancied her generous defence of an unfortunate woman; and with an air of unembarrassed dignity she gave him her hand to lead her into an adjoining apartment.

"This is very good of you," cried colonel Mordaunt: "but you are all goodness!—My dear miss Douglas, had I not gone away as I did last night, I believe I should have fallen down and worshipped you, or committed some other extravagance."

"Indeed!—What could I say to excite such enthusiasm?" replied Emma, deeply blushing.

"What!—Oh, miss Douglas!"—Then after a few more ohs, and other exclamations, he related to her the whole progress of his acquaintance with and attachment to Adeline, adding as he concluded, "Now then judge what feelings you must have excited in my bosom:—yes, miss Douglas, I reverenced you before for your own sake, I now adore you for that of my lost Adeline."

"So!" thought Emma, "the kiss of the hand is explained,"—and she sighed as she thought it; nor did she much like the word *reverenced*: but she had ample amends for her mortification by what followed.

"Really," cried colonel Mordaunt, gazing very earnestly at her, "I do not mean to flatter you, but there is something in your countenance that reminds me very strongly of Adeline."

"Is it possible?" said Emma, her cheeks glowing and her eye sparkling as she spoke: "you may not mean to flatter me, but I assure you I am flattered; for I never saw any woman whom in appearance I so much wished to resemble."

"You do resemble her indeed," cried colonel Mordaunt, "and the likeness grows stronger and stronger."

Emma blushed deeper and deeper.

"But come," exclaimed he, "let us go; and I will—no, *you* shall—relate to the party in the next room what I have been telling you, for I long to shame those d—"

"Fye!" said Emma smiling, and holding up her hand as if to stop the coming word. And she did stop it; for colonel Mordaunt conveyed the reproving hand to his lips; and Emma said to herself, as she half-frowning withdrew it, "I am glad my brother was not present."

Their return to the breakfast-room was welcome to every one, from different causes, as colonel Mordaunt's motives for requesting a tête-à-tête had given rise to various conjectures. But all conjecture was soon lost in certainty: for Emma Douglas, with more than usual animation of voice and countenance, related what colonel Mordaunt had authorised her to relate; and the envious sisters heard, with increased resentment, that Adeline, were she unmarried, would be the choice of the man whose affections they were eagerly endeavouring to captivate.

"You can't think," said colonel Mordaunt when Emma had concluded, leaving him charmed with the manner in which she had told his story, and with the generous triumph which sparkled in her eyes at being able to exhibit Adeline's character in so favourable a point of view, "you can't think how much miss Douglas reminds me of Mrs. Berrendale!"

"Lord!" said miss Maynard with a toss of the head, "my brother told us that she was handsome!"

"And so she is," replied the colonel, provoked at this brutal speech: "she has one of the finest countenances that I ever saw,—a countenance never distorted by those feelings of envy, and expressions of spite, which so often disfigure some women,—converting even a beauty into a fiend; and in this respect no one will doubt that miss Douglas resembles her:

> 'What's female beauty—but an air divine,
> Thro' which the mind's all gentle graces shine?'[1]

says one of our first poets: therefore, in Dr. Young's opinion, madam," continued Mordaunt, turning to Emma, "you would have been a perfect beauty."

This speech, so truly gratifying to the amiable girl to whom it was addressed, was a dagger in the heart of both the sisters. Nor was Emma's pleasure unalloyed by pain; for she feared that Mordaunt's attentions might become dangerous to her peace of mind, as she could not disguise to herself, that his visits at Mr. Maynard's had been the chief cause of

---

1   Edward Young, *Love of Fame, the Universal Passion* (1728), satire 6, "On Women," 151-52.

her reluctance to return to Scotland whenever their journey home was mentioned. For, always humble in her ideas of her own charms, Emma Douglas could not believe that Mordaunt would ever entertain any feeling for her at all resembling love, except when he fancied that she looked like Adeline.

But however unlikely it seemed that Mordaunt should become attached to her, and however resolved she was to avoid his society, certain it is that he soon found he could be happy in the society of no other woman, since to no other could he talk on the subject nearest his heart; and Emma, though blaming herself daily for her temerity, could not refuse to receive Mordaunt's visits: and her patient attentions* to his conversation, of which Adeline was commonly the theme, seemed to have a salutary effect on his wounded feelings.

But the time for their departure arrived, much to the joy of Mrs. Wallington and her sister, who hoped when Emma was gone to have a chance of being noticed by Mordaunt.

What then must have been their confusion and disappointment, when colonel Mordaunt begged to be allowed to attend the Douglases on their journey home, as he had never seen the Highlands, and wished to see them in such good company! Major Douglas and his charming wife gave a glad consent to this proposal: but Emma Douglas heard it with more alarm than pleasure; for, though her heart rejoiced at it, her reason condemned it.

A few days, however, convinced her apprehensive delicacy, that, if she loved colonel Mordaunt, it was not without hope of a return.

Colonel Mordaunt declared that every day seemed to increase her resemblance to Adeline in expression and manner; and in conduct his reason told him that she was her superior; nor could he for a moment hesitate to prefer as a wife, Emma Douglas who had never erred, to Adeline who had.

Colonel Mordaunt felt, to borrow the words of a celebrated female writer,[1] that "though it is possible to love and esteem a woman who has expiated the faults of her youth by a sincere repentance; and though before God and man her errors may be obliterated; still there exists one being in whose eyes she can never hope to efface them, and that is her lover or her husband." He felt that no man of acute sensibility can be happy with a woman whose recollections are not pure: she must necessarily be jealous

---

1 Madame de Stael, Recueil de Morceaux détachés, page 208 (Opie's note); Germaine de Stael, "The Story of Pauline," *Recueil de morceaux détachés* (1796): "Je crois … que devant Dieu et devant les hommes tous ses torts sont effacés; il existe un seul object aux yeux duquel elle ne peut les réparer, c'est son amant ou son époux" ("Histoire de Pauline," in *Zulma, et Trois Nouvelles* [London, 1813], 177).

of the opinion which he entertains of her; and he must be often afraid of speaking, lest he utter a sentiment that may wound and mortify her. Besides, he was, on just grounds, more desirous of marrying a woman whom he "admired, than one whom he forgave";[1] and therefore, while he addressed Emma, he no longer regretted Adeline.

In short, he at length ceased to talk of Emma's resemblance to Adeline, but seemed to admire her wholly for her own sake; and having avowed his passion,* and been assured of Emma's in return, by major Douglas, he came back to England in the ensuing autumn, the happy husband of one of the best of women.

### CHAPTER 25

We left Adeline preparing to address Mrs. Mowbray and recommend her child to her protection:—but being deeply impressed with the importance of the task which she was about to undertake, she timidly put it off from day to day; and having convinced herself that it was her duty to endeavour to excite her husband to repentance, and make him acknowledge Editha as his legitimate child, she determined to write to him before she addressed her mother, and also to bid a last farewell to colonel Mordaunt, whose respectful attachment had soothed some of the pangs which consciousness of her past follies had inflicted, and whose active friendship deserved her warmest acknowledgments.†—Little did she think the fatal effect which one instance of his friendly zeal in her cause had had on Berrendale; unconscious was she that the husband, whose neglect she believed to be intentional, great as were his crimes against her, was not guilty of the additional crime of suffering her to pine in poverty without making a single inquiry concerning her, but was convinced that both she and her child were no longer in existence.

In her letter to him, she conjured him by the love which he *always* bore Glenmurray, by the love he *once* bore her, and by the remorse which he would sooner or later feel for his conduct towards her and her child, to acknowledge Editha to be his lawful heir, but to suffer her to remain under that protection to which she meant to bequeath her; and on these conditions she left him her blessing, and her pardon.

The letter to colonel Mordaunt was long, and perhaps diffuse: but Adeline was jealous of his esteem, though regardless of his love; and as he had known her while acting under the influence of a fatal error of opinion, she

---

1  Edouard comments, "je veux m'unir à celle que j'admire plutôt qu'à celle à qui je pardonne" ("Histoire de Pauline," 177).

wished to show him that on conviction she had abandoned her former way of thinking, and was candid enough to own that she had been wrong.

"You, no doubt," she said, "are well acquainted with the arguments urged by different writers in favour of marriage. I shall therefore only mention the argument which carried at length full conviction to *my* mind, and conquered even my deep and heartfelt reverence for the opinions of one who long was, and ever will be, the dearest object of my love and regret. But *he*, had he lived, would I am sure have altered his sentiments; and had he been a parent, the argument I allude to, as it is founded on a consideration of the interest of children, would have found its way to his reason, through his affections.

"It is evident that on the education given to children must depend the welfare of the community; and, consequently, that whatever is likely to induce parents to neglect the education of their children must be *hurtful* to the welfare of the community. It is also certain, that though the agency of the *passions* be necessary to the existence of all society, it is on the cultivation and influence of the *affections* that the happiness and improvement of social life depend.

"Hence it follows that marriage must be more beneficial to society in its consequences, than connections capable of being dissolved at pleasure; because it has a tendency to call forth and exercise the affections, and control the passions.—It has been said, that, were we free to dissolve at will a connection formed by love, we should not wish to do it, as constancy is natural to us, and there is in all of us a tendency to form an exclusive attachment. But though I believe, from my own experience, that the few are capable of unforced constancy, and could love for life one dear and honoured object, still I believe that the many are given to the love of change;—that, in men especially, a new object can excite new passion; and, judging from the increasing depravity of both sexes, in spite of existing laws, and in defiance of shame,—I am convinced, that if the ties of marriage were dissolved, or it were no longer to be judged infamous to act in contempt of them, unbridled licentiousness would soon be in general practice.—What then, in such a state of society, would be the fate of the children born in it?—What would their education be?—Parents continually engrossed in the enervating but delightful egotism of a new and happy love, lost in selfish indulgence, the passions awake, but the affections slumbering, and the sacred ties of parental feeling not having time nor opportunity to fasten on the heart,—their offspring would either die the victims of neglect, and the very existence of the human race be threatened; or, without morals or instruction, they would grow up to scourge the world by their vices, till the whole fabric of civilized society was gradually destroyed.

"On this ground, therefore, this strong ground, I venture to build my present opinion, that marriage is a wise and ought to be a sacred institution; and I bitterly regret the hour when, with the hasty and immature judgment of eighteen, and with a degree of presumption scarcely pardonable at any time of life, I dared to think and act contrary to this opinion and the reverend experience of ages, and became in the eyes of the world an example of vice, when I believed myself the champion of virtue."

She then went on to express the following sentiments. "You will think, perhaps, that I ought to struggle against the weakness which is hurrying me to the grave, and live for the sake of my child.—Alas! it is for her sake that I most wish to die.

"There are two ways in which a mother can be of use to her daughter: the one is by instilling into her mind virtuous principles, and by setting her a virtuous example: the other is, by being to her in her own person an awful warning,—a melancholy proof of the dangers which attend a deviation from the path of virtue. But, oh! how jealous must a mother be of her child's esteem and veneration! and how could she bear to humble herself in the eyes of the beloved object, by avowing that she had committed crimes against society, however atoned for by penitence and sorrow! I can never, now, be a correct example for my Editha, nor could I endure to live to be a warning to her.—Nay, if I lived, I should be most probably a dangerous example to her; for I should be (on my death-bed I think I may be allowed the boast) respected and esteemed; while the society around me would forget my past errors, in the sincerity of my repentance.

"If then a strong temptation should assail my child, might she not yield to it from an idea that 'one false step may be retrieved,'[1] and cite her mother as an example of this truth? while, unconscious of the many secret heart-aches of that repentant mother, unconscious of the sorrows and degradations she had experienced, she regarded nothing but the present respectability of her mother's life, and contented herself with hoping one day to resemble her.

"Believe me, that were it possible for me to choose between life and death, for my child's sake, the choice would be the latter. Now, when she shall see in my mournful and eventful history, written as it has been by me in moments of melancholy leisure, that all my sorrows were consequent on one presumptuous error of judgment in early youth, and shall see a long and minute detail of the secret agonies which I have endured,—those agonies wearing away my existence, and ultimately hurrying me to an untimely grave; she will learn that the woman who feels justly, yet has been

---

1  Cf. Thomas Gray, "On the Death of a Favourite Cat, Drowned in a Tub of Goldfishes" (1748), 38: the line actually reads, "Know, one false step is ne'er retrieved."

led even into the practice of vice, however she may be forgiven by others, can never forgive herself; and though she may dare to lift an eye of hope to that Being who promises pardon on repentance, she will still recollect with anguish the fair and glorious course which she might have run; and that, instead of humbly imploring forbearance and forgiveness, she might have demanded universal respect and esteem.

"True it is, that I did not act in defiance of the world's opinion, from any depraved feelings,* or vicious inclinations: but the world could not be expected to believe this, since motives are known only to our own hearts, and the great Searcher of hearts:[1] therefore, as far as example goes, I was as great a stumbling block[2] to others as if the life I led had been owing to the influence of lawless desires; and society was right in making, and in seeing, no distinction between me and any other woman living in an unsanctioned connection.

"But methinks I hear you say, that Editha might never be informed of my past errors. Alas! wretched must that woman be whose happiness and respectability depend on the secrecy of others! Besides, did I not think the concealment of crime in itself a crime, how could I know an hour of peace while I reflected that a moment's malice, or inadvertency, in one of Editha's companions might cause her to blush at her mother's disgrace?— that, while her young cheek was flushed perhaps with the artless triumphs of beauty, talent, and virtue, the parent who envied me, or the daughter who envied her, might suddenly convert her joy into anguish and morti- fication, by artfully informing her, with feigned pity for my sorrows and admiration of my penitence, that I had once been a *disgrace* to that family of which I was now the pride?—No—even if I were not for ever separated in this world from the only man whom I ever loved with passionate and well-founded affection, united for life to the object of my just aversion, and were I not conscious (horrible and overwhelming thought!) of having by my example led another into the path of sin,—still, I repeat it, for my child's sake I should wish to die, and should consider, not early death, but lengthened existence, as a curse."

So Adeline reasoned and felt in her moments of reflection: but the heart had sometimes dominion over her; and as she gazed on Editha, and thought that Mrs. Mowbray might be induced to receive her again to her favour, she wished even on any terms to have her life prolonged.

---

1   God: cf. Romans 8.27.
2   Cf. Leviticus 19.14.

# CHAPTER 26

HAVING finished her letter to colonel Mordaunt and Berrendale, she again prepared to write to her mother; a few transient fears overcoming every now and then those hopes of success in her application, which, till she took up her pen, she had so warmly encouraged.

Alas! little did she know how erroneously for years she had judged of Mrs. Mowbray. Little did she suspect that her mother had long forgiven her; had pined after her; had sought, though in vain, to procure intelligence of her, and was then wearing away her existence in solitary woe, a prey to self-reproach, and to the corroding fear that her daughter, made desperate by her renunciation of her, had, on the death of Glenmurray, plunged into a life of shame, or sunk, broken-hearted, into the grave! for not one of Adeline's letters had ever reached Mrs. Mowbray; and the mother and the* daughter had both been the victims of female treachery and jealousy.

Mrs. Mowbray, as soon as she had parted with Adeline for the last time, had dismissed all her old servants, the witnesses of her sorrows and disgrace, and retired to her estate in Cumberland,—an estate where Adeline had first seen the light, and where Mrs. Mowbray had first experienced the transports of a mother. This spot was therefore ill calculated to banish Adeline from her mother's thoughts, and to continue her exclusion† from her affections.‡ On the contrary, her image haunted Mrs. Mowbray:—whithersoever she went, she still saw her in an attitude of supplication; she still heard the plaintive accents of her voice;—and often did she exclaim, "My child, my child! wretch that I am! must I never, never§ see thee more!"

These ideas increased to so painful a degree, that, finding her solitude insupportable, she invited an orphan relation in narrow circumstances to take up her abode with her.

This young woman, whose ruling passion was avarice, and whose greatest talent was cunning, resolved to spare no pains to keep the situation which she had gained, even to the exclusion of Adeline, should Mrs. Mowbray be weak enough to receive her again. She therefore intercepted all the letters which were in or like Adeline's hand-writing; and having learnt to imitate Mrs. Mowbray's, she enclosed them in a blank cover to Adeline; who, thinking the direction was written in her mother's hand, desisted, as the artful girl expected she would do, from what appeared to her a hopeless application.

And she exulted in her contrivance;—when Mrs. Mowbray, on seeing in a magazine that Glenmurray was dead, (full a year after his decease,) bursting into a passion of tears, protested that she would instantly invite Adeline to her house.

"Yes," cried she, "I can do so without infringement of my oath.—She is disgraced in the eye of the world by her connection with Glenmurray, and she is wretched in love; nay, more so, perhaps, than I have been; and I can, I will invite her to lose the remembrance of her misfortunes in my love!"

Thus did her ardent wish to be re-united to Adeline deceive her conscience; for, by the phrase "wretched in love," she meant, forsaken by the object of her attachment,—and that Adeline had not been: therefore her oath remained in full force against her. But where could she seek Adeline?—Dr. Norberry could, perhaps, give her this information; and to him she resolved to write—though he had cast her from his acquaintance: "but her pride," as she said, "fell with her fortunes"; and she scrupled not to humble herself before the zealous friend of her daughter. But this letter would never have reached him, had not her treacherous relation been ill at the time when it was written.

Dr. Norberry had recovered the illness of which Adeline supposed him to have died: but as her letter to him, to which she received no answer, alluded to the money transaction between her and Mrs. Norberry; and as she commented on the insulting expressions in Mrs. Norberry's note, that lady thought proper to suppress the second letter as well as the first; and when the doctor, on his recovery, earnestly demanded to know whether any intelligence had been received of miss Mowbray, Mrs. Norberry, with pretended reluctance, told him that she had written to him in great distress, while he was delirious, to borrow money; that she had sent her *ten pounds*,[*] which Adeline had returned, reproaching her for her parsimony, and saying that she had found a friend who would not suffer her to want.

"But did you tell her that you thought me in great danger?"

"I did."

"Why, zounds,[†] woman! did she not, after that, write to know how I was?"

"Never."

"Devil take me if I could have thought it of her!"[‡] answered the doctor—who could not but believe this story for the sake of his own peace, as it was less destructive to his happiness to think Adeline in fault, than his wife or children guilty of profligate falsehood: he therefore, with a deep sigh, begged Adeline's name might never be mentioned to him again; and though he secretly wished to hear of her welfare, he no longer made her the subject of conversation.

But Mrs. Mowbray's letter recalled her powerfully both to his memory and affections, while, with many a deep-drawn sigh, he regretted that he had no possible means of discovering where she was;—and with a heavy heart he wrote the following letter, which miss Woodville, Mrs. Mowbray's relation, having first contrived to open, and read it, ventured to give into her hands, as it contained no satisfactory information concerning Adeline.

"'I look on the separation of my mother and me in this world to be eternal,' said the poor dear lost Adeline to me, the last time we met. 'You do!' replied I: 'then, poor devil! how miserable will your mother be when her present* resentment subsides!—Well, when that time comes, I may perhaps see her again,' added I, with a d——d† queer something rising in my throat as I said it, and your poor girl blessed me for the kind intention.—(Pshaw! I have blotted the paper: at my years it is a shame to be so watery-eyed.) Well,—the time above mentioned is come—you are miserable, you are repentant—and you ask me to forget and forgive.—I do forget, I do forgive: some time or other, too, I will tell you so in person; and were the lost Adeline to know that I did so, she would bless me for the act, as she did before for the intention. But, alas! where she is, what she is, I know not, and have not any means of knowing. To say the truth, her conduct to me and mine has been devilish *odd*, not to say *wrong*.‡ But, poor thing! she is either dead or miserable, and I forgive her:—so I do you, as I said before, and the Lord give you all the consolation which you so greatly need!

"Yours once more,
"In true kindness of spirit,
"JAMES NORBERRY."

This letter made Mrs. Mowbray's wounds bleed afresh, at the same time that it destroyed all her expectations of finding Adeline; and the only hope that remained to cheer her was, that she might perhaps, if yet alive, write sooner or later, to implore forgiveness. But month after month elapsed, and no tidings of Adeline reached her despairing mother.

She then put an advertisement in the paper, so worded that Adeline, had she seen it, must have known to whom it alluded; but it never met her eyes, and Mrs. Mowbray gave herself up to almost absolute despair; when accident introduced her to a new acquaintance, whose example taught her patience, and whose soothing benevolence bade her hope for happier days.

One day as Mrs. Mowbray, regardless of a heavy shower, and lost in melancholy reflections, was walking with irregular steps on the road to Penrith, with an unopened umbrella in her hand, she suddenly raised her eyes from the ground, and beheld a quaker-lady pursued by an over-driven bullock, and unable any longer to make an effort to escape its fury.

At this critical moment Mrs. Mowbray, from a sort of irresistible impulse, as fortunate in its effects as presence of mind, yet scarcely perhaps to be denominated such, sudden opened her umbrella; and, approaching the animal, brandished it before his eyes. Alarmed at this unusual appearance, he turned hastily and ran towards the town, where she saw that he was immediately met and secured.

"Thou hast doubtless saved my life," said the quaker, grasping Mrs. Mowbray's hand, with an emotion which she vainly tried to suppress; "and I pray God to bless thine!"*

Mrs. Mowbray returned the pressure of her hand, and burst into tears; overcome with joy for having saved a fellow-creature's life; with terror, which she was now at leisure to feel for the danger to which she had herself been exposed; and with mournful emotion from the consciousness how much she needed the blessing which the grateful quaker invoked on her head.

"Thou tremblest even more than I do," observed the lady, smiling, but seeming ready to faint; "I believe we had better, both of us, sit down on the bank: but it is so wet that perhaps we had better† endeavour to reach my house, which is only at the end of yon field." Mrs. Mowbray bowed her assent; and, supporting each other, they at length arrived at a neat white house, to which the quaker cordially bade her welcome.

"It was but this morning," said Mrs. Mowbray, struggling for utterance, "that I called upon Death to relieve me from an existence at once wretched and useless."—Here she paused:—and her new acquaintance, cordially pressing her hand, waited for the conclusion of her speech;— "but now," continued Mrs. Mowbray, "I revoke, and repent my idle and vicious impatience of life. I have‡ saved your life, and something like enjoyment now seems to enliven mine."

"I suspect," replied the lady, "that thou hast known deep affliction; and I rejoice that at this moment, and in so providential a manner, I have been introduced to thy acquaintance:—for I too have known sorrow, and the mourner knows how to speak comfort to the heart of the mourner. My name is Rachel Pemberton; and I hope that when I know thy name, and thy story, thou wilt allow me to devote to thy comfort some hours of the existence which thou hast preserved." She then hastily withdrew, to pour forth in solitary prayer§ the breathings of devout gratitude:—while Mrs. Mowbray, having communed with her own thoughts, felt a glow of un-wonted satisfaction steal over her mind; and by the time Mrs. Pemberton returned, she was able to meet her with calmness and cheerfulness.

"Thou knowest my name," said Mrs. Pemberton as she entered, seating herself by Mrs. Mowbray, "but I have yet to learn thine."

"My name is Mowbray," she replied, sighing deeply.

"Mowbray!—The lady of Rosevalley in Gloucestershire; and the mother of Adeline Mowbray?" exclaimed Mrs. Pemberton.

"What of Adeline Mowbray? What of my child?" cried Mrs. Mowbray, seizing Mrs. Pemberton's hand. "Blessed woman! tell me,—Do you indeed know her?—can you tell me where to find her?"

"I will tell thee all that I know of her," replied Mrs. Pemberton in a faltering voice; "but thy emotion overpowers me.—I—I was once a mother, and I can feel for thee." She then turned away her head to conceal a starting tear; while Mrs. Mowbray, in incoherent eagerness, repeated her questions, and tremblingly awaited her answer.

"Is she well? Is she happy?—say but that!" she exclaimed, sobbing as she spoke.

"She was well and contented when I last heard from her," replied Mrs. Pemberton calmly.

"Heard from her? Then she writes to you! Oh, blessed, blessed woman! show me her letters, and tell me only that she has forgiven me for all my unkindness to her—" As she said this, Mrs. Mowbray threw her arms round Mrs. Pemberton, and sunk half-fainting on her shoulder.

"I will tell thee all that has ever passed between us, if thou wilt be composed," gravely answered Mrs. Pemberton; "but this violent expression of thy feelings is unseemly and detrimental."

"Well—well—I will be calm," said Mrs. Mowbray; and Mrs. Pemberton began to relate the interview which she had with Adeline at Richmond.

"How long ago did this take place?" eagerly interrupted Mrs. Mowbray.

"Full six years."

"Oh, God!" exclaimed she, impatiently,—"Six years! By this time then she may be dead—she may——"

"Thou art incorrigible, I fear," said Mrs. Pemberton, "but thou art afflicted, and I will bear with thy impatience:—sit down again and attend to me, and thou wilt hear much later intelligence of thy daughter."

"How late?" asked Mrs. Mowbray, with frantic eagerness;—and Mrs. Pemberton, overcome with the manner in which she spoke, could scarcely falter out, "Within a twelvemonth I have heard of her."

"Within a twelvemonth!" joyfully cried Mrs. Mowbray: but, recollecting herself, she added mournfully—"but in that time what—what may not have happened!"

"I know not what to do with thee nor for thee," observed Mrs. Pemberton; "but do try, I beseech thee, to hear me patiently!"

Mrs. Mowbray then re-seated herself; and Mrs. Pemberton informed her of Adeline's premature confinement at Richmond; of her distress on Glenmurray's death, and of her having witnessed it.

"Ah! you acted a mother's part—you did what I ought to have done," cried Mrs. Mowbray, bursting into tears,—"but, go on—I will be patient."

Yet that was impossible; for, when she heard of Adeline's insanity, her emotions became so strong that Mrs. Pemberton, alarmed for her life, was obliged to ring for assistance.

When she recovered,—"Thou hast heard the worst now," said Mrs. Pemberton, "and all I have yet to say of thy child is satisfactory."

She then related the contents of Adeline's first letter, informing her of her marriage:—and Mrs. Mowbray, clasping her hands together, blessed God that Adeline was become a wife. The next letter Mrs. Pemberton read informed her that she was the mother of a fine girl.

"A mother!" she exclaimed, "Oh, how I should like to see her child!"—But at the same moment she recollected how bitterly she had reviled her when she saw her about to become a mother, at their last meeting; and, torn with conflicting emotions, she was again insensible to aught but her self-upbraidings.

"Well—but where is she now? where is the child? and when did you hear from her last?" cried she.

"I have not heard from her since," hesitatingly replied Mrs. Pemberton.

"But can't you write to her?"

"Yes;—but in her last letter she said she was going to change her lodgings, and would write again when settled in a new habitation."

Again Mrs. Mowbray paced the room in wild and violent distress: but her sorrows at length yielded to the gentle admonitions and soothings of Mrs. Pemberton, who bade her remember, that when she rose in the morning she had not expected the happiness and consolation which she had met with that day; and that a short time might bring forth still greater comfort.

"For," said Mrs. Pemberton, "I can write to the house where she formerly lodged, and perhaps the person who keeps it can give us intelligence of her."

On hearing this, Mrs. Mowbray became more composed, and diverted her sorrow by a thousand fond inquiries concerning Adeline, which none but a mother could make, and none but a mother listen* to with patience.

While this conversation was going on, a knock at the door was heard, and miss Woodville entered the room in great emotion; for she had heard, on the road, that a mad bullock had attacked a lady; and also that Mrs. Mowbray, scarcely able to walk, had been led into the white house in the field by the road side.

Miss Woodville was certainly as much alarmed as she pretended to be: but there was a somewhat in the expression of her alarm which, though it gratified Mrs. Mowbray, was displeasing to the more penetrating Mrs.

Pemberton. She could not indeed guess that miss Woodville's alarm sprung merely from apprehension lest Mrs. Mowbray should die before she had provided for her in her will: yet, notwithstanding, she felt that her expressions of concern and anxiety had no resemblance to those of real affection; and in spite of her habitual candour, she beheld miss Woodville with distrust.

But this feeling was considerably increased on observing, that when Mrs. Mowbray exultingly introduced her, not only as the lady whose life she had been the means of preserving, but as the friend and correspondent of her daughter, she evidently changed colour; and, in spite of her habitual plausibility, could not utter a single coherent sentence of pleasure or congratulation:—and it was also evident, that, being conscious of Mrs. Pemberton's regarding her with a scrutinizing eye, she was not easy till, on pretence of Mrs. Mowbray's requiring rest after her alarm, she had prevailed on her to return home.

But she could not prevent the new friends from parting with eager assurances of meeting again and again: and it was agreed between them, that Mrs. Pemberton should spend the next day at the Lawn.

Mrs. Pemberton, who is thus again introduced to the notice of my readers, had been, as well as Mrs. Mowbray, the pupil of adversity. She had been born and educated in fashionable life; and she united to a very lovely face and elegant form, every feminine grace and accomplishment.

When she was only eighteen, Mr. Pemberton, a young and gay quaker,[1] fell in love with her; and having inspired her with a mutual passion, he married her, notwithstanding the difference of their religious opinions, and the displeasure of his friends. He was consequently disowned by the society: but being weaned by the happiness which he found at home from those public amusements which had first lured him from the strict habits of his sect, he was soon desirous of being again admitted a member of it; and in process of time he was once more received into it; while his amiable wife, having no wish beyond her domestic circle, and being disposed to think her husband's opinions right, became in time, a convert to the same profession of faith, and exhibited in her manners the rare union of the easy elegance of a woman of the world with the rigid decorum and unadorned dress of a strict quaker.

But in the midst of her happiness, and whilst looking forward to a long continuance of it, a fever, caught in visiting the sick bed of a cottager, carried off her husband, and next two lovely children; and Mrs. Pemberton would have sunk under the stroke, but for the watchful care and affection-

---

1  I.e., a member of the Society of Friends who did not follow the strictest tenets of the religion.

ate attentions of the friend of her youth, who resided near her, and who, in time, prevailed on her to receive with becoming fortitude and resignation the trials which she was appointed to undergo.

During this season of affliction, as we have before stated, she became a teacher* in the quaker's society:† but at the time of her meeting Adeline at Richmond, she had been called from the duties of her public profession to watch over the declining health of her friend and consoler, and to accompany her to Lisbon.

There, during four long years, she bent over her sick couch, now elated with hope, and now sunk into despondence; when, at the beginning of the fifth year, her friend died in her arms, and she returned to England, resolved to pass her days, except when engaged in the active duties of her profession,‡ on a little estate in Cumberland, bequeathed to her by her friend on her death-bed. But ill health and various events had detained her in the west of England since her return; and she had not long taken possession of her house near Penrith, when she became introduced in so singular a manner to Mrs. Mowbray's acquaintance—an acquaintance which would, she hoped, prove of essential service to them both; and as soon as her guest departed, Mrs. Pemberton resolved to inquire what character Mrs. Mowbray bore in the neighbourhood, and whether her virtues at all kept pace with her misfortunes.

Her inquiries were answered in the most satisfactory manner; as, fortunately for Mrs. Mowbray, with the remembrance of her daughter had recurred to her that daughter's benevolent example. She remembered the satisfaction which used to beam from Adeline's countenance when she returned from her visits to the sick and the afflicted; and she resolved to try whether those habits of charitable exertion which could increase the happiness of the young and light-hearted Adeline, might not have power to alleviate the sorrows of her own drooping age, and broken, joyless heart.

"Sweet are the uses of adversity!"[1]—She who, while the child of prosperity, was a romantic, indolent theorist, an inactive speculator, a proud contemner of the dictates of sober experience, and a neglecter of that practical benevolence which can in days produce more benefit to others than theories and theorists can accomplish in years—this erring woman, awakened from her dreams and reveries to habits of useful exertion by the stimulating touch of affliction, was become the visitor of the sick, the consoler of the sorrowful, the parent of the fatherless, while virtuous industry looked up to her with hope; and her name, like that of Adeline in happier days, was pronounced with prayers and blessings.

---

1  Shakespeare, *As You Like It* 2.1.12.

But, alas! she felt that blessing could reach her only in the shape of her lost child: and, though she was conscious of being useful to others, though she had the satisfaction of knowing that she had but the day before been the means of preserving a valuable life, she met Mrs. Pemberton, when she arrived at the Lawn, with a countenance of fixed melancholy, and was at first disposed to expect but little success from the project of writing to Adeline's former lodgings in order to inquire.

The truth was, that miss Woodville had artfully insinuated the improbability of such an inquiry's succeeding; and, though Mrs. Mowbray had angrily asserted her hopes when miss Woodville provokingly asserted her *fears*, the treacherous girl's insinuations had sunk deeply into her mind, and Mrs. Pemberton saw, with pain and wonder, an effect produced of which the cause was wholly unseen. But she at length succeeded in awakening Mrs. Mowbray's hopes; and in a letter written by Mrs. Pemberton to the mistress of the house whence Adeline formerly dated, she inclosed one to her daughter glowing with maternal tenderness, and calculated to speak peace to her sorrows.

These letters were sent, as soon as written, to the post by Mrs. Mowbray's footman; but miss Woodville contrived to meet him near the post-office, and telling him she would put the letter in the receiver, she gave him a commission to call at a shop in Penrith for her, at which she had not time to call herself.

Thus was another scheme for restoring Adeline to her afflicted mother frustrated by the treachery of this interested woman; who, while Mrs. Pemberton and Mrs. Mowbray looked anxiously forward to the receipt of an answer from London, triumphed with malignant pleasure in the success of her artifice.—But, spite of herself, she feared Mrs. Pemberton, and was not at all pleased to find that, till the answer from London could arrive, that lady was to remain at the Lawn.

She contrived, however, to be as little in her presence as possible; for, contrary to Mrs. Pemberton's usual habits, she felt a distrust of miss Woodville, which her intelligent eye could not help expressing, and which consequently alarmed the conscious heart of the culprit. Being left therefore, by miss Woodville's fears, alone with Mrs. Mowbray, she drew from her, at different times, ample details of Adeline's childhood, and the method which Mrs. Mowbray had pursued in her education.

"Ah! 'tis as I suspected," interrupted Mrs. Pemberton during one of these conversations. "Thy daughter's *faults* originated in thee! her education was cruelly defective."

"No!" replied Mrs. Mowbray with almost angry eagerness, "whatever my errors as a mother have been, and for the rash marriage which I made I own myself culpable in the highest degree, I am sure that I paid the greatest attention to my daughter's education. If you were but to see the voluminous manuscript on the subject, which I wrote for her improvement——"

"But where was thy daughter; and how was she employed during the time that thou wert writing a book by which to educate her?"

Mrs. Mowbray was silent; she recollected that, while she was gratifying her own vanity in composing her system of education, Adeline was almost banished her presence; and, but for the humble instruction of her grandmother, would, at the age of fifteen, have run a great risk of being both an ignorant and useless being.

"Forgive me, friend Mowbray," resumed Mrs. Pemberton, aware in some measure of what was passing in Mrs. Mowbray's mind—"forgive me if I venture to observe, that till of late years, a thick curtain of self-love seems to have been dropped between thy heart and maternal affection. It is now, and now only that thou hast learned to feel like a true and affectionate mother!"

"Perhaps you are right," replied Mrs. Mowbray mournfully, "still, I always meant well; and hoped that my studies would conduce to the benefit of my child."

"So they might, perhaps, to that of thy second, third, or fourth child, hadst thou been possessed of so many; but, in the mean while, thy first-born must have been fatally neglected. A child's education begins almost from the hour of its birth; and the mother who understands her task, knows that the circumstances which every moment calls forth, are the tools with which she is to work in order to fashion her child's mind and character.—What would you think of the farmer who was to let his fields lie fallow for years, while he was employed in contriving a method of cultivating land to increase his gains ten-fold?"

"But I did not suffer Adeline's mind to lie fallow.—I allowed her to read, and I directed her studies."

"Thou didst so; but what were those studies? and didst thou acquaint thyself with the deductions which her quick mind formed from them? No—thou didst not, as parents should do, inquire into the impressions made on thy daughter's mind by the books which she perused. Prompt to feel, and hasty to decide, as Adeline was, how necessary was to her the warning voice of judgment and experience!"

"But how could I imagine that a girl so young should dare to act, whatever her opinions might be, in open defiance of the opinions of the world?"

"But she had not lived in the world; therefore, scarcely knew how repugnant to it her opinions were; nor, as she did not mix in general society, could she care sufficiently for its good opinion, to be willing to act contrary to her own ideas of right, rather than forfeit it: besides, thou ownest that thou didst openly profess thy admiration of the sentiments which she adopted; nor, till they were confirmed irrevocably her's, didst thou declare, that to act up to them was, in thy opinion, vicious. And then it was too late: she thought thy timidity, and not thy wisdom, spoke, and she set thee the virtuous example of acting up to the dictates of conscience. But Adeline and thou are both the pupils of affliction and experience; and I trust that, all your errors repented of, you will meet once more to expiate your past follies by your future conduct."

"I hope so too," meekly replied Mrs. Mowbray, whose pride had been completely subdued by self-upbraidings and distress: "Oh! when—when will an answer arrive from London?"


## CHAPTER 27

ALAS! day after day elapsed, and no letter came; but while Mrs. Mowbray was almost frantic with disappointment and anxiety, Mrs. Pemberton thought that she observed in miss Woodville's countenance a look of triumphant malice, which ill accorded with the fluent expressions of sympathy and regret with which she gratified her unsuspicious relation, and she determined to watch her very narrowly; for she thought it strange that Adeline, however she might respect her mother's oath, should never, in the bitterness of her sorrows, have unburthened her heart by imparting them to her: one day, when, as usual, the post had been anxiously expected, and, as usual, had brought no letter from London concerning Adeline; and while miss Woodville was talking on indifferent subjects with ill suppressed gaiety, though Mrs. Mowbray, sunk into despondence, was lying on the sofa by her; Mrs. Pemberton suddenly exclaimed—"There is only one right way of proceeding, friend Mowbray,—thou and I must go to London, and make our inquiries in person, and then we shall have a great chance of succeeding." As she said this, she looked stedfastly at miss Woodville, and saw her turn very pale, while her eye was hastily averted from the penetrating glance of Mrs. Pemberton; and when she heard Mrs. Mowbray, in a transport of joy, declare that they had better set off that very evening, unable to conceal her terror and agitation, she hastily left the room.

Mrs. Pemberton instantly followed her into the apartment to which she had retired, and the door of which she had closed with great* violence.—She found her walking to and fro, and wringing her hands, as if in agony. On seeing Mrs. Pemberton, she started, and sinking into a chair, she complained of being very ill, and desired to be left alone.

"Thou art ill, and thy illness is of the worst sort, I fear," replied Mrs. Pemberton; "but I will stay, and be thy physician."

"*You*, my physician?" replied miss Woodville, with fury in her looks; "You?"

"Yes—*I*—I see that thou art afraid lest Adeline should be restored to her paternal roof."

"Who told you so, officious, insolent woman?" returned miss Woodville.

"Thy own looks—but all this is very natural in thee: thou fearest that Adeline's favour should annihilate thine."

"Perhaps I do"; cried miss Woodville, a little less alarmed, and catching at this plausible excuse for her uneasiness; "for, should I be forced to leave my cousin's house, I shall be reduced to comparative poverty, and solitude again."

"But why shouldest thou be forced to leave it? Art thou not Adeline's friend?"

"Ye—yes," faltered out miss Woodville.

"But it is uncertain whether we can find Adeline—still we shall be very diligent in our enquiries; yet it is so strange that she should never have written to her mother, if alive, that perhaps—"

"Oh, I dare say she is dead," hastily interrupted miss Woodville.

"Has she been dead long? thinkest thou."

"No—not long—not above six months, I dare say."

"No!—Hast thou any reason then for knowing that she was alive six months ago?" asked Mrs. Pemberton, looking steadily at miss Woodville, as she spoke.

"I?—Lord—no—How should I know?" she replied, her lip quivering, and her whole frame trembling.

"I tell thee how.—Art thou not conscious of having intercepted letters from thy cousin, to her relenting parent?"

Mrs. Pemberton had scarcely uttered these words, when miss Woodville fell back nearly *insensible* in her chair—a proof that the accusation was only too well founded. As soon as she recovered, Mrs. Pemberton said, with great gentleness, "Thou art ill,—ill indeed, but, as I suspected, thy illness is of the mind; there is a load of guilt on it; throw it off then by a full confession, and be the sinner that repenteth."[1]

In a few moments miss Woodville, conscious that her emotion had betrayed her, and suspecting that Mrs. Pemberton had by some means or other received hints of her treachery, confessed that she had intercepted and destroyed letters from Adeline to her mother; and also owned, to the great joy of Mrs. Pemberton, that Adeline's last letter, the letter in which she informed Mrs. Mowbray that all the conditions were then fulfilled,

---

1  See Luke 15.7.

without which alone she had sworn never to forgive her, had arrived only two months before; and that it was dated from such a street, and such a number, in London.

"My poor friend will be so happy!" said Mrs. Pemberton; and, her own eyes filling with tears of joy, she hastened to find Mrs. Mowbray.

"But what will become of *me*?" exclaimed miss Woodville, detaining her— "*I* am ruined—ruined for ever!"

"Not so," replied Mrs. Pemberton, "thou art *saved*,—saved, I trust, *for*<sup>*</sup> *ever*.—Thou hast confessed thy guilt, and made all the atonement now in thy power. Go to thine own room, and I will soon make known to thee thy relation's sentiments towards thee."

So saying, she hastened to Mrs. Mowbray, whom she found giving orders, with eager impatience, to have post horses sent for immediately.

"Then thou art full of expectation, I conclude, from the event of our journey to town?" said Mrs. Pemberton smiling.

"To be sure I am," replied Mrs. Mowbray.

"And so am I," she answered—"for I think that I know the present abode of thy daughter."

Mrs. Mowbray started—her friend's countenance expressed more joy and exultation than she had ever seen on it before; and, almost breathless with new hope, she seized her hand and conjured her to explain herself.

The explanation was soon given; and Mrs. Mowbray's joy, in consequence of it, unbounded.

"But what is thy will," observed Mrs. Pemberton, "with regard to thy guilty relation?"

"I cannot—cannot see her again now, if ever;—and she must immediately leave my house."

"Immediately?"

"Yes,—but I will settle on her a handsome allowance; for my conscience tells me, that, had I behaved like a mother to my child, no one could have been tempted to injure her thus.—I put this unhappy woman into a state of temptation, and she yielded to it:—but I feel only too sensibly, that no one has been such an enemy to my poor Adeline as I have been; nor, conscious of my own offences toward her, dare I resent those of another."

"I love, I honour thee for what thou hast now uttered," cried Mrs. Pemberton with unusual animation.—"I see that thou art now indeed a christian; such are the breathings of a truly contrite spirit;[1] and, verily, she who can so easily forgive the crimes of others may hope to have her own forgiven."

---

1  See Psalm 34.18 (and many other passages in the Bible).

Mrs. Pemberton then hastened to speak hope and comfort to the mind of the penitent offender, while Mrs. Mowbray ran to meet her servant, who, to her surprise, was returning without horses, for none were to be procured; and Mrs. Mowbray saw herself obliged to delay her journey till noon the next day, when she was assured of having horses from Penrith. But when, after a long and restless night, she arose in the morning, anticipating with painful impatience the hour of her departure, Mrs. Pemberton entered her room, and informed her that she had passed nearly all the night at miss Woodville's bed-side, who had been seized with a violent delirium at one o'clock in the morning, and in her ravings was continually calling on Mrs. Mowbray, and begging to see her once more.

"I will see her directly," replied Mrs. Mowbray, without a moment's hesitation; and hastened to miss Woodville's apartment, where she found the medical attendant whom Mrs. Pemberton had sent for just arrived. He immediately declared the disorder to be an inflammation on the brain, and left them with little or no hope of her recovery.

Mrs. Mowbray, affected beyond measure at the pathetic appeals for pardon addressed to her continually by the unconscious sufferer, took her station at the bed-side; and, hanging over her pillow, watched for the slightest gleam of returning reason, in order to speak the pardon so earnestly implored: and while thus piously engaged, the chaise that was to convey her and her friend to London, and perhaps to Adeline, drove up to the gate.

"Art thou ready?" said Mrs. Pemberton, entering the room equipped for her journey.

At this moment the poor invalid reiterated her cries for pardon, and begged Mrs. Mowbray not to leave her without pronouncing her forgiveness.

Mrs. Mowbray burst into tears; and though sure that she was not even conscious of her presence, she felt herself almost unable to forsake her:— still it was in search of her daughter that she was going—nay, perhaps, it was to her daughter that she was hastening; and, as this thought occurred to her, she hurried to the door of the chamber, saying she should be ready in a moment.

But the eye of the phrensied sufferer followed her as she did so, and in a tone of unspeakable agony she begged, she entreated that she might not be left to die in solitude and sorrow, however guilty she might have been.— Then again she implored Mrs. Mowbray to speak peace and pardon to her drooping soul; while, unable to withstand these solicitations, though she knew them to be the unconscious ravings of the disorder, she slowly and mournfully returned to the bed-side.

"It is late," said Mrs. Pemberton—"we ought ere now to be on the road."

"How can I go, and leave this poor creature in such a state?—But then should we find my poor injured child at the end of the journey! Such an expectation as that!——"

"Thou must decide quickly," replied Mrs. Pemberton gently.

"Decide! Then I will go with you.—Yet still, should Anna recover her senses before her death, and wish to see me, I should never forgive myself for being absent—it might sooth the anguish of her last moments to know how freely I pardon her.—No, no:—after all, if pleasure awaits me, it is only delaying it a few days; and this, this unhappy girl is on her *death-bed.*—You, you must go *without* me."

As she said this, Mrs. Pemberton pressed her hand with affectionate eagerness, and murmured out in broken accents, "I honour thy decision, and may I return with comfort to thee!"

"Yet though I wish you to go," cried Mrs. Mowbray, "I grieve to expose you to such fatigue and trouble in your weak state of health, and——"

"Say no more," interrupted Mrs. Pemberton, "I am only doing my duty; and reflect on my happiness if I am allowed to restore the lost sheep to the fold again!"[1]—So saying she set off on her journey, and arrived in London only four days after Adeline had arrived in Cumberland.

Mrs. Pemberton drove immediately to Adeline's lodgings, but received the same answer as colonel Mordaunt had received; namely, that she was gone no one knew whither. Still she did not despair of finding her: she, like the colonel, thought that a mulatto, a lady just recovered from the small-pox, and a child, were likely to be easily traced; and having written to Mrs. Mowbray, owning her disappointment, but bidding her not despair, she set off on her journey back, and had succeeded in tracing Adeline as far as an inn on the high North road,—when an event took place which made her further inquiries needless.

CHAPTER 28

ADELINE, after several repeated trials, succeeded in writing the following letter to her mother:

"Dearest of Mothers,

"When this letter reaches you, I shall be no more; and however I may hitherto have offended you, I shall then be able to offend you no longer; and that child, whom you bound yourself by oath never to see or forgive but on the most cruel of conditions while living,

---

1 See Luke 15.1-7.

dead you may perhaps deign to receive to your pardon and your love.—Nay, my heart tells me that you will do more,—that you will transfer the love which you once felt for me, to my poor help-less orphan; and in full confidence that you will be thus indulgent, I bequeath her to you with my dying breath.—O! look on her, my mother, nor shrink from her with disgust, although you see in her my features; but rather rejoice in the resemblance, and fancy that I am restored to you pure, happy, and beloved as I once was.—Yes, yes,—it will be so: I have known a great deal of sorrow—let me then indulge the little ray of pleasure that breaks in upon me when I think that you will not resist my dying prayer, but bestow on my child the long arrears of tenderness due to me.

"Yes, yes, you will receive, you will be kind to her; and by so do-ing you will make me ample amends for all the sorrow which your harshness caused me when we met last.—That was a dreadful day! How you frowned on me! I did not think you could have frowned so dreadfully—but then I was uninjured by affliction, unaltered by illness. Were you to see me now, you would not have the heart to frown on me: and yet my letters, being repeatedly returned, and even the last unnoticed and unanswered, though it told you that even on your own conditions I could now claim your pardon, for that I had been 'wretched in love,' and had experienced 'the anguish of being forsaken, despised, and disgraced in the eye of the world,'[1] proves but too surely that the bitterness of resentment is not yet past!—But on my *death-bed* you promised to see and forgive me— *and I am there, my mother*!! Yet will I not claim that promise;—I will not weaken, by directing it towards myself, the burst of sorrow, of too late regret, of self-upbraidings, and long-restrained affection, which must be directed towards my child when I am not alive to profit by it. No:—though I would give worlds to embrace you once more, for the sake of my child I resign the gratification.

"Oh, mother! you little think that I saw you, only a few days ago, from the stile by the cottage which overlooks your house: you were walking with a lady, and my child was with me (my Editha, for I have called her after you). You seemed, methought, even cheerful, and I was so selfish that I felt shocked to think I was so entirely forgotten by you; for I was sure that if you thought of me you could not be cheer-ful. But your companion left you; and then you looked so very sad, that I was wretched from the idea that you were then thinking too much of me, and I wished you to resume your cheerfulness again.

---

1   See 139; cf. 223.

"*I* was not cheerful, and Editha by her artless prattle wounded me to the very soul.—She wished, she said, to live in that sweet house, and asked why she should not live there? *I could* have told her why, but dared not do it; but I assured her, and do not for mercy's sake prove that assurance false! that she *should* live there *one day.*

"'But when—when?' she asked.

"'When I am in my grave,' replied I: and, poor innocent! throwing herself into my arms with playful fondness, she begged me to go to my grave directly. I feel but too sensibly that her desire will soon be accomplished.

"But must I die unblest by you? True, I am watched by the kindest of human beings! but then she is not my mother—that mother, who, with the joys of my childhood and my home, is so continually recurring to my memory. Oh! I forget all your unkindness, my mother, and remember only your affection. How I should like to feel your hand supporting my head, and see you perform the little offices which sickness requires.—And must I never, never see you more? Yes! you will come, I am sure you will, but come, come quickly, or I shall die without your blessing.

"I have had a fainting fit—but I am recovered, and can address you again.—Oh! teach my Editha to be humble, teach her to be slow to call the experience of ages contemptible prejudices; teach her no opinions that can destroy her sympathies with general society, and make her an alien to the hearts of those amongst whom she lives.

"Be above all things careful that she wanders not in the night of scepticism. But for the support of religion, what, amidst my various sorrows, what would have become of *me*?

"There is something more that I would say. Should my existence be prolonged even but a few days, I shall have to struggle with poverty as well as sickness; and the anxious friend (I will not call her servant) who is now my all of earthly comfort, will scarcely have money sufficient to pay me the last sad duties; and I owe her, my mother, a world of obligation! She will make my last moments easy, and *you* must reward her. From her you will receive this letter when I am no more, and to your care and protection I bequeath her. She is—my eyes grow dim, and I must leave off for the present."

On the very evening in which Adeline had written this address to her mother, Mrs. Mowbray had received Mrs. Pemberton's letter; and as miss Woodville had been interred that morning, she felt herself at liberty to join Mrs. Pemberton in her search after Adeline, while various plans for this purpose presented themselves to her mind, and each of them was dismissed in its turn as fruitless or impracticable. Full* of these thoughts she pensively walked along the lawn before her door, till sad and weary she leaned on a little gate at the bottom of it; which, as she did so, swung slowly backwards and forwards, responsive as it were to her feelings.

But, as she continued to muse, and to recall the varied sorrows of her past life, the gate on which she leaned began to vibrate more quickly; till, unable to bear the recollections which assailed her, she was hastening with almost frantic speed towards the house, when she saw a cottager approaching, to whose sick daughter and helpless family she had long been a bountiful benefactress.

"What is the matter, John?" cried Mrs. Mowbray, hastening forward to meet him—"you seem agitated."

"My poor daughter, madam!" replied the man, bursting into tears.

At the sight of his distress, his *parental* distress, Mrs. Mowbray sighed deeply, and asked if Lucy was worse.

"I doubt she is dying," said the afflicted father.

"God† forbid!" exclaimed Mrs. Mowbray, throwing her shawl over her shoulders; "I will go and see her myself."

"What, really?—But the way is so long, and the road so miry!"‡

"No matter—I must do my duty."

"God bless you, and reward you!" cried the grateful father—"that is so like you! Lucy said you would come!"

Mrs. Mowbray then filled a basket with medicine and refreshments, and set out on her charitable visit.

She found the poor girl in a very weak and alarming state; but the sight of her benefactress, and the tender manner in which she supported her languid head, and administered wine and other cordials to her, insensibly revived her; and while writhing under the feelings of an unhappy parent herself, Mrs. Mowbray was soothed by the blessings of the parent whom she comforted.

At this moment they were alarmed by a shriek from a neighbouring cottage, and a woman who was attending on the sick girl ran out to inquire into the cause of it.

She returned, saying that a poor sick young gentlewoman, who lodged at the next house, was fallen back in a fit, and they thought she was dead.

"A young gentlewoman," exclaimed Mrs. Mowbray, "at the next cottage!" rising up.

"Aye sure," cried the woman, "she looks like a lady for certain, and she has the finest child I ever saw."

"Perhaps she is not dead," said Mrs. Mowbray:—"let us go see."

# CHAPTER 29

LITTLE did Mrs. Mowbray think that it was her own child whom she was hastening to relieve; and that, while meditating a kind action, recompense was so near.

Adeline, while trying to finish her letter to her mother, had scarcely traced a few illegible lines, when she fell back insensible on her pillow; and at the moment of Mrs. Mowbray's entering the cottage, Savanna, who had uttered the shriek which had excited her curiosity, had convinced herself that she was gone for ever.

The woman who accompanied Mrs. Mowbray entered the house first; and opening a back chamber, low-roofed, narrow, and lighted only by one solitary and slender candle, Mrs. Mowbray beheld through the door the lifeless form of the object of her solicitude, which Savanna was contemplating with loud and frantic sorrow.

"Here is a lady come to see what she can do for your mistress," cried the woman, while Savanna turned hastily round:—"Here she is—here is good madam Mowbray."

"Madam Mowbray!" shrieked Savanna, fixing her dark eyes fiercely on Mrs. Mowbray, and raising her arm in a threatening manner as she approached her: then snatching up the letter which lay on the bed,— "Woman!" she exclaimed, grasping Mrs. Mowbray's arm with frightful earnestness, "read dat—'tis for you!"

Mrs. Mowbray, speechless with alarm and awe, involuntarily seized the letter—but scarcely had she read the first words, when uttering a deep groan she sprung forward, to clasp the unconscious form before her, and fell beside it equally insensible.

But she recovered almost immediately to a sense of her misery; and while, in speechless agony, she knelt by the bed-side, Savanna, beholding her distress, with a sort of dreadful pleasure exclaimed, "Ah! have you at last learn to feel?"

"But is she, is she *indeed* gone?" cried Mrs. Mowbray, "is there *no* hope?" and instantly seizing the cordial which she had brought with her, assisted by the woman, she endeavoured to force it down the throat of Adeline.

Their endeavours were for some time vain: at length, however, she exhibited signs of life, and in a few minutes more she opened her sunk eye, and gazed unconsciously around her.

"My God! I thank you!" exclaimed Mrs. Mowbray, falling on her knees; while Savanna, laying her mistress's head on her bosom, sobbed with fearful joy.

"Adeline! my child, my dear, dear child!" cried Mrs. Mowbray, seizing her clammy hand.

That voice, those words which she had so long wished to hear, though hopeless of ever hearing them again, seemed to recall the fast fading recollection of Adeline; she raised her head from Savanna's bosom, and, looking earnestly at Mrs. Mowbray, faintly smiled, and endeavoured to throw herself into her arms,—but fell back again exhausted on the pillow.

But in a few minutes she recovered so far as to be able to speak; and while she hung round her mother's neck, and gazed upon her with eager and delighted earnestness, she desired Savanna to bring Editha to her immediately.

"Will you, will you—," said Adeline, vainly trying to speak her wishes, as Savanna put the sleeping girl in Mrs. Mowbray's arms: but she easily divined them; and, clasping her to her heart, wept over her convulsively— "She shall be dear to me as my own soul!" said Mrs. Mowbray.

"Then I die contented," replied Adeline.

"Die!" exclaimed Mrs. Mowbray hastily: "no, you must not, shall not die; you must live to see me atone for—"

"It is in vain," said Adeline faintly. "I bless God that he allows me to enjoy this consolation—say that you forgive me."

"Forgive you! Oh, Adeline! for years have I forgiven and pined after you: but a wicked woman intercepted all your letters; and I thought you were dead, or had renounced me for ever."

"Indeed!" cried Adeline. "Oh! had I suspected that!"—*

"Nay more, Mrs. Pemberton is now in London, in search of you, in order to bring you back to happiness!" As Mrs. Mowbray said this, Savanna, drawing near, took her hand and gently pressed it.

Adeline observed the action, and seeing by it that Savanna's heart relented towards her mother, said, "I owe that faithful creature more than I can express; but to your care I bequeath her."

"I will love her as my child," said Mrs. Mowbray, "and behave to her better than I did to—"

"Hush!" cried Adeline, putting her hand to Mrs. Mowbray's lips.

"But you *shall* live! I will send for Dr. Norberry; you shall be moved to my house, and all will be well—all our past grief be forgotten," returned Mrs. Mowbray with almost convulsive eagerness.

Adeline faintly smiled, but repeated that every hope of that kind was over, but that her utmost wish was gratified in seeing her mother, and receiving her full forgiveness.

"But you must live for my sake!" cried Mrs. Mowbray: "and for mine," sobbed out Savanna.

"Could you not be moved to my house?" said Mrs. Mowbray. "There every indulgence and attention that money can procure shall be yours. Is this a place,—is this poverty—this—" here her voice failed her, and she burst into tears.

"Mother, dearest mother," replied Adeline, "I see you, I am assured of your love again, and I have not a want beside. Still, I could like, I could wish, to be once more under a *parent's roof.*"

In a moment, the cottager who was present, and returning with usury to Mrs. Mowbray's daughter the anxious interest which she had taken in his, proposed various means of transporting Adeline to the Lawn; a difficult and a hazardous undertaking; but the poor invalid was willing to risk the danger and the fatigue; and her mother could not but indulge her. At length the cottager, as it was for the *general benefactress*, having with care procured even more assistance than was necessary, Adeline was conveyed on a sort of a litter, along the valley, and found herself once more in the house of her mother; while Savanna, sharing in the joy which Adeline's countenance expressed, threw herself on Mrs. Mowbray's neck, and exclaimed, "Now I forgive you!"

"Mother, dear mother," cried Adeline, after having for some minutes vainly endeavoured to speak—"I am so happy! no more an outcast, but under my mother's roof!—Nay, I even think I *can* live now," added she with a faint smile.

Had Adeline risen from her bed in complete health and vigour, she would scarcely have excited more joy in her mother, and in Savanna, than she did by this expression.

"Can live!" cried Mrs. Mowbray, "O! you shall, you must live."—And an express was sent off immediately to Dr. Norberry too, who was removed to Kendal,[1] to be near his elder daughter, lately married in the neighbourhood.

Dr. Norberry arrived in a few hours. Mrs. Mowbray ran out meet him; but a welcome died on her tongue, and she could only speak by her tears.

"There, there, my good woman, don't be foolish," replied he: "it is cursed* silly to blubber, you know: besides, it can do no good,"—giving her a kiss, while tears trickled down his rough cheek.—"So, the lost sheep is found?"[2]

"But, O! she will be lost again," faltered Mrs. Mowbray; "I doubt nothing can save her!"

"No!" cried the old man, with a gulp, "no! not my coming so many miles on purpose?—Well, but where is she?"

"She will see you presently, but begged to be excused for a few minutes."—"You see," said he, "by my dress, what has happened," gulping as he spoke. "I have lost the companion of thirty years!—and—and—" here he paused, and after an effort went on to say, that his wife in her

---

1   A town in Westmoreland (now in Cumbria), south of Penrith.

2   Another reference to Luke 15.1-7 (cf. 270).

last illness had owned that she had suppressed Adeline's letters, and had declared the reason of it—"But, poor soul!" continued the doctor, "it was the only sin against me, I believe, or any one else, that she ever committed—so I forgave her; and I trust that God will."

Soon after they were summoned to the sick room, and Dr. Norberry beheld with a degree of fearful emotion, which he vainly endeavoured to hide under a cloak of pleasantry, the dreadful ravages which sorrow and sickness had made in the face and form of Adeline.

"So, here you are at last!" cried he, trying to smile while he sobbed audibly, "and a pretty figure you make, don't you?—But we have you again, and we will not part with you soon,* I can tell you," (almost starting as the faint but rapid pulse met his fingers,) "that is, I mean," added he, "unless it please God."—Mrs. Mowbray and Savanna, during this speech, gazed on his countenance in breathless anxiety, and read in it a confirmation of their fears.—"But who's afraid?" cried the doctor, forcing a laugh, while his tone and his looks expressed the extreme of apprehension, and his laugh ended in a sob.

Mrs. Mowbray turned away in a sort of desperate silence; but the mulatto still kept her penetrating eye fixed upon him, and with a look so full of woe!

"I'll trouble you, mistress, to take those formidable eyes of yours off my face," cried the doctor, pettishly; "for, by the Lord,† I can't stand their inquiry!—But who the devil are you?"

"She is my nurse, my consoler, and my friend," said Adeline. .

"Then she is mine of course," cried the doctor, "though she has a devilish‡ terrible stare with her eyes:—but give me your hand, mistress. What is your name?"

"Me be name Savanna," replied the mulatto; "and me die and live wid my dear mistress," she added, bursting into tears.

"Zounds!"§ cried the doctor, "I can't bear this—here I came as a physician, and these blubberers melt me down into an old woman.—Adeline, I must order all these people out of the room, and have you to myself, or I can do nothing."

He was obeyed; and on inquiring into all Adeline's symptoms, he found little to hope and every thing to fear—"But your mind is relieved, and you have youth on your side; and who knows what good air, good food, and good nurses may do for you!"

"Not to mention a good physician," added Adeline, smiling, "and a good friend in that physician."

"This it be to have money," said Savanna, as she saw the various things prepared and made to tempt Adeline's weak appetite:—"poor Savanna mean as well—her heart make all these, but her hand want power."

During this state of alarming suspense Mrs. Pemberton was hourly expected, as she had written word that she had traced Adeline into Lancashire, and suspected that she was in her mother's neighbourhood.—It may be supposed that Mrs. Mowbray, Adeline, and Savanna, looked forward to her arrival with eager impatience; but not so Dr. Norberry—he said that no doubt she was a very good sort of woman, but that he did not like pretensions to righteousness over much, and had a particular aversion to a piece of formal drab coloured morality.[1]

Adeline only laughed at these prejudices, without attempting to confute them; for she knew that Mrs. Pemberton's appearance and manners would soon annihilate them. At length she reached the Lawn; and Savanna, who saw her alight, announced her arrival to her mistress, and was commissioned by her to introduce her immediately into the sick chamber.—She did so; but Mrs. Pemberton, almost overpowered with joy at the intelligence which awaited her, and ill fortified by Savanna's violent and mixed emotions against the indulgence of her own, begged to compose herself a few moments before she met Adeline: but Savanna was not to be denied; and seizing her hand she led her up to the bed-side of the invalid.—Adeline smiled affectionately when she saw her; but Mrs. Pemberton started back, and, scarcely staying to take the hand which she offered her, rushed out of the room, to vent in solitude the burst of uncontrollable anguish which the sight of her altered countenance occasioned her.—Alas! her eye had been but too well tutored to read the characters of death in the face, and it was some time before she recovered herself sufficiently to appear before the anxious watchers by the bed of Adeline with that composure which on principle she always endeavoured to display.—At length, however, she re-entered the room, and, approaching the poor invalid, kissed in silence her wan yet* flushed cheek.

"I am very different now, my kind friend, to what I was when you *first* saw me," said Adeline, faintly smiling.

To the moment when they *last* met, Adeline had not resolution enough to revert, for then she was mourning by the dead body of Glenmurray.

Mrs. Pemberton was silent for a moment; but, making an effort, she replied, "Thou art now more like what thou wert in *mind*, when I *first* saw† thee at Rosevalley, than when I first met‡ thee at Richmond. At Rosevalley I beheld thee innocent, at Richmond guilty, and here I see thee penitent, and, I hope, resigned to thy fate."—She spoke the word *resigned* with emphasis, and Adeline *understood* her.

---

1   "Drab" means "colourless" or "dull"; it was also the name of a kind of fabric. Dr. Norberry associates the sombre clothing worn by Quakers with their strict moral code.

"I am indeed resigned," replied Adeline in a low voice: "nay, I feel that I am much favoured in being spared so long. But there is one thing that weighs heavily on my mind; Mary Warner is leading a life of shame, and she told me when I last saw her, that she was corrupted by my precept and example: if so—"

"Set thy conscience at rest on that subject," interrupted Mrs. Pemberton: "while she lived with me, I discovered, long before she ever saw thee, that she had been known to have been faulty."

"Oh! what a load have you removed from my mind!" replied Adeline. "Still it would be more relieved, if you would promise to find her out; and she may be heard of at Mr. Langley's chambers in the Temple. Offer her a yearly allowance for life, provided she will quit her present vicious habits; I am sure my mother will gladly fulfil my wishes in this respect."

"And so will I," replied Mrs. Pemberton. "Is there any thing else that I can do for thee?"

"Yes: I have two pensioners at Richmond,—a poor young woman, and her orphan boy,—an illegitimate child," she added, deeply sighing, as she recollected what had interested her in their fate. "I bequeath them to your care; Savanna knows where they are to be found. And now, all that disturbs my thoughts at this awful moment is, the grief which my poor mother and Savanna will feel;—nay, they will be quite unprepared for it; for they persist to hope still, and I believe that even Dr. Norberry allows his wishes to deceive his judgment."

"They will suffer, indeed!" cried Mrs. Pemberton: "but I give thee my word, that I will never leave thy mother, and that Savanna shall be our joint care."

"It is enough—I shall now die in peace," said Adeline; and Mrs. Pemberton turned away to meet Mrs. Mowbray, who with Dr. Norberry at that moment entered the room. Mrs. Mowbray met her, and welcomed her audibly and joyfully: but Mrs. Pemberton, aware of the blow which impended over her, vainly endeavoured to utter a congratulation; but throwing herself into Mrs. Mowbray's extended arms, she forgot her usual self-command, and sobbed loudly on her bosom.

Dr. Norberry gazed at the benevolent quaker with astonishment. True, she was "*drab-coloured*"; but where was the repulsive formality that he had expected? "Zounds!" thought he, "this* woman can feel like other women, and is as good a hand at a crying-bout as myself." But Mrs. Pemberton did not long give way to so violent an indulgence of her feelings; and gently withdrawing herself from Mrs. Mowbray's embrace, she turned to the window, while Mrs. Mowbray hastened to the bedside of Adeline. Mrs. Pemberton then turned round again, and, seizing Dr. Norberry's hand, which she fervently pressed, said in a faltering voice, "Would thou couldst *save* her!"* "And—and *can't* I? can't I?" replied he, gulping. Mrs. Pemberton looked at him with an expression which he could neither mistake nor endure; but muttering in a low tone, "No! dear, sweet soul! I doubt I can't, I doubt I can't, by the Lord!" he rushed out of the room.

From that moment he never was easy but when he could converse with Mrs. Pemberton; for he knew that she, and she only, sympathized in his feelings, as she only knew that Adeline was not likely to recover. The invalid herself observed his attention to her friend, nor could she forbear to rally him on the total disappearance of his prejudices against the fair quaker; for, such was the influence of Mrs. Pemberton's dignified yet winning manners, and such was the respect with which she inspired him, that, if he had his hat on, he always took it off when she entered the room, and never uttered any thing like an oath, without humbly begging her pardon; and he told Adeline, that were all quakers like Mrs. Pemberton, he should be tempted to cry, "Drab is your only wear."[1]

Another, and another day elapsed, and Adeline still lived.—On the evening of the third day, as she lay half-slumbering with her head on Savanna's arm, and Mrs. Mowbray, lulling Editha to sleep on her lap, was watching beside her, glancing her eye alternately with satisfied and silent affection from the child to the mother, whom she thought in a fair way of recovery; while Dr. Norberry, stifling an occasional sob, was contemplating the group, and Mrs. Pemberton, her hands clasped in each other, seemed lost in devout contemplation, Adeline awoke, and as she gazed on Editha, who was fondly held to Mrs. Mowbray's bosom, a smile illumined her sunk countenance. Mrs. Mowbray at that moment eagerly and anxiously pressed forward to catch her weak accents, and inquire how she felt. "I have seen that fond and anxious look before," she faintly articulated, "but in happier times! and it assures me that you love me still."

"Love you still!" replied Mrs. Mowbray with passionate fondness:— "never, never were you so dear to me as now!"

Adeline tried to express the joy which flushed her cheek at these words, and lighted up her closing eyes: but she tried in vain. At length she grasped Mrs. Mowbray's hand to her lips, and in imperfect accents exclaiming "I thank thee, gracious Heaven!"† she laid her head on Savanna's bosom, and expired.

THE END.

---

1 Cf. Shakespeare, *As You Like It* 2.7.34. In "The Hard Summer" (*Our Village*, introd. Anne Thackeray Ritchie [London: Macmillan, 1910], 161), Mary Mitford appears to be quoting Opie's version.

# Textual Variants

The copy-text for this edition, as I explain in A Note on the Text, is the first edition of 1805. The notes that follow indicate the major variants between that edition and the two subsequent editions published in Britain during Opie's lifetime: that of 1810 and that of 1844. (The "second edition" of 1805 appears not to be a new edition, but a second printing identical to the first.)

I do not include changes between hyphenated and unhyphenated forms of the same word (e.g., "reenter" and "re-enter") and between two-word and one-word spellings (e.g., "any thing" and "anything"); nor do I record minor spelling changes (e.g., "O" and "Oh," "authorised" and "authorized," "enquiries" and "inquiries," "sooth" and "soothe," "stedfastly" and "steadfastly," "past" and "passed").

Some spellings and conventions of capitalization characteristic of the 1805 edition are consistently (or almost consistently) revised in 1810; these revisions are usually consistent with those in 1844. Examples, none of which are individually noted below, include the change of "connection" to "connexion," "antient" to "ancient," "christian" to "Christian," "quaker" to "Quaker," "visiter" to "visitor," "œconomy" to "economy." In 1844, "*l*." ("pound") is consistently changed to "£." I have not noted such changes as the substitution of £1,000 for 1000*l*.; however, where changes in punctuation and capitalization—however minor—might affect interpretation, I have conscientiously recorded them. The attentive reader may be interested to note that substantive revisions in the 1810 text are not usually retained in 1844.

**PAGE 43**
* whig] Whig (1844)
† tory] Tory (1844)

**PAGE 46**
* *new paragraph* 1844

**PAGE 47**
* there] *omitted* 1844
† orders, saying, that "as their mistress was a learned lady, and that, and so could not be spoken with except here and there on occasion, they wished their young mistress, who was more easy spoken, would please to order:"] orders: (1810)
‡ her;] her grandmother; (1810)
§ And though] Therefore, though (1810)

**PAGE 48**
* pray God] pray to God (1844)
† prevailed upon] prevailed on (1844)
‡ perfectly."] perfectly well." (1844)

**PAGE 49**
* always] *omitted* 1844

† Lord bless me! my] My (1844)

‡ Lord bless] bless (1844)

§ or child] or a child (1844)

** is] has (1844)

†† And God forgive me, and you too,] And forgive me, (1844)

**PAGE 50**

* Lord help us and save us!] *omitted* 1844

† very well] *omitted* 1844

‡ Conduct of the Human Understanding; (1844)

**PAGE 52**

* writer.] writer, especially as he also laid it down as a rule, that it was the serious duty of every one to act up to their belief on every subject, however that belief might militate against the received opinions of the world. (1810)

**PAGE 54**

* *bouts rimes* (1844)

† "Zounds!] "Why [1844]

**PAGE 55**

* *no paragraph break* 1844

† his] her (1844)

**PAGE 56**

* "Zounds!"] "Pshaw!" (1844)

† devilish] very (1810); sadly (1844)

‡ God] Heaven (1844)

§ Nature] nature (1844)

**PAGE 57**

* her] *omitted* 1844

† her] the (1810)

‡ had] *omitted* 1844

§ on the discussion] on discussions (1810)

**PAGE 58**

* to him almost every door and every heart was shut;] almost every door and every heart was

shut to him; (1810); to him almost every door and heart was shut; (1844)

† whatever] what (1844)

**PAGE 59**

* a] the (1844)

† was] *omitted* 1844

**PAGE 60**

* the] *omitted* 1844

† at the pump-room,] in the shop of a fashionable bookseller, (1810)

**PAGE 62**

* "My good gracious! and] "And (1844)

† the] a (1810)

**PAGE 63**

* his] her (1810)

† Adeline;] Adeline neither; (1810)

**PAGE 64**

* the daughter's person;] the daughter; (1810)

† the daughter's person.] the daughter. (1844)

‡ formed for the service and amusement of men;] *omitted* 1844

**PAGE 65**

* soul!"] word!" (1844)

† of her daughter,—eloquence] *omitted* 1844

**PAGE 66**

* rose,] arose, (1844)

† "Upon my soul,] "Really (1844)

‡ confoundedly] confounded (1844)

**PAGE 67**

* chastity;] purity; (1844)

† chastity] purity (1844)

‡ No, no, thank God!] No, no! (1844)

PAGE 69

\* and] and she (1810)

† love!"] dear!" (1844)

‡ "Retire!.... Aye, by all means,"] "Not so fast," (1810); "Retire!——No, indeed" (1844)

PAGE 72

\* concluded] conclude (1810)

† principles] principle (1844)

‡ a] *omitted* 1844

PAGE 73

\* even of influencing] of influencing even (1844)

PAGE 74

\* that God] He (1844)

† heaven] Heaven (1810)

PAGE 76

\* to confine himself within] *omitted* 1844

† passion] love (1844)

PAGE 78

\* hoped,] hope (1844)

PAGE 79

\* her (1805); *corrected* 1810, 1844.

† her hand out] out her hand (1844)

‡ all they say] all they say are (1844)

PAGE 80

\* addresses."] addresses?" (1810, 1844)

PAGE 81

\* this] that (1844)

PAGE 82

\* the] *omitted* 1844

PAGE 83

\* I] I (1844)

† As to the concluding paragraph——"] As to the last paragraph but one——" (1810)

PAGE 84

\* last paragraph] last paragraph but one (1810)

PAGE 85

\* a] *omitted* 1844

† that my fatherly attentions shall be of the warmest kind.] well—that is—I— (1810)

PAGE 86

\* "Thank God!" replied Adeline. The girl sighed still more deeply.] *omitted* 1844

PAGE 88

\* *dearest*] dearest (1844)

† *to spare*] to spare (1810, 1844)

PAGE 89

\* *interpret,*] interpret, (1844)

† soul] word (1844)

PAGE 90

\* till she] till she had (1844)

† day] *omitted* 1844

‡ were] was (1844)

§ Glenmurray] the man whom she loved (1810)

\*\* him.] Glenmurray. (1810)

PAGE 92

\* companion] companion whom (1810)

† pure] *omitted* 1844

‡ of his Candide.] of his romances. (1844)

PAGE 93

\* Here the sentence and the paragraph end in 1844. The text resumes three paragraphs later, at "Disappointed in her hopes...."

PAGE 96

\* , —not doubting but that opportunity was alone wanting to enable him to succeed in his abandoned wishes.] *omitted* 1844

**PAGE 97**

* and protestations that she should that moment be his,] *omitted* 1844
† Great God! what] What (1844)

**PAGE 98**

* have] has (1844)
† less] more (1844)

**PAGE 101**

* *him,*] him, (1844)
† affection.] affections. (1844)

**PAGE 103**

* her (1805); *corrected* 1810, 1844
† most salutary to] most salutary, in one respect at least, to (1810)
‡ [*new paragraph*] But the connexion that is founded on a guilty disregard of sound and positive institutions cannot long be productive of happiness, even though the reasonings of perverted intellect and the persuasions of self-love have convinced the offending parties that such an union is wise and virtuous.

Adeline and Glenmurray, while secluded from society, might fancy themselves happy, and be so perhaps in some measure, although they had violated those sacred ties by which society's best interests are kept together: but as soon as society could resume in any way its power, and opportunity of operating on their happiness, that happiness must necessarily vanish; as a dead body which has been preserved from decay by being entirely excluded from the external air, moulders into dust immediately on being exposed to its influence. (1810)

**PAGE 105**

* away.] away? (1810)

**PAGE 106**

* for *them*, not they for *me!*"] for them, not they for me!" (1844)

**PAGE 108**

* had] *omitted* 1844
† ever I] I ever (1844)
‡ *prodigies,*"] prodigies," (1844)

**PAGE 109**

* he (1805); *corrected* 1810, 1844.
† *no*] no (1844)

**PAGE 111**

* confounded] *omitted* 1844

**PAGE 112**

* causes] cause (1810)

**PAGE 116**

* her] *omitted* 1844

**PAGE 119**

* , and be hanged to you] *omitted* 1844
† I swore a good oath] I almost swore (1844)
‡ Lord] Heaven (1844)
§ cursed] *omitted* 1810, 1844
** (an old blockhead!)] *omitted* 1810, 1844

**PAGE 123**

* the devil] *omitted* 1844
† o'] of (1844)
‡ d——d] *omitted* 1810; vile (1844)
§ Zounds,] Why, (1844)

**PAGE 124**

* Zounds! what] What (1810, 1844)
† 'Sdeath,] *omitted* 1844
‡ cursed] great (1810, 1844)
§ the] your (1810)

**PAGE 125**

* by the Lord ] *omitted* 1844
† Odzooks,] Why, (1844)

PAGE 127

* *fellow*-creature,] fellow creature, (1844)

† "but God grant, Jane," (seizing her hand) "that your soul may not] "Jane,"(seizing her hand) "may your soul never (1844)

PAGE 129

* could] did (1844)

† suspected] suspected, though unjustly, (1844)

‡ Zounds,] *omitted* 1844

§ cursed] *omitted* 1844

PAGE 130

* a young] a single young (1844)

† to lie-in of a bastard child."] to lie-in." (1844)

‡ sdeath,] 'sdeath (1810); *omitted* 1844

§ having any more."] further harm." (1844)

** *cruel*] cruel (1844)

†† Norberry," (pushing her pillow vehemently towards the valance as she spoke,) "while] Norberry, while (1844)

‡‡ unrefreshed] *omitted* 1844

§§ Zounds,] Hold, (1844)

PAGE 131

* put] put it (1844)

† Zounds!—] *omitted* 1844

‡ *that,*"] that," (1844)

PAGE 132

* devilish] very (1844)

† that d——d dog.] that—but I forbear (1810, 1844)

‡ the good lad looks as ashamed of what he has done as any modest miss in Christendom;] *omitted* 1844

§ consent,] consent, he (1844)

PAGE 133

* Lord! Lord! that] That (1844)

† *child*] child (1844)

‡ "Why, zounds!"] "Why!" (1844)

§ "Zounds!"] "There," (1844)

PAGE 134

* "Gadzooks, give] "Give (1844)

PAGE 135

* d——d] very (1810)

† doctor; "it is d——d ill, sir."] doctor. (1844)

‡ mother,"] mother?" (1810, 1844)

§ and—Lord have mercy upon us!" cried the doctor, turning round and seeing the situation into which his words had thrown Adeline, who was then] and here the doctor, turning round, saw Adeline (1844)

PAGE 136

* devilish] pretty (1844)

† friend. Zounds, it] friend; and it (1844)

PAGE 137

* God's] mercy's (1844)

PAGE 138

* 'tis] it is (1844)

PAGE 139

* "and I call on God to witness my oath,] *omitted* 1844

† being forsaken and despised as I have been,] having lost the man whom you adore, (1810, 1844)

‡ you shall be] *you* shall have been (1810, 1844)

§ world,] world, as I have been, (1810, 1844)

** God's] pity's (1844)

PAGE 140

* recollection] recollections (1844)

† coach,] coach, which Glenmurray had called, (1844)

PAGE 141

\* misery, but of misery inflicted] misery inflicted (1844)

PAGE 142

\* "Yet—no. Girl, girl, your virtue only heaps coals of fire on that devoted woman's head."

"For pity's sake, Dr. Norberry!" cried Adeline.

"Well, well, I have done.] *omitted* 1844

† Zounds, girl!] Girl! (1844)

‡ d——d] *omitted* 1810, 1844

§ God knows] I know not (1844)

PAGE 143

\* had] *omitted* 1844

† d——d] *omitted* 1810, 1844

PAGE 144

\* conveniencies] conveniences (1844)

PAGE 145

\* and] *omitted* 1844

PAGE 146

\* you] you have (1844)

PAGE 147

\* "Merciful heaven!"] "Heaven!" (1844)

† "Thank God!"] "Thank Heaven!" (1844)

PAGE 148

\* say] says (1844)

PAGE 149

\* pertend] pretend (1844)

PAGE 151

\* she felt that she was going to appear before a fellow-creature as an object of scorn, and, though an enthusiast for virtue, to be] she was going to appear before a fellow creature, conscious she was become an object of scorn, and, though an enthusiast for virtue, would be (1844)

† her."] her?" (1810, 1844)

‡ worse."] worse?" (1810)

§ Glenmurray?"] Glenmurray!" (1844)

PAGE 152

\* principles."] principles?" (1810)

PAGE 153

\* , I bless God,] *omitted* 1844

PAGE 159

\* child] child which (1810)

† her] the (1844)

PAGE 160

\* ardently] evidently (1810, 1844)

PAGE 162

\* life!"] love!" (1844)

PAGE 163

\* an] and (1844)

† was] had (1844)

‡ this] the (1810)

PAGE 165

\* "I] "*I* (1844)

PAGE 166

\* bought] brought (1810, 1844)

† a] that (1844)

‡ the] that (1844)

PAGE 167

\* six] ten (1810, 1844)

† half] part (1810)

‡ half."] part." (1810, 1844)

PAGE 168

\* black b——h!"] black toad!" (1844)

† own] *omitted* 1844

PAGE 170

\* and] and a (1810)

PAGE 171

\* Dr., as he feel] doctor, as he feels (1844)

290    TEXTUAL VARIANTS

PAGE 172
* 300*l*.] three hundred pounds. (1844)

PAGE 173
* fewel] fuel (1844)
† metought] me tought (1844)
‡ got] *omitted* 1844

PAGE 174
* noting] nothing (1844)
† her] the (1844)

PAGE 177
* in] of (1810, 1844)

PAGE 178
* that] the (1844)

PAGE 179
* then] than (1810)
† at] *at* (1810, 1844)
‡ my dearest girl;] my dearest; (1844)

PAGE 183
* to] *omitted* 1810, 1844

PAGE 184
* Glenmurray;] Glenmurray! (1810, 1844)

PAGE 185
* to] of (1844)

PAGE 187
* in becoming] was enabled to become (1844)

PAGE 192
* Punctuation here follows the 1810 text, which clarifies the meaning obscured by punctuation in 1805 (and 1844).

PAGE 194
* then] *omitted* 1844
† then] *omitted* 1810, 1844

PAGE 197
* wat will appen,"] what will happen," (1844)
† ave] have (1844)
‡ Savanna?" (1844)

PAGE 199
* recollections (1844)

PAGE 200
* that] that which (1810, 1844)
† her,] to her, (1810, 1844)
‡ money] money for fees (1810, 1844)

PAGE 201
* at sight] at the sight (1844)

PAGE 202
* mistress] companion (1844)

PAGE 203
* here; at present I am particularly engaged," (with a significant smile;) "but—"] here; (with a significant smile); (1844)
† "And so do I.—] "And I think so too.— (1810)
‡ "And so do I.—O zounds! by] "And I think so too!—by (1844)

PAGE 204
* gentlemen, patting her on the back as he spoke:] gentlemen: (1810, 1844)
† but, perhaps your favours are all bespoken.—Pray] but pray (1810, 1844)
‡ "Oh! I have but few friends," cried Adeline mournfully.
 "Few! the devil!" replied the young templar; "and how many would you have?" Here he put his arm around her waist: and his companion giving way to a loud fit of laughter,] Here, as his companion gave way to a loud fit of laughter, (1810, 1844)

PAGE 207
* was to him *tout simple*;] seemed to him quite natural and proper; (1810, 1844)

PAGE 208
* but] and (1810, 1844)
† confession] confessions (1844)
PAGE 209
* pampered] *omitted* 1810, 1844
PAGE 210
* Glenmurray; and as expiations also.] Glenmurray. (1844)
† heaven] her God and Saviour, (1844)
‡ *no paragraph break* 1805
PAGE 211
* God!] Heaven! (1844)
PAGE 212
* directly."] directly?" (1810, 1844)
† Ye,] Yes, (1844)
‡ *no paragraph break* 1844
PAGE 213
* A minute, and more perhaps,] A minute more perhaps, (1844)
† *new paragraph* (1844)
PAGE 214
* indulgences] indulgencies (1844)
PAGE 215
* card!] cards! (1844)
† perhaps,] *omitted* 1844
‡ though, God knows, I never speak] though I never speak (1844)
PAGE 216
* remit] remit to (1844)
PAGE 217
* preservative,] preservation, (1844)
PAGE 218
* as] as a (1844)
† God] Heaven (1844)
‡ noting,] nothing, (1844)
PAGE 219
* making atonement] making some atonement (1844)
† at] of (1844)

PAGE 220
* to] *omitted* 1844
PAGE 225
* heaven,] Heaven, (1844)
† the slave of women,] a slave of woman, (1844)
‡ a countenance more in sorrow than in anger.] "a countenance more in sorrow than in anger." (1810, 1844)
PAGE 226
* ignominy.] infamy. (1810, 1844)
† "Good God! this] "This (1844)
‡ she have made you believe that she think] she has made you believe that she thinks (1844)
PAGE 227
* curse] hang (1810, 1844)
PAGE 228
* God's] mercy's (1844)
† for God's sake] *omitted* 1844
PAGE 229
* and pollution] *omitted* 1810; and infection (1844)
PAGE 231
* life-guards,"] guards," (1810, 1844)
PAGE 233
* missess?] mistress? (1844)
PAGE 235
* now] *omitted* 1810, 1844
† fearfully] fearful of (1810, 1844)
PAGE 236
* distress,] distress, poured (1844)
PAGE 237
* her] her even (1810, 1844)
† latent blessings,] merciful chastisements (1844)
‡ required of] inflicted on (1844)
PAGE 238
* from] from a (1844)
† more an] *omitted* 1844

‡ musquet] musket (1844)

§ and] and that it (1810, 1844)

** *fallacy*] fallacy (1844)

**PAGE 239**

* "For God's sake,] "In pity, (1844)

**PAGE 240**

* hang; if you can] hang, if you can; (1810); hang; if you can; (1844)

**PAGE 241**

* had I had such] had I such (1844)

**PAGE 242**

* "You first will stay and close my eyes,] "You will stay and close my eyes first, (1810, 1844)

**PAGE 244**

* in] on (1810, 1844)

**PAGE 247**

* search,] search of her, (1844)

† , though capable of charming the senses,] *omitted* 1844

‡ disgusted with an intercourse in which the heart had no share,] *omitted* 1844

**PAGE 248**

* a] the (1810, 1844)

† *wonder,*] wonder, (1844)

**PAGE 249**

* motive] motives (1810, 1844)

**PAGE 250**

* disrespect,] respect, (1844)

† he] *omitted* 1844

**PAGE 251**

* *you,*] you, (1844)

† colonel (1805); *corrected* 1810, 1844

**PAGE 254**

* attentions] attention (1810, 1844)

**PAGE 255**

* passion,] attachment, (1844)

† acknowledgments.] acknowledgment. (1844)

**PAGE 258**

* feelings,] feeling, (1844)

**PAGE 259**

* the] *omitted* 1844

† exclusion] seclusion (1844)

‡ *new paragraph* 1844

§ must I never, never] must I never (1844)

**PAGE 260**

* *ten pounds,*] ten pounds (1844)

† zounds,] what, (1844)

‡ "Devil take me if I could have thought it of her!"] "I could not have thought it of her!" (1844)

**PAGE 261**

* present] *omitted* 1844

† d——d ] *omitted* 1810, 1844

‡ devilish *odd, not to say* wrong.] odd, not to say wrong. (1844)

**PAGE 262**

* "and I pray God to bless thine!"] "and I pray that thine may be blest!" (1844)

† had better] may as well (1810, 1844)

‡ have] have probably (1844)

§ solitary prayer] solitude (1844)

**PAGE 264**

* listen] could listen (1844)

**PAGE 266**

* teacher] minister (1844)

† quaker's society:] Quaker society: (1844)

‡ in the active duties of her profession,] in active duties, (1844)

**PAGE 269**

* great] much (1844)

**PAGE 271**

* *for*] for (1844)

**PAGE 276**

* Adeline, while various plans for this purpose presented them-

selves to her mind, and each of them was dismissed in its turn as fruitless or impracticable. Full] Adeline. While various plans for this purpose presented themselves to her mind, and each of them was dismissed in its turn as fruitless or impracticable,—full (1810, 1844)

† "God] "Heaven (1844)

‡ miry!"] miry?" (1844)

**PAGE 278**

* *no paragraph break* 1844

**PAGE 279**

* cursed] very (1844)

**PAGE 280**

* soon,] so soon (1844)

† , by the Lord,] *omitted* 1844

‡ devilish] *omitted* 1844

§ "Zounds!"] "Pshaw!" (1844)

**PAGE 281**

* yet] *omitted* 1844

† saw] met (1844)

‡ met] saw (1844)

**PAGE 282**

* "Zounds!" thought he, "this] "This (1844)

**PAGE 283**

* *new paragraph* 1844

† gracious Heaven!"] blessed Lord!" (1844)

# Appendix A: Contemporary Reviews

## 1. *Critical Review*, 3rd series, 4 (1805): 219-21

We opened with great pleasure a new novel from the entertaining pen of Mrs. Opie, a lady whose uncommon talents do honour to her sex and country. She displayed, in her pathetic tale of "the Father and Daughter,"[1] a power of working upon the passions we think unrivalled (perhaps with the single exception of Mrs. Inchbald,)[2] by any writer of the present day. Nor has she failed to affect her readers with many heart-rending scenes in the work before us.

The story of "the Mother and Daughter" may be comprised in few words. The former imbibes and supports *in theory* the principles of the new code of morality; the latter carries them into *practice*, and becomes the mistress of one of the authors who broached them to the world. Upon this her mother, inconsistently, but naturally, renounces her; and by the death of her lover she is driven to seek support in the exercise of those accomplishments her education had bestowed upon her. But her course of virtuous industry is interrupted by the scandalous reports of those who remembered her in her former vicious situation; and she is awakened to a sense of her misguided conduct. She is in consequence married; but her husband using her ill, after much misery she is restored to her mother, and dies contented.

But this scanty outline Mrs. Opie has most ably filled up with a variety of characters and incidents, well conceived, and adroitly introduced. She keeps up the attention of her readers to the end. The moral of her work is declared in the following passage: (Vol. iii. p. 13).[3]

The example of Adeline is held up "as a warning to all young people; for her story inculcates most powerfully how vain are personal graces, talents, sweetness of temper, and even active benevolence, to ensure respectability, and confer happiness, without a strict regard to the long established rules for conduct, and a continuance in those paths of virtue and decorum which the wisdom of ages has pointed out to every one."

But we cannot avoid remarking that the effect of this moral does not seem to have been consulted, when the state in which Adeline and Glen-

---

1   Opie's very popular tale of a mad father and a seduced and repentant daughter, published in 1801.

2   Elizabeth Inchbald (1753-1821), novelist and actress, author of *A Simple Story* (1791) and *Nature and Art* (1796).

3   Above, 196.

murray lived was represented as perfectly happy, as far as their happiness rested in themselves; but the instant that Adeline marries, she becomes miserable from the conduct of her husband. Rightly considered, this reflects nothing upon the marriage state; but what we have to object to are the fascinating colours thrown over the erroneous virtues of Adeline and Glenmurray, "making" (as the benevolent quaker observes, Vol. ii. page 109) "vice more dangerous by giving it an air of respectability."[1]

We have to remark a few inaccuracies in Mrs. Opie's style: solely from a regard to her reputation as a writer, for we doubt not her good sense will profit by our hints. "Gulping down sobs and sighs" is an expression that occurs too often throughout the three volumes; "a fine moral tact" we cannot help thinking a silly and affected phrase; "it was the dark hour" means nothing but "it was dark;" and why should "the maternal feeling" be substituted for the feelings of a mother?

The interesting interview between the mother of Adeline and the benevolent quaker, in which the latter gives the former tidings of her daughter, is successfully imitated from the scene between Lady Randolph and the Stranger, in the play of Douglas.[2]

But the description of the death of Adeline may bear a comparison with that of Richardson's Clarissa, or Rousseau's Heloise. Her last letter to her mother, where she bequeaths her infant daughter to her care, must move every reader to tears who can melt at the recital of unmerited distress; and that to colonel Mordaunt, recanting her false principles, and strongly contending in favour of marriage for the sake of the children and their education, is an honourable proof of Mrs. Opie's powers of argument in the defence of the good old cause....[3]

## 2. *Annual Review* 4 (1805): 653

Novels in former days were nothing but love stories, or works professing, often indeed falsely enough, to exhibit pictures of real life and manners. The importance that they have lately been allowed to usurp in the republic of letters, is at once a curious and an alarming symptom of the frivolity of the age. There was a time when a person wishing to inform himself in the higher branches of literature or philosophy, would have been obliged to undergo the labour of perusing dry crab-bed treatises, written profess-

---

1  Above, 152 (paraphrase).

2  The most famous of the tragedies by John Home (1722-1808), first performed in Edinburgh in 1756.

3  The review concludes by quoting with great approval Mrs. Pemberton's contrast between Adeline as she was at Rosevalley and Adeline as she is at Richmond (155).

edly on serious and important subjects. Now, happy revolution! he may luxuriantly imbibe, in the tempting form of a novel, the beauties of history embellished with all the eloquence of fiction, encumbered by no dates, and perplexed with no documents. Through the same medium he may see the happy effects of a new scheme of education, illustrated by the example of children who were never born; or the advantages of a new system of morals displayed, or its evil consequences exposed, on the unexceptionable authority of characters that have never existed. The work before us undertakes to shew, from the example of miss Adeline Mowbray, that a young lady who ventures to ridicule and condemn the marriage-tie, will expose herself to insult; that if she consents, though from the purest motives imaginable, to live with a man as his mistress, she will assuredly be driven out of decent company; that her children, being illegitimate, will be destitute of the right of inheritance, and subject to a thousand affronts; and that she cannot do better, if deprived of her lover by death, than to accept the first legal protector that offers. From the adventures of the mother is taught, the folly of neglecting all the duties of life for the study of metaphysics and politics; the ill consequences attendant on a complete ignorance of the world in the mother of a grown up daughter; and the madness of a rich widow's falling in love with and marrying a profligate young Irishman overwhelmed with debt, from whom she forgets to demand a settlement. It must be confessed that these great truths are sufficiently familiar; and in spite of the rage for experiment in moral conduct, which some years ago prevailed to a considerable extent, we hope there are few ladies "so to seek in virtue's lore,"[1] as to be inclined to put in practice the extravagances of poor Adeline. As for the faults and follies of her mother, we fear the causes of most of them are too deeply wrought into the constitution of the human race, to be removed by the united eloquence of all moralists, novelists, and divines, who have ever written, preached, or taught. If, therefore, it was Mrs. Opie's wish, by the present work, to establish her name among the great guides of female conduct and promoters of practical wisdom, she has assuredly failed of her object; but if she has adopted the vehicle of system only for the sake of placing interesting characters in new and striking situations, contenting herself with the more appropriate task of amusing the fancy and touching the heart, she may certainly lay claim to a pretty large portion of applause. In drawing characters indeed we do not think she has been very successful, for both Adeline and her mother appear to us considerably out of nature; but there are situations and incidents of great effect. Glenmurray, the hero, is a most interesting being; and several well-imagined circumstances serve to set in a strong light the native benevo-

---

1 Unidentified.

lence and sensibility of his mind, triumphing first over the stoical pride of system, and afterwards over the fretful selfishness produced by lengthened sickness. The account of Adeline's meeting with the illegitimate child at Richmond is natural and striking, and the speech of the quaker over the body of the misguided Glenmurray is quite in character. There are other passages of considerable merit interspersed throughout, and some of deep pathos; but we should have been better pleased if the tale had ended with the death of the hero, before the odious Berrendale had appeared to put us out of love with husbands.

### 3. *Literary Journal* 5 (1805): 171-75

[The review begins with a lengthy plot summary.]

Such is the substance of the story before us. It will readily appear that its object is to point out the consequences of opinions that have been propagated by certain persons calling themselves philosophers, especially respecting the institution of marriage. The tale itself is simple, elegant, and highly interesting throughout. The style is perspicuous, and though it cannot be said to be always pure and correct, yet it does not deserve the epithets of harsh and unpleasant. The characters are ably drawn and well preserved. Adeline is represented with all those qualities that can command our esteem, or gain our affection. Her faults arise from the want of an enlightened instructor, a circumstance over which she herself had no controul. She is young and beautiful, possessed of the most benevolent heart and of the most pleasing manners. Her mind is invigorated by exertion. Having once adopted erroneous principles, she acts upon them with ardour and decision. While we condemn her conduct, we pity her as a martyr to mistaken notions of virtue. The fortitude with which she bears her distresses is exemplary. The change in her sentiments is sufficiently accounted for, and the sincerity of her repentance consistent with her character. It may perhaps be supposed that such a character as this must be prejudicial to the interests of morality, by giving vice the appearance of respectability. Here the address of our authoress is conspicuous. The error in Adeline's education is constantly kept in view, and all her miseries are clearly exhibited as its natural consequence. By its operation we find a being, formed to adorn society, rejected as an outcast; and our abhorrence of the vice almost rises in proportion to our esteem for her virtues, and our pity for her misfortunes. The character next in importance is Glenmurray, a young man who is also formed to adorn society, but whose opinions have rendered him an isolated and useless being. He had published one of the works which had perverted the mind of Adeline. His mind is constantly tormented with the idea of the miseries which his opinions brought upon the object of his affection. When we find him *blaming* his own rashness and youthful presumption, and brought by anxiety to an early grave, we are forced to confess that his punishment is adequate to his offence. The character of Mrs. Mowbray is also well drawn, but her continued affection for a man who deceived and married her, while he had another wife alive, does not seem to be altogether natural. Her virulent hatred against her daughter for having been an object of preference to such a wretch, is equally objectionable. Instances, however, are not wanting that might at first view appear to justify such a departure from probability. But unless all the circumstances could be brought under our view that contributed to produce such instances, they cannot be considered as decisive in favour of our authoress. Doctor Norberry is represented as a man of the highest benevolence, with a dash of eccentricity, which adds considerably to the effect of his character.

The moral of the story is unobjectionable. It points out the fatal consequences of an improper education, and the danger of acting upon principles contrary to the established rules of society. It shews the folly of forming rash and presumptuous opinions in our youth, and propagating them before they have received the sanction of our maturer years. The tale is throughout a lively representation of the incompatibility of a disregard of the institution of marriage with the happiness of the individual and the good of society.

Upon the whole this work must be allowed to rank considerably higher than the ordinary productions of the same kind. The interest of the story is well preserved to the end. The incidents in general follow naturally from the causes assigned, and are wrought up with uncommon skill. The tale is for the most part close and connected. We only recollect one instance of what appeared an unnecessary digression from the principal story. It is the rise and progress of Colonel Mordaunt's love for the sister of Major Douglas. But this digression, though it detracts from the uniformity of the tale, is in itself so agreeable that we cannot wish it away.

### 4. *Monthly Review*, ns 51 (1806): 320-21

These volumes are, both in their design and execution, so superior to those which we usually encounter under the title of novels, that we can safely recommend them to the perusal of our readers. We wish, nevertheless, to hint to Mrs. Opie, that her work would be improved by a more strict attention to the propriety of some of her expressions, which at times are affected, and at others inelegant: but we forbear to point out instances, under the persuasion that our caution is already sufficient to a writer who possesses so much good sense.

It is the intention of this work to portray the lamentable consequences, which would result from an adoption of some lax principles relative to a rejection of matrimonial forms, which have been inculcated by certain modern writers.

## 5. *European Magazine* 47 (1805): 129–30

Mrs. Mowbray is a learned lady, and a widow, devoted altogether to abstruse and metaphysical speculations. While this ill-judging mother is occupied in preparing a voluminous system of education, Adeline her daughter, for whom she entertains nevertheless the most parental and tender regard, remains in the mean time neglected and uninstructed; and had she not found in Mrs. Woodville, the mother of Mrs. Mowbray, a teacher after "the old fashion," her mind at fifteen would have been without improvement and without knowledge; the important system of Mrs. M[owbray] being still imperfect and incomplete. Adeline, who has the highest respect for her mother's literary talents, about this period, and after Mrs. Woodville's death, becomes emulous of similar pursuits. Totally inexperienced, and without any proper director of her studies, she obtains the perusal of her mother's books, and unfortunately, in the writings of an author who is called Glenmurray, she discovers objections which she deems invincible against the institution of marriage. Upon the strength of this conviction, she forms a solemn compact with herself, and resolves never to marry. At Bath she meets with this Glenmurray, and, of course, they are mutually enamoured. He is reasonable enough, notwithstanding the public avowal of her sentiments, to offer her marriage; but this she disclaims, and in defiance of a parent's command, of the sense of the world, and the solicitation of Glenmurray himself, she unites herself to him, on her own baneful and absurd principles "of love and honour:"—a step this, it must be admitted, not consistent with that delicate feeling, and those exalted notions of filial affection and duty, which she is represented to possess; and although her conduct, with this single exception, be considered faultless, yet such an obstinate pertinacity of opinion must be conceived as belonging rather to the bold and lawless innovator, than to the submissive, the gentle, the benevolent, Adeline Mowbray.

This unlicensed union could only produce misery, shame, and disgrace; and of this Adeline is an eminent, and, it may be hoped, a useful, example. By no means so much can be said for Glenmurray; a man without any fixed notions of religion, or indeed of any thing else, "for he doubts of all things,"[1] who dies without any renunciation of his errors,

---

1  Cf. Samuel Johnson's definition of "sceptic" in *A Dictionary of the English Language* (1755): "One who doubts, or pretends to doubt of everything."

and yet is exhibited in the fascinating colours of splendid talents and attractive excellence and virtue. On the death of Glenmurray, Adeline is
brought to some acknowledgment of her great mistake; and, in obedience
to his dying request, resolutely struggling with her feelings, she marries
his relation, Mr. Berrendale. By him she is deserted; and at length, after
some additional evidences, she relinquishes, *on conviction*, her former way
of thinking;—she is convinced, that if the ties of marriage were dissolved,
or it were no longer to be judged infamous to act in contempt of them, unbridled licentiousness would soon be in general practice. The remainder of
the tale is short. Mrs. M[owbray], by a wild sort of conditional oath, had
renounced her daughter; and after many mutual attempts at reconciliation,
which were frustrated by a malicious *Miss Woodville*, Adeline, in a declining state, retires with her child, an only daughter, by Mr. Berrendale, to
a cottage within two miles of her native place, where her mother resides.

Here they casually meet; Adeline in a dying condition, and Mrs. Mowbray full of unabated affection: the former is conveyed, at her particular
entreaty, to the shelter of a parent's roof; and the whole concludes, "in the
German stile," at the moment of her death.

Mrs. Opie is well known as "a mighty mistress of pathetic song;" and
though the above outlines seem unpromising, because the sufferings
of Adeline are deserved; yet so many affecting incidents, so many little
circumstances, are skilfully introduced, that this tale cannot be perused
without strong emotion, even by those "unused to the melting mood."[1]

The character of Mrs. Pemberton, a quaker, merits unqualified praise;
and Dr. Norberry, a physician, blunt, and rather vulgar, is well drawn.

The language of Mrs. Woodville, the early instructress of Adeline, is
rather overcharged; it is "downright vulgar;" and therefore scarcely correct enough for "the sole surviving daughter of an opulent merchant of
London."[2]

---

1  Shakespeare, *Othello* 5.2.135.

2  The review concludes by quoting Opie's narrator's criticism of Mrs. Mowbray's
   "[f]atal and unproductive studies" (42).

# Appendix B: On Education

[*Adeline Mowbray* can be read as one among many novels of the late eighteenth and early nineteenth centuries warning about the effects on young women of a bad or inadequate education. Among many others, Helen Maria Williams (*Julia*, 1790), Mary Wollstonecraft (*The Wrongs of Woman, or Maria*, posthumously published in 1798), and Mary Hays (*The Victim of Prejudice*, 1799), all present heroines whose education has been deficient—leaving the reader to consider what would constitute a proper education for a girl destined for adult life in a society where, whatever her attainments, she could hardly expect to be treated as the equal of a man. The two excerpts from writers on education that follow are particularly relevant to the discussion of Adeline's education in *Adeline Mowbray*.

John Locke is mentioned in the novel by name (though Mrs. Mowbray asks her parents to read the *Essay Concerning Human Understanding*, not *Some Thoughts Concerning Education*). Yet Mrs. Mowbray has evidently been reading *Some Thoughts*, and Opie brings Locke into the discussion of Adeline's education less because she wants to argue with his ideas than because she wants to illustrate Mrs. Mowbray's pedantry. Mrs. Mowbray treats educational theory as prescriptive and she follows it blindly: she, not Locke, is the main object of Opie's satire.

Hannah More, on the other hand, is never mentioned in Opie's novel, but More's enlightened conservatism is certainly an influence on Opie's changing ideas: the discussion in More's *Strictures on the Modern System of Female Education* (1799) of Jean-Jacques Rousseau—especially about whether *La Nouvelle Héloïse* is appropriate reading for young women—is particularly relevant if one wants to understand the ideological context of *Adeline Mowbray*. Rousseau, like Locke, was an important and influential writer on education (see *Emile* [1762], which Wollstonecraft attacks in *A Vindication of the Rights of Woman* for its unenlightened attitude to the education of girls).][1]

## 1. From John Locke, *Some Thoughts Concerning Education* (1693)[2]

1.7. I would also advise [the child's] *Feet to be wash'd* every Day in cold Water, and to have his *Shoes* so thin, that they might leak and *let in Water*, whenever he comes near it. Here, I fear, I shall have the Mistress and

---

1    On education and on reading Rousseau, see also Introduction, especially 31-32.
2    The text is from the 9th ed. (London: A. Bettesworthy and C. Hitch, 1732).

Maids too against me. One will think it too filthy, and the other perhaps too much Pains to make clean his Stockings. But yet Truth will have it, that his Health is much more worth, than all such Considerations, and ten times as much more. And he that considers how mischievous and mortal a Thing taking *Wet in the Feet* is, to those who have been bred nicely, will wish he had, with the poor People's Children, gone *bare-foot*, who, by that Means, come to be so reconcil'd by Custom to Wet in their Feet, that they take no more Cold or Harm by it, than if they were wet in their Hands....

1.[13]. As for his *Diet*, it ought to be very plain and simple; and, if I might advise, Flesh should be forborn as long as he is in Coats, or at least 'till he is two or three Years old. But whatever Advantage this may be to his present and future Health and Strength, I fear it will hardly be consented to by Parents, misled by the Custom of eating too much Flesh themselves, who will be apt to think their Children, as they do themselves, in Danger to be starv'd, if they have not Flesh at least twice a-day. This I am sure, Children would breed their Teeth with much less Danger, be freer from Diseases whilst they were little, and lay the Foundations of an healthy and strong Constitution much surer, if they were not cramm'd so much as they are by fond Mothers and foolish Servants, and were kept wholly from Flesh, the first three or four Years of their Lives.

But if my young Master must needs have Flesh, let it be but once a-day, and of one Sort at a Meal. Plain Beef, Mutton, Veal, *&c.* without other Sauce than Hunger, is best; and great Care should be us'd, that he eat *Bread* plentifully, both alone and with every thing else; and whatever he eats that is solid, make him chew it well. We *English* are often negligent herein; from whence follow Indigestion, and other great Inconveniences.

1.14. For *Breakfast* and *Supper, Milk, Milk-Pottage, Water-Gruel, Flummery,* and twenty other things, that we are wont to make in *England,* are very fit for Children; only, in all these, let Care be taken that they be plain, and without much Mixture, and very sparingly season'd with Sugar, or rather none at all; especially all *Spice,* and other things that may heat the Blood, are carefully to be avoided. Be sparing also of *Salt* in the seasoning of all his Victuals, and use him not to high-season'd Meats. Our Palates grow into a Relish, and liking of the Seasoning and Cookery, which by Custom they are set to; and an over-much Use of Salt, besides that it occasions Thirst, and over-much Drinking, has other ill Effects upon the Body. I should think, that a good Piece of well-made and well bak'd *brown Bread,* sometimes with, and sometimes without *Butter* or *Cheese,* would be often the best Breakfast for my young Master. I am sure 'tis as wholsome, and will make him as strong a Man as greater Delicacies; and if he be us'd to it, it will be as pleasant to him. If he at any time calls for Victuals between Meals, use him to nothing but dry Bread. If he be hungry more than wanton, Bread alone will down; and if he be not hungry, 'tis not fit he should eat. By this you will obtain two good Effects.... That by Custom he will come to be in love with *Bread*; for, as I said, our Palates and Stomachs too are pleas'd with the things we are us'd to. Another Good you will gain hereby, is, That you will not teach him to eat more nor oftner than Nature requires.... [M]any are made *Gourmands* and *Gluttons* by Custom, that were not so by Nature.... You cannot imagine of what Force Custom is; and I impute a great Part of our Diseases in *England*, to our eating too much *Flesh*, and too little *Bread*.

## 2. From Hannah More, *Strictures on the Modern System of Female Education* (1799)[1]

From Chapter 1, "On the Effects of Influence"

Novels, which used chiefly to be dangerous in one respect, are now become mischievous in a thousand. They are continually shifting their ground, and enlarging their sphere, and are daily becoming vehicles of wider mischief. Sometimes they concentrate their force, and are at once employed to diffuse destructive politics, deplorable profligacy, and impudent infidelity. Rousseau was the first popular dispenser of this complicated drug,[2] in which the deleterious infusion was strong, and the effect proportionably fatal. For he does not attempt to seduce the affections but through the medium of the principles. He does not paint an innocent woman, ruined, repenting, and restored; but with a far more mischievous refinement, he annihilates the value of chastity, and with pernicious subtlety attempts to make his heroine appear almost more amiable without it. He exhibits a virtuous woman, the victim not of temptation but of reason, not of vice but of sentiment, not of passion but of conviction; and strikes at the very root of honour by elevating a crime into a principle. With a metaphysical sophistry the most plausible, he debauches the heart of woman, by cherishing her vanity in the erection of a system of male virtues, to which, with a lofty dereliction of those that are her more peculiar and characteristic praise, he tempts her to aspire; powerfully insinuating, that to this splendid system chastity does not necessarily belong: thus corrupting the

---

1  The text is from the first edition: *Strictures on the Modern System of Female Education, with a View of the Principles and Conduct Prevalent among Women of Rank and Fortune,* 2 vols. (London: T. Cadell, 1799).

2  In *Julie, ou La Nouvelle Héloïse* (1761). See 32-32, 93 above.

judgment and bewildering the understanding, as the most effectual way to inflame the imagination and deprave the heart.

The rare mischief of this author consists in his power of seducing by falsehood those who love truth, but whose minds are still wavering, and whose principles are not yet formed. He allures the warm-hearted to embrace vice, not because they prefer vice, but because he gives to vice so natural an air of virtue: and ardent and enthusiastic youth, too confidently trusting in their integrity and in their teacher, will be undone, while they fancy they are indulging in the noblest feelings of their nature. Many authors will more infallibly complete the ruin of the loose and ill-disposed; but perhaps (if I may change the figure) there never was a net of such exquisite art and inextricable workmanship, spread to entangle innocence and ensnare inexperience, as the writings of Rousseau: and, unhappily, the victim does not even struggle in the toils, because part of the delusion consists in imagining that he is set at liberty.

Some of our recent popular publications have adopted all the mischiefs of this school, and the principal evil arising from them is, that the virtues they exhibit are almost more dangerous than the vices. The chief materials out of which these delusive systems are framed, are characters who practise superfluous acts of generosity, while they are trampling on obvious and commanded duties; who combine sentiments of honour with actions the most flagitious: a high-tone of self-confidence, with a perpetual breach of self-denial: pathetic apostrophes to the passions, but no attempt to resist them. They teach that no duty exists which is not prompted by feeling: that impulse is the main spring of virtuous actions, while laws and principles are only unjust restraints; the former imposed by arbitrary men, the latter by the absurd prejudices of timorous and unenlightened conscience. In some of the most splendid of these characters, compassion is erected into the throne of justice, and justice is degraded into the rank of plebeian virtues. Creditors are defrauded, while the money due to them is lavished in dazzling acts of charity to some object that affected their senses; which fits of charity are made the sponge of every sin, and the substitute of every virtue: the whole indirectly tending to intimate how very *benevolent people are who are not Christians*. From many of these compositions, indeed, Christianity is systematically, and always virtually excluded; for the law and the prophets and the gospel *can* make no part of a scheme in which this world is looked upon as all in all; in which poverty and misery are considered as evils arising solely from human governments, and not from the dispensations of God: this poverty is represented as the greatest of evils, and the restraints which tend to keep the poor honest, as the most flagrant injustice. The gospel can have nothing to do with a system in which sin is reduced to a little human imperfection, and Old Bailey[1] crimes are softened down into a few engaging weaknesses; and in which the turpitude of all the vices a man himself commits, is done away by his *candour* in tolerating all the vices committed by others.

But the most fatal part of the system to that class whom I am addressing is, that even in those works which do not go all the lengths of treating marriage as an unjust infringement on liberty, and a tyrannical deduction from general happiness; yet it commonly happens that the hero or heroine, who has practically violated the letter of the seventh commandment, and continues to live in the allowed violation of its spirit, is painted as so amiable and so benevolent, so tender or so brave; and the temptation is represented as so *irresistible*, (for all these philosophers are fatalists,) the predominant and cherished sin is so filtered and purged of its pollutions, and is so sheltered and surrounded, and relieved with shining qualities, that the innocent and impressible young reader is brought to lose all horror of the awful crime in question, in the complacency she feels for the engaging virtues of the criminal.

... The writings of the French infidels were some years ago circulated in England with uncommon industry, and with some effect: but the good sense and good principles of the far greater part of our countrymen resisted the attack, and rose superior to the trial. Of the doctrines and principles here alluded to, the dreadful consequences, not only in the unhappy country where they originated and were almost universally adopted, but in every part of Europe where they have been received, have been such as to serve as a beacon to surrounding nations, if any warning can preserve them from destruction. In this country the subject is now so well understood, that every thing which issues from the French press is received with jealousy; and a work, on the first appearance of its exhibiting the doctrines of Voltaire and his associates, is rejected with indignation.

... About the same time that this first attempt at representing an adultress in an exemplary light was made by a German dramatist,[2] which forms an aera in manners; a direct vindication of adultery was for the first time attempted by a *woman*, a professed admirer and imitator of the German

---

1  The criminal courts in London.

2  August Friedrich Ferdinand von Kotzebue (1761-1819), a prolific playwright whose *Menschenhass und Reue* (*Misanthropy and Repentance*) was pirated in 1798 as *The Stranger* and performed at Drury Lane. Elizabeth Inchbald adapted the same play as *Lovers' Vows* (1798), the play chosen for the controversial theatricals in Jane Austen, *Mansfield Park* (1814).

suicide Werter.[1] The Female Werter, as she is styled by her biographer,[2] asserts in a work, intitled "The Wrongs of Woman,"[3] that adultery is justifiable, and that the restrictions placed on it by the laws of England constitute part of the *wrongs of woman*.

But let us take comfort. These fervid pictures are not yet generally realised. These atrocious principles are not yet adopted into common practice. Though corruptions seem to be pouring in upon us from every quarter, yet there is still left among us a discriminating judgment. Clear and strongly marked distinctions between right and wrong still subsist. While we continue to cherish this sanity of mind, the case is not desperate. Though the crime above alluded to, the growth of which always exhibits the most irrefragable proof of the dissoluteness of public manners; though this crime, which cuts up order and virtue by the roots, and violates the sanctity of vows, is awfully increasing,

'Till senates seem,
For purposes of empire less conven'd
Than to release the adult'ress from her bonds;[4]

Yet, thanks to the surviving efficacy of a holy religion, to the operations of virtuous laws, and the energy and unshaken integrity with which these laws are *now* administered; and still more perhaps to a standard of morals which continues in force, when the principles which sanctioned it are no more; this crime, in the female sex at least, is still held in just abhorrence; if it be practised, it is not honourable; if it be committed, it is not justified; we do not yet affect to palliate its turpitude; as yet it hides its abhorred head in lurking privacy; and reprobation hitherto follows its publicity.

From Chapter 7, "On Female Study, and Initiation into Knowledge.—Error of Cultivating the Imagination to the Neglect of the Judgment.—Books of Reasoning Recommended."

... Perhaps there is some analogy between the mental and bodily conformation of women. The instructor should therefore imitate the physician. If the latter prescribe bracing medicines for a body of which delicacy is the

---

1  Johann Wolfgang von Goethe, *The Sorrows of Young Werther* (1774), an epistolary novel in which the hero, in love with a married woman, eventually kills himself.
2  William Godwin, *Memoirs of the Author of "A Vindication of the Rights of Woman"* (1798), chapter 7. See *Memoirs*, ed. Richard Holmes, 242.
3  See Appendix D4.
4  Cf. William Cowper, *The Task*, Book 3 ("The Garden"), 61-63.

disease, the former would do well to prohibit relaxing reading for a mind which is already of too soft a texture, and should strengthen its feeble tone by invigorating reading.

By softness, I cannot be supposed to mean imbecility of understanding, but natural softness of heart, with that indolence of spirit which is fostered by indulging in seducing books and in the general habits of fashionable life.

I mean not here to recommend books which are immediately religious, but such as exercise the reasoning faculties, teach the mind to get acquainted with its own nature, and to stir up its own powers. Let not a timid young lady start if I should venture to recommend to her, after a proper course of preparation, to swallow and digest such strong meat, as Watts's or Duncan's little book of Logic, some parts of Mr. Locke's Essay on the Human Understanding, and Bishop Butler's Analogy.[1] Where there is leisure, and capacity, and an able counsellor, works of this nature might be profitably substituted in the place of so much English Sentiment, French Philosophy, Italian Poetry, and fantastic German imagery and magic wonders. While such enervating or absurd books sadly disqualify the reader for solid pursuit or vigorous thinking, the studies here recommended would act upon the constitution of the mind as a kind of alterative, and, if I may be allowed the expression, would help to brace the intellectual stamina.

This is however by no means intended to exclude works of taste and imagination, which must always make the ornamental part, and of course a very considerable part of female studies. It is only suggested that they should not form them entirely. For what is called dry tough reading, independent of the knowledge it conveys, is useful as an habit and wholesome as an exercise. Serious study serves to harden the mind for more trying conflicts; it lifts the reader from sensation to intellect; it abstracts her from the world and its vanities; it fixes a wandering spirit, and fortifies a weak one; it divorces her from matter; it corrects that spirit of trifling which she naturally contracts from the frivolous turn of female conversation, and the petty nature of female employments; it concentrates her attention, assists her in a habit of excluding trivial thoughts, and thus even helps to qualify her for religious pursuits. Yes; I repeat it, there is to woman a Christian use to be made of sober studies; while books of an opposite cast, however unexceptionable they may be sometimes found in point of expression; however free from evil in its more gross and palpable shapes, yet by their

---

1  Isaac Watts, *Logic: or, The Right Use of Reason in the Inquiry After Truth* (1724); William Duncan, *The Elements of Logic. In Four Books* (9th ed., 1800); John Locke, *Essay Concerning Human Understanding* (1689); Joseph Butler, *Analogy of Religion* (1736).

very nature and constitution they excite a spirit of relaxation, by exhibiting scenes and ideas which soften the mind; they impair its general powers of resistance, and at best feed habits of improper indulgence, and nourish a vain and visionary indolence, which lays the mind open to error and the heart to seduction.

... Far be it from me to desire to make scholastic ladies or female dialecticians; but there is little fear that the kind of books here recommended, if thoroughly studied, and not superficially skimmed, will make them pedants or induce conceit; for by shewing them the possible powers of the human mind, you will bring them to see the littleness of their own, and to get acquainted with the mind and to regulate it, does not seem the way to puff it up. But let her who is disposed to be elated with her literary acquisitions, check her vanity by calling to mind the just remark of Swift, "that after all her boasted acquirements, a woman will, generally speaking, be found to possess less of what is called learning than a common school-boy."[1]

Neither is there any fear that this sort of reading will convert ladies into authors. The direct contrary effect will be likely to be produced by the perusal of writers who throw the generality of readers at such an unapproachable distance. Who are those ever multiplying authors, that with unparalleled fecundity are overstocking the world with their quick succeeding progeny? They are novel writers; the easiness of whose productions is at once the cause of their own fruitfulness, and of the almost infinitely numerous race of imitators to whom they give birth. Such is the frightful facility of this species of composition, that every raw girl while she reads, is tempted to fancy that she can also write.

---

1    Jonathan Swift, *A Letter to a Young Lady, on Her Marriage* (1723).

# Appendix C: On Duelling

[*Adeline Mowbray* engages in the contemporary debate about the legality of duelling, a traditional way for gentlemen to settle their grievances and assert their "honour": the opposition of the "law of honour" to civil law persisted well into the nineteenth century. Nevertheless, death as a result of premeditated duelling was sometimes regarded as murder: this was the jurist William Blackstone's interpretation in his *Commentaries on the Laws of England* (1765). Unlike the debate about marriage, which tends to divide proponents and opponents along religious lines, opponents of duelling display a range of political and theological positions. Godwin's argument, reprinted below, is similar in many respects to that of other opponents of duelling, some of whom offer religious arguments. See, for example, William Hunter, *An Essay on Duelling. Written with a view to discountenance this barbarous and disgraceful practice* (London, 1792); Edward Barry, *Theological, Philosophical, and Moral Essays* (London, 1799); and William Paley, *The Principles of Moral and Political Philosophy*, 12th ed. (London, 1799). In *Adeline Mowbray*, Glenmurray, the author of a (Godwinian) book on duelling—and Sir Patrick's opponent in a duel—eventually learns to take his own good advice and turn down Major Douglas's challenge to a duel.]

## 1. From **William Godwin, *Enquiry Concerning Political Justice and Its Influence on Morals and Happiness*, 3rd ed. (1798)**

Appendix to Book 2, Chapter 2: *Of Duelling*

It may be proper in this place to bestow a moment's consideration upon the trite, but very important case of duelling. A short reflection will suffice to set it in its true light.

This despicable practice was originally invented by barbarians for the gratification of revenge. It was probably at that time thought a very happy project, for reconciling the odiousness of malignity with the gallantry of courage.

But in this light it is now generally given up. Men of the best understanding who lend it their sanction, are unwillingly induced to do so, and engage in single combat merely that their reputation may sustain no slander.

In examining this subject we must proceed upon one of two suppositions. Either the lives of both the persons to be hazarded are worthless, or they are not. In the latter case, the question answers itself, and cannot stand in need of discussion. Useful lives are not to be hazarded, from a view to the partial and contemptible obloquy that may be annexed to the refusal of such a duel, that is, to an act of virtue.

When the duellist tells me, that he, and the person that has offended him, are of no possible worth to the community, I may reasonably conclude that he talks the language of spleen. But, if I take him at his word, is it to be admitted, though he cannot benefit the community, that he should injure it? What would be the consequence, if we allowed ourselves to assail everyone that we thought worthless in the world? In reality, when he talks this language, he deserts the ground of vindicating his injured honour, and shows that his conduct is that of a vindictive and brutalised savage.

"But the refusing a duel is an ambiguous action. Cowards may pretend principle to shelter themselves from a danger they dare not meet."

This is partly true and partly false. There are few actions indeed that are not ambiguous, or that with the same general outline may not proceed from different motives. But the manner of doing them, will sufficiently show the principle from which they spring.

He, that would break through a received custom because he believes it to be wrong, must no doubt arm himself with fortitude. The point in which we principally fail, is in not accurately understanding our own intentions, and taking care beforehand to purify ourselves from every alloy of weakness and error. He, who comes forward with no other idea but that of rectitude, and who expresses, with the simplicity and firmness which conviction never fails to inspire, the views with which he is penetrated, is in no danger of being mistaken for a coward. If he hesitate, it is because he has not an idea perfectly clear of the sentiment he intends to convey. If he be in any degree embarrassed, it is because he has not a feeling, sufficiently generous and intrepid, of the demerit of the action in which he is urged to engage.

If courage have any intelligible nature, one of its principal fruits must be the daring to speak truth at all times, to all persons, and in every possible situation in which a well informed sense of duty may prescribe it. What is it but the want of courage that should prevent me from saying, "Sir, I will not accept your challenge. Have I injured you? I will readily and without compulsion repair my injustice to the uttermost mite. Have you misconstrued me? State to me the particulars, and doubt not that what is true I will make appear to be true. I should be a notorious criminal, were I to attempt your life, or assist you in an attempt upon mine. What compensation will the opinion of the world make, for the recollection of so vile and brutal a proceeding? There is no true applause, but where the heart of him that receives it beats in unison. There is no censure terrible, while the heart repels it with conscious integrity. I am not the coward, to do a deed that my soul detests, because I cannot endure the scoffs of the mistaken. Loss of reputation is a serious evil. But I will act so, that no man shall suspect me of irresolution and pusillanimity." He that should firmly hold this language, and act accordingly, would soon be acquitted of every dishonourable imputation.

# Appendix D: On Marriage and Divorce

[Like duelling, at the turn of the eighteenth century marriage was an institution that revealed the difficulty of reconciling law with codes of conduct outside the law. Appendix D1 is an excerpt from the Act against clandestine marriages (1753), included here to emphasize the relatively recent insistence in this period on accurate record-keeping, and to demonstrate that altering the record of a marriage had become a capital crime. Before 1753, marriages had often been contracted secretly or informally; the Act provided for clear legal definition. Mrs. Mowbray marries Sir Patrick by licence: hers is not a clandestine marriage, but it is certainly an unwisely discreet one, soon revealed as bigamous. Considering her mother's fate, Adeline might have insisted on the banns being publicly read when she married Berrendale. He keeps their marriage, which eventually turns out to be legal, a secret; but he does not interfere with the marriage registry. Nevertheless, the reader informed about contemporary marriage law might well, from Adeline's difficulty in obtaining proof of her marriage, suspect him of having done so. Here, Opie's interest in and understanding of the law is particularly evident: her attendance at the law courts—and, possibly, her own marriage to a divorced man—evidently inform her treatment of marriage in the novel.

The late eighteenth-century debate about marriage coincides with the revolution debate and the anxiety about so-called French ideas. Wollstonecraft's *The Wrongs of Woman, or Maria* (first published in *Posthumous Works*, 1798) uses fiction to demonstrate how marriage can imprison ("bastille") women. The anonymous *Letters on Love, Marriage, and Adultery, Addressed to the Right Honorable The Earl of Exeter* (London: Ridgway, 1789), one of which is reprinted as Appendix D2, makes some of the same points that Adeline makes: church and law "have enjoined, that men and women must continue together; not because they love each other, or are likely to be happy; but because they are united; because mystical words have been pronounced over them; and heaven has been supposed to witness their contract" (318). William Godwin's attack on marriage in *Enquiry Concerning Political Justice* (reprinted as Appendix D3) is the most notorious contemporary critique of marriage as an institution.

Mary Wollstonecraft's Maria (in *Maria, or, The Wrongs of Woman*, Appendix D4) pleads in court against the double standard that has made her little better than her degraded husband's property: she soon discovers that unfair marriage laws—and no access to divorce, especially for women—leave her with no way of living respectably with her lover, Darnford. Men of social standing could obtain divorces by petitioning Parliament; but there are almost no eighteenth-century cases of women doing so successfully. Maria is, in the eyes of the court, an adulteress; her lover is a seducer.]

## 1. From *An Act for the Better Preventing of Clandestine Marriages* (1753)[1]

Provided always, and be it enacted by the Authority aforesaid, That no Parson, Minister, Vicar or Curate solemnizing Marriages after the Twenty fifth Day of *March*, One thousand seven hundred and fifty four, between Persons, both or One of whom shall be under the Age of Twenty one Years, after Banns published, shall be punishable by Ecclesiastical Censures for solemnizing such Marriages without Consent of Parents or Guardians, whose Consent is required by Law, unless such Parson, Minister, Vicar or Curate, shall have Notice of the Dissent of such Parents or Guardians; and in case such Parents or Guardians, or One of them, shall openly, and publickly declare, or cause to be declared, in the Church or Chapel, where the Banns shall be so published, at the Time of such Publication, his, her, or their Dissent to such Marriage, such Publication of Banns shall be absolutely void.

... And for preventing undue Entries and Abuses in Registers of Marriages; be it enacted by the Authority aforesaid, That on or before the Twenty fifth Day of *March*, in the Year One thousand seven hundred and fifty four, and from time to time afterwards as there shall be Occasion, the Churchwardens and Chapelwardens of every Parish or Chapelry shall provide proper Books of Vellum, or good and durable Paper, in which all Marriages and Banns of Marriage respectively there published or solemnized, shall be registered, and every Page thereof shall be marked at the Top, with the Figure of the Number of every such Page, beginning at the Second Leaf with Number One; and every Leaf or Page so numbered, shall be ruled with Lines at proper and equal Distances from each other, or as near as may be; and all Banns and Marriages published or celebrated in any Church or Chapel, or within any such Parish or Chapelry, shall be respectively entered, registered, printed, or written upon, or as near as conveniently may be to such ruled Lines, and shall be signed by the Parson, Vicar, Minister or Curate, or by some other Person in his Presence, and by his Direction; and such Entries shall be made as aforesaid, on or near such Lines in successive Order, where the Paper is not damaged or decayed by Accident or Length of Time, until a new Book shall be thought proper or

---

1 The text is from from *Anno Regni Georgii II.... At the Parliament begun and holden at Westminster ... [1747-1753]* (London: Thomas Baskett, 1753), 471-78.

necessary to be provided for the same Purposes, and then the Directions aforesaid shall be observed in every such new Book; and all Books provided as aforesaid, shall be deemed to belong to every such Parish or Chapel respectively, and shall be carefully kept and preserved for publick Use.

And in order to preserve the Evidence of Marriages, and to make the Proof thereof more certain and easy, and for the Direction of Ministers in the Celebration of Marriages and registering thereof, be it enacted, That from and after the Twenty fifth Day of *March*, in the Year One thousand seven hundred and fifty four, all Marriages shall be solemnized in the Presence of Two or more credible Witnesses, besides the Minister who shall celebrate the same; and that immediately after the Celebration of every Marriage, an Entry thereof shall be made in such Register to be kept as aforesaid; in which Entry or Register it shall be expressed, That the said Marriage was celebrated by Banns or Licence; and if both or either of the Parties married by Licence, be under Age, with Consent of the Parents or Guardians, as the Case shall be; and shall be signed by the Minister with his proper Addition, and also by the Parties married, and attested by such Two Witnesses....

... And be it further enacted by the Authority aforesaid, That if any Person shall, from and after the Twenty fifth Day of *March*, in the Year One thousand seven hundred and fifty four, with Intent to elude the Force of this Act, knowingly and willfully insert, or cause to be inserted in the Register Book of such Parish or Chapelry as aforesaid, any false Entry of any Matter or Thing relating to any Marriage; or falsely make, alter, forge, or counterfeit, or cause or procure to be falsely made, altered, forged, or counterfeited, or act or assist in falsely making, altering, forging or counterfeiting any such Entry in such Register; or falsely make, alter, forge, or counterfeit, or cause or procure to be falsely made, altered, forged, or counterfeited, or assist in falsely making, altering, forging, or counterfeiting any such Licence of Marriage as aforesaid; or utter or publish as true any such false, altered, forged, or counterfeited Register as aforesaid, or a Copy thereof, or any such false altered, forged, or counterfeited Licence of Marriage, knowing such Register or Licence of Marriage respectively to be false, altered, forged, or counterfeited; or if any Person shall, from and after the said Twenty Fifth Day of *March*, willfully destroy, or cause or procure to be destroyed, any Register Book of Marriages, or any Part of such Register Book, with Intent to avoid any Marriage, or to subject any Person to any of the Penalties of this Act; every Person so offending, and being thereof lawfully convicted, shall be deemed and adjudged to be guilty of Felony, and shall suffer Death as a Felon, without benefit of Clergy.

## 2. From Anon., *Letters on Love, Marriage, and Adultery* (1789)[1]

From Letter 6, "Marriage"

My Lord,
We have considered the union of man and woman, as intended to be brought on by inclination and choice. Inclination, and the power of chusing, give rise to the affection of love; which is the best and most useful affection in the human mind. But it is with affections, as with the productions of the earth; they cannot be cherished in improper soils. Constitutions of government, and systems of religion, are to principles of morality, what climates are to trees or herbs or flowers; and in the moral as well as the natural world, things alter and even change by a change of circumstances or situation. This we have seen in the kind of history which we have given of the passion of love; or the principle which has united men and women. At one time, it has been, a brutal appetite, consistent with brutal and savage cruelty. At another, it has mounted into the sublimity and madness of romantic adoration; from which it has again fallen into a civilized kind of brutality called gallantry, intrigue, and debauchery. For the difference between a state of savage brutality, and civilized gallantry, is not so great in fact as in appearance. Women are the mere instruments of low and temporary sensuality; they are in common, possessed by as many persons as will flatter or purchase them; and they are slaves nearly alike in both cases: for they hold their influence, their pleasures, and even their support, by the precarious tenure of the caprice of men....

Where laws, prejudices, and customs are in opposition to nature, it will seek a kind of indemnification in gallantry, libertinism, or debauchery. Indeed the vices arising in modern governments from the effects of love, seem to be all owing to unnatural or iniquitous customs and laws; and gallantry and intrigue are the indemnities which men and women reserve to themselves for the injustice or injuries they have received.— Though the idea of being property, or parts of our goods and chattels, be exploded from our philosophy and from some of our laws, it still remains in our prepossessions or customs, counteracting by a little senseless and romantic gallantry. It does not offend a man's conscience; it is not reprehensible by his parents; it is not dishonorable; it is not punishable by law—that he should seduce an unsuspicious, artless, or affectionate girl; that he should deprive her of that character, without which even he would disesteem or dislike her; that he should involve her in dishonor

---

1   The text is from Anon., *Letters on Love, Marriage, and Adultery, Addressed to the Right Honorable The Earl of Exeter* (London: Ridgway, 1789).

and infamy, which no repentance, no good behaviour can remove: while he would be executed, if he forcibly entered her habitation, or took away some paltry parts of her dress or property. The crime is always contrived and committed by the man; the punishment and the infamy are borne by the woman. These are the principles of Europe; on these all the nations of it act in respect to women; whatever may be their laws or their religions....

... Brutes live promiscuously; because they have not acquired talents and reason to render domestic society, or domestic virtue, the source of pleasure. Savages act in a similar manner for a similar reason. Men and women of gallantry, in all the variations of what is called a state of civilization, adopt the usages of savages and brutes, because they have not sufficient experience and reason to discern that by adopting the genuine principles and rational regulations of domestic society, they heighten and multiply their pleasures.

They who have studied the laws of nature, not only in the simple propensities by which she first acts, but in those combinations which form social principles; who have felt their pleasures heighten, become more interesting and more numerous as they advanced in paths of virtue; who have found themselves becoming more free by observing the regulations of reason, and more happy by sacrificing present and single pleasures to those which may be at some distance, but of great importance, complicated with gratifications of the most interesting nature:—these persons have ever held the promiscuous commerce of savage brutality, or of civilized gallantry, in abhorrence; and have sought the virtues, as the instruments of pleasure....

These claims ... have influenced the principles of the barbarous, as well as licentious forms of governments; they have had the sanctions of all religions; they have checked the profligacy of public manners; they have been avowed and acted upon by the wisest and most excellent persons who have ever appeared in the world.

We need not therefore be afraid of the sarcasms of licentious wit; we need not apprehend being ridiculed as superstitious, if we assert, that love is not designed to be a temporary pastime; or the instrument of gratification merely sensual; but a principle of union in man and woman to continue during life.

Religious legislators have imagined they perceived this truth; and they have enjoined, under the sanction of penalties in this world and of damnation in another, that when man and woman are united, they shall never be separated but by one offence. Nothing could have been imagined more effectually to counteract the intentions of marriage, than such a law. Nature plainly intimates, the only method to secure domestic and social happiness, is to form our connections on affection or principle; which, in producing conjugal love, the most sincere and most interesting friendship, the reciprocal and tender attachments of parents and children, brothers and sisters heighten and multiply all our pleasures. If we obey this direction, we are sure to be happy; if we disobey, we have no reason to expect happiness. But nature is not sufficiently wise or prudent, according to the church or the law. They have enjoined, that men and women must continue together; not because they love each other, or are likely to be happy; but because they are *united*; because mystical words have been pronounced over them; and heaven has been supposed to witness their contract.

The very breath of a priest has ever seemed malignant to the happiness of man. This is the triumph of superstitious artifice over reason and the affections of the heart. Nothing has ever been contrived so effectually to oppose the intentions of reason; to destroy the best affections of men; to warp them by authority and interest; or to drive them by despair into all the excesses of prostitution or debauchery as the impolitic, the barbarous custom of forcing those whose folly has made them wretched, to continue wretched to the end of life....

... [A]ll connections, without that affection, which may truly and properly be called love; whether effected by the authority of parents, by views of interest, or by lust, however sanctioned by superstitious or legal forms, are PROSTITUTIONS; offences against nature; and therefore necessarily productive of misery. The Deity hath provided, when the first enchanting links of mutual affection and parental love have united us; we should be more endeared to each other, by the instance of care and affection in the education of our children.... We view the progress of an infant mind, the sources and growth of its affections, with more pleasure than is experienced by itself. We interest ourselves in those great passions which determine the events of life; we forget our infirmities, we imagine ourselves in love again because our children are enamoured; and we become fathers and mothers a second time, when they assume those happy denominations. Compare, if you can, the events of what is called a life of pleasure, with such as these. And when nature is decomposing; when infirmities or disorders menace dissolution—you may see the man who has acted on the selfish and brutal principle of gratifying himself at the expence of truth, honour, and the happiness of others, cursing a world which detests or despises him; deserted by all, by the very instruments of his pleasures, because universally disesteemed; and sinking into the grave in ignominy or frantic wretchedness: while those men and women who have gone hand in hand in the pleasing duties of life, will not only have a firm support in honorable recollections; but will be led down its rugged declivity, by the tenderest care of an affectionate offspring; and will consign themselves to rest, like useful labourers, a little weary, but satisfied with the work of the day.

> I have the honor to be,
>> My Lord,
>> Your Lordship's,
>>> Most obedient,
> And most humble servant,
>> THE AUTHOR

### 3. From William Godwin, *Enquiry Concerning Political Justice and Its Influence on Morals and Happiness*, 3rd ed. [1798]

From Appendix to Book 8, chap. 8: *Of Cooperation, Cohabitation and Marriage*

... Another article which belongs to the subject of cooperation, is cohabitation. The evils attendant on this practice, are obvious. In order to the human understanding's being successfully cultivated, it is necessary, that the intellectual operations of men should be independent of each other. We should avoid such practices as are calculated to melt our opinions into a common mould. Cohabitation is also hostile to that fortitude, which should accustom a man, in his actions, as well as in his opinions, to judge for himself, and feel competent to the discharge of his own duties. Add to this, that it is absurd to expect the inclinations and wishes of two human beings to coincide, through any long period of time. To oblige them to act and to live together, is to subject them to some inevitable portion of thwarting, bickering and unhappiness. This cannot be otherwise, so long as men shall continue to vary in their habits, their preferences and their views. No man is always chearful and kind; and it is better that his fits of irritation should subside of themselves, since the mischief in that case is more limited, and since the jarring of opposite tempers, and the suggestions of a wounded pride, tend inexpressibly to increase the irritation. When I seek to correct the defects of a stranger, it is with urbanity and good humour. I have no idea of convincing him through the medium of surliness and invective. But something of this kind inevitably obtains, where the intercourse is too unremitted.

The subject of cohabitation is particularly interesting, as it includes in it the subject of marriage. It will therefore be proper to pursue the enquiry in greater detail. The evil of marriage, as it is practised in European countries, extends further than we have yet described. The method is, for a thoughtless and romantic youth of each sex, to come together, to see each other, for a few times, and under circumstances full of delusion, and then to vow to eternal attachment. What is the consequence of this? In almost every instance they find themselves deceived. They are reduced to make the best of an irretrievable mistake. They are led to conceive it is their wisest policy, to shut their eyes upon realities, happy, if, by any perversion of intellect, they can persuade themselves that they were right in their first crude opinion of each other. Thus the institution of marriage is made a system of fraud; and men who carefully mislead their judgments in the daily affair of their life, must be expected to have a crippled judgment in every other concern.

Add to this, that marriage, as now understood, is a monopoly, and the worst of monopolies. So long as two human beings are forbidden, by positive institution, to follow the dictates of their own mind, prejudice will be alive and vigorous. So long as I seek, by despotic and artificial means, to maintain my possession of a woman, I am guilty of the most odious selfishness. Over this imaginary prize, men watch with perpetual jealousy; and one man finds his desire, and his capacity to circumvent, as much excited, as the other is excited, to traverse his projects, and frustrate his hopes. As long as this state of society continues, philanthropy will be crossed and checked in a thousand ways, and the still augmenting stream of abuse will continue to flow.

The abolition of the present system of marriage, appears to involve no evils. We are apt to represent that abolition to ourselves, as the harbinger of brutal lust and depravity. But it really happens, in this, as in other cases, that the positive laws which are made to restrain our vices, irritate and multiply them. Not to say, that the same sentiments of justice and happiness, which, in a state of equality, would destroy our relish for expensive gratifications, might be expected to decrease our inordinate appetites of every kind, and to lead us universally to prefer the pleasures of intellect to the pleasures of sense.

It is a question of some moment, whether the intercourse of the sexes, in a reasonable state of society, would be promiscuous, or whether each man would select for himself a partner, to whom he will adhere, as long as that adherence shall continue to be the choice of both parties. Probability seems to be greatly in favour of the latter. Perhaps this side of the alternative is most favourable to population. Perhaps it would suggest itself in preference, to the man who would wish to maintain the several propensities of his frame, in the order due to their relative importance, and to prevent a merely sensual appetite from engrossing excessive attention. It is scarcely to be imagined, that this commerce, in any state of society, will be stripped of its adjuncts, and that men will as willingly hold it, with a woman whose personal and mental qualities they disapprove, as with one of a different description. But it is the nature of the human mind, to persist, for a certain length of time, in its opinion or choice. The parties therefore, having acted upon selection, are not likely to forget this selection when the interview is over. Friendship, if by friendship we understand that affection for an individual which is measured singly by what we know of his worth, is one of the most exquisite gratifications, perhaps one of the most improving exercises, of a rational mind. Friendship therefore may be expected to come in aid of the sexual intercourse, to refine its grossness, and increase its delight. All these arguments are calculated to determine our judgment in favour of marriage as a salutary and respectable institution, but not of that species of marriage, in which there is no room for repentance, and to which liberty and hope are equally strangers.

Admitting these principles therefore as the basis of the sexual commerce, what opinion ought we to form respecting infidelity to this attachment? Certainly no ties ought to be imposed upon either party, preventing them from quitting the attachment, whenever their judgment directs them to quit it. With respect to such infidelities as are compatible with an intention to adhere to it, the point of principal importance is a determination to have recourse to no species of disguise. In ordinary cases, and where the periods of absence are of no long duration, it would seem, that any inconstancy would reflect some portion of discredit on the person that practised it. It would argue that the person's propensities were not under that kind of subordination, which virtue and self-government appear to prescribe. But inconstancy, like any other temporary dereliction, would not be found incompatible with a character of uncommon excellence. What, at present, renders it, in many instances, peculiarly loathsome, is its being practised in a clandestine manner. It leads to a train of falshood and a concerted hypocrisy, than which there is scarcely anything that more eminently depraves and degrades the human mind.

The mutual kindness of persons of an opposite sex will, in such a state, fall under the same system as any other species of friendship. Exclusively of groundless and obstinate attachments, it will be impossible for me to live in the world, without finding in one man a worth superior to that of another. To this man I shall feel kindness, in exact proportion to my apprehension of his worth. The case will be the same with respect to the other sex. I shall assiduously cultivate the intercourse of that woman, whose moral and intellectual accomplishments strike me in the most powerful manner. But "it may happen, that other men will feel for her the same preference that I do." This will create no difficulty. We may all enjoy her conversation; and her choice being declared, we shall all be wise enough to consider the sexual commerce as unessential to our regard. It is a mark of the extreme depravity of our present habits, that we are inclined to suppose the sexual commerce necessary to the advantages arising from the purest friendship. It is by no means indispensable, that the female to whom each man attaches himself in that matter, should appear to each the most deserving and excellent of her sex.

Let us consider the way in which this state of society will modify education. It may be imagined, that the abolition of the present system of marriage, would make education, in a certain sense, the affair of the public; though, if there be any truth in the reasonings of this work, to provide for it by the positive institutions of a community, would be extremely inconsistent with the true principles of an intellectual nature. Education may be regarded as consisting of various branches. First, the personal cares which the helpless state of an infant requires. These will probably devolve upon the mother; unless, by frequent parturition, or by the nature of these cares, that be found to render her share of the burthen unequal; and then it will be amicably and willingly participated by others. Secondly, food and other necessary supplies. These will easily find their true level, and spontaneously flow, from the quarter in which they abound, to the quarter that is deficient. Lastly, the term education may be used to signify instruction. The task of instruction, under such a form of society, will be greatly simplified and altered from what it is at present. It will then scarcely be thought more necessary to make boys slaves, than to make men so. The business will not then be, to bring forward so many adepts in the egg-shell, that the vanity of parents may be flattered by hearing their praises. No man will think of vexing with premature learning the feeble and inexperienced, lest, when they came to years of discretion, they should refuse to be learned. The mind will be suffered to expand itself, in proportion as occasion and impression shall excite it, and not tortured and enervated by being cast in a particular mould. No creature in human form will be expected to learn any thing, but because he desires it, and has some conception of its value; and every man, in proportion to his capacity, will be ready to furnish such general hints and comprehensive views, as will suffice for the guidance and encouragement of him who studies from the impulse of desire....

## 4. From Mary Wollstonecraft, *The Wrongs of Woman: or, Maria: A Fragment* (1798)[1]

Chapter 17

Such was [Maria's] state of mind when the dogs of law were let loose on her. Maria took the task of conducting Darnford's defence upon herself. She instructed his counsel to plead guilty to the charge of adultery; but to deny that of seduction.

The counsel for the plaintiff opened the cause, by observing, "that his client had ever been an indulgent husband, and borne with several defects of temper, while he had nothing criminal to lay to the charge of his wife. But that she left his house without assigning any cause. He could not assert that she was then acquainted with the defendant; yet, when he was once endeavouring to bring her back to her home, this man put the peace-officers to flight, and took her he knew not whither. After the birth of her child, her conduct was so strange, and a melancholy malady having afflicted one of the family, which delicacy forbade the dwelling on, it was necessary to confine her. By some means the defendant enabled her to make her escape, and they had lived together, in despite of all sense of order and decorum. The adultery was allowed, it was not necessary to bring any witnesses to prove it; but the seduction, though highly probable from the circumstances which he had the honour to state, could not be so clearly proved.—It was of the most atrocious kind, as decency was set at defiance, and respect for reputation, which shows internal compunction, utterly disregarded."

A strong sense of injustice had silenced every emotion, which a mixture of true and false delicacy might otherwise have excited in Maria's bosom. She only felt in earnest to insist on the privilege of her nature. The sarcasms of society, and the condemnation of a mistaken world, were nothing to her, compared with acting contrary to those feelings which

---

1  The text is from *Posthumous Works of the Author of "A Vindication of the Rights of Woman,"* [ed. William Godwin] (London: J. Johnson), 1798, vols. 1 and 2. Chapter 17 is the last completed chapter of this unfinished work. Maria has been separated from her infant daughter and imprisoned in a madhouse by her mercenary, unfaithful, and abusive husband. There, she meets and eventually forms a relationship with Henry Darnford. Maria's husband, George Venables, prosecutes Darnford for adultery and seduction—a usual first step if Venables were later to seek a parliamentary divorce. This final chapter of Wollstonecraft's unfinished novel illustrates women's inequality under the law: divorces were granted to men (but not to women) who could prove their spouses' adultery; a husband's infidelity was comparatively trivial, and men's right to their wives' property was protected in law.

were the foundation of her principles. [She therefore eagerly put herself forward, instead of desiring to be absent, on this memorable occasion.]

Convinced that the subterfuges of the law were disgraceful, she wrote a paper, which she expressly desired might be read in court:

"Married when scarcely able to distinguish the nature of the engagement, I yet submitted to the rigid laws which enslave women, and obeyed the man whom I could no longer love. Whether the duties of the state are reciprocal, I mean not to discuss; but I can prove repeated infidelities which I overlooked or pardoned. Witnesses are not wanting to establish these facts. I at present maintain the child of a maid servant, sworn to him, and born after our marriage. I am ready to allow, that education and circumstances lead men to think and act with less delicacy, than the preservation of order in society demands from women; but surely I may without assumption declare, that, though I could excuse the birth, I could not the desertion of this unfortunate babe:—and, while I despised the man, it was not easy to venerate the husband. With proper restrictions however, I revere the institution which fraternizes the world. I exclaim against the laws which throw the whole weight of the yoke on the weaker shoulders, and force women, when they claim protectorship as mothers, to sign a contract, which renders them dependent on the caprice of the tyrant, whom choice or necessity has appointed to reign over them. Various are the cases, in which a woman ought to separate herself from her husband; and mine, I may be allowed emphatically to insist, comes under the description of the most aggravated.

"I will not enlarge on those provocations which only the individual can estimate; but will bring forward such charges only, the truth of which is an insult upon humanity. In order to promote certain destructive speculations, Mr. Venables prevailed on me to borrow certain sums of a wealthy relation; and, when I refused further compliance, he thought of bartering my person; and not only allowed opportunities to, but urged, a friend from whom he had borrowed money, to seduce me. On the discovery of this act of atrocity, I determined to leave him, and in the most decided manner, for ever. I consider all obligation as made void by his conduct; and hold, that schisms which proceed from want of principles, can never be healed.

"He received a fortune with me to the amount of five thousand pounds. On the death of my uncle, convinced that I could provide for my child, I destroyed the settlement of that fortune. I required none of my property to be returned to me, nor shall enumerate the sums extorted from me during six years that we lived together.

"After leaving, what the law considers as my home, I was hunted like a criminal from place to place, though I contracted no debts, and demanded no maintenance—yet, as the laws sanction such proceeding, and make women the property of their husbands, I forbear to animadvert. After the birth of my daughter, and the death of my uncle, who left a very considerable property to myself and child, I was exposed to new persecution; and, because I had, before arriving at what is termed years of discretion, pledged my faith, I was treated by the world, as bound for ever to a man whose vices were notorious. Yet what are the vices generally known, to the various miseries that a woman may be subject to, which, though deeply felt, eating into the soul, elude description, and may be glossed over! A false morality is even established, which makes all the virtue of women consist in chastity, submission, and the forgiveness of injuries.

"I pardon my oppressor—bitterly as I lament the loss of my child, torn from me in the most violent manner. But nature revolts, and my soul sickens at the bare supposition, that it could ever be a duty to pretend affection, when a separation is necessary to prevent my feeling hourly aversion.

"To force me to give my fortune, I was imprisoned—yes; in a private mad-house.—There, in the heart of misery, I met the man charged with seducing me. We became attached—I deemed, and ever shall deem, myself free. The death of my babe dissolved the only tie which subsisted between me and my, what is termed, lawful husband.

"To this person, thus encountered, I voluntarily gave myself, never considering myself as any more bound to transgress the laws of moral purity, because the will of my husband might be pleaded in my excuse, than to transgress those laws to which [the policy of artificial society has] annexed [positive] punishments.——While no command of a husband can prevent a woman from suffering for certain crimes, she must be allowed to consult her conscience, and regulate her conduct, in some degree, by her own sense of right. The respect I owe to myself, demanded my strict adherence to my determination of never viewing Mr. Venables in the light of a husband, nor could it forbid me from encouraging another. If I am unfortunately united to an unprincipled man, am I for ever to be shut out from fulfilling the duties of a wife and mother?—I wish my country to approve of my conduct; but, if laws exist, made by the strong to oppress the weak, I appeal to my own sense of justice, and declare that I will not live with the individual, who has violated every moral obligation which binds man to man.

"I protest equally against any charge being brought to criminate the man, whom I consider as my husband. I was six-and-twenty when I left Mr. Venables' roof; if ever I am to be supposed to arrive at an age to direct my own actions, I must by that time have arrived at it.—I acted with deliberation.—Mr. Darnford found me a forlorn and oppressed woman, and promised the protection women in the present state of society want.—But the man who now claims me—was he deprived of my society by this conduct? The question is an insult to common sense, considering where Mr. Darnford met me.—Mr. Venables' door was indeed open to me—nay, threats and intreaties were used to induce me to return; but why? Was affection or honour that motive?—I cannot, it is true, dive into the recesses of the human heart—yet I presume to assert, [borne out as I am by a variety of circumstances,] that he was merely influenced by the most rapacious avarice.

"I claim then a divorce, and the liberty of enjoying, free from molestation, the fortune left to me by a relation, who was well aware of the character of the man with whom I had to contend.—I appeal to the justice and humanity of the jury—a body of men, whose private judgment must be allowed to modify laws, that must be unjust, because definite rules can never apply to indefinite circumstances— and I deprecate punishment [upon the man of my choice, freeing him, as I solemnly do, from the charge of seduction].

"I did not put myself into a situation to justify a charge of adultery, till I had, from conviction, shaken off the fetters which bound me to Mr. Venables.—While I lived with him, I defy the voice of calumny to sully what is termed the fair fame of woman.—Neglected by my husband, I never encouraged a lover; and preserved with scrupulous care, what is termed my honour, at the expence of my peace, till he, who should have been its guardian, laid traps to ensnare me. From that moment I believed myself, in the sight of heaven, free—and no power on earth shall force me to renounce my resolution."

The judge, in summing up the evidence, alluded to "the fallacy of letting women plead their feelings, as an excuse for the violation of the marriage-vow. For his part, he had always determined to oppose all innovation, and the new-fangled notions which incroached on the good old rules of conduct. We did not want French principles in public or private life—and, if women were allowed to plead their feelings, as an excuse or palliation of infidelity, it was opening a flood-gate for immorality. What virtuous woman thought of her feelings?—It was her duty to love and obey the man chosen by her parents and relations, who were qualified by their experience to judge better for her, than she could for herself. As to the charges brought against the husband, they were vague, supported by no witnesses, excepting that of imprisonment in a private mad-house. The proofs of an insanity in the family, might render that however a prudent measure; and indeed the conduct of the lady did not appear that of a person of sane mind. Still such a mode of proceeding could not be justified, and might perhaps entitle the lady [in another court] to a sentence of separation from bed and board, during the joint lives of the parties;[1] but he hoped that no Englishman would legalize adultery, by enabling the adulteress to enrich her seducer. Too many restrictions could not be thrown in the way of divorces, if we wished to maintain the sanctity of marriage; and, though they might bear a little hard on a few, very few individuals, it was evidently for the good of the whole."

---

1 Not a divorce, but a legal separation, according to which any financial settlement would depend on the woman living a celibate life.

# Appendix E: On Godwin and Wollstonecraft

[The emphasis in *Adeline Mowbray* on the heroine's adoption of the "new philosophy" associated with William Godwin led to an assumption that the novel represented the relationship of Godwin and Mary Wollstonecraft. This, as the Introduction argues (22-25), is not an adequate or accurate description of the relationship between Adeline Mowbray and Frederic Glenmurray. Nevertheless, the notorious relationship of Godwin and Wollstonecraft, made more notorious by Godwin's attempt to justify and explain it, is an important context for the novel.

A long excerpt from Godwin's memoir of Wollstonecraft, in which he describes their relationship, followed by a review that attacks not just Godwin's book but his character and that of his dead wife, provides some insight into the passionate intensity both of Godwin and of those who opposed him.]

## 1. From William Godwin, *Memoirs of the Author of "A Vindication of the Rights of Woman"* [1st ed.] (1798)[1]

Chapter 9, 1796-1797

I am now led, by the progress of the story, to the last branch of her history, the connection between Mary and myself. And this I shall relate with the same simplicity that has pervaded every other part of my narrative. If there ever were any motives of prudence or delicacy, that could impose a qualification upon the story, they are now over. They could have no relation but to factitious rules of decorum. There are no circumstances of her life, that, in the judgment of honour and reason, could brand her with disgrace.[2] Never did there exist a human being, that needed, with less fear, expose all their actions, and call upon the universe to judge them. An event of the most deplorable sort,[3] has awfully imposed silence upon the gabble of frivolity.

We renewed our acquaintance in January 1796, but with no particular effect, except so far as sympathy in her anguish, added in my mind to

---

1 Godwin revised the *Memoirs* for the 2nd ed., also published in 1798. Variant readings from the second edition are given in the footnotes.

2 The second edition adds: "She had errors; but her errors, which were not those of a sordid mind, were connected and interwoven with the qualities most characteristic of her disposition and genius."

3 Wollstonecraft's death on 10 September 1797.

the respect I had always entertained for her talents. It was in the close of that month that I read her Letters from Norway;[1] and the impression that book[2] produced upon me has been already related.

It was on the fourteenth of April that I first saw her after her excursion into Berkshire. On that day she called upon me in Somers Town, she having, since her return, taken a lodging in Cumming-street, Pentonville, at no great distance from the place of my habitation.[3] From that time our intimacy increased, by regular, but almost imperceptible degrees.[4]

The partiality we conceived for each other, was in that mode, which I have always regarded as the purest and most refined style of love. It grew with equal advances in the mind of each. It would have been impossible for the most minute observer to have said who was before, and who was after. One sex did not take the priority which long-established custom has awarded it, nor the other overstep that delicacy which is so severely imposed. I am not conscious that either party can assume to have been the agent or the patient, the toil-spreader or the prey, in the affair.[5] When, in the course of things, the disclosure came, there was nothing, in a manner, for either party to disclose to the other.

In July 1796 I made an excursion into the county of Norfolk, which occupied nearly the whole of that month.[6] During this period Mary removed, from Cumming-street, Pentonville, to Judd-place West, which may be considered as the extremity of Somers Town. In the former situation, she had occupied a furnished lodging. She had meditated a tour

---

1   *Letters Written During a Short Residence in Sweden, Norway, and Denmark* (1796), rpt. in Mary Wollstonecraft and William Godwin, *A Short Residence in Sweden* and *Memoirs of The Author of "The Rights of Woman,"* ed. Richard Holmes (Harmondsworth: Penguin, 1987).

2   that book] they (2nd ed.).

3   Both Somers Town and Pentonville are in London. The second edition adds: "Her visit, it seems, is to be deemed a deviation from etiquette; but she had through life trampled on those rules which are built on the assumption of the imbecility of her sex; and had trusted to the clearness of her spirit for the direction of her conduct, and to the integrity of her views for the vindication of her character. Nor was she deceived in her trust. If, in the latter part of her life, she departed from the morality of vulgar minds too decidedly to be forgiven by its abettors, be it remembered that, till this offense was given, calumny itself had not dared to utter an insinuation against her."

4   From that time our intimacy ... imperceptible degrees. ] *omitted* 2nd edition.

5   prey, in the affair.] prey. (2nd edition).

6   Godwin had gone to school in Norwich, and retained connections both with that city and with the county of Norfolk: his friendship with Amelia Alderson had developed during an earlier visit there in June 1794.

to Italy or Switzerland, and knew not how soon she should set out with that view. Now however she felt herself reconciled to a longer abode in England, probably without exactly knowing why this change had taken place in her mind. She had a quantity of furniture locked up at a broker's ever since her residence in Store-street, and she now found it adviseable to bring it into use. This circumstance occasioned her present removal.

The temporary separation attendant on my little journey, had its effect on the mind of both parties. It gave a space for the maturing of inclination. I believe that, during this interval, each furnished to the other the principal topic of solitary and daily contemplation. Absence bestows a refined and aërial delicacy upon affection, which it with difficulty acquires in any other way. It[1] seems to resemble the communication of spirits, without the medium, or the impediment, of this earthly frame.

When we met again, we met with new pleasure, and, I may add, with a more decisive preference for each other. It was however three weeks longer, before the sentiment which trembled upon the tongue, burst from the lips of either. There was, as I have already said, no period of throes and resolute explanation attendant on the tale. It was friendship melting into love. Previously to our mutual declaration, each felt half-assured, yet each felt a certain trembling[2] anxiety to have assurance complete.[3]

Mary rested her head upon the shoulder of her lover, hoping[4] to find a heart with which she might safely treasure her world of affection; fearing to commit a mistake, yet, in spite of her melancholy experience, fraught with that generous confidence, which, in a great soul,[5] is never extinguished. I had never loved till now; or, at least, had never nourished a passion to the same growth, or met with an object so consummately worthy.

We did not marry. It is difficult to recommend any thing to indiscriminate adoption, contrary to the established rules and prejudices of mankind; but certainly nothing can be so ridiculous upon the face of it, or so contrary to the genuine march of sentiment, as to require the overflowing of the soul to wait upon a ceremony, and that at which, wherever

---

1  It] The sentiment produced, thus (2nd edition).

2  trembling] *omitted* 2nd edition.

3  The second edition adds: "The sort of connection of which I am here speaking, between parties of whom the intercourse of mind, and not sordid and casual gratification, is the object proposed, is certainly the most important choice in the departments of private life."

4  Mary rested her head upon the shoulder of her lover, hoping] Mary trusted (2nd edition).

5  great soul] liberal spirit (2nd edition).

delicacy and imagination exist, is of all things most sacredly private, to blow a trumpet before it, and to record the moment when it has arrived at its climax.[1]

There were however other reasons why we did not immediately marry. Mary[2] felt an entire conviction of the propriety of her conduct.[3] It would be absurd to suppose that, with a heart withered by desertion, she was not right to give way to the emotions of kindness which our intimacy produced, and to seek for that support in friendship and affection, which could alone give pleasure to her heart, and peace to her meditations. It was only about six months since she had resolutely banished every thought of Mr. Imlay;[4] but it was at least eighteen that he ought to have been banished, and would have been banished, had it not been for her scrupulous pertinacity in determining to leave no measure untried to regain him. Add to this, that the laws of etiquette ordinarily laid down in these cases, are essentially absurd, and that the sentiments of the heart cannot submit to be directed by the rule and square.[5] But Mary[6] had an extreme aversion to be made the topic of vulgar discussion; and, if there be any weakness in this, the dreadful trials through which she had recently passed, may well plead in[7] its excuse. She felt that she had been too much, and too rudely spoken of, in the former instance; and she could not resolve to do any thing that should immediately revive that painful topic.

For myself, it is certain that I had for many years regarded marriage with so well-grounded an apprehension, that, notwithstanding the partiality for Mary that had taken possession of my soul, I should have felt it very difficult, at least in the present stage of our intercourse, to have resolved on such a measure. Thus, partly from similar, and partly from

---

1   We did not marry ... its climax.] We did not immediately marry. Ideas which I am now willing to denominate prejudices, made me by no means eager to conform to a ceremony as an individual, which, coupled with the conditions our laws annex to it, I should undoubtedly, as a citizen, be desirous to abolish. Fuller examination however has since taught me to rank this among those cases, where an accurate morality will direct us to comply with customs and institutions, which, if we had had a voice in their introduction, it would have been incumbent on us to negative. (2nd edition).

2   There were ... marry. Mary] The motives of Mary, were not precisely those which influenced my judgment. She (2nd edition).

3   Second edition adds: "in forming this connection."

4   Gilbert Imlay (1754-1828), an American whom Wollstonecraft met in France in 1793 and with whom she had a daughter, Frances ("Fanny"), born in 1794.

5   It was only about six months ... rule and square.] *omitted* 2nd edition.

6   But Mary] But she (2nd edition).

7   in] *omitted* 2nd edition.

different motives, we felt alike in this, as we did perhaps in every other circumstance that related to our intercourse.[1]

I have nothing further that I find it necessary to record, till the commencement of April 1797. We then judged it proper to declare our marriage, which had taken place a little before. The principal motive for complying with this ceremony, was the circumstance of Mary's being in a state of pregnancy. She was unwilling, and perhaps with reason, to incur that exclusion from the society of many valuable and excellent individuals, which custom awards in cases of this sort. I should have felt an extreme repugnance to the having caused her such an inconvenience. And, after the experiment of seven months of as intimate an intercourse as our respective modes of living would admit, there was certainly less hazard to either, in the subjecting ourselves to those consequences which the laws of England annex to the relations of husband and wife. On the sixth of April we entered into possession of a house, which had been taken by us in concert.

In this place I have a very curious circumstance to notice, which I am happy to have occasion to mention, as it tends to expose certain regulations of polished society, of which the absurdity vies with the odiousness. Mary had long possessed the advantage of an acquaintance with many persons of genius, and with others whom the effects of an intercourse with elegant society, combined with a certain portion of information and good sense, sufficed to render amusing companions. She had lately extended the circle of her acquaintance in this respect; and her mind, trembling between the opposite impressions of past anguish and renovating tranquillity, found ease in this species of recreation. Wherever Mary appeared, admiration attended upon[2] her. She had always displayed talents for conversation; but maturity of understanding, her travels, her long residence in France,[3] the discipline of affliction, and the smiling, new-born peace which awaked a corresponding smile in her animated countenance, inexpressibly increased them. The way in which the story of Mr. Imlay was treated in these polite circles, was probably the result of the partiality she excited. These elegant personages were divided between their cautious adherence to forms, and the desire to seek their own gratification. Mary made no secret of the nature of her connection with Mr. Imlay; and in one instance, I well know, she put herself to the trouble of explaining it to a person totally indifferent to her, because he never failed to publish every thing he knew, and, she was sure, would repeat her explanation to his numerous acquaintance. She was of too proud and generous a spirit to stoop to hypocrisy. These persons

---

1   For myself ... intercourse. ] *omitted* 2nd edition.
2   upon] *omitted* 2nd edition.
3   From 1792-94.

however, in spite of all that could be said, persisted in shutting their eyes, and pretending they took her for a married woman.

Observe the consequence of this! While she was, and constantly professed to be, an unmarried mother; she was fit society for the squeamish and the formal. The moment she acknowledged herself a wife, and that by a marriage perhaps unexceptionable,[1] the case was altered. Mary and myself, ignorant as we were of these elevated refinements, supposed that our marriage would place her upon a surer footing in the calendar of polished society, than ever. But it forced these people to see the truth, and to confess their belief of what they had carefully been told; and this they could not forgive. Be it remarked, that the date of our marriage had nothing to do with this, that question being never once mentioned during this period. Mary indeed had, till now, retained the name of Imlay which had first been assumed from necessity in France; but its being retained thus long, was purely from the aukwardness that attends the introduction of a change, and not from an apprehension of consequences of this sort. Her scrupulous explicitness as to the nature of her situation, surely sufficed to make the name she bore perfectly immaterial.

It is impossible to relate the particulars of such a story, but in the language of contempt and ridicule. A serious reflection however upon the whole, ought to awaken emotions of a different sort. Mary retained the most numerous portion of her acquaintance, and the majority of those whom she principally valued. It was only the supporters and the subjects of the unprincipled manners of a court, that she lost. This however is immaterial. The tendency of the proceeding, strictly considered, and uniformly acted upon, would have been to proscribe her from all valuable society. And who was the person proscribed? The firmest champion, and, as I strongly suspect, the greatest ornament her sex ever had to boast! A woman, with sentiments as pure, as refined, and as delicate, as ever inhabited a human heart! It is fit that such persons should stand by, that we may have room enough for the dull and insolent dictators, the gamblers and demireps[2] of polished society!

Two of the persons, the loss of whose acquaintance Mary principally regretted upon this occasion, were Mrs. Inchbald and Mrs. Siddons.[3] Their acquaintance, it is perhaps fair to observe, is to be ranked among her recent acquisitions. Mrs. Siddons, I am sure, regretted the necessity, which she conceived to be imposed on her by the peculiarity of her situation, to

---

1   and that by a marriage perhaps unexceptionable,] *omitted* 2nd edition.
2   Women of doubtful reputation ("half reputable").
3   Elizabeth Inchbald (1753-1821), playwright, novelist, and actress; and Sarah Siddons (1755-1831), the most famous actress of her day.

conform to the rules I have described. She is endowed with that rich and generous sensibility, which should best enable its possessor completely to feel the merits of her deceased friend. She very truly observes, in a letter now before me, that the Travels in Norway were read by no one, who was in possession of "more reciprocity of feeling, or more deeply impressed with admiration of the writer's extraordinary powers."

Mary felt a transitory pang, when the conviction reached her of so unexpected a circumstance, that was rather exquisite. But she disdained to sink under the injustice (as this ultimately was)[1] of the supercilious and the foolish, and presently shook off the impression of the first surprize. That once subsided, I well know that the event was thought of, with no emotions, but those of superiority to the injustice she sustained; and was not of force enough, to diminish a happiness, which seemed hourly to become more vigorous and firm.

I think I may venture to say, that no two persons ever found in each other's society, a satisfaction more pure and refined. What it was in itself, can now only be known, in its full extent, to the survivor. But, I believe, the serenity of her countenance, the increasing sweetness of her manners, and that consciousness of enjoyment that seemed ambitious that every one she saw should be happy as well as herself, were matters of general observation to all her acquaintance. She had always possessed, in an unparalleled degree, the art of communicating happiness, and she was now in the constant and unlimited[2] exercise of it. She seemed to have attained that situation, which her disposition and character imperiously demanded, but which she had never before attained; and her understanding and her heart felt the benefit of it.

While we lived as near neighbours only, and before our last removal, her mind had attained considerable tranquillity, and was visited but seldom with[3] those emotions of anguish, which had been but too familiar to her. But the improvement in this respect, which accrued upon our removal and establishment, was extremely obvious. She was a worshipper of domestic life. She loved to observe the growth of affection between me and her daughter, then three years of age, as well as my anxiety respecting the child not yet born. Pregnancy itself, unequal as the decree of nature seems to be in this respect, is the source of a thousand endearments. No one knew better than Mary how to extract sentiments of exquisite delight, from trifles, which a suspicious and formal wisdom would scarcely deign to remark. A little ride into the country with myself and the child, has

---

1   (as this ultimately was)] (as this, when traced ... will be found to be) (2nd edition).
2   and unlimited] *omitted* 2nd edition.
3   with] by (2nd edition).

sometimes produced a sort of[1] opening of the heart, a general expression of confidence and affectionate soul, a sort of infantile, yet dignified endearment, which those who have felt may understand, but which I should in vain attempt to pourtray.

In addition to our domestic pleasures, I was fortunate enough to introduce her to some of my acquaintance of both sexes, to whom she attached herself with all the ardour of approbation and friendship.

Ours was not an idle happiness, a paradise of selfish and transitory pleasures. It is perhaps scarcely necessary to mention, that, influenced by the ideas I had long entertained upon the subject of cohabitation,[2] I engaged an apartment, about twenty doors from our house in the Polygon, Somers Town, which I designed for the purpose of my study and literary occupations. Trifles however will be interesting to some readers, when they relate to the last period of the life of such a person as Mary. I will add therefore, that we were both of us of opinion, that it was possible for two persons to be too uniformly in each other's society. Influenced by that opinion, it was my practice to repair to the apartment I have mentioned as soon as I rose, and frequently not to make my appearance in the Polygon, till the hour of dinner. We agreed in condemning the notion, prevalent in many situations in life, that a man and his wife cannot visit in mixed society, but in company with each other; and we rather sought occasions of deviating from, than of complying with, this rule. By these means, though, for the most part, we spent the latter half of each day in one another's society, yet we were in no danger of satiety. We seemed to combine, in a considerable degree, the novelty and lively sensation of a visit, with the more delicious and heart-felt pleasures of domestic life.

Whatever may be thought, in other respects, of the plan we laid down to ourselves, we probably derived a real advantage from it, as to the constancy and uninterruptedness of our literary pursuits. Mary had a variety of projects of this sort, for the exercise of her talents, and the benefit of society; and, if she had lived, I believe the world would have had very[3] little reason to complain of any remission of her industry. One of her projects, which has been already mentioned, was of a series of Letters on the Management of Infants. Though she had been for some time digesting her ideas[4] on this subject with a view to the press, I have found comparatively nothing that she had committed to paper respecting it. Another project, of longer standing, was of a series of books for the instruction of

---

1    a sort of] an (2nd edition).
2    See Appendix D3.
3    very] *omitted* 2nd edition.
4    ideas] views (2nd edition).

children. A fragment she left in execution of this project, is inserted in her Posthumous Works.[1]

But the principal work, in which she was engaged for more than twelve months before her decease, was a novel, entitled, The Wrongs of Woman.[2] I shall not stop here to explain the nature of the work, as so much of it as was already written, is now given to the public. I shall only observe that, impressed, as she could not fail to be, with the consciousness of her talents, she was desirous, in this instance, that they should effect what they were capable of effecting. She was sensible how arduous a task it is to produce a truly excellent novel; and she roused her faculties to grapple with it. All her other works were produced with a rapidity, that did not give her powers time fully to expand. But this was written slowly and with mature consideration. She began it in several forms, which she successively rejected, after they were considerably advanced. She wrote many parts of the work again and again, and, when she had finished[3] what she intended for the first part, she felt herself more urgently stimulated to revise and improve what she had written, than to proceed, with constancy of application, in the parts that were to follow.

## 2. From Robert Bisset, et al., *The Historical, Biographical, Literary, and Scientific Magazine.... for ... 1799*[4]

... [B]y no means the ablest, yet by far the most singular biography of 1798 was the philosopher Godwin's History of the Propensities, Amours, and Adventures of his own Wife.[5] Speculative men have often, in theory, supported principles inconsistent with the common sense of mankind, and the well-being of society; without reducing their speculations to practice. A reader of the Political Justice[6] must have reprobated doctrines that tended, if admitted, to destroy our respect for marriage, property, promises; our conviction of the immortality of the soul; the ties of natural affection, gratitude, friendship; every cement of civil and social duty; to overturn monarchy, laws, government, and every political institution. But it might have been supposed that the author of the Political Justice merely

---

1   See *Posthumous Works* (1798) 4: 53-57.
2   *The Wrongs of Woman, or Maria*, published in *Posthumous Works* (1798), vols. 1 and 2. See Appendix D4.
3   finished] gone through (2nd edition).
4   The complete title is *The Historical, Biographical, Literary, and Scientific Magazine. The History of Literature and Science for the Year 1799*, vol. 1 (London: G. Cawthorn, n.d.).
5   William Godwin's *Memoirs of the Author of "A Vindication of the Rights of Woman"* (1798): see previous excerpt (Appendix E1).
6   Godwin's *Enquiry Concerning Political Justice* (1793, 3rd ed. 1798).

advanced paradoxes, for the sake of displaying ingenuity; that he himself was convinced, as much as any other, endowed with reason, must be, of the total incompatibility of such *ravings* with any thing that could actually exist. The present publication proves that this supposition would have been wrong, and shews the effect of such theories when reduced to practice. The author sets out with saying, "that there are not many individuals with whose character the public welfare and improvement are more intimately connected than the author of a Vindication of the Rights of Woman."[1] Mr. Godwin, indeed, considers her as a *model* for imitation! and her life as *peculiarly* useful, on account of the *precept and example* it affords. We coincide with him in his opinion of the *utility* of a life of Miss Wollstonecraft, though for a very different reason. If it does not teach what it is wise to pursue, it manifests what it is wise to avoid. It illustrates both the sentiments and conduct resulting from such principles as those of Miss Wollstonecraft and Mr. Godwin. As her biographer holds up her opinions and conduct to adoption and imitation, we must allow him great credit for his candour in explaining, with the most exact precision, what the opinions and conduct were.... Perhaps those who were acquainted with Miss Wollstonecraft might have very little doubt on the subject before: for her public notoriety she was indebted to her husband: as Fielding observes, describing a female friend of Tom Jones, Ensign Northerton, Mrs. Fitzpatrick, and others, *who* this Mrs. Waters was, the reader pretty well knows; WHAT she was, he can have no manner of doubt.[2]

... The opinions, sentiments, and consequent conduct of this pair of votaries of the new philosophy [Wollstonecraft and Godwin] deserve repeated quotation.[3] "*We did not marry. It is difficult to recommend any thing to indiscriminate adoption, contrary to the established rules and prejudices of mankind; but certainly nothing can be so ridiculous upon the face of it, or so contrary to the genuine march of sentiments, as to require the overflowing of the soul to wait upon a ceremony; and that which, wherever delicacy and imagination exist, is of all things most sacredly private, to blow a trumpet before it, and to record the moment when it arrived at its climax.*"[4]

---

1  Godwin, Preface to *Memoirs*, ed. Richard Holmes, 204.

2  Henry Fielding, *The History of Tom Jones, a Foundling*, ed. Thomas Keymer and Alice Wakely, introd. Thomas Keymer (Harmondsworth; Penguin, 2005), 809.

3  "It has been quoted in the Anti-Jacobin of August, and the British Critic of September, both which criticisms we earnestly recommend to the perusal of our readers, as both contain very clear elucidations of the consequences to individuals and to society from the philosophy of Godwin" (RB).

4  Quoted from Chapter 9 of Godwin's *Memoirs of the Author of "A Vindication of the Rights of Woman"*; see above, Appendix E1 and *Memoirs*, ed. Richard Holmes, 258.

This passage not only illustrates, but fully displays the *morality* of the Godwin system. We have next its *religious doctrines*. Mr. Godwin by no means wants dexterity, and with much art intermingles doctrinal reflections with narrative.... As she advanced in philosophy, her attendance on public worship became less and less constant, and was soon wholly discontinued. On this the philosopher makes the following remark, equally wise and pious: "*I believe it may be admitted as a maxim, that no person of a well-furnished mind, that has shaken off the implicit subjection of youth, and is not the zealous partisan of a sect, can bring himself to conform to the public and regular routine of sermons and prayers.*"[1]

After seven months intercourse between this moral and religious lady, and a gentleman no less moral and religious than herself; an intercourse of which the philosopher gives a very circumstantial account, he, contrary to the declarations of the Political Justice, agreed to marry his mistress. We think here a reviewer, whom we much respect, the British Critic, is too hasty in charging the philosopher with inconsistency in this marriage.[2] It is true he had declared, as quoted by that reviewer, so long as he should seek to engross one woman to himself, and to prohibit his neighbour from *proving* his *superior desert* and *reaping the fruits of it*, he would be guilty of the *most odious of all monopolies.*[3]

We have too good an opinion of Mr. Godwin's discernment to suppose he ever entertained an idea of a *monopoly* in a subject such as he has described.

About three months after their marriage, Mrs. Godwin died in childbed, a circumstance to be the more lamented, as her wise husband *intreated her to recover*; and she, equally wise, had *promised* not to die![4]

Such is the extraordinary narrative published by the philosopher concerning his own wife! *Such*, according to her panegyrist, *in morals and religion, was the pattern he holds up to imitation!* Such is the species of sentiment and conduct which Wollstonecraft and Godwin inculcate! Parents may, in this exhibition, see *what sort of sons and daughters* would be formed for them by the philosophy of this pair, if adopted; and, as Godwin desires, made the rule of their lives. Statesmen may observe its tendency to produce obedience to the laws and benefit to the community; philosophers, the conduciveness of impiety, concubinage, and irreligion to the general

---

1  Godwin, *Memoirs*, ed. Richard Holmes, 215-16.
2  See the review of Godwin's *Memoirs* in the *British Critic* 12 (1798): 228-33.
3  The *British Critic* reviewer is alluding to *Enquiry Concerning Political Justice*. See the 3rd edition (1798), Appendix to Book 8, chap. 8; cf. Appendix D3, above.
4  See *British Critic* 12 (1798): 233. The reviewer quotes from *Memoirs*, ed. Richard Holmes, 266, 268.

*good* of mankind! ... The great point at which he [Godwin] aims [in *Political Justice*], as the practical inference to be drawn from the whole of his reasonings, is the EQUALIZATION of PROPERTY; which reform, however, he readily admits, is not to be effected until men shall have made much greater progress in intelligence.[1] Under this general head may be comprehended the abolition of marriage, and every other positive institution. It appears, however, from Political Justice, that he imitates the economists in also considering his theory of government and morals as applicable to this perfect state of his own creation, and not to the present imperfect state of society. So far as his system is not intended or calculated for present use, or for use at any future period previous to the arrival of the philosophical millennium, it is mere waste of time, and perhaps not much more absurd and culpable than a man would be, who, adopting the mythology of the Arabian Nights Entertainment, should write a treatise on the best mode of decorating and furnishing a house, to be built by Alladin's Genie. The Political Justice, as referable to a perfect state, is neither more nor less than a piece of pseudo-philosophical castle-building. But should a man, depending upon the performances of this perfect Genie, to make way for that ideal architecture, purpose to pull down our palaces, our churches, all our public and private edifices, we should consider the proposal not merely as insane, but mischievous, and should resist it to the utmost of our power.

In the Life of Mary, Godwin appears the practiser of those principles which, he had before said, were only applicable to a state of perfection, and proposes concubinage as a substitute for marriage; holds up as an example a character, which detested all existing establishments and institution. As long as Mr. Godwin confined himself to mere theory, and did not attempt to reduce his notions to practice, he might excite regret for misemployed ingenuity; but now that he has publicly avowed himself the practical advocate of concubinage and the abuser of marriage; has held up to imitation a woman whose conduct was habitually, and by principle, at variance with virtue and religion; who has made that deviation from piety and morality the chief theme of his praise, we think his doctrines and lessons deserving of the reprobation of every one who regards the happiness of individuals and of society....

---

1  See *Enquiry Concerning Political Justice*, 3rd ed. (1798), Book 8, Chapter 10 ("Reflections").

# Appendix F: On Mothers and Daughters

[The two poems that follow will speak for themselves as expressions outside the novel of Opie's interest in the relationships of mothers and daughters. The first has evident similarities with the plot of *Adeline Mowbray*. The second is more obviously autobiographical, referring to Opie's mother's childhood in India, her arrival in England, her black nurse Savannah, and the circumstances of her death. The tone of grief, loss, piety, and remorse in both poems may give the reader insight into how Opie understood Adeline's fate in the novel.]

## 1. From Amelia Opie, *Poems by Mrs. Opie* (1802)[1]

*The Dying Daughter to Her Mother*

Mother! when these unsteady lines
Thy long averted eyes shall see,
This hand that writes, this heart that pines,
Will cold, quite cold, and tranquil be.

That guilty child so long disowned
Can then, blest thought! no more offend;
And, shouldst thou deem my crimes atoned,
O deign my orphan to befriend: ...

That orphan, who with trembling hand
To thee will give my dying prayer; ...
Canst thou my dying prayer withstand,
And from my child withhold thy care?

O raise the veil which hides her cheek,
Nor start her mother's face to see,
But let her look thy love bespeak, ...
For once that face was dear to thee.

Gaze on, ... and thou'lt perchance forget
The long, the mournful lapse of years,
Thy couch with tears of anguish wet,
And e'en the guilt which caused those tears.

---

1   The text is from *Poems by Mrs. Opie* (London: T.N. Longman and O. Rees), 1802.

And in my pure and artless child
Thou'lt think her mother meets thy view;
Such as she was when life first smiled,
And guilt by name alone she knew.

Ah! then I see thee o'er her charms
A look of fond affection cast;
I see thee clasp her in thine arms,
And in the present lose the past.

But soon the dear illusion flies;
The sad reality returns;
My crimes again to memory rise,
And, ah! in vain my orphan mourns:

Till suddenly some keen remorse,
Some deep regret, her claims shall aid,
For wrath that held too long its course,
For words of peace too long delayed.

For pardon (most, alas! denied
When pardon might have snatched from shame)
And kindness, hadst thou kindness tried,
Had checked my guilt, and saved my fame.

And then thou'lt wish, as I do now,
Thy hand my humble bed had smoothed,
Wiped the chill moisture off my brow,
And all the wants of sickness soothed.

For, oh! the means to sooth my pain
My poverty has still denied;
And thou wilt wish, ah! wish in vain,
Thy riches had those means supplied.

Thou'lt wish, with keen repentance wrung,
I'd closed my eyes, upon thy breast
Expiring, while thy faltering tongue
Pardon in kindest tones expressed.

O sounds which I must never hear!
Through years of woe my fond desire!

O Mother, spite of all most dear!
Must I unblest by thee expire?

Thy love alone I call to mind,
And all thy past disdain forget, ...
Each keen reproach, each frown unkind,
That crushed my hopes when last we met.

But when I saw that angry brow,
Both health and youth were still my own:
O mother! couldst thou see me now,
Thou wouldst not have the heart to frown.

But see! my orphan's cheek displays
Both youth, and health's carnation dies,
Such as on mine in happier days
So fondly charmed thy partial eyes.

Grief o'er her bloom a veil now draws,
Grief her loved parent's pangs to see;
And when thou think'st upon the cause,
That paleness will have charms for thee:

And thou wilt fondly press that cheek,
Bid happiness its bloom restore,
And thus in tenderest accents speak,
"Sweet orphan, thou shalt mourn no more."

But wilt thou thus indulgent be?
O! am I not by hope beguiled?
The long long anger shown to me,
Say, will it not pursue my child?

And must she suffer for my crime?
Ah! no;.... forbid it gracious Heaven!
And grant, O grant! In thy good time,
That she be loved, and I forgiven.

## 2. From *Lays for the Dead* (1834)[1]

*In Memory of My Mother*

An orphan'd babe, from India's plain
She came, a faithful slave her guide!
Then, after years of patient pain,
That tender wife and mother *died*.
Where gothic windows dimly throw
O'er the long aisles a dubious day,
Within the time-worn vaults below,
Her relics join their kindred clay—
And I, in long departed days,
Those dear, though solemn, precincts sought,
When evening shed her parting rays,
And twilight lengthening shadows brought—
There, long I knelt beside the stone
Which veils thy clay, lamented shade!
While memory, years for ever gone,
And all the distant past portray'd!

I saw thy glance of tender love!
Thy cheek of suffering's sickly hue!
Thine eye, where gentle sweetness strove
To look the ease it rarely knew.
I heard thee speak in accents kind,
And promptly praise, or firmly chide;
Again admir'd that vigorous mind
Of power to charm, reprove, and guide.
Hark! clearer still thy voice I hear!
Again reproof, in accents mild,
Seems whispering in my conscious ear,
And pains, yet sooths, thy kneeling child!
Then, while my eyes I weeping raise,
Again thy shadowy form appears;
I see the smile of other days,
The frown that melted soon in tears!
Again I'm exiled from thy sight
Alone my rebel will to mourn;

---

1   The text is from *Lays for the Dead* (London: Longman, Rees, Orme, Brown, Green, and Longman, 1834).

Again I feel the dear delight
When told I may to thee return!

But oh! too soon the vision fled,
With all of grief, and joy it brought:
And as I slowly left the dead,
And gayer scenes still musing sought,
Oh! how I mourn'd my heedless youth
Thy watchful care repaid so ill—
Yet joy'd to think some words of truth
Sank in my soul, and teach me still:
Like lamps along life's fearful way
To me at times those truths have shone;
And oft, when snares around me lay,
That light has made that danger known.
Then, how thy grateful child has blest
Each wise reproof thy accents bore!
And now she longs, in worlds of rest
To dwell with thee for evermore!

# Appendix G: On Slavery and Jamaica

[In order to understand Berrendale's business dealings in Jamaica and Savanna's recapture into slavery, it is necessary to understand that the slave-trade was abolished in the British colonies only in 1807, two years after *Adeline Mowbray* was published, and that slavery itself was not abolished in the British Empire until 1833. The Mansfield decision of 1772 meant that Savanna could not be enslaved while on English soil; but, as a former slave, she could be taken back into slavery when she went to Jamaica. Knowing this, her self-sacrificial behaviour in going to nurse William during his illness and in standing up to Berrendale over his treatment of Adeline is all the more admirable.

The second excerpt below is from an account of Jamaica published in 1823, after the abolition of the slave-trade but before emancipation. Stewart's book is heavily indebted to Bryan Edwards, *History, Civil and Commercial, of the British Colonies in the West Indies* (1793): its attitudes to race, gender, and culture are typical of those held even by some liberal thinkers at the time.]

## 1. From the Mansfield Decision, 22 June 1772[1]

On the part of Sommersett, the case which we gave notice should be decided this day, the Court now proceeds to give its opinion. I shall recite the return to the writ of Habeas Corpus, as the ground of our determination; omitting only words of form. The captain of the ship on board of which the negro was taken, makes his return to the writ in terms signifying that there have been, and still are, slaves to a great number in Africa; and that the trade in them is authorized by the laws and opinions of Virginia and

---

1 From Thomas B[ayly] H[owell], *A Complete Collection of State Trials and Proceedings for High Treason and Other Crimes and Misdemeanors, from the Earliest Period to the Present Time* (London: Longman et al., 1814), vol. 20 (1771-77), columns 80-82. James Somerset (or Sommersett), a black slave, was brought from America to England, where he escaped from his master. On 26 November 1771 he was recaptured and imprisoned in chains on a ship bound for Jamaica. A writ of habeas corpus ("you may have the body"—a demand that Somerset be brought before the court) was granted to his supporters (including the abolitionist Granville Sharp) by William Murray, first Earl of Mansfield (1705–93), the Lord Chief Justice. Somerset's lawyers argued in their "return" or response to the writ that although slavery was tolerated in the colonies, there was no such institution in England. Lord Mansfield came back with this ruling, which granted Somerset his freedom.

Jamaica; that they are goods and chattels; and, as such, saleable and sold. That James Sommersett is a negro of Africa, and long before the return of the king's writ was brought to be sold, and was sold to Charles Steuart, esq. then in Jamaica, and has not been manumitted since; that Mr. Steuart, having occasion to transact business, came over hither, with an intention to return; and brought Sommersett to attend and abide with him, and to carry him back as soon as the business should be transacted. That such intention has been, and still continues; and that the negro did remain till the time of his departure in the service of his master Mr. Steuart, and quitted it without his consent; and thereupon, before the return of the king's writ, the said Charles Steuart did commit the slave on board the Anne and Mary, to safe custody, to be kept till he should set sail, and then to be taken with him to Jamaica, and there sold as a slave.... The only question before us is, whether the cause on the return is sufficient? If it is, the negro must be remanded; if it is not, he must be discharged. Accordingly, the return states, that the slave departed and refused to serve; whereupon he was kept, to be sold abroad. So high an act of dominion must be recognized by the law of the country where it is used. The power of a master over his slave has been extremely different, in different countries. The state of slavery is of such a nature, that it is incapable of being introduced on any reasons, moral or political, but only by positive law, which preserves its force long after the reasons, occasion, and time itself from whence it was created, is erased from memory. It is so odious, that nothing can be suffered to support it, but positive law. Whatever inconveniences, therefore, may follow from the decision, I cannot say this case is allowed or approved by the law of England; and therefore the black must be discharged.

## 2. From J. Stewart, *A View of the Past and Present State of the Island of Jamaica* (1823)[1]

From Chapter 20, "The People of Colour—Their Character, Manners, and Amusements—Their Political Situation"

Between the whites and the blacks, in the West Indies, a numerous race has sprung up, which goes by the general appellation of *people of colour.* These are subdivided into mulattoes, the offspring of a white and a black; samboes, the offspring of a black and a mulatto; quadroons, the offspring of a white and a mulatto; and mestees, the offspring of a white and a quad-

---

1   *A View of the Past and Present State of the Island of Jamaica; with Remarks on the Moral and Physical Condition of the Slaves, and on the Abolition of Slavery in the Colonies* (London: Oliver and Boyd, 1823. Rpt. New York: Negro Universities P, 1969).

roon. Below this last-mentioned grade the distinction of colour is hardly perceptible; and those who are thus far removed from the original negro stock are considered in law as whites, on obtaining their manumission if born slaves, and competent of course to enjoy every privilege as such. Between these particular *castes* an endless variety of non-descript shades exist, descending from the deep jet to the faintest tinge of the olive, by gradations which it would be difficult to trace and designate.

The people of colour may be supposed to possess the mingled natures of the two original stocks from whence they spring; and the more or less they are removed from one or the other, they seem to be imbued in proportion with their particular qualities. The sambo differs little in manners, habits, &c. from the negro; while the mestee and his descendants approximate as near in these particulars to the white as it is possible for a mingled race to do; and when polished by a genteel education, that little distinction ceases to exist.

... A few men of colour have been so far elevated above their *caste* by the advantages of fortune and a liberal education, as to be received into white society; but it very rarely happens that a brown female is so admitted, whatever her merit or acquired advantages. If she has one drop of African blood in her veins, however remotely derived, it operates as effectually to shut her out from the society of the white ladies, as a moral stain in her character would do in European society.

# Appendix H: On Religion

[Opie's friend John Joseph Gurney of Norwich was a cousin of Joseph Gurney Bevan (1753–1814), who wrote this account of the religious beliefs of the Society of Friends, also known as Quakers. After a lengthy correspondence with Gurney and other Quaker friends, Opie eventually converted to the Quakers in 1825. The excerpt that follows demonstrates the Christian faith of the Society—but it also emphasizes certain characteristic Quaker beliefs and practices: plain dress, plain speech, belief that women as well as men could be called to preach, pacifism, prohibition of oaths, and a belief in the equality of all human beings.]

## 1. From Joseph Gurney Bevan, *A Refutation of Some of the More Modern Misrepresentations of the Society of Friends, Commonly Called Quakers* (1800)[1]

From Chapter 2

We agree with other professors of the Christian name, in the belief of one eternal God, the Creator and Preserver of the universe; and in Jesus Christ his Son, the Messiah, and Mediator of the new covenant.[2]

... We reverence those most excellent precepts which are recorded in Scripture to have been delivered by our great Lord, and we firmly believe that they are practicable, and binding on every Christian; and that in the life to come, every man will be rewarded according to his works.[3] And further it is our belief, that, in order to enable mankind to put in practice these sacred precepts, many of which are contradictory to the unregenerate will of man,[4] every man coming into the world, is endued with a measure of the light, grace, or good Spirit of Christ; by which, as it is attended to, he is enabled to distinguish good from evil, and to correct the disorderly passions and corrupt propensities of his nature, which mere reason is altogether insufficient to overcome. For all that belongs to man is fallible, and within the reach of temptation; but this Divine grace, which comes by him who hath overcome the world,[5] is, to those who humbly and sincerely seek it, an all-sufficient and present help in time of need....

---

1   The text is from *A Refutation of Some of the More Modern Misrepresentations of the Society of Friends, Commonly Called Quakers ... also, ... A Summary of the History, Doctrine and Discipline of Friends* (London: William Phillips, 1800).
2   "Heb. xii. 24." (JGB)
3   "Mat. xvi. 27." (JGB)
4   "John i. 9." (JGB)
5   "Ibid. xvi. 33." (JGB)

... As we dare not encourage any ministry, but that which we believe to spring from the influence of the Holy Spirit, so neither dare we attempt to restrain this influence to persons of any condition in life, or to the male sex alone; but, as male and female are one in Christ, we allow such of the female sex as we believe to be endued with a right qualification for the ministry, to exercise their gifts for the general edification of the church: and this liberty we esteem a peculiar mark of the gospel dispensation, as foretold by the prophet Joel,[1] and noticed by the apostle Peter.[2]

... There are not many of our tenets more generally known than our testimony against Oaths, and against War. With respect to the former of these, we abide literally by Christ's positive injunction, delivered in his sermon on the mount, "Swear not at all."[3] From the same sacred collection of the most excellent precepts of moral and religious duty, from the example of our Lord himself,[4] and from the correspondent convictions of his Spirit in our hearts, we are confirmed in the belief that wars and fightings are, in their origin and effects, utterly repugnant to the gospel; which still breathes peace and good-will to men. We also are clearly of the judgment, that if the benevolence of the Gospel were generally prevalent in the minds of men, it would effectually prevent them from oppressing, much more enslaving, their brethren (of whatever colour or complexion), for whom, as for themselves, Christ died; and would even influence their conduct in their treatment of the brute creation: which would no longer groan, the victims of their avarice, or of their false ideas of pleasure.

... It is well known that the society, from its first appearance, has disused those names of the months and days, which having been given in honour of the heroes or false gods of the heathen, originated in their flattery or superstition; and the custom of speaking to a single person in the plural number, as having arisen also from motives of adulation. Compliments, superfluity of apparel and furniture, outward shews of rejoicing and mourning, and the observation of days and times, we esteem to be incompatible with the simplicity and sincerity of a Christian life; and public diversions, gaming, and other vain amusements of the world, we cannot but condemn. They are a waste of that time which is given us for nobler purposes; and divert the attention of the mind from the sober duties of life, and from the reproofs of instruction, by which we are guided to an everlasting inheritance.

---

1   "Joel ii. 28, 29." (JGB)
2   "Acts ii. 16, 17." (JGB)
3   "Matt. v. 34." (JGB)
4   "Mat. v. 39, 44, &c. ch. xxvi. 52. 53. Luke xxii. 51. John xviii. 11." (JGB)

# Select Bibliography

Eighteenth-century editions in this bibliography are available through Eighteenth-Century Collections Online. Gale Group. <http://galenet.galegroup.com.ezproxy.lib.ucalgary.ca/servlet/ECCO>

## Selected Works by Amelia Alderson Opie

Opie, Amelia Alderson. *Adeline Mowbray.* Introd. Jeanette Winterson. London: Pandora, 1986.

——. *Adeline Mowbray, or The Mother and Daughter; A Tale.* Introd. Gina Luria. 3 vols. New York: Garland, 1974 (vol. 1, 1805; vol. 2, 1810; vol. 3, 1810).

——. *Adeline Mowbray, or The Mother and Daughter; A Tale.* Ed. Shelley King and John B. Pierce. Oxford: Oxford UP, 1999.

——. *Adeline Mowbray, or The Mother and Daughter; A Tale.* 1805. New York: Woodstock Books, 1995. [Facsimile of Bodleian Library copy.]

——. *Illustrations of Lying, in All Its Branches.* 2 vols. London: Longman, Hurst, Rees, Orme, Brown, and Green, 1825.

——. *Lays for the Dead.* London: Longman, Rees, Orme, Brown, Green, and Longman, 1834.

——. *Poems by Mrs. Opie.* London: T.N. Longman and O. Rees, 1802.

——. *Temper, or Domestic Scenes: a Tale,* 3 vols. London: Longman, Hurst, Rees, Orme, and Brown, 1812.

——. *The Black Man's Lament; or, How to Make Sugar.* London: Harvey and Darton, 1826.

——. *The Father and Daughter* with *Dangers of Coquetry.* Ed. Shelley King and John B. Pierce. Peterborough: Broadview P, 2003.

——. "The Quaker, and the Young Man of the World." *New Tales,* 1818. Rpt. *Adeline Mowbray. A New and Illustrated Edition.* London: Longman, 1844.

——. *The Warrior's Return, and Other Poems.* London: Longman, Hurst, Rees, and Orme, 1808.

## Reviews of *Adeline Mowbray*

*Critical Review,* 3rd series, 4 (1805): 219-21.
*Annual Review* 4 (1805): 653.
*Literary Journal* 5 (1805): 171-75.
*Monthly Review* ns 51 (1806): 320-21.
*European Magazine* 47 (1805):129-30.

## Contextual Works and Works by Opie's Contemporaries

*An Act for the Better Preventing of Clandestine Marriages* [1753]. Anno *Regni Georgii II. ... At the Parliament begun and holden at Westminster* ... [1747–1753]. London: Thomas Baskett, 1755. 471–78.

Anon. *Letters on Love, Marriage, and Adultery, Addressed to the Right Honorable The Earl of Exeter.* London: Ridgway, 1789.

Barbauld, Anna Laetitia. *Poems.* London: Joseph Johnson, 1773.

Barry, Edward. *Theological, Philosophical, and Moral Essays.* London: C. Wittingham, 1799.

Bevan, Joseph Gurney. *A Refutation of Some of the More Modern Misrepresentations of the Society of Friends, Commonly Called Quakers ... also, ... A Summary of the History, Doctrine and Discipline of Friends.* London: William Phillips, 1800.

Bisset, Robert, et al. *The Historical, Biographical, Literary, and Scientific Magazine. The History of Literature and Science for the Year 1799.* London: G. Cawthorn, n.d. 1: 27–35.

Buchan, William. *Domestic Medicine: or, A Treatise on the Prevention and Cure of Diseases....* 17th ed. London: A. Strahan, T. Cadell, Jun., and W. Davies, 1800.

Godwin, William. *Enquiry Concerning Political Justice and Its Influence on Morals and Happiness.* 3rd ed. [1798]. Ed. F.E.L. Priestley. 3 vols. Toronto: U of Toronto P, 1946.

———. *Fleetwood: or, The New Man of Feeling.* Ed. Gary Handwerk and A.A. Markley. Peterborough: Broadview P, 2001.

———. *Memoirs of the Author of "A Vindication of the Rights of Woman."* 1798. Rpt. Mary Wollstonecraft and William Godwin. *A Short Residence in Sweden, Norway and Denmark* and *Memoirs of the Author of "The Rights of Woman."* Ed. Richard Holmes. London: Penguin, 1987.

———. *Things As They Are, or, The Adventures of Caleb Williams.* Ed. Gary Handwerk and A.A. Markley. Peterborough: Broadview P, 2000.

Hayley, William. *The Triumphs of Temper, A Poem. In Six Cantos.* 10th ed. London: T. Cadell, Jun., and W. Davies, 1799.

Hays, Mary. *Memoirs of Emma Courtney.* Ed. Marilyn L. Brooks. Peterborough: Broadview P, 2000.

———. *The Victim of Prejudice.* Ed. Eleanor Ty. 2nd ed. Peterborough: Broadview P, 1998.

H[owell], T[homas] B[ayly]. *A Complete Collection of State Trials and Proceedings for High Treason and Other Crimes and Misdemeanors, from the Earliest Period to the Present Time.* Vol. 20. London: Longman et al., 1814.

Hunter, William. *An Essay on Duelling. Written with a View to Discountenance this Barbarous and Disgraceful Practice.* London: J. Debrett, 1792.

Locke, John. *Some Thoughts Concerning Education.* 9th ed. London: A. Bettesworthy and C. Hitch, 1732.

More, Hannah. *Strictures on the Modern System of Female Education, with a View of the Principles and Conduct Prevalent among Women of Rank and Fortune.* 2 vols. London: T. Cadell, 1799.

Paley, William. *The Principles of Moral and Political Philosophy.* 12th ed. London: R. Faulder, 1799.

Rousseau, Jean-Jacques. *La Nouvelle Héloïse, ou Julie.* 1761. Trans. and abridged Judith H. McDowell. University Park: Pennsylvania State UP, 1968.

Shelley, Percy Bysshe. *The Complete Works of Percy Bysshe Shelley: Vol. 8, Letters, 1803-1812.* Ed. Walter E. Peck and Roger Ingpen. New York: Gordian, 1965.

Smith, Charlotte. *Elegiac Sonnets and Other Poems.* 8th ed. 2 vols. London: Cadell and Davies, 1797.

Staël, Germaine de. "L'Histoire de Pauline." *Recueil de morceaux détachés.* 1796. Rpt. *Zulma, et Trois Nouvelles.* London, 1813.

Stewart, J. *A View of the Past and Present State of the Island of Jamaica; with Remarks on the Moral and Physical Condition of the Slaves, and on the Abolition of Slavery in the Colonies.* London: Oliver and Boyd, 1823. Rpt. New York: Negro Universities P, 1969.

Wollstonecraft, Mary. *Posthumous Works of the Author of "A Vindication of the Rights of Woman."* [Ed. William Godwin.] 4 vols. London: J. Johnson, 1798.

——. *Letters Written During a Short Residence.* 1796. Rpt. Mary Wollstonecraft and William Godwin. *A Short Residence in Sweden, Norway and Denmark* and *Memoirs of the Author of "The Rights of Woman."* Ed. Richard Holmes. London: Penguin, 1987.

——. *Mary, a Fiction and Maria, or The Wrongs of Woman.* Ed. Gary Kelly. London: Oxford UP, 1976.

——. *The Vindications: "A Vindication of the Rights of Men" and "A Vindication of the Rights of Woman."* Ed. D.L. Macdonald and Kathleen Scherf. Peterborough: Broadview P, 1997.

——. *The Wrongs of Woman, or Maria. Posthumous Works.* Vols. 1 and 2.

## Secondary Works

Anderson, Stuart. "Legislative Divorce—Law for the Aristocracy?" *Law, Economy and Society: Essays in History of English Law, 1750-1914.* Ed. G.R. Rubin and David Sugarman. Abingdon: Professional Books, 1984: 412-43.

Bailey, Joanne. *Unquiet Lives: Marriage and Marriage Breakdown in England, 1660-1800*. Cambridge: Cambridge UP, 2003.

Bannet, Eve Tavor. "The Marriage Act of 1753: 'A Most Cruel Law for the Fair Sex.'" *Eighteenth-Century Studies* 30 (1997): 233-50.

Brightwell, Cecilia Lucy. *Memorials of the Life of Amelia Opie, Selected and Arranged from her Letters, Diaries, and Other Manuscripts*. Norwich: Fletcher and Alexander, 1854.

Bunnell, Charlene E. "Breaking the Tie That Binds: Parents and Children in Romantic Fiction." Andrea O'Reilly Herrera, Elizabeth Mahn Nollen, Sheila Reitzel Foor, eds. *Family Matters in the British and American Novel*. Bowling Green, OH: Popular, 1997. 31-53.

Cooper, Christine M. "Reading Otherwise: The Abortive Politics of *Adeline Mowbray; or The Mother and Daughter*." *European Romantic Review* 12 (2001): 1-42.

Eberle, Roxanne. "Amelia Opie's *Adeline Mowbray*: Diverting the Libertine Gaze; or, The Vindication of a Fallen Woman." *Studies in the Novel* 26 (1994): 121-52.

Ferguson, Moira. *Subject to Others: British Women Writers and Colonial Slavery, 1670-1834*. New York: Routledge, 1992.

Garside, Peter, et al. "Opie, Amelia Alderson, *Adeline Mowbray* (1805)." *British Fiction, 1800-1829: Publishing Papers*. <http://www.british-fiction.cf.ac.uk/publishing/adelo5-57.html>

Grenby, M.O. *The Anti-Jacobin Novel: British Conservatism and the French Revolution*. Port Chester, NY: Cambridge UP, 2001.

Harth, Erica. "Virtue of Love: Lord Hardwicke's Marriage Act." *Cultural Critique* 9 (1988): 123-54.

Hirsch, Marianne. *The Mother/Daughter Plot: Narrative, Psychoanalysis, Feminism*. Bloomington: Indiana UP, 1989.

Howard, Carol. "The Story of the Pineapple: Sentimental Abolitionism and Moral Motherhood in Amelia Opie's *Adeline Mowbray*." *Studies in the Novel* 30.3 (1998): 355-76.

Jones, Vivien. "Placing Jemima: Women Writers of the 1790s and the Eighteenth-Century Prostitution Narrative." *Women's Writing* 4 (1997): 201-20.

Kelly, Gary. "Amelia Opie, Lady Caroline Lamb, and Maria Edgeworth: Official and Unofficial Ideology." *Ariel* 12.4 (1981): 3-24.

——. *English Fiction of the Romantic Period, 1789-1830*. London: Longman, 1989.

——. "Amelia Opie." *Oxford Dictionary of National Biography*. <http://www.oxforddnb.com/view/article/20799>

——. "Discharging Debts: The Moral Economy of Amelia Opie's Fiction." *Wordsworth Circle* 11 (1980): 198-203.

Lemmings, David. "Marriage and the Law in the Eighteenth Century: Hardwicke's Marriage Act of 1753." *Historical Journal* 39 (1996): 339-60.

Leneman, Leah. "The Scottish Case that led to Hardwicke's Marriage Act." *Law and History Review* 17 (1999): 161-69. < http://www.history-cooperative.org/journals/lhr/17.1/leneman.html>

Lorch, Jennifer. *Mary Wollstonecraft and the Making of a Radical Feminist.* New York: Berg, 1990.

MacDonald, Susan Peck. "Jane Austen and the Tradition of the Absent Mother." *The Lost Tradition: Mothers and Daughters in Literature.* Ed. Cathy N. Davidson and E.M. Broner. New York: Ungar, 1980. 58-69.

Macfarlane, Alan. *Marriage and Love in England: Modes of Reproduction 1300-1840.* New York: Basil Blackwell, 1986.

Mahon, Penny. "In Sermon and Story: Contrasting Anti-War Rhetoric in the Work of Anna Barbauld and Amelia Opie." *Women's Writing* 7 (2000): 23-38.

McCormick, Marjorie. *Mothers in the English Novel: From Stereotype to Archetype.* New York: Garland, 1991.

McKee, Kenneth N. "Voltaire's *Brutus* During the French Revolution," *Modern Language Notes* 56 (1941): 100-06.

Mellor, Anne K. "English Women Writers and the French Revolution." Melzer and Rabine, eds. 255-72.

Melzer, Sara E. and Leslie W. Rabine, eds. *Rebel Daughters: Women and the French Revolution.* Oxford: Oxford UP, 1992.

Menzies-Wilson, Jacobine, and Helen Lloyd. *Amelia—The Tale of a Plain Friend.* London: Oxford UP, 1937.

Mueller, Gerhard O.W. "Inquiry into the State of a Divorceless Society: Domestic Relations, Law, and Morals in England from 1660 to 1857." *University of Pittsburgh Law Review* 18.3 (Spring 1957): 545-78.

Nussbaum, Felicity A. *Torrid Zones: Maternity, Sexuality and Empire in Eighteenth-Century English Narratives.* Baltimore: Johns Hopkins UP, 1995.

O'Connell, Lisa. "Marriage Acts: Stages in the Transformation of Nuptial Culture." *Differences: A Journal of Feminist Cultural Studies* 11.1 (Spring 1999): 68-111.

Scott, Iaian Robertson. "'Things As They Are': The Literary Response to the French Revolution." *Britain and the French Revolution, 1789-1815.* Ed. H.T. Dickinson. London: Macmillan, 1989.

Shumaker, Jeanette. "Gaskell's Ruth and Hardy's Tess as Novels of Free Union." *Dickens Studies Annual: Essays on Victorian Fiction* 28 (1999): 151-72.

Spencer, Jane, "'Of Use to Her Daughter': Maternal Authority and Early Women Novelists." *Living by the Pen.* Ed. Dale Spender. New York: Teachers College P, 1992.

Stone, Laurence. *Road to Divorce: England 1530-1987.* Oxford: Oxford UP, 1990.

Tong, Joanne. "The Return of the Prodigal Daughter: Finding the Family in Amelia Opie's Novels." *Studies in the Novel* 36 (2004): 465-83.

Ty, Eleanor. *Empowering the Feminine: The Narratives of Mary Robinson, Jane West, and Amelia Opie, 1796-1812.* Toronto: U of Toronto P, 1998.

Wolfram, Sybil. "Divorce in England 1700-1857." *Oxford Journal of Legal Studies* 5 (1985): 155-86.